PRAISE FOR SUSAN ELIA MacNEAL

Princess Elizabeth's Spy

"MacNeal's sophomore historical outing (after *Mr. Churchill's Secretary*) synchronizes perfectly with the 60th anniversary of Queen Elizabeth II's reign. With a smart, code-breaking mathematician heroine, abundant World War II spy intrigue, and a whiff of romance, this series has real luster. The author leaves readers with a mind-boggling conclusion that hints at Maggie's next assignment."

—*Library Journal* (starred review)

"MacNeal provides a vivid view of life both above and below stairs at Windsor Castle."

—*Publishers Weekly*

Mr. Churchill's Secretary

"Susan Elia MacNeal perfectly captures the spirit of wartime Britain in *Mr. Churchill's Secretary*, a delightful mystery that follows the adventures of an appealing heroine who is both secretary and spy. This wonderful debut is intelligent, richly detailed, and filled with suspense."

—STEFANIE PINTOFF, Edgar Award–winning author of *In the Shadow of Gotham*

"Chock-full of fascinating period details and real people, including Winston Churchill, MacNeal's fast-paced thriller gives a glimpse of the struggles, tensions, and dangers of life on the home front during World War II. A terrific read."

—RHYS BOWEN, author of *Royal Blood* and
winner of the Agatha, Anthony,
and Macavity awards

"Think early Ken Follett, amp it up with a whipsmart young American not averse to red lipstick and vintage cocktails, season it with espionage during the London Blitz. Add to that her boss Churchill and War Room intrigue, and you've got a heart-pounding, atmospheric debut in *Mr. Churchill's Secretary*. I loved it."

—CARA BLACK, author of *Murder in Passy*

"Brave, clever Maggie's debut is an enjoyable mix of mystery, thriller and romance that captures the harrowing experiences of life in war-torn London."

—*Kirkus Reviews*

"[A] solid historical cozy debut. MacNeal squeezes in plenty of World War II facts but never slows the pace."

—*Library Journal* (starred review, debut of the month)

"Delightful may seem a strange word to describe a novel that takes place against the backdrop of the bombings of London during World War II, but it's appropriate for this debut novel. . . . Family secrets, a bevy of adorable roommates, a budding romance and Maggie's role in a sting operation make this novel as sweet as it is intriguing."

—*USA Today*

"MacNeal, whose prodigious research results in an accurate depiction of the historical context, fashions a page-turner of a story, complete with a plucky heroine and other well-conceived characters—real and fictional, good and evil. A ripping good yarn, *Mr. Churchill's Secretary* enthralls and satisfies."

—*Richmond Times-Dispatch*

BY SUSAN ELIA MacNEAL

His Majesty's Hope
Princess Elizabeth's Spy
Mr. Churchill's Secretary

HIS MAJESTY'S HOPE

A Bantam Books Trade Paperback Original

Copyright © 2013 by Susan Elia MacNeal

Excerpt from *The Prime Minister's Secret Agent* by Susan Elia MacNeal
copyright © 2013 by Susan Elia MacNeal.

All rights reserved.

Published in the United States by Bantam Books,
an imprint of The Random House Publishing Group,
a division of Random House, Inc., New York.

BANTAM BOOKS and the rooster colophon are registered trademarks of Random House, Inc.

This book contains an excerpt from the forthcoming novel *The Prime Minister's Secret Agent* by Susan Elia MacNeal. This excerpt has been set for this edition only and may not reflect the final content of the forthcoming edition.

LIBRARY OF CONGRESS CATALOGING-IN-PUBLICATION DATA
MacNeal, Susan Elia.
His Majesty's Hope: a Maggie Hope mystery/Susan Elia MacNeal.
pages   cm
Includes bibliographical references.
ISBN 978-0-345-53673-0
eBook ISBN 978-0-345-53875-8
1. Americans—England—London—Fiction. 2. World War, 1939–1945—Great Britain—
Fiction. 3. Historical fiction. 4. Spy stories. I. Title.
PS3613.A2774H57 2013
813'.6—dc23   2012043224

Printed in the United States of America

www.bantamdell.com

2 4 6 8 9 7 5 3 1

Book design by Dana Leigh Blanchette
Title-page image: © iStockphoto.com

To Idria Barone Knecht
Thank you

The right of personal freedom recedes before the duty to pre-serve the race. There must be no half-measures.

—Adolf Hitler

In the higher ranges of Secret Service work, the actual facts in many cases were in every respect equal to the most fantastic inventions of romance and melodrama. Tangle within tangle, plot and counter-plot, ruse and treachery, cross and double-cross, true agent, false agent, double agent, gold and steel, the bomb, the dagger and the firing party, were interwoven in many a texture so intricate as to be incredible and yet true. The Chief and the High Officers of the Secret Service reveled in these subterranean labyrinths, and pursued their task with cold and silent passion.

—Winston Churchill

HIS MAJESTY'S HOPE

Prologue

The urn the ashes came in was beautiful—shiny and black, with an enamel swastika on one side. It was small, so very small, Jens Hartmann thought. How could it possibly hold the remains of his son?

Jens launched their small boat, the *Lorelei,* from the dock of their summer home on the lake. It was still spring; most of the villas ringing the lake were empty, their doors locked and curtains drawn, ballrooms and great halls quiet, boats dry-docked for the winter in carriage houses. A breeze rustled the branches of the linden trees near the shore as the rising sun burned off the morning mist.

Neither Jens nor his wife, Mena, had asked the housekeeper to take the sheets off the furniture. It had seemed appropriate last night, when they'd arrived from Berlin-Charlottenburg, that everything was shrouded in white, like apparitions in the dark.

Their seven-year-old son, Gregor, had loved their summer house. He'd spent hours playing tag near the shore with his friends, sailing across the sparkling water, or climbing the tall oak trees in the garden. On rainy days, he curled up in a window seat with a book—Hoffmann's *Struwwelpeter* or the Grimm brothers' fairy tales. The fact that he was different seemed to matter much less in the summer, away from school and the heart of Berlin. He even seemed to have fewer seizures.

The family doctor had treated Gregor's epilepsy by prescribing phenobarbital and phenytoin, and putting him on a ketogenic diet. For a while, the program had seemed to work. But then the sei- zures came back, worse than ever, and the doctor told them to take Gregor to Charité Hospital, Mitte-Berlin, and see Dr. Karl Brandt, the Führer's personal physician.

Events proceeded quickly, too quickly, after that.

Gregor had been admitted, then scheduled for tests. From there, he'd been taken to the Hadamar Institute, for yet more tests. Jens and Mena had received a letter not long after, informing them that Gregor had died of pneumonia. Everything possible had been done, of course. And that the urn, with their son's ashes, would be arriving the next day.

"Mein liebling!" Mena had wailed, tearing at the letter. "My baby!"

"Shhh," Jens had said, patting her arm, taking the heavy, cream-colored piece of paper with the embossed swastika out of her hand. "They probably had to cremate"—it was hard for him to form the words—"his body immediately. To make sure the pneu- monia didn't spread."

Which was why they were on the *Lorelei* on the Großer Wann- see, the glossy black urn in Mena's arms as Jens steered, then an- chored in the middle of the lake. The planks of the boat creaked, waves lapped softly against the shore, and across the lake, a black heron gave a deep, ragged cry that echoed through the mist.

"He'll be happy here." Mena shivered in her black shawl. "He always loved the lake."

"He did," Jens said, stepping to her and reaching for the urn. He took off the cap. *"Let nothing disturb thee,"* he intoned, reciting the prayer of St. Teresa: *"Let nothing dismay thee. All things pass. God never changes."* His fingers pressed against the urn's sides. *"Patience attains all that it strives for. He who has God finds he lacks nothing. God alone suffices."*

He tipped the urn and poured the gray ashes onto the water, then put the urn down on the wooden seat. The boat rocked, nearly tipped over, with his movements. *"Heil Hitler!"* he cried, raising his right arm in the sharp Caesar-style *Hitlerguss* salute.

"Heil Hitler," his wife whispered, her hands grabbing at the boat's sides, knuckles white.

Jens sat and they both bent their heads in prayer.

When they were finished, Mena picked up the urn. "Jens," she said, peering inside, "there's something still in here."

"What?"

She tipped it over. Some gritty gray ash fell into her gloved palm, along with a charred piece of black metal, the white pearl tip scorched black.

"Mein Gott," she said, brows creasing. "Why, in heaven's name, would there be a girl's hairpin in Gregor's ashes?"

Chapter One

Maggie Hope was feeling her way through thick darkness. She was panting after shimmying up a rickety drainpipe, knocking out a screen in an upper-story window, avoiding several trip wires, and then sliding silently onto the floor of a dark hallway. She took a deep breath and rose to her feet, every nerve alert.

Beneath her foot, a parquet floorboard creaked. *Oh, come now,* she thought. She waited for a moment, slowing her breathing, feeling her heart thunder in her chest. All around her was impenetrable black. The only sounds were the creaks of an ancient manor house.

Nothing.

All clear.

Maggie could feel dampness under her arms and hot drops of sweat trickling down the small of her back. Aware of each and every sound, she continued down the hall until she reached the home's library. The door was locked. *Well, of course it is,* Maggie thought. She picked the lock in seconds with one of her hairpins.

Once she'd ascertained no one was there, she turned on her tiny flashlight and made her way to the desk. The safe was supposed to be under it. And it was, just as her handler had described.

Good, she thought, sitting down on the carpet next to it. *All right, let's talk.* That was how she pictured safecracking: a nice little chat with the safe. It was how the Glaswegian safecracker Johnny Ramensky—released from prison to do his part for the war effort—had taught her. She spun the dial and listened. When she could hear the tumblers dropping into place—not hear, but *feel* the vibrations with her fingertips—she knew she had the first number correct. *Now, for the second.*

Biting her lower lip in concentration, immersed in safecracking, Maggie didn't hear the room's closet door open.

Out from the shadows emerged a man. He was tall and lean, and wearing an SS uniform. "You're never going to get away with this, you know," he lisped, like Paul Lukas in *Confessions of a Nazi Spy*.

Maggie didn't bother to answer, saving her energy for the last twist of the dial, the safe's thick metal door clicking open.

In a single move, she gathered the files from the safe under her arm and sprang to her feet. She turned the flashlight on the intruder. He squinted at the light in his eyes.

Maggie ran at him, kneeing him in the groin, hard. While he was doubled over, she elbowed him in the back of the head. Satisfied he was unconscious, she ran to the door, folders still in hand.

Except that he *wasn't* unconscious. An arm shot out and a hand grabbed Maggie's ankle. She fell, files sliding across the floor. She kicked his hand off and scrambled for the door.

He struggled to his feet and ran after her, catching and holding her easily with his left arm while he wrapped his right hand around her throat. She gasped for breath, trying to throw him off, but she couldn't get the proper leverage. He threw her up against the wall, pinning her—

"*Stop! Stop!*"

Then, again—the voice amplified by a megaphone, louder this time: "OH, FOR HEAVEN'S SAKE, STOP!"

The man's arms around Maggie relaxed and released her.

"What on earth . . . ?" she muttered in exasperation.

The hall's lights blinked on, bare bulbs in elaborate molded ceilings. It wasn't actually the home of a high-ranking Nazi in Berlin but the Beaulieu Estate in Hampshire, England. Beaulieu was considered the "finishing school" of SOE—Special Operations Executive—Winston Churchill's black ops division. Some of the recruits joked that SOE didn't stand for Special Operations Executive as much as "Stately 'omes of England," where all the training seemed to take place.

"What now?" Maggie grumbled and started to pace the hallway.

A severe-looking man in his late forties with a full head of gray hair walked out into the hall with a clipboard. "All right, Miss Hope—would you like to tell us what you did wrong?"

Maggie stopped, hands on hips. "Lieutenant Colonel Ronald Thornley." Maggie had to remember *not* to call him Thorny, which was his unfortunate nickname among the trainees. "I picked the lock, cracked the safe, took the folders, disarmed the enemy—"

"Disarmed. Didn't kill."

Maggie stopped herself from rolling her eyes. "I was just about to do the honors, sir."

"You were about to be killed yourself, young lady," Thornley barked.

The tall man in the SS uniform walked up behind Maggie, rubbing the back of his head. "Not bad technique there, Maggie. But they told me that if you only knocked me out and didn't fake-kill me I'd have to come after you again."

She gave him her most winning smile. "Sorry about the knee, Phil."

"Not at all."

Thornley was not amused. "Not killing the enemy is the worst mistake *because* . . ."

Maggie and Phil looked at each other.

From behind Thornley came a loud, high-pitched nasal voice: "*Because the only safe enemy is a dead enemy.*"

"Oh, Colonel Gubbins—we didn't know you were there," Thornley said, as Gubbins stepped out of the shadows.

"There is nothing more deadly than an angry Nazi—remember that—you're not killing a person, you're killing a Nazi. A Kraut. A Jerry."

Colonel Colin McVean Gubbins was Head of Training and Operations at Beaulieu—a haunted-looking man with dark, recessed eyes, thick eyebrows, and wispy mustache. "Only sixty percent of agents dropped behind enemy lines survive, Miss Hope. You're the first woman to be dropped into Germany—the *first woman* to be dropped behind enemy lines in this war, period. Lord only knows what your odds are. We're taking an ungodly risk. And we want you to be prepared."

Maggie's frustration cooled. This wasn't about her—it was about the mission succeeding. "Yes, sir."

"You're going in to deliver a radio part to a resistance group in Berlin, and also to plant a bug at a high-ranking Abwehr officer's home. For whatever reason, the Prime Minister has asked for you for this mission specifically. And if you take out a Nazi or two in the process, so be it. This is no time to be squeamish or sentimental. Do you understand?"

The P.M. asked for me specifically for this mission! Maggie glowed with pride but tried to damp it down so Gubbins wouldn't notice. "I do, sir."

"With your fluency in German, and the skills you've been working on, you just *might* pull it off," he said. "But it's dangerous work and that's why you can leave nothing—and no one—to chance."

"Yes, sir." Maggie had dreamed about becoming a spy sent on

a foreign mission. She'd dreamed of it working as a typist to Prime Minister Winston Churchill and she dreamed about it while she was acting as a maths tutor to the Princess Elizabeth. Now, finally, was her chance.

"Let's try it again," Gubbins said. "And this time, Miss Hope, I want you to finish the Nazi off. Kill the damned Kraut."

It was ungodly hot and humid, even though it was still early morning. The skies were dark and swollen with bloated clouds. Above the buildings soared the baroque verdigris roof of the Berliner Dom, its golden cross pointing heavenward like an accusing finger.

Elise Hess navigated the narrow cobblestone side streets of Berlin-Mitte in order to avoid the parade on Unter den Linden, fast approaching the Brandenburg Gate.

The Nazis had reason to celebrate. Not only had they already seized Holland, Belgium, and France, but now German troops had invaded Russia, destroying Russia's 16th and 20th Armies in the "Smolensk pocket" and triumphing at Roslavl, near Smolensk. The German military seemed invincible. Despite the Atlantic Charter with the United States, Britain's defeat was clearly only a matter of time.

Elise could hear the steady beating drums of the Hitler Youth and the coarse clamor of the crowd in the distance, singing the Horst Wessel Song. She could see the scarlet banners with their white circles and black *hakenkreuz*—broken crosses—which the *Volk* had hung from their windows. Papering the limestone walls were tattered posters of Adolf Hitler in medieval armor, on horseback like a Teutonic knight, captioned *Dem Führer die Treue:* Be True to the Führer. Trash, cigarette butts, and broken glass from the rally the night before lined the gutters, and the air stank of stale beer and urine.

The ground was marked with chalk squares for the children's hopping game Heaven and Hell. Boys and girls were playing, throwing a small stone, then hopping on the chalked squares, trying to make it from one end to the other and back again. The boys were well scrubbed, the girls had intricate braids. All had round, rosy cheeks.

As one, they spied a small boy with a clubfoot, walking with a crutch, twisted ankle dragging behind him. He hobbled as close to the wall as he could, trying not to be noticed. But like a pack, the group set on him, herding him away from the wall. They formed a circle around him, holding hands, as the boy's eyes darted, trying to find a way to escape. One of the older boys started singing a familiar nursery rhyme:

> *Fox, you've stolen the goose*
> *Give it back!*
> *Give it back!*
> *Or the hunter will get you*
> *With his gun,*
> *Or the hunter will get you*
> *With his gun.*

The other children joined in:

> *His big, long gun,*
> *Takes a little shot at you,*
> *Takes a little shot at you,*
> *So, you're tinged with red*
> *And then you're dead.*
> *So, you're tinged with red*
> *And then you're dead.*

In the distance, church bells tolled the hour.

"Children!" Elise said, clapping her hands together. "Stop! That's enough!" They looked over at her, angry.

The boy with the clubfoot took their momentary distraction as an opportunity to burst through the circle and make a hard right into an alley, staggering as fast as he could with his crutch. The children picked up rocks and flung them after him but didn't bother to give chase. "Are you going to the parade, *Fräulein?*" one girl called to Elise.

"*Nein,*" she replied. "I have to work."

"Too bad!" the girl called back, skipping and laughing, as the boys slapped one another's backs.

Walking away, Elise shook her head. "*Gott im Himmel* help us."

Elise took one of the many bridges over the Spree and arrived at Charité Mitte Hospital damp with sweat.

She went to the nurses' changing room. It was small, with walls of gray lockers and a low wooden bench. There was a poster on the wall, of a handsome doctor and a mentally disabled man in a wheelchair, with the caption *This hereditarily sick person costs the Volksgemeinschaft 60,000 R.M. for life. Comrade, it's your money, too.*

Elise slipped out of her skirt and blouse. She kept on her necklace with the tiny gold cross, a diamond chip in its center. The door opened. It was Frieda Klein, another nurse. "*Hallo!*" Elise said, smiling. Shifts were always better when Frieda was working.

"*Hallo,*" Frieda replied. She put down her things and began to change. "*Gott,* I wish I had breasts like yours, Elise," she said, looking down at her own flat chest. "You're the perfect Rhine maiden."

"I'm too fat," Elise moaned. "As my mother *loves* to remind me. Often. I wish I had collarbones like yours—so elegant."

Whereas Elise was curvaceous, Frieda was thin and all angles. Whereas Elise had dark blue eyes and chestnut-brown curls, Frieda was blond and pale. And whereas Frieda was phlegmatic, Elise had a habit of speaking too quickly and bouncing up and down on her toes when she became excited about a finer point of medicine, swing music, or anything at all to do with American movie stars. The two young women, friends since school, had both wanted to be nurses since they were young girls.

They put on their gray uniforms, with starched white aprons and linen winged caps. "Do you mind?" Elise asked, indicating the back strings on her apron.

"Not at all," Frieda said and tied them into a bow. She turned around. "Now do mine?"

Elise did, then slapped Frieda on the bottom. They laughed as they walked out together to the nurses' station to begin their shift.

In an examination room that smelled of rubbing alcohol and lye soap, a tiny blond girl in a hospital gown asked, "Will there be blood?"

The only picture on the wall was Heinrich Knirr's official portrait of Adolf Hitler—the Führer's figure stiff, his hard eyes gazing impassively over the proceedings.

Elise smiled and shook her head. *"Nein,"* she answered. "No blood work today. The doctor just wants to take a look at your ears. To make sure the infection's gone."

The girl, Gretel Paulus, was sitting on a hospital bed. She held a small brown, well-loved teddy bear and spoke with a slight speech impediment. Her thick lower lip protruded and glistened with saliva, her tongue overlarge. She had a round face, pointy chin, and almond-shaped eyes behind thick, distorting eyeglasses.

Elise smiled. "What goes ninety-nine *thump*, ninety-nine *thump*, ninety-nine *thump*?"

Gretel shrugged.

"A centipede with a wooden leg, of course!"

That won a weak smile out of the young girl. Elise took an otoscope from the cabinet, cleaned the earpiece with alcohol, and then put it to the girl's right ear. Then the left.

"Nurse Hess?"

"When it's just you and I, you may call me Elise."

"Elise—why do my ears always hurt?" Gretel wanted to know.

Elise knew all too well that ear infections were common with Down syndrome patients. "It's just something that happens sometimes," she said, putting the otoscope away and returning to rub the girl's back. "And you feel better now, yes? The medicine worked?"

"If I feel better, why do I still have to see the doctor? The new doctor?"

Gretel didn't miss a thing, Elise realized. "His name is Doktor Brandt. And he wants to make sure you don't have any more ear infections."

The door to the examination room opened, and in walked Dr. Karl Brandt. He was relatively new to Charité, one of the SS doctors who came in the late winter of 1941, with their red armbands with black swastikas, and their new rules and regulations. Young, handsome, with thick, dark hair and impeccable posture, Brandt radiated authority.

Elise handed Gretel's chart to him. Without preamble, he marked the black box in the lower left-hand corner of the medical history chart with a bold red *X*, the last of three. He looked out the door and beckoned. Two orderlies arrived, strong and broad-shouldered in white coats with swastika armbands.

"Am I going home?" Gretel asked the doctor.

"Not yet, *Mäuschen*," Brandt replied, smiling. "We're going to make sure this never happens to you again."

Gretel beamed. "Oh, thank you, *Herr Doktor*!" she lisped as the two orderlies escorted her back to her room to get dressed. She hugged her teddy bear to her small body.

"Take this to the nurses' station," Dr. Brandt said to Elise, handing her the file. He headed toward the door.

"What should I tell her father and mother?" During the course of Gretel's multiple ear infections, Elise had come to know the child's parents.

He eyed the cross she wore around her neck. "Just deliver the paperwork to the nurses' station. They will take care of everything."

Elise was stung by his brusque tone. *"Jawohl, Herr Doktor,"* she replied, following behind him.

Dr. Brandt turned and frowned in response but did not discipline her. "Go," he said. "There are forms to fill out."

Elise made her way down the hallways to the nurses' station. She handed the file to the nurse on duty. *"Another* one?" the gray-haired woman grumbled, looking at the three red *X*s on the chart.

"What does that mean?" Elise asked.

"It means a lot of paperwork."

"What kind of paperwork?"

The gray-haired woman, Nurse Flint, gave Elise a sharp look. "The kind that keeps me here, instead of at home with my husband and children, that's what kind," she snapped, stacking Gretel's file on top of similar folders.

Elise caught sight of Frieda, rounding the corner; her friend pointed up with one finger. Elise caught her meaning and nodded. She held up one hand, palm out—their code for meeting on the roof in five minutes.

Before she met up with Frieda, Elise wanted to check on someone. She walked down the corridor and into a ward filled with wounded soldiers in narrow white beds. Some moaned in their sleep, some stared listlessly out the windows at the leaden sky, others sat up in their wheelchairs and played cards.

Elise wanted to check on the temperature of a young man all the nurses called *Herr Geheimnis*—Herr Mystery. He'd been running an intermittent fever over the past few days. The patient had curly brown hair, an angular face, shoulders full of tension, and eyes wild with fear. Who was he? Where was he from? Did he have a girlfriend? Was he married? Why couldn't—or wouldn't— he speak?

"Is he all right?" Flight Lieutenant Emil Eggers asked, indicating with his chin the bandaged body asleep in the narrow bed next to him. Eggers, a beefy, blond man with the face of a cherub, was a Luftwaffe commander. He'd had a close call in France but survived his crash landing and had been brought back to Berlin to convalesce.

"Is that any business of yours, Lieutenant Eggers?" Elise admonished as she shook a thermometer and slipped it into Herr Mystery's mouth. She might be young, but she was strict with the men, who often seemed grateful to be ordered about as they convalesced.

"Well, there's not much to do in here . . ." Eggers said, trying his best to look winsome and failing.

"True," Elise agreed in gentler tones, picking up the chart hanging at the end of the bed frame. "He's one of yours—a pilot. Had quite a bad crash landing. A veterinarian from somewhere outside Berlin found him and patched him up as best he could and brought him in, but he had a lot of internal injuries."

"Is he going to make it?" Eggers asked. He didn't recognize the man, but there was a code of solidarity among pilots.

Elise may have been young, but she was also a realist. "I hope so." She removed the thermometer from his mouth and looked. A hundred and one. "His temperature's still a bit elevated." She made a note in the pilot's chart, then walked over to Eggers. "And how's your leg today, Lieutenant?"

Eggers pulled back the rough sheet and gray wool blanket to reveal a bandaged stump. "Still gone, I'm afraid."

After, Elise met up with Frieda on the hospital's roof. The tar paper was littered with cigarette butts. A crumpled packet of Milde Sorte was stuck under a drainpipe. The sun was blisteringly hot— 1941 was turning into Berlin's warmest summer on record. Frieda lit a cigarette and took a puff, then handed it to Elise. "I hate this place."

Elise accepted the cigarette and took a long inhale. "Charité? Berlin? All of Germany?" she asked, blowing out rings of pale blue smoke.

"Everything. All of it."

They leaned over the railing. The city of Berlin spread out before them: the river Spree glittering in the harsh sunlight, long red Nazi banners snapping in the breeze, the black, burned-out dome of the Reichstag.

The parade was still marching down Unter den Linden, the sounds of cheering and music and hobnailed black boots goose-stepping on the pavement muted now by height and distance. Directly below them in the hospital's circular driveway, a bus idled. It was dark gray, with white-painted windows.

"Especially since Dr. Brandt and his cronies arrived here."

"You don't know the half of it." Frieda's slim fingers shook as she took another drag on her cigarette.

"What do you mean?"

"Have you noticed how patient charts now have the attending physician mark a red *X* or a blue minus sign on them?"

"Yes," Elise replied. "I had a third red *X* on a patient's chart today. I asked Dr. Brandt about it—he said it had something to do with paperwork."

"Paperwork, right." Frieda picked a stray fleck of tobacco from her tongue. From below, the noxious bus fumes drifted upward in the heat. The two young nurses watched as a cluster of children was herded inside a bus by orderlies in white coats.

"Maybe it has to do with the compulsory sterilization," Elise suggested. Under the Law for the Prevention of Hereditarily Diseased Offspring, all Reich doctors were required to report the retarded, mentally ill, epileptic, blind, deaf, physically deformed, and homosexual—and make sure they were unable to procreate. As a Catholic, Elise was adamantly opposed.

"Something like that."

"How's Ernst?" Elise asked, deliberately changing the subject.

Frieda's face, pale as milk, flushed red in anger. "He's all right—at least as all right as a surgeon who's not allowed to operate anymore can be." Ernst Klein, Frieda's husband, was Jewish, and now prohibited from practicing medicine.

"I'm sorry. I can only imagine how hard it's been."

Frieda pressed her lips together. "The Codex Judaicum is a nightmare. They're taking away our pets, now—can you believe? Pets! No Jew is allowed to own a dog, cat, or bird. And they're not just given to some nice gentile family—no, they might be 'racially contaminated' somehow—God forbid! So, they're all killed instead." Frieda kicked some of the gravel with her foot. "Four SA officers came to take Widow Kaufman's cat last night. Can you imagine—four men for *one* cat? Widow Kaufman was crying, but little Bärli didn't go without a fight. We didn't dare open our door, of course. But from the noise, I think she managed a few good scratches."

"And Marthe?" Elise asked. Marthe was Frieda and Ernst's small white dove, named after Marguerite's guardian in Charles Gounod's *Faust*.

"She's safe—for now."

"Would you like me to take Marthe in? I'd take good care of her until she can return to you."

"Of course, *you* can still have a pet. *You* can do whatever you want." Frieda brushed some loose, pale hair out of her eyes and wiped away hot tears. Then her face softened. "Of course, it's not your fault, Elise." She added, "Have you heard anything?"

Berlin's Jews were slowly but surely being called to ghettos and work camps. Letters told them where to report, what to bring with them, and which train to take.

"I'll ask my mother," Elise said. "I know she can help."

Elise's mother actually had refused to look into it. But Elise, normally cowed by her domineering mother, was determined to bring it up again, and not take no for an answer this time.

"Thank you," Frieda said with palpable relief.

The two young women smoked in silence, passing the cigarette back and forth, as a long-necked heron flew by in the distance.

Elise ventured, "Do you ever—"

The words hung in the air for long seconds.

"Think about divorcing him?" Frieda finished. "*Nein*. Never. We love each other. I just wish we'd left Germany when we still had the chance. To think I was afraid to move to Hong Kong." She gave a bitter laugh.

"Sorry." Elise crushed the cigarette out under her heel. "I

shouldn't have even asked." In the glint of the morning sunlight, Elise caught a glimpse of a young girl with blond hair in the line to board the bus below, holding a tattered brown teddy bear.

"I think that girl's my patient," Elise said, blue eyes darkening. Together they watched as the patients and nurses boarded, then the bus's engine revved. It pulled away, belching thick, black smoke from the exhaust pipe as it made its way down the drive. "Those buses," Elise said, "they call them the Ravens. Why?"

Frieda shrugged. "The color."

Elise was confused. Surely the child she'd glimpsed below was Gretel. Had she missed something? Had the girl taken a turn for the worse?

Chapter Two

Clara Hess was wearing a mask. It was pure white, like Kabuki makeup. Her eyes were closed.

She was draped, catlike, over a divan in her office at the Abwehr, the German Military Intelligence agency, wearing only the mask, a scarlet silk robe, and Chanel No. 5. One woman was painting her toenails, while another was rubbing lotion into her hands. Still another was taking curlers out of her hair, leaving glistening platinum ringlets.

Taller than most women and slim as a ballerina, Clara looked like Jean Harlow crossed with the warrior-goddess Brünnhilde, as seen through the lens of Horst P. Horst. She favored Chanel's androgynous suits in jersey, which she wore with ropes of pearls and gold chains. It was a look not often seen on women in Berlin. But with her height, excellent posture, and entitled attitude, she was never questioned. Being good friends with Adolf Hitler, Hermann Göring, and Joseph Goebbels, and being photographed with them frequently at the Opera or Philharmonic, didn't hurt either.

Although lately, such photographs were less frequent. Clara Hess's last mission, the assassination of King George VI and the kidnapping of Princess Elizabeth, intending to pave the way for the eventual German invasion of England and the crowning of Edward and Wallis Simpson as Great Britain's new King and Queen, hadn't happened. In fact, it had been a complete and total failure. Since her fall from grace, it was whispered about the halls of the Abwehr that Clara was losing her magic touch—as well as the Führer's favor.

The heavy door opened and her secretary announced, "Admiral Canaris to see you, as you requested, Frau Hess."

"Come in," Clara said.

Wilhelm Canaris, head of the Abwehr, was a distinguished-looking man with white hair and shaggy white eyebrows. He walked in and stopped in front of her divan. *"Heil Hitler!"* Images of Clara were reflected back to him in the many beveled mirrors the office had on the walls, along with an oil portrait of Adolf Hitler.

Her eyes were still closed. "Our agent in London is in place, Wilhelm. He's just waiting for my go-ahead."

"Good," Canaris said, taking a seat as one of the women finished massaging Clara's hands and began to remove the mask with cotton pads soaked with witch hazel. "We'll coordinate with Göring and Halder. It's high time Britain surrendered. And Operation Aegir plays an important role."

"I'm no admirer of Mother Russia," Clara said, sitting upright, the mask now removed, glacier-blue eyes open. While they were undisputedly beautiful, one wandered just slightly, the gaze of each pupil focusing on a different point in space. "But when we went into Poland, the Russian General Staff shared their methods for population control with us. And what they accomplished with their workers in the gulags is nothing short of inspiring."

One of the women opened a black crocodile makeup case, extracting pans of foundation, compacts of powder, tins of rouge, and tubes of lipstick.

"Yes, I've heard they've already started using it in the camps," Canaris said, as the woman began to paint Clara's face.

"We can control any population through medication of its drinking water supply. And by our releasing this poison into London's water supply before the invasion, British morale will be destroyed. Churchill's great speeches will be useless. The population will put up no resistance."

"Just by adding a chemical to the water supply?" Canaris didn't sound convinced. "This is all on you, you know. If this mission should fail . . ." The silence turned ominous.

Clara didn't answer as the woman finished applying her makeup; then she barked, "Mirror!" The woman handed Clara a silver hand mirror. She studied her visage in the reflection, turning this way and that. "It will do," she said to the woman, who nodded and began packing up.

"Aegir won't fail," Clara assured Canaris. "I went over the facts with one of the top chemists at I.G. Farben." She smiled, a gorgeous smile of crimson lipstick and pearly teeth, a smile that used to bring audiences at the Berlin Opera House to their feet, applauding madly, back in the day when she was a soprano famed for her Wagnerian roles. "And now, I must get dressed to meet Herr Goebbels at the cinema. We're seeing a preview of *Ich klage. an*—it's his favorite."

Frieda knocked on the door to the servants' entrance to the Hess house in Grunewald, a leafy, wealthy suburb of Berlin. Joseph Goebbels's family lived in a large house nearby.

Unlike her Jewish husband, Frieda was allowed to be out after curfew. Even so, and even with her Aryan features and identity card, it terrified her to be in such close proximity to high-ranking Nazi families.

Elise, who'd been waiting for her friend, opened the door within moments. "Good to see you," she said, giving her friend a hug the best she could, considering the other woman was carrying a covered birdcage and a brown paper bag filed with seed.

"And you, too," Frieda said, wiping her feet on a coconut mat and then walking into the kitchen, which smelled of baking bread. "And here is the lovely Marthe." She set the cage down on the long wooden table and pulled back the protective covering. Marthe, a white-feathered dove, stared back at the two young women with shiny black eyes and cocked her head.

Elise bent down to the cage to address the bird. "Hello, little Marthe. I hope you'll be happy here. That is, until you can get back to your real home."

Frieda snorted. "As if that's going to happen anytime soon."

"Come, sit down," Elise urged, pulling out a chair for her friend. "I'll get us something to eat."

Frieda sat as Elise made ham sandwiches with dark, grainy mustard and poured two glasses of milk.

Although many foods in Germany were rationed, for the well-placed Hess family nothing was in short supply. Along the shelves, Frieda could see the tribute from the conquered: long, slim bottles of apricot schnapps from Austria, stout bottles of horseradish vodka from Poland, boxes of chocolates from Belgium, and magnums of champagne from France.

As Elise sat down, Frieda took a huge bite, cramming as much as she could of the sandwich into her mouth. With a pang, Elise realized how hungry her friend must be. "I'll give you some to take home, for you and Ernst."

"Thank you," Frieda said through her mouthful, reaching for the milk.

"Marthe and I are going to have a lovely time, aren't we?" Elise said to the bird, who looked at her quizzically, and then began pecking an errant seed on the bottom of the cage. She turned back to her friend. "And Ernst, how is he?"

"Not well," Frieda managed between mouthfuls. "Since he's married to a blond shiksa, he's safe, for now, but they're making him . . ." She swallowed. "He has to deliver letters to Jews, telling them to report for deportation to the camps. It's the letter everyone dreads. After a day of delivering, all he can do is sleep. It's all he does anymore—sleep. Sleeping is preferable to this new reality, I think."

"I can imagine." Elise pictured Ernst, once a pediatric surgeon, so full of vitality and energy. She wondered how he looked now, not a surgeon anymore, banned from the hospital.

"But enough about me." Frieda took another sip of milk. "How are you? How's your piano playing?"

"Fair," Elise said. "I'd rather be studying for the boards, even if we can't take them until the war's over. But Mother has this party coming up and wants me to accompany her, so . . ." Whatever her mother wanted, Elise usually did. Although not without a fair amount of resentment.

Frieda gave a grim smile. She knew exactly who Elise's mother was in the Reich, and her reputation at the Abwehr. She was terrified of her. But keeping her husband alive and in Berlin was her biggest and most overwhelming challenge now. "And . . . how is she?" Frieda managed, trying to sound normal.

Elise did her best to distance herself from her mother's Nazi affiliations, saying that medicine and science had no politics, and thus she had no politics—certainly not her mother's. . . . But she and Frieda both knew the truth. They did their best, for the sake of their friendship, to avoid talking about it.

"I haven't seen her yet today, Frieda. But I promise you—I'll speak to her about Ernst tonight."

"I know the Abwehr's not in charge of deportations, but I saw a picture of her in the newspaper, at a concert with Himmler. . . . She must have some sort of influence?"

"I promise you, Frieda, I will do everything in my power to help you and Ernst." Elise made the sign of a cross over her chest.

"Hand aufs Herz," she vowed. Her stomach lurched as she said the words, for she remembered how her mother had screamed and shouted the last time she'd brought up protection for Ernst.

Frieda also made the sign. "Cross my heart."

SOE was no ordinary spy organization. It was unconventional, fluid, rogue. And its goals were not military. No, the goals of SOE were sabotage and subversion, often collaborating with local resistance groups in enemy territories to thwart the enemy, working toward the ultimate liberation of Nazi-occupied Europe. Based at 64 Baker Street in London, its motley crew of administrators and agents were sometimes called the Baker Street Irregulars, after Sherlock Holmes's men. They were charged by Churchill to "set Europe ablaze!"

Sir Frank Nelson, the Director of SOE, was at his massive wooden desk in his office. He had high cheekbones, thin lips, and fine hair held fast with a copious amount of Brylcreem. He pulled over a heavy file labeled MARGARET HOPE. Stamped on it, in thick red letters, was TOP SECRET.

The papers in the file were typed, single-spaced. British by birth, but raised in the United States for most of her life, Margaret Rose Hope had started off in May 1940 as one of Prime Minister Winston Churchill's secretaries. She'd cracked a secret code that a Nazi sleeper spy had put in a newspaper advertisement, and saved not just the Prime Minister's life but also St. Paul's Cathedral from destruction.

These strengths, along with her fluency in French and German, led to her being recruited by Peter Frain, head of MI-5. Her increased strength and endurance, honed at Windsor Castle while protecting the young Princess Elizabeth from a kidnapping threat, had convinced Frain to put her name forward as a candidate for

SOE. She'd been accepted, and had spent much of the winter and spring of 1941 at various training camps.

Surviving those, she'd moved on to six weeks of "finishing school" at Lord Montagu's Beaulieu Estate in the New Forest, in the Station X–Germany division. Passing her final test at Beaulieu was what led Maggie Hope to SOE's sandbagged Baker Street office.

Maggie stepped around a Salvation Army soldier ringing an iron bell, an older woman in the requisite navy-blue uniform, and dropped a coin into the basket. Air Raid wardens in tin helmets were sweeping up broken glass from the bombing the night before.

She entered the building, showed her papers to the guard on duty, and was led by a young woman in uniform to Nelson's office. He rose when she entered. "Please sit down, Miss Hope."

Maggie had endured a long day. Her cartwheel hat, with its low crown and wide, stiff brim, was askew. She had a run in her last good pair of stockings. Her dark red hair was slipping from its bun, and her lipstick had worn off long ago. She'd taken three different trains to get from Beaulieu to Baker Street in London, and had lost her gas mask on one of them, her gloves on another, and her temper on the third. She'd only had time to drop her valise in her room at David's flat in Knightsbridge before making her way to Marylebone and SOE's offices.

"Thank you," she replied, as she took a seat in the hard-backed wooden chair, crossing her ankles and folding her gloveless hands in her lap.

It was summer in London. Outside Nelson's taped windows, Maggie could see the glossy leaves of a hawthorn tree. The office itself was austere, with only a green banker's lamp and two framed photographs: King George VI and Prime Minister Winston Churchill. Nelson turned back to finish reading her folder. "I'd love a cup of tea, Miss Hope."

Tea? Maggie thought, as she clenched her hands. *He expects me to parachute into Germany* and *make tea?* Still, her voice remained even. "Why, I'd love a cup of tea, too, sir. One sugar, if you have it. Of course, I understand if you don't."

Nelson looked up, blinked, then recovered. He cleared his throat. "I know you've just returned from Beaulieu, Miss Hope, but it's time."

"Yes, sir?"

"Two missions in one." He peered at her over the rim of his glasses. "The first is to deliver desperately needed radio crystals to one of a resistance circle in Berlin. The other, a more difficult task, is to gain entrance to a high-level Nazi officer's study and bug it."

"I see." Maggie considered. "Who's the officer?"

"A Commandant Hess." He looked down at the file. "I understand Hess was the mastermind behind the attempted assassination of the King and the kidnapping of the Princess last December?"

"Yes," Maggie said, aware that Nelson was scrutinizing her face for any reaction. She gave none.

"So it's personal for you."

"You might say." *If there's no notation in your little file that Commandant Clara Hess of the Abwehr had once been known as Clara Hope, my allegedly dead-in-a-car-crash mother, I'm not about to enlighten you, Nellie.*

"I will tell you, Miss Hope, that as of yet, no women have been sent to the Continent. The Prime Minister has serious issues with the thought of women spooks. As do I. But, as I said, the P.M. asked for you specifically for this job, and so here we are." He flipped the folder closed, then rose and went to the window. "Feels a woman will be able to slip in and out more easily. As the war goes on, any young man we send in looks more and more suspicious— 'Why isn't he off fighting?' Et cetera, et cetera."

Maggie raised her chin. "Of course. However, I can assure

you, sir, that I've been well trained. I can carry out any missions assigned as well as any man."

Nelson turned back toward Maggie. "I realize the personal angle might give you extra impetus, but it's important not to let emotions cloud your vision. You go in, perform your mission, and leave. That's it. Clean and fast. In fact, the job is quick—no more than four nights."

"What's my cover?"

Nelson found another folder on his desk and opened it, his eyes scanning the page. "Let's see—you'll pose as a mistress to an Abwehr officer. He's part of the resistance circle that's been working with us. He'll be your way into Berlin. You'll deliver the radio crystals to him. And then he will also be your entree to Commandant Hess's home."

"Sounds straightforward."

He flipped a page. "You'll parachute into the German countryside, where one of our people will meet you and take you to a safe house. From there you'll take the train to Berlin, where your contact will meet you. Your cover story is that you met while he was in Rome, at a conference the Abwehr was having with the Vatican. You were assigned to be his temporary secretary there, and you fell madly in love."

"Does this new love of my life have a name?"

"Let's see." Nelson riffled through the papers. "Here we are—Gottlieb Lehrer."

"Gottlieb Lehrer," Maggie repeated.

"And you'll need this." Nelson opened his desk drawer and riffled inside until he found what he was looking for: a gold lipstick tube, which he handed to Maggie.

No stranger to the methods of SOE, she unscrewed the bottom. There, in a hidden compartment, was a tablet encased in rubber.

"Cyanide, I presume?" she asked, returning the pill to its chamber and screwing the cap back on tightly.

"Indeed. I hope you won't have to use it."

"Thank you. I hope I don't either." Maggie gave a grim smile. "When do I leave?"

"Because of the urgency of the mission, and the fact we're coming up on a full moon, you'll be leaving tomorrow night. I assume you can get everything in order? You do have a will, yes?"

Tomorrow night! Maggie thought. *But I've only just returned! I haven't even seen Hugh yet.* . . . Still, there was no arguing with the phases of the moon. If she didn't leave now, she'd have to wait another month. And she wanted to go. It was what she'd dreamed of, trained for. . . . "Yes, I have a will. And yes, I'll be ready, sir."

"Excellent, Miss Hope." They both stood and shook hands across Nelson's wooden desk.

"Report here tomorrow morning at nine sharp," he said, walking her out. "First you'll get all your paperwork together and then head to Wardrobe. You'll be dropped into Germany tomorrow night."

"Ah," Maggie said. *"Das Eisen schmieden, solange es heiß ist."*

"Yes, let's strike while the iron is still hot. And, Miss Hope?"

"Yes?"

"I hope your skills are up to par. Your life, and the lives of the brave people of the resistance group in Berlin, depend on them."

Maggie replied, with the confidence of youth, "You can count on me, sir."

Frieda returned to the apartment she and her husband shared, carrying two loaves of bread, a thick slab of ham, a tin of coffee, and a bag of sugar. In addition, she had large bars of Neuhaus chocolate from Belgium and a bottle of schnapps.

It was a cramped, dingy, airless flat, so different from the one they had shared when they'd first been married, in 1934. Frieda had always felt that, somehow, because they were married before the Nuremberg Laws passed, they were still safe. Even when the SS took their spacious, sunlit apartment near the Tiergarten, along with their furnishings and artwork, even when they were relocated to a small, dark one in the ghetto, even when Ernst lost his job, even when he started having to send out the letters. They were together. And Ernst was still alive. That was the only thing that mattered.

She set the rucksack full of food on the table. "Look, love," she said, feigning cheer. "Finally, something decent to eat!"

"I don't want any damned Nazi food," Ernst said, shirtsleeves rolled up, sorting through envelopes. "I'd rather starve."

"And we just may." Both Ernst and Frieda had become gaunt in the last few years, due to fear as well as bad nutrition. "Well, *I'm* not going to let this go to waste," Frieda declared, peeling back the foil on the chocolate bar and taking a greedy bite. The intense creamy sweetness nearly caused her to tear up—it had been so long since she'd had candy.

"The Belgian storekeeper that bar was stolen from was probably shot," Ernst said. "Doesn't that bother you at all?"

"Well, he may be dead, but I'm still alive," Frieda countered through her mouthful. "And if I throw out this beautiful chocolate, who wins? It doesn't affect the shopkeeper either way."

Ernst stood up from his wobbly chair and walked over to Frieda, giving her a gentle kiss on the cheek. Then he rifled through the bag. "Oh, and I see she gave you ham. How thoughtful, to give a Jew *ham*."

"You're lucky to be eating at all." Frieda was exhausted and losing patience. "They now expect two weeks' worth of rations to last for three. When the war's over, we can keep kosher again."

Ernst didn't want to argue further. "Yes, of course," he said. "I'm sorry. I know you're doing your best." Then, "I have a joke for you."

Frieda didn't smile. "Really?"

"What do you call one Englishman?"

She cocked one pale eyebrow. "I don't know, what?"

"An idiot. What do you call two Englishmen?"

"No idea."

"A club. And what do you call three Englishmen?"

Frieda sighed in disapproval. "Oh, Ernst."

"An empire!" When Ernst smiled, he looked like less of a gaunt old man and more of the dashing young doctor with whom Frieda had fallen in love. Her lips twitched.

"Now, what do you call one German?" he asked.

"Stop, Ernst." She started giggling.

"A damned fine man." He held up two fingers. "What do you call two Germans?"

"Stop!" She clapped her hands over her lips, as though trying to cram the rare laughter back inside.

"A putsch," he said, grabbing her by the waist, pulling her close. He held up three fingers. "And three Germans?"

Tears were rolling down her cheeks. "Stop! Stop! Stop!" she cried.

"A war!" he thundered, spinning her around in his arms.

After a few moments of laughter, Frieda began to hiccup. "This is your fault," she scolded, shaking a finger at him.

He kissed her. When they broke apart, she looked down at what he was doing. "More letters?"

He nodded. "Do you know what they call me now? *Der Schreck-ensträger*. 'Carrier of horror.' It has a certain ring to it."

"As long as no letter comes for you. You'll get through it. All we need to do is survive. I look Death in the face every day and say, 'Not today, Death. Not today, you bastard.'" She took another bite of chocolate. "So, no letters for you, right? Because we're still married. And I'm having Elise speak with her mother."

"Yes, darling," Ernst told his wife. "Of course I'm still safe."

Chapter Three

Maggie arrived, breathless, at the glossy green door of Hugh's garden-level flat in Kensington. It had been months since they had last seen each other, and all she knew was how much she wanted to be in his arms again.

She knocked and the door swung open, as though he had been waiting. They stared at each other, reality piercing memory. Then they embraced, Maggie smelling shaving soap and bay rum cologne as she kissed his warm neck.

Finally, they drew apart. "Look at you," Maggie said, as she walked into his flat and set her handbag on the entryway table, then took off her hat.

"Look at *you!*" he countered. "All that country air's been good for you. Would you like a drink?"

"I'd love one, thank you."

Maggie slipped off her pumps and sat down on the sofa, tucking her stockinged feet up under her. Hugh went into his efficiency kitchen and came back with two glasses of gin.

"I'm leaving tomorrow," Maggie told him. "I know it's fast, but it's almost a full moon, after all."

"I can't ask you what you're doing." Hugh smoothed back her hair, then took out the hairpins, one by one.

"And I can't ask you about what you're doing. Although, how's Frain?"

Hugh had Maggie's hair down and was pulling her close. "Can we not talk about my boss for the moment, please?" he murmured against her ear. "You must be starving. Do you want dinner?"

"Yes—anything, though. Don't go to any trouble."

But Hugh had gone to trouble, lots of it. China and silver were laid out on his dining table. He lit new tapered candles as she watched, drink in hand. "We're having vegetable turnovers, straight out of the war ration cookbook. Not exactly a Sunday roast, but I've been practicing just for this occasion."

"I'm honored," she said. "What can I do to help?"

"Everything's done. But you can pour the wine, if you'd like."

Maggie watched him through dinner, not sure whether she could trust her vision. They had written to each other, of course, long letters, while she was at the various training camps, where they knew whatever they wrote would be seen by censors, but they didn't really care. They kept gazing at each other, as though wanting to make sure each was not a mirage.

At eleven o'clock, Maggie had to leave. In the light of one candle, she gazed down at Hugh on his bed, wrapped in a sheet. She thought about waking him, then decided just to kiss him on the forehead and let him sleep. She found herself not wanting to leave, almost physically unable to put on her hat and open the front door. To stall for time, she wrote a note. *Dearest Hugh, Off on yet another adventure. I'll be back as soon as I can.*

She contemplated writing *I love you,* then decided on *xxoo Maggie.*

Unwilling to deal with the vast sea of humanity settled into the Tube stations for the night to escape the Blitz, Maggie splurged and took a taxi from Westminster to Knightsbridge. In the damp darkness, she realized how much she'd missed London. The people. The narrow, winding streets. Pubs with names such as The Bag o' Nails and Hat and Feathers.

When she finally arrived at David's flat, she let herself in with the iron key she kept in her handbag. Inside, it was inky black. She made sure the door was closed completely, so no light would escape and alert the ARP warden, and only then switched on the foyer light. From the parlor, she heard a soft scuffling. "Hello?" she called, body tense, months of combat training triggered instinctively.

David Greene appeared in the French double doorway to the parlor, his tie undone, wire-framed glasses askew, shirt unbuttoned, fair hair uncharacteristically mussed. He looked like a guilty choirboy. "Merciful Minerva! What are you doing home?" Then he collected himself and grinned. "Not that I'm not thrilled to see you, of course, darling Mags," he said, walking toward her and kissing her on both cheeks.

Maggie took in his appearance. "Good to see you, too, David." He had the grace to blush. "Are you . . . *alone?*" she asked in a sisterly tone.

"Well, ah, you see—the strangest thing happened—"

Another man stepped from the darkened parlor to the French doors. He'd already taken the time to button up his shirt and fix his tie. "How do you do?" he said to Maggie. "I'm Freddie Wright. You must be Maggie Hope. David's told me all about you."

Has he now? Maggie stepped past David and extended her hand. "Lovely to meet you. Now that I know you're not a burglar." They shook. Maggie was impressed; it was a good handshake, firm and confident. "Mr. . . . Wright, is it?"

She glanced back at David, who shot her a significant look. Maggie smiled back at him. After all, he'd had many, many Mr. Wrongs in his life. Maybe it was time for Mr. Right? Or, at least, Mr. Wright? "From the Treasury?"

"Call me Freddie, please. And yes, I work at the Treasury."

"Freddie. Of course. David's mentioned you."

There was another moment of awkward silence. "Oh dear!" Maggie made herself yawn. "It's late, and I'm absolutely knackered—so I'm going to turn in. Good night, David. Again, lovely to meet you, Freddie." She began to walk down the long hallway that led to the bedrooms. "I hope you don't mind, but I'm going to go to sleep. I sleep soundly," she added, significantly. "*Quite* soundly."

"Good night, Mags," David called after her with affection. "It's good to have you home again—even if you do have terrible timing."

"Elise?" Clara Hess called.

She strode into the lavish master bedroom, dressed in satin and rubies. She flung her beaded evening purse on the dressing table, then sat down on the small stool at her vanity and took off her high heels. Her feet were red and angry-looking, with blood blisters beginning to form. "Elise!" Clara called again, shrill this time.

Elise appeared in her mother's doorway, wearing a white cotton nightgown and robe.

"Oh, *there* you are," her mother said, stretching her back like a cat. "Get me some aspirin, *Mausi*, won't you? Mutti's had too much champagne."

Elise did as she was bade, going to the large black-marble bathroom and taking out two white tablets from the mirrored medicine cabinet. Then she filled a heavy crystal glass with cold water from the tap and brought it and the aspirin to her mother.

"And would you fetch me a cold cloth, too?" Clara asked. She began to remove her heavy jewelry. "Oh, it was a wonderful night—but there's a price for everything, isn't there?"

"Where were you tonight, Mutti?" Elise asked.

"Out with Joseph. We saw *Ich klage an*—it's his favorite, you know."

"I read the book." Elise frowned, remembering how much she'd disliked it. The controversial bestseller was about a woman suffering from multiple sclerosis. The woman had pleaded with doctors to help end her suffering; when they refused, her husband gave her a fatal overdose. He was arrested and put on trial, where he argued that he'd committed an act of mercy, not murder. He had been acquitted. The novel had been denounced by the Catholic Church.

"What?" Clara said. "Darling, you're mumbling, I can't hear you. What have I told you, again and again, about the mumbling?"

Elise gritted her teeth. "Sorry, Mother."

"Only people who don't trust what they have to say mumble, you know."

Biting her lip, Elise went back to the marble bathroom, took one of the thick washcloths folded on the counter, and ran it under the cold water. She wrung it out in the sink, then brought it back into the bedroom.

"How's the piano practice coming along?" Clara asked. "My party's this weekend, after all, and I want there to be fantastic music. A small orchestra, of course, but I've chosen a few pieces to sing—just me with piano accompaniment. I'll have my secretary draw up a list of possible songs for you." She gave Elise an up-and-down look. "And perhaps we could cut back on the marzipan for the next few days?" she suggested, patting the young woman's cheek. "Your face is looking a bit full, not to mention your bottom. And I've picked out an appropriate dress for you to wear. . . ."

Elise's face crumpled under the weight of her mother's criticism. It had been a long day. She was worried about Gretel, she was worried about Frieda and Ernst, and now she was worried about how to approach her mother. Tears pricked at her blue eyes and threatened to overflow.

"Oh, for heaven's sake—don't cry, darling. You're so sensitive sometimes. I feel I can't say *anything* around you. You take everything so personally—really, you must get over that."

Elise blinked her eyes, hard. As she often did, she decided to change the subject. "Is Papa coming to the party?" Alaric Hess was one of the Reich's most famous opera conductors, and often away on tour.

"I don't know, *Mausi*." Clara unhooked the clips from her silk stockings and, one after the other, rolled them down her legs. "Why don't you telephone and ask him yourself?" She stripped out of her dress, then out of her girdle, garter belt, and bra. There were red welts where the elastic had bitten into her skin. With a sigh of relief, she slipped on a black silk nightgown. She lay on the bed and draped a slender arm over her eyes. "Where's that washcloth, *Mausi*?"

Elise laid the wet cloth over her mother's temples. "Ah, that's better," Clara sighed. "It's good to have a nurse in the family. If you recall, I wasn't too thrilled about it at first, but it does have some perks. As does your piano playing. I do wish you'd take it more seriously, though. Wouldn't you rather be touring as a pianist, instead of cleaning up God-knows-what at the hospital?"

"I've told you," Elise said, sitting down on the gray satin duvet covering the bed. "I don't like classical German music. I like jazz."

"Jazz!" Clara groaned. "Why listen to that *scheisse*?"

"Well, I can't, actually—not since you broke all of my records." Elise spoke in a neutral tone, but her point was made. Clara had thrown all of Elise's records from her window in a fit of anger when she'd discovered them, then had the gardener toss the broken pieces into the trash. She and Elise hadn't spoken for weeks after that.

"It's not right for *my* daughter, of all people, to own such things—let alone play them."

Elise gave a tight smile. Little did her mother know that she'd replaced all the broken records with exact duplicates—but this time labeled Bach, Beethoven, and Bruckner, instead of Benny Goodman, Dizzy Gillespie, and Louis Armstrong.

"And where's your swastika necklace?" Clara asked, lifting the wet washcloth and peering at Elise with one eye. "The one with the diamonds and rubies? Why are you still wearing that pathetic old cross?"

"I love the cross—and besides, it belonged to Grandmother."

Clara lowered the towel back over her eyes. "You're not still planning on becoming a nun, are you?" She sighed. "Poverty, chastity, and obedience—you were raised for so much more. Extraordinary—I raised you to be nothing short of extraordinary."

But this wasn't the argument Elise wanted to have. Especially now. She took a breath. "Mother, I want to talk to you about something. My friend from the hospital, Frieda, is married to a man named Ernst Klein—"

"The Jew. Yes. You've mentioned. They don't have any half-breeds now, do they?"

"No," Elise said, setting her jaw, "Frieda's not having a baby. Truth be told, she's concerned because she thinks Ernst might be called away soon, to a work camp." The words tumbled out of Elise's mouth. "He's a wonderful man—a good husband, honorable, responsible. An excellent surgeon—I used to work with him, at Charité. I know I asked you about this before, but it seems as though being married to an Aryan isn't enough to keep you in Berlin anymore. And—if there's anything—anything at all—that you can do . . . ." Her words hung in the air.

Clara was silent.

Elise tried again. "Mother, he's her husband. She loves him."

Clara exhaled. "If she loves him, she should be proud of his going to a labor camp and working hard for the *Volk*." Clara folded her hands over her chest. "Now, leave me. I'm tired. And I have to get up early tomorrow."

"Yes, Mother." Elise bit her tongue, wanting to say so much more. But she knew the tone in her mother's voice all too well. This conversation was finished. "Good night."

It's not over, Elise thought.

Back in her own room, Elise sat at a dressing table covered with her old porcelain-faced Kessel dolls keeping watch over a well-worn copy of Dietrich Bonhoeffer's *The Cost of Discipleship*. She brushed out her braids and curled the loose hair with a hot iron, the way the American movie stars did. She painted a matte cherry bow on her lips and changed from her demure frock to a blue dress with a circle skirt, with ruffled petticoats beneath.

She gave herself a spritz of Tosca behind each ear and between her breasts. Then she placed her pillows under her bedcovers, to look like a sleeping body, tossed a pair of Cuban heeled pumps out the window, and climbed out and made her way down a rose trellis.

A voice whispered from a cluster of trees. "What took you so long?" A young man stepped out of the shadows. Fritz Frommel's long blond hair covered his eyes, and he was dressed in a loose-fitting suit with pegged trousers and two-toned oxford wingtip shoes in beige and black. He carried a cane tucked under his arm, just like an English Dandy. He held out her shoes.

"You look divine, Fritz," Elise said, giving him a peck on the cheek, then taking the proffered shoes and slipping them on her feet.

"Not as glorious as you," he replied, going for her lips. Finally, they broke apart. "Are you ready?" he said, grabbing her hand. Together, they slipped out of the bushes and ran down the street, to the Grunewald S-Bahn station. He began singing, *"It don't mean a thing, if it ain't got that swing—"*

Together, they ran down the dark and deserted street, singing, *"Doo-ah, doo-ah, doo-ah, doo-ah, doo-ah, doo-ah, doo-ah, doo-ah!"*

The Berlin Swing Parties were never held twice in the same place. The dates and locations were always changing. Only secret whistles and passed notes gave information to those in the know.

This night's party was being held in an abandoned art deco theater in Schöneberg. A slim man wearing a top hat and a monocle was taking contributions at the door. However, when Elise and Fritz made it to the front of the line, they realized he was really a woman, dressed in drag and chewing on a cigar.

Inside, it was hot, close, and loud. The air smelled of smoke and sweat and sweet ylang-ylang perfume. A swing orchestra—men in white coats and black bow ties—was assembled onstage, playing, "Hep! Hep! The Jumpin' Jive." The brass wailed, the cymbals crashed, and drums beat time in a way that shook the floorboards. There were young people sitting on the sidelines at café tables with wrought-iron chairs snapping their fingers and keeping time, but most were up and dancing, jumping, and flying through the air in lifts and twists.

Across the dance floor, a few couples at a table spied Elise and Fritz and waved. They threaded their way through the crowd. There was only one seat, so Fritz took it and Elise perched in his lap. One of the women took a drag on her Trommler and stared out at the dancers. "It's like rearranging chairs on the deck of the *Titanic*," she remarked in a husky voice.

Elise took the woman's cigarette, then realized she was a young man with makeup. "I think it's brave!" Elise shouted over the noise.

"Listen to that scat," Fritz said, leaning back and snapping his fingers. "He might be German, but he sounds just like Cab Calloway." He gave Elise a gentle slap on the bottom. "Want to dance?"

She smiled and passed the cigarette back. "Of course!"

Fritz led Elise into the crowd as the orchestra segued into Louis Prima's "Sing, Sing, Sing." The other dancers were also young: boys with vests and Windsor knots, girls in floral dresses and flowing curls freed from braids.

It was crowded, so they started out with sugar pushes, skip ups, and side passes. "The King and Queen of Harlem!" someone shouted, and the crowd began to move aside, circling around Elise and Fritz as they started aerials: Lindy flips, candlesticks, Frankie snatches, frogs, and belly cherries.

"Go! Go! Go!" the other dancers shouted in English as Elise and Fritz kicked, jumped, and spun, her skirt flipping up to reveal her garters as the saxophones sang and trumpets blared.

When it was done, the crowd applauded, and the orchestra began "Take the 'A' Train." Fritz, breathing heavily, led Elise back to the table, where he pulled out a flask. He opened it and offered it to her. She took a gulp.

"*Mein Gott,* there's only one thing better than dancing," Elise said breathlessly, pushing back damp hair and giving Fritz a significant look.

He winked at her. "I'll go now. Meet me in five minutes."

In the alley behind the theater, Elise gave a contented sigh and pulled her panties back up and her skirt back down.

"Someday, I'd like to do it with you in a bed, not just a wall job," Fritz said, leaning against the postered brick wall.

"Oh stop!" Elise protested, flushed and laughing. "Someone will hear us!"

Fritz pulled off the condom he was wearing and began to pee, hitting the soldier in black featured on an SS recruitment poster square in the face. "Swing Heil!" he shouted, as he shook his penis and zipped up his trousers.

"Fritz!"

"What! You weren't so shy a few minutes ago."

"Well, that was different."

"For a girl who wants to be a nun, I'll say."

"I haven't taken any vows yet, remember," Elise said, straightening the seams on her stockings. "And, until I do, I see nothing wrong with enjoying life."

The metal doors of the theater were flung open as people ran out. "H.J.!" one girl shouted. Elise gasped. The *Jugend*—Hitler Youth—often stalked the swing parties and shut them down for being "un-German." They were violent and unpredictable, like the leaders they followed. More people poured out as Elise and Fritz watched in shock.

They heard shouting over a megaphone from inside. "We are closing this club! Give your names at the door!" A group of H.J., dressed in black, swarmed out into the alley to corral people back inside. Through the open doorway, Elise could see fights had broken out between the H.J. and the swing dancers as the *Jugends'* hard rubber batons met flimsy umbrellas.

"Come on!" Elise called, grabbing Fritz's hand. "We must go!" The two ran as fast and as hard as they could away from the H.J. and the club, finally finding an open church, St. Michael's.

Once inside, they slammed the doors shut. Then, breathless,

they took seats in hard wooden pews, a still and silent world away from the riotous dance club. The church smelled of incense. An organist was practicing Bach's *"Wachet auf, ruft uns die Stimme."* A priest, preparing the altar for the next day's Mass, shot them a baleful look but said nothing.

Then the doors banged open—the H.J. with their red swastika armbands. Elise turned in the pew, waiting, ready. Fritz stood, holding his umbrella. The air felt charged, the way it did before a thunderstorm.

The priest, an older man with silver hair combed over large ears, looked up and assessed the situation. "This is a place of worship," he intoned to the boys in uniforms, his voice filling the soaring space as it did on Sunday mornings. "This is no place for you."

"This is no place for *you*!" one of the older boys rejoined, spitting on the floor with contempt. "The Germans are God's chosen people and Hitler is our Savior! We don't need churches and priests and ministers telling us what to do anymore." He looked back to his comrades and began chanting: "Hang the Jews! Put the priests against the walls!"

One by one, the other boys joined in. "Hang the Jews! Put the the priests against the walls! Hang the Jews! Put the priests against the walls!"

"Stop!" the priest thundered from the altar.

The ugly face-off was interrupted by the menacing howl of an air-raid siren.

The H.J. boys looked at one another, then back to the priest. *"Heil Hitler,"* they said in near unison, saluting.

"Gute nacht," he replied.

The head H.J. boy took one step toward the priest, then another. The siren wailed. "Say *'Heil Hitler.'*"

The priest held his ground. "Good evening."

"Say *'Heil Hitler,'* old man!"

The priest didn't flinch.

The boy reached behind the priest and pulled off his skullcap, throwing it to the floor. He spat on it, then ground it under his black boot. As the other boys cheered and the sirens continued their wail, he turned and left, the rest following after.

The priest nodded to Elise and Fritz, leaving the defiled skullcap on the floor. "You can come with me—we have a crypt that doubles as a bomb shelter."

Elise and Fritz followed, meeting up with him at the altar. The organist, a stout older woman with large hands perfect for bridging octaves, came, too.

As they walked together, Elise said, "You didn't say *'Heil Hitler'* to them. Weren't you afraid of being arrested?"

"My dear," the priest replied, opening the door behind the altar that led down into the crypt and letting them all enter first. "I made the decision a very long time ago not to say *'heil'* to anyone but God."

Chapter Four

The next morning, Maggie cornered David in the dining room over his breakfast and newspaper. It was dim, so she pushed aside the blackout curtains and opened a few of the windows, letting in lemony sunlight and warm morning air.

"Mr. Wright, hmm?" she teased, sitting down and pouring herself a cup of weak tea.

"Jumping Jupiter, stop—just stop!" David said, turning red. It was one of the few times in their four years of friendship that Maggie had ever seen him blush.

"When did all . . . this . . . happen?" she asked.

"While you were off—doing, well, whatever it is you've been doing for the last few months."

Maggie spread margarine on a piece of toast. "And is it serious?" she asked. David had had numerous romances and love affairs, flirtations and flings—including one with a British traitor at Windsor Castle—but never had anyone serious in his life. *Perhaps he's growing up?* Maggie wondered. *Goodness knows, living through these last few years has changed us all.* Maggie was one of the very, very, *very* few people who knew David was homosexual, and she took the responsibility of keeping his secret seriously.

"It is, actually," David said, through a large mouthful of toast.

Maggie looked down at her nightgown and ratty plaid flannel

robe. "He's not still here, is he?" she asked, patting her disheveled hair and glancing to the doorway.

"Oh, goodness, no. He took off before dawn."

"Well, congratulations to both of you. I think it's absolutely wonderful." Maggie stood to give David a huge embrace, causing him to choke on a crumb.

"Careful there, Mags. It would be a shame to survive all those air raids, only to be taken out by an overenthusiastic flatmate and a wayward piece of toast."

Maggie returned to her seat, beaming. "I'm just so happy for you, David."

"Well, it's not all hearts and flowers, you know."

"Really? Why on earth not?"

"Oh, nothing at all to do with Freddie." David sighed. "It's my parents, you see. They think it's high time I should get married. To a nice Jewish girl. Have babies and suchlike things. I blame the war for it. Before, I might have managed my bachelor existence. Now, they're suddenly quite concerned with their potential progeny."

Maggie took a sip of tea. "Well, can't you just put them off?"

"That's the sticky part. They're not religious at all, just go to temple on the High Holidays. One of my father's favorite foods is bacon, for heaven's sake. But ever since the Nuremberg Laws passed, they're twitchy. And now they've given me an ultimatum. Find a bride and get married by my thirtieth birthday, or be completely cut off. In case you don't remember, I'll be thirty on—"

"September third. Yes, of course I know when your birthday is, you lout." Maggie contemplated David's parents' ultimatum. It was horrible, of course, but still just a bit funny. She snorted a little. David did love his luxuries so. The idea of his making do without seemed . . . interesting. "You know, the rest of us seem to survive without vast sums from rich relatives."

"I'm cursed with exquisite taste, Mags! Cursed, I say! Plus, this flat is in their name. I'd have to find somewhere else to live." He leaned in toward her. "We'd *all* have to find somewhere else to live," he said pointedly.

Maggie did still own her late grandmother's house on Portland Place in Marylebone, but there were too many ghosts there, so she had rented it out. "I understand." She put on her best serious face. "So what do you plan to do?"

"No idea." He took an enormous bite of toast. "Speaking of love, how's what's-his-name?"

David had been best friends with Maggie's late almost-fiancé, John Sterling. They had all worked together at Number 10 for Mr. Churchill, before John joined the RAF. His Lancaster had crashed somewhere near Berlin and he was officially classified as "missing and presumed dead." His family had held a memorial service a few months ago; Maggie had taken the train from Scotland to London to attend and mourn, along with David. Loyal to the core to his late friend, David wasn't enamored of Maggie's current beau, Hugh Thompson. "What's his name again? Stew? Lou? Prue?"

Maggie frowned. "You know perfectly well what his name is. And *Hugh* is fine, thank you. In fact, I was coming from his flat last night. Not that it's any of your business."

"You're right, Mags." David had the decency to look ashamed. "You're a grown woman—you have the right to live your life."

"David, I loved John," Maggie said. "I did. He was my first love. And it nearly killed me to find out his plane had been shot down. To have Nigel write to me to say that they'd given up hope. I was at the memorial service if you recall, holding up his mother." Maggie raised her chin. "But life *does* go on."

"I know, I know," David amended. "So—how is *Hugh*?"

She smiled. "*I* don't kiss and tell. Besides, it's the last time we'll see each other, for a while."

"Really?" David didn't know exactly what Maggie was up to, but as Winston Churchill's head private secretary, he had a fair amount of clearance; he knew she'd been training with SOE. "Off so soon? No rest for the weary, apparently."

"You know I can't give details."

"Well, I hope I still have the flat whenever it is you return. If I can't figure anything else out—" David stood and walked over to Maggie, then dropped down dramatically on one knee. He took her hand in both of his. "Maggie, my redheaded shiksa goddess, would you do me the supreme honor of marrying me?" He grinned. "After you convert, of course."

Maggie nearly spat out her tea. "I'm, ah, very flattered, David, and will keep it in mind. But as one of the 'overlooked people'— and a Jeffersonian agnostic at that—I'm not sure marriage to me specifically would do the trick. Not that I don't appreciate the lovely offer, of course."

David looked serious as he stood up. "Far safer to be one of the overlooked at this point, I should think. By the way, give 'em hell, Mags."

She gave him a tight smile. "I certainly intend to."

Hell was just what Maggie Hope had trained for.

When she returned to the SOE office later that morning, she was directed to Noreen Baxter, a woman about Maggie's age, with pale skin, rosebud lips, and crimped brown hair. "Don't be nervous, darling," she said, slipping her arm through Maggie's as they walked the corridors of 64 Baker. She drew close and whispered in Maggie's ear. "You're the first woman to be dropped— we're all rooting for you."

"Thank you," Maggie whispered back as they reached Noreen's office. They both sat down on a worn sofa.

"Now, your cover story is the most important part of the operation," Noreen told her, picking up a folder from the low table and handing it to Maggie. "Here you are. Your name is Margareta Hoffman. You were born on the second of June, 1916, in Frankfurt, to a German businessman and his wife. You were educated in Switzerland, which will explain any inconsistencies with your accent or verbiage. You met Gottlieb Lehrer in Rome, where you were hired as his typist."

For the next two hours, Maggie read and memorized the file, including names and addresses of contacts in Berlin, and Noreen quizzed her on it, even adding in trick questions, such as "Who does your hair?" "What's your doctor's name and address?" and "How do you do laundry?"

Then Maggie wrote letters to her family and friends, telling them that, once again, she would be away on official business, and would contact them when she returned. To Aunt Edith, in Wellesley, Massachusetts. To her father, Edmund Hope, at Bletchley Park. To Sarah, on tour, care of the Sadler's Wells Ballet. To the newly wed Nigel and Charlotte Ludlow. David and Hugh knew, more or less, what she was doing, but she wrote to them anyway.

In case she didn't come back. She'd already made out her will, leaving her most precious possession, her slide rule, to David.

Afterward, Maggie was quizzed by another agent named Kim Philby, a dashing young Cambridge graduate, who was wearing a gray pin-striped suit with a deep red tie and red double-point pocket square. He was tough but thorough, and when she'd finished with him, she felt more secure with her cover. "Remember," Philby admonished, "you are now Margareta Hoffman. Let your life here melt away. The more comfortable you are in Margareta's skin, the safer you'll be."

Maggie nodded. She wasn't at all against the idea of leaving Maggie Hope in England. Maggie had problems—a bluestocking aunt who'd lied about her father's death while raising her, a father who'd kept his existence a secret until she uncovered it, and a mother who—well, Maggie was still wrestling with the ugly truth of that. John, the man whom she'd loved and turned away, was dead. And Hugh was . . . confusing. Margareta was free from all that.

Noreen swept back in. "Open your mouth," she ordered.

Maggie raised one eyebrow but complied.

Noreen peered inside. "Well, I can see you've had good American dentistry, but on the Continent, fillings are gold, not silver. We'll need to switch them out. I'll make you an appointment for our dentist."

"You're going to change my *fillings*?"

Noreen nodded, walking to the telephone. "You only have two, so it shouldn't be that bad."

"We leave nothing to chance," Philby added.

Just after noon, her fillings replaced with gold by an SOE dentist, Maggie returned to the office. Her teeth hurt. But the pain took her mind off her nerves.

In Noreen's office, there were clothes on hangers on a hook behind the closed wooden door. "Go ahead, put them on," Noreen told her. "They're quite nice, actually."

Maggie locked the door, then stripped down to nothing and first put on the underthings. At one time, she would have asked Noreen to leave, but her time at paramilitary camps had done away with modesty. The lingerie was German-made and quite luxurious, compared to what she usually wore. Next came a Jaeger suit and blouse, broken-in Rieker shoes with the soles rubbed in German soil, and an elegant leather handbag.

"Quite cosmopolitan," Maggie commented.

"Forget bombs—letting that gorgeous bag go may quite literally kill me," Noreen said.

"I promise to bring it back, safe and sound."

"Inside, you'll find a wallet with some Reichsmarks, face powder, keys to your flat, Goethe's *Faust*, and Hitler's *Mein Kampf*. You'll be given a suitcase with a few changes of clothes, your gown for the party, more undergarments, a nightgown, and toiletries, including German-brand sanitary towels, just in case."

Noreen appraised Maggie's face. "You don't wear much makeup—that's good. Nazi women don't, just like they're not supposed to smoke and drink—not that that stops them, of course." She laughed. "Oh, all this luxury is wasted on you! You should see what we have picked out for the girls parachuting into France later this month—hideous dowdy things—no style at all. Smelly and scratchy. You're very lucky." Without missing a beat, she continued, "Nelson gave you the lipstick with the cyanide pill in it, yes? Let's put that in there."

Maggie transferred the gold tube with the false bottom from her bag to Margareta's. She sniffed—the bag smelled of something both beautiful and disarming. "Oh, that's wonderful," she said. "What is it?"

"Jicky," Noreen said. "There *are* benefits to conquering France—Jicky is Guerlain, of course. There's a small bottle in your purse. And this is one of our best toys." Noreen handed Maggie a red and white box of Milde Sorte cigarettes. Maggie turned it this way and that to see what it really was. "It's a subminiature spy camera with a film cartridge, small enough to fit into a cigarette pack. Just in case you find anything useful."

Noreen patted a chair. "Now, come, sit down. I'm going to teach you how to do your hair." With deft fingers, she fashioned Maggie's coppery tresses into an intricately braided updo, the latest in Germanic elegance.

"I feel like I should be dancing around a solstice bonfire," Maggie said, turning her head back and forth and looking in the mirror of her compact. "I just hope I can replicate it."

"You'll have plenty of downtime with nothing to do, so you can practice." Noreen scooped up Maggie's clothes and folded them, then wrapped them in brown paper. "We'll keep these safe for you," she promised. "And it's only four days. You'll be back before you know it."

Then Noreen handed Maggie a scrap of silk with writing on it. Maggie's codes. For her to use each time she communicated, and then tear off and destroy. "And what happens if you don't have the silk and you need to radio us?"

"Then I have to use a poem instead," Maggie answered. "A poem I've memorized."

"If the enemy knows you've destroyed this code, it will be in their power to make you tell them your poem." Noreen's eyes were grave. "Remember it's what would allow the Germans to transmit to England and endanger the lives of all who come after you. That's why you have the pill." Then she smiled. "Now, here's your 'poem'—we chose it especially for you."

Maggie was expecting something from Shakespeare, Milton, or even the King James Bible—but not what Noreen passed her. *"We hold these truths to be self-evident, that all men are created equal, that they are endowed by their Creator with certain unalienable Rights, that among these are Life, Liberty and the pursuit of Happiness."*

Maggie smiled, delighted to see the words again. As she'd been taught, she picked five words at random: *equal, rights, life, liberty,* and *happiness.* Noreen copied the words down, then created Maggie's code. And so the five words became:

e q u a l r i g h t s l i f e l i b e r t y h a p p

which corresponded to the code alphabet of

a b c d e f g h i j k l m n o p q r s t u v w x y z

"You're our honorary Yank," Noreen said. "So we wanted something appropriate." She pointed to Maggie's skirt. "There's a secret pocket in the hem."

Maggie found it and tucked the scrap of silk away.

"Oh, and there's one more thing." From a shelf, Noreen pulled a bag full of black yarn and long knitting needles. She drew out a scarf in progress. "Margareta is a knitter."

"All right . . ." Maggie said, not seeing the point but willing to play along.

"Do you know why?"

Maggie's forehead creased. "Knitting socks for German soldiers?"

"Yes, many German women do that in their spare time. But," Noreen said, holding the half-done scarf in one hand, "this knitting might save your life. Do you see the pattern?"

Maggie squinted. It was hard to see any sort of a pattern in pearl stitches against flat stockinet in black yarn; it all looked like mistakes. "Not a great knitting job."

"Look closer," Noreen said.

Maggie did. "It's *code*," she said, realizing. *Ah, brilliant!* "Morse code."

"In an emergency, if you can't get to a radio, knit a message into your scarf, then go to Hasenheideplatz, located just outside your contact's flat. There will be an older woman there, every morning, sitting on a bench and working on her knitting—Berlin's answer to Madame Defarge. She'll see the code you've knit in and copy it, to get it back to us. Likewise, she may provide information for you. When you're done, rip the coded stitching out." Noreen looked hard at Maggie. "You *do* knit, don't you?"

"Yes," Maggie replied. "I do. Not well, and I can't turn heels, but enough to knit some code, certainly." It was one of the few traditionally feminine crafts that Aunt Edith had taught her. Knitting had a structural logic based on geometry and proportion that had always appealed to her. She accepted the needles and ball of yarn from Noreen, and tucked them into her handbag.

There was a sharp rap at the door. "The car's here, ladies," a woman called.

Maggie and Noreen made their way downstairs. A glossy black Riley had pulled up in front of the door and was idling. The driver, a FANY in her brown uniform, exited the car. "Good afternoon, ladies," she said as she walked around to open the trunk.

"Thank you," Maggie said, handing over her valise. "You *are* coming with me?" she said to Noreen in what she hoped was a strong and confident voice.

"Absolutely," Noreen answered, opening the car door. "Come on, hop in."

It was getting dark by the time they reached the Whitley airport in Reading, the night air chill after the warm summer day. The car went through security and then out to the airfield.

They pulled into the parking lot. Maggie and Noreen exited the car and entered the building. "Why don't you use the loo? It's a long way to Berlin." Noreen touched Maggie's shoulder. "Don't worry—they won't leave without you."

Maggie found the ladies' W.C. Her face in the mirror was gray. *What am I doing?* she wondered. But it was too late to go back now.

"Almost ready!" Noreen chirped to Maggie when she returned. She pulled papers from her purse. "Now, here are your passport, identity card, proof of Aryan descent, and your ration card. Put them in your wallet. You'll need to sign them, as Margareta Hoffman, of course. Let's see, and clothing coupons and some more Reichsmarks. Don't spend them all in one place."

Maggie accepted the fountain pen, a Lamy, and practiced her new signature in German script a few times before actually signing her name. "Did this actually come from Germany?" she asked as she signed numerous documents and official papers.

"It's German, but it came from the Lower East Side of New York City."

Maggie finally finished signing everything. Her stomach was doing flips in nervous anticipation.

"Goodbye, Margareta," Noreen said, kissing her on both cheeks. "We don't say 'good luck' in this business, so I'll just say 'cheers.' We'll see you soon."

Maggie took a shaky breath as her heart thudded in her chest. "Don't worry about me," she said, kissing Noreen back. "Piece of cake." It was now time to board the plane.

This moment was exactly what she'd trained for. Still, now that she was climbing the narrow ladder to the Westland Lysander's hinged door, she was having second thoughts. *I'm stupid, I'm so ridiculously stupid—why couldn't I have stayed a secretary? Or a governess? I was actually good at those things* . . . Maggie reflected as she took off her shoes and put them in her suitcase. Then she bandaged her ankles, rolled up her skirt, zipped up her padded jumpsuit, and pulled on heavy boots.

It's just like training, it's just like training . . . she repeated to herself, like a mantra.

"Your parachute's up there." The RAF sergeant, a young man with high color, low voice, and a Scottish accent, wore a shearling jacket. He helped her up the ladder through the trapdoor in the midsection of the plane, a converted Halifax bomber, with the underside gun turret removed and replaced by a hatch. *The belly of the beast,* Maggie thought. Her nostrils flared as she detected the scent of oil.

The RAF sergeant boarded behind her; he would be her dispatcher when they reached the drop zone. Her folded-up parachute was at one end of the plane. Her suitcase, now packed into a crate, was attached to another parachute.

The engines started up with a roar. Maggie strapped herself in next to the sergeant, in the walled-off area that was just behind the nose, where the flight crew sat. "You doing all right there, miss?" he said. "If you need to be sick, there's a bucket in the corner."

"I won't need it, Sergeant," Maggie assured him. *At least I really, truly hope not.*

The plane began moving, slowly at first, then gaining speed as it finally achieved liftoff, and Maggie could hear the wheels being retracted with a loud crash and a corresponding tremor.

"Now, I have some hot tea," the sergeant said, pulling out a green-and-silver Thermos. "But I also have some gin if you'd prefer."

"Tea, please," she said, thankful for a civilized beverage in strange circumstances. "Just a little," she amended, realizing the plane had no toilet.

"We also have some cheese sandwiches. Oh, look, a bar of chocolate!"

Maggie's stomach turned a few somersaults. "Really—you have it."

"Nervous?" he asked, not unkindly.

"No. Well—maybe a little."

"It's good to be nervous," he said, clapping her on the shoulder. "Means you're alive. Now, we'll be flying over the Netherlands and then into Germany. Might try to get in a catnap while we're up here. They're going to turn the lights off soon, anyway."

Maggie finished her tea, crossed her legs and arms, and closed her eyes. She internally recited Canto III of Longfellow's translation of Dante's *Inferno*—it seemed appropriate, after all—

Through me the way is to the city dolent;
Through me the way is to eternal dole;
Through me the way among the people lost.

Justice incited my sublime Creator;
Created me divine Omnipotence,
The highest Wisdom and the primal Love.

Before me there were no created things,
Only eterne, and I eternal last.
All hope abandon, ye who enter in!

She was sure she'd never sleep on the plane, but before long her eyes had closed and her mind was filled with images of burning swastikas and the sound of howling wolves. And then she felt the sergeant poke her arm. "Wake up, miss," he said. "We're almost there."

Maggie was so groggy and dazed by her nightmare that she didn't have time to panic as she stood and let him help her on with her parachute. "Now remember what they taught you in training," he told her. "Keep your legs together when you jump and tuck your chin. And, most important, bend your knees when you land."

He went to the hatch in the floor and opened the doors. A great gush of icy wind came up, nearly knocking her over. Maggie took a few steps toward it and peered down into the darkness.

"They're under blackout, too," the sergeant said. "But, look—that's our man on the ground. He's giving the signal. Don't worry—he'll take good care of you."

Maggie felt her heart starting to beat faster and faster. She forced herself to take deep breaths. "It's time now, miss."

The plane circled lower and slowed. Maggie walked, with tiny steps, closer to the hole. She and the sergeant squatted down at the edge. Below, they could see a bonfire glittering orange in the darkness. "You all right, miss? Do you want to jump, or should I push you? No shame in it—done it for lots of the boys."

That made Maggie twist her mouth in a half smile. "No, I want to jump on my own."

"That's right," he said, clapping her on the shoulder again. Maggie was suddenly overwhelmed with gratitude for his touch. "Now, just remember—bend your knees. Five, four, three, two . . ."

Maggie jumped, or rather stepped, into the hole and dropped straight down. It felt as if there was no air in her lungs as she fell, her body pushed almost sideways by the contrast in speed, as she plummeted through the air. $S = D/T$, Maggie thought in the logical part of her brain, even as the other parts screamed in fear and excitement, a trick she'd learned on practice jumps. *Speed = Distance divided by Time*.

She pressed the button on her harness to release the parachute, heard it engage, then open, and felt a painful tug on her legs and rear where the straps were attached.

Her descent into darkness began to slow and she almost, almost, had a split second to enjoy the feeling of flying before she hit the ground—sooner than she expected.

And much harder.

She lay on her side, in pain. Slowly the burning feeling subsided, although her knees still throbbed. From a long way off, she heard voices. *"Gute nacht, gnädiges Fräulein!* So glad you could 'drop in,' " a male voice said. She saw the glare of flashlights.

I bet he's been working on that all day. Maggie spat out dirt and grass and sat up, grabbing the hand in front of her and coming up to her feet. There she swayed, unsteady, testing her limbs and joints for damage. But as she hit the disk on her belt to disengage the parachute, she smiled.

"Thank you. Next time, I'll remember to bend my knees," she said in perfect German.

One of the men detached the parachute from the crate protecting Maggie's suitcase, then retrieved the suitcase itself from the padding. "You will be needing this, Fräulein Hoffman," he said, handing it to her.

"*Danke schön,*" Maggie said, trying not just to speak but to *think* in German, as she extricated herself from her jumpsuit. Her ankles and knees were sore, but her left hip had taken the brunt of the impact. She brushed grass from her face and hair and continued to spit out dust and dirt. "What's your name?"

"Herr Karl. If you can walk now, the auto is over this way." He picked up her valise and led the way to a waiting truck, its headlights dimmed by blackout slats.

"In you go," he said, opening the door for her. "I'll put this in the back." He also folded both parachutes and broke down the crate, pulling nails from the wood until it collapsed, then putting everything into the truck bed.

As Maggie sat in the front seat, she realized her legs were shaking. And her hands. She was overwhelmed, but part of her was still thrilled. *I'm in Germany!*

They drove down a dark and twisting road, to a small farmhouse. There Maggie was introduced to Frau Karl, Herr Karl's wife, and a young man, their son, called Carl. *Carl Karl.* Maggie tried not to smile.

Herr Adelwin Karl was in his late fifties, with pale, thinning hair and a weather-burned face. His light eyes were filled with fear, and darted back and forth, as though he expected the Gestapo to break down the door at any moment. Frau Karl was small and dark, with a no-nonsense air that indicated she was the boss of the operation. Carl was young, sixteen at the most, and had an eager, round face. He was solidly built and somewhat clumsy in the way most teenagers are, with large hands and large feet, like a puppy's.

"Sit down, sit down!" Frau Karl called to all of them as she bustled about the warm and delicious-smelling kitchen. "Dinner is almost ready." Maggie did as she was bid, sitting at a rough-hewn wooden table, already set.

Sure enough, there were onions sizzling in a cast-iron pan; Frau Karl turned them over with a pair of tongs. Carl took a loaf of brown bread from the cupboard, and Adelwin filled three glasses with milk and brought them to the table. Frau Karl brought a large bowl of mashed vegetables. *"Himmel und Hölle,"* she told them, putting it down. "Apples from heaven and potatoes from the earth."

Maggie was surprised to find that she had a voracious appetite. She downed everything, mopping up the onion grease with the bread, as well as a good portion of the *Himmel und Hölle*. What she couldn't finish, Carl Karl tucked into with abandon.

When they were done, and the table was cleared, Adelwin brought out train schedules and maps, to make certain that Maggie knew where she was going in the morning. Herr Karl would drive her to the station early; there Maggie would take the train to Berlin, where she would meet up with Gottlieb Lehrer.

"There aren't many SS here in our tiny town," Frau Karl told her, "but you still need to be careful. Anyone can turn you in for anything, at any time. Always assume you're being watched."

Maggie gave an enormous yawn; it was well after midnight. "Excuse me."

"Come, let me show you to your room," Frau Karl said.

Maggie bade good night to the men, then followed Frau Karl

up the narrow wooden stairs. "Your suitcase is in there," she said, indicating a guest room. "*Schlafen Sie gut.* I will see you in the morning."

The first thing Maggie did was open her suitcase, checking for the radio transmitter crystals and the microphone. She breathed a sigh of relief: both seemed undamaged.

She was able to undress and put on her nightgown before the first wave of exhaustion engulfed her. She barely had time to pull the quilt over her before she was fast asleep.

Downstairs, Frau Karl cleaned up the kitchen, washing the last of the dishes. "Do you think she'll make it? She's a woman after all. She might have an advantage. No Nazi would ever believe that a woman could be a spy."

"I hope so," Herr Karl said, drinking ersatz coffee. "I certainly hope so."

Chapter Five

Elise had been shocked to receive the invitation to Gretel Paulus's memorial service. The card stock was thick and bone-white, the text engraved in black ink.

HERR AND FRAU ODWIN PAULUS

REQUEST THE HONOR OF YOUR PRESENCE

AT THE MEMORIAL SERVICE FOR

OUR BELOVED DAUGHTER, GRETEL ADA PAULUS

ON SUNDAY, THE 5TH OF JUNE

AT TWELVE O'CLOCK NOON

KAISER WILHELM MEMORIAL CHURCH

BREITSCHEIDPLATZ 10789

RECEPTION TO FOLLOW

NIEBUHRSTRASSE 27

BERLIN-CHARLOTTENBURG

The day of the memorial service, Elise donned her best black crepe dress, hat, and gloves. It was hot; Elise's dress stuck to the small of her back. Underneath the hat, her hair was damp.

The service was traditional, and the priest sounded truly sorrowful to have lost the little girl from his congregation. Afterward, Elise, with the rest of the mourners, went to the Pauluses' nearby home. It was a large and comfortable third-floor apartment in a

baroque limestone building. Inside, Bauhaus furniture was juxta-
posed against nineteenth-century herringbone wood floors. The
wide windows looked out over a courtyard garden, where roses
bloomed and a raven croaked in an apple tree. People dressed in
black milled about, clutching delicate cups and saucers, speaking in
subdued voices.

"Ah, Nurse Hess," said Gretel's father, finding her in the crowd.
His eyes were blank and his voice was a monotone. "How good of
you to come. Gretel always spoke so well of you. Won't you have
something to drink? Eat?" He indicated a plantation table in the
dining room, swathed in white linen, piled high with fruit, cold
cuts, cheeses, breads, and pastries. A fat black housefly buzzed
over the table, finally landing on a sticky, almond-covered
ʒuckerkuchen.

"I'm fine, thank you, Herr Paulus," Elise replied. "I want you
to know how sorry I am for your loss. I didn't know Gretel for
long, but she was a lovely child. She was always so brave and
cheerful."

"Thank you for your kind words, Nurse Hess," he said, his
eyes trying to focus.

Elise wondered whether to press on. The girl was dead, after
all. Why upset a grieving father? Then she remembered Gretel
holding her little bear, and took a breath. "If I may ask, Herr Paulus, what was the cause of her death?"

"Pneumonia," he said flatly. "They told us she died of pneumonia."

"They 'told you'?" Elise repeated, confused. "Gretel didn't die
at home? I wasn't aware that she'd been readmitted to Charité."

Herr Paulus blinked. "No, no—she left Charité and was sent to
the Hadamar Institute, for additional evaluation. While she was
there, she caught pneumonia. They sent us her ashes in an urn. We
didn't even have time to see her. We don't even have her body to

bury. They sent her away to Hadamar without telling us. It was only later that we were informed. And then it was too late." He turned to the urn on the mantel, in front of a framed oil painting of Hitler. It was shiny and black, an enameled swastika facing front.

"I'm so sorry," Elise repeated to Herr Paulus, thinking of the little blond girl with the teddy bear who'd been on the gray bus. Hadamar? *Why on earth had Gretel been sent to Hadamar?* Elise gave her condolences to Gretel's mother as well and left, taking the S-Bahn to Charité. Something was wrong.

And she was determined to look at Gretel's files.

Despite the war, football continued in Britain.

Under a gunpowder-gray sky, Chelsea, in royal blue uniforms, took the grassy green field, representing West London. They were facing off against Sunderland, in red, white, and black.

Peter Frain, head of MI-5, might have looked as though he'd be more at home at the ballet or opera, but he was a lifelong Chelsea fan. The crowd, mostly Londoners, was busy booing Sunderland star footballer Horatio "Raich" Carter, who'd joined the Sunderland Fire Service. Although most of the prominent professional players left in the leagues had already volunteered for or been drafted to the armed forces, the fire service was a reserved occupation, and some thought it was a tactic to avoid military service. As a result, Carter was often jeered by the opposing team's fans.

Far, far up in the stands, well away from the crowd, Frain and his younger protégé, Hugh Thompson, booed Carter along with the crowd. As the game commenced, Frain lit a cigarette. "Did you see Maggie Hope before she left?" he asked, squinting.

"Briefly," Hugh replied. "She'd just returned from training. And she was assigned immediately."

Frain smoked impassively, until one of the Chelsea midfielders lost control of the ball, allowing one of the Sunderland players to move it toward Chelsea's goal. "Damn it! Come on, boys!"

Hugh had worked with Frain for several years, ever since Winston Churchill had appointed Frain to the post, and had never seen him in any context that was not professional. He was somewhat amused by his boss's demeanor at the game.

"You and she did well with the Windsor situation," Frain remarked.

"Thank you, sir," Hugh replied. He was proud of his work with Maggie at Windsor Castle. They had indeed worked well together—saving the Princess Elizabeth from being kidnapped by Nazis and carried off to Germany. And the experience had made them grow closer.

But that had been months ago. He'd been officially promoted, but still—nothing really had changed. He was itching for another big assignment. And more work to help him keep his mind off things. When he and Maggie had worked the Windsor case, they'd discovered that Maggie's mother had been a German Sektion agent, one who'd killed Hugh's father, an MI-5 operative, among others. Hugh didn't hold what he'd learned against Maggie; after all, she'd never known her mother. Still, he was having a hard time grappling with the truth about his father's murder, battling insomnia and lack of appetite.

"You know Robertson."

"Of course." Lieutenant Colonel T. A. Robertson was the MI-5 agent in charge of finding and turning over German spies captured in Britain.

"Robertson works with a chap named John Cecil Masterman, who's the chairman of the Twenty Committee. Do you know about the Twenty Committee?"

"No, sir. At least, only rumors."

"The Twenty Committee is known by the Roman numerals XX—Operation Double Cross, you see." Frain rolled his eyes. "Masterman thinks he's quite clever. It's an anti-espionage operation. Nazi agents in Britain who are captured by Robertson are used to broadcast disinformation to their Nazi controllers. I want you to meet with him."

"Sir?"

"Tomorrow. Eight A.M., at Tower Bridge."

Hugh felt a prickle of excitement on the back of his neck. He'd been so depressed for so long. But the Twenty Committee was real, and he'd be part of it. "Meet with John Cecil Masterman tomorrow. I understand, sir." He beamed.

"Wipe that idiotic grin off your face," Frain muttered, before turning his attention back to the game. "Oh, Chelsea, you're breaking my heart," he yelled. "Get the damned ball!"

It was late morning and Patient No. 1564, also known as Herr Mystery, opened his eyes for the first time since his latest surgery.

He took in his surroundings: the whitewashed ceilings, the gray walls, the glossy wainscoting. He looked up and down lines of narrow beds inhabited by wounded men. Some were sleeping; some were conversing quietly. A few moaned in pain. The air was pungent with the scents of rubbing alcohol and bleach. High windows admitted shafts of yellow sunlight.

Still groggy from pain medication, he didn't remember where he was—and then, all at once, he did. Terror twisted at his guts. He tried to move and pain washed over him. A groan escaped from his parched lips; he didn't recognize the sound of his own voice.

Flight Lieutenant Eggers turned over in his bed. "Steady there," he said to the man. "You've had a rough time of it." He looked around and spied Elise passing by in the hallway. "Nurse!"

Elise, still in her black dress from the memorial service, looked in. "Yes?"

"Oh, it *is* you—almost didn't recognize you in civilian clothing."

Elise wanted nothing more than to get to Gretel's files, but she was nothing if not professional. "Yes, Lieutenant Eggers?"

Eggers pointed to the man in the bed next to his. "Our 'Herr Mystery'—he's awake!"

Elise walked quickly to Patient No. 1564, heels tapping on the floor. At his bedside, she checked the size of his pupils and how they reacted to light. "Hello," she said in soothing tones. "You're in Berlin, at Charité Mitte Hospital. You were in a plane crash and sustained a number of internal injuries. You've had two surgeries to repair them." Nothing. Just a blank, almost panicked look.

She took his temperature; it was normal. Whatever infection he'd had, he'd fought it off. "Can you tell me your name?" she asked.

His eyes darted around, as though looking for the nearest escape.

"I'll let the doctors know you're awake now," she said, tucking the blanket around him. "They'll be so pleased. We all are."

The man blinked, his eyes struggling to focus on Elise's.

"Don't let this one get you in any trouble." Elise indicated Eggers with her thumb. "And I'll be right back with the doctor." She patted his shoulder. "Hold tight."

His hand grabbed for hers, gripping it as his eyes searched hers. It was as if he recognized her. The two locked eyes for a long moment.

"It looks like he knows you!" Eggers was watching avidly. "Do you know him?"

Elise laughed, breaking the tension. "No. Maybe. At any rate, I'll be back."

At the nurses' station, Elise called Dr. Brandt, to tell him that Patient No. 1564 was awake and alert, then hung up the receiver and made a few notes in the chart.

Nurse Flint, sitting next to her, looked up. "Can he talk?"

"No," said Elise. "At least, not yet. But his temperature's normal and he seems aware of his surroundings, if a little disoriented."

Elise finished her notes and then put the chart back in a pile. She turned to Nurse Flint. "By the way, whatever happened to Gretel Paulus?" she asked casually. "I thought she was going to be released."

Nurse Flint looked heavenward. "I can't keep track of them all the way you can," she said, organizing the doctors' telephone message slips.

"Do you mind if I check her file?"

"You know that's not allowed."

"She was such a sweet girl. I just need to know what happened," Elise said, with her most beguiling smile.

"Neugier ist der Katze Tod." Curiosity killed the cat.

"Please?" Elise wheedled. *"Na Bittchen?"*

"The keys are in the top right-hand drawer." Nurse Flint shrugged. "But I didn't tell you that."

Elise grinned. "Tell me what?"

The record keeping in all German hospitals was excellent and Charité's was no exception. And that was why there were files upon files upon files, all in perfect order. It wasn't hard for Elise to find the proper key and pull out the red file on Gretel Paulus.

She noted the treatments for chronic ear infections, lengths of hospital stays, medications prescribed. Nothing out of the ordinary. At the end of the file was the form Dr. Brandt had marked with a red *X*. Behind this form was a copy of a letter sent to Gretel's parents.

> *Dear Herr and Frau Paulus,*
>   *We are writing to inform you that Gretel Paulus has been transferred to the Hadamar Institute, for assessment and possible additional treatment in a Special Section for Children.*
>   *We will keep you informed of her progress.*
>
>

Heil Hitler!
Nurse Aloïsa Herrmann
Charité Campus Mitte

How strange, Elise thought. *How very, very strange.*

To the best of her knowledge, no one named Aloïsa Herrmann worked as a nurse at Charité.

Elise returned the key to the drawer. "What time is the next trip to Hadamar?" she asked Nurse Flint.

The woman didn't look up from her paperwork. "There's a bus leaving today, at five o'clock."

The buses used to transport the children from Charité to the Hadamar Institute were dark gray, with white painted-over windows, like milky blind eyes. At five o'clock that evening, when the bus was ready to pull away from Charité, Elise—who'd now changed into her nurse's uniform—slipped onto it.

"Are you working this shift now?" one of the other nurses asked. "Do you have your papers?"

"In my bag," Elise lied, thinking quickly. From the back of the bus, a boy began to wail.

"I'm Brigitta Graff," the young woman told her. "We can deal with that later; for now, just help me." Wafting through the bus was the unmistakable odor of urine. Several other children began to cry.

"What can I do to help?" Elise asked.

Together, they looked at the children in their seats, about fifteen in all. Some were drooling, some were moaning, some were waving their limbs spastically. There were children with Down syndrome, neurological diseases, and malformations of all kinds. Some sat quietly and appeared as any other child, but Elise recognized them—they were blind, deaf, or epileptic. And some were *mischlinge*—mixed Jewish and Aryan, but classified as Jewish according to the Nuremberg Laws of 1935.

Elise began gathering up damp cloths and fresh clothes for the wailing boy, who'd wet himself and was sobbing. She felt a stab of irritation at Brigitta, who seemed slow to help.

"I'd say just let it go," said Brigitta to Elise, "but it's a long drive to Hadamar."

" 'Let it go'? Why on earth would you ever do that?"

"As soon as they get there, they'll be taking a shower."

Still, Elise felt that was no reason for the boy to have to sit in soiled clothes. She made her way to the back of the bus. The wailing child was about four, with sandy hair and freckles across his nose. Elise recognized him from Charité. He was deaf.

She tapped him on the shoulder to get his attention, and he looked up at her. "It's all right, Friedrich," she said, enunciating her words carefully so that he could read her lips. "It could happen to anyone." She smiled, a reassuring smile. "Look, we have clean clothes for you to wear."

She helped him change out of his wet trousers and underthings and into hospital-issued pajama bottoms. "Thank you," he said in a thick, hard-to-understand voice—the voice of one who had never actually heard language. Elise rolled up the wet clothes and tucked them into a bag. Then she wiped her hands on a damp cloth.

"You're welcome, *Liebling*," she replied, ruffling his fair hair.

Brigitta remained silent.

The bus traveled southwest, from Berlin to the Hadamar Psychiatric Institute, located in Hadamar, a small town in the Limburg-Weilburg district in Hesse, between the cities of Cologne and Frankfurt. The longer they drove, the more uneasy Elise grew.

Halfway into the journey, Brigitta began distributing small cups of liquid medicine. "What is this?" Elise asked, as she was given some to pass out.

"Just a little something to keep them calm," Brigitta answered.

Elise gave one to Friedrich, and he rewarded her with a huge grin. When they were done distributing the medicine, Elise took her seat at the front of the bus and tried to look out the window. There was a small crack in the white paint, where she could see through to the darkening sky. She had the disconcerting realization that while they couldn't see out, no one could see in. She hadn't told anyone where she was going. No one had seen her leave; no one could see her now.

Finally, at almost midnight, they reached Hadamar and pulled up the drive to the institute. Out the driver's window, Elise could see a series of redbrick buildings. They drove past the main entrance and went to what seemed to be a garage for the buses.

"All right then, stand up, everyone!" Brigitta called, clapping her hands. The children, groggy from their medicine and tired from the late hour, rose to their feet.

Brigitta and Elise, along with some orderlies from the institute, guided the children from the bus garage through what Brigitta called "the sluice"—a narrow, fenced-in path—to a large building. They went inside what looked like a gymnasium locker room in the basement. All of the windows were sealed.

"You're all going to take showers now," Brigitta called to the group. "Please find a locker. You will leave your clothes there. Remember the number—you'll need it to get dressed again. Any jewelry and valuables should be handed over to one of the doctors for safekeeping."

Friedrich looked at Elise, and she pointed to the other children, then pointed back at him. He smiled and followed the lead of the others.

When the children were naked, they were walked past a long table for registration and a superficial inspection by a doctor in a white lab coat and swastika armband. Each had to open his mouth for inspection. Those with gold crowns were marked with black crosses on their backs. Each child was then photographed, a startled second of flash.

Afterward, they were given bars of soap as they entered the white-tiled shower room. The door closed behind them with a loud bang. The sound startled Elise, and she turned to see one of the SS doctors dead-bolt it closed and twist the lock.

"Where are the towels?" Elise asked. "Where are the hospital gowns?"

"No need." Brigitta's expression was impassive.

Elise didn't understand. "No need?" She walked to the door and slid the peephole cover open. She leaned forward and peered in. Then she pulled her eye away as though it had been burned. "My God," she whispered. "The children—" She shook her head, unable to process what she had just seen. Brigitta made her way to Elise's side as she began to pound on the door and try to unlock it. "Friedrich . . ." Then, louder this time, to Brigitta, "They're *dying* in there!"

"I know." Brigitta lit a cigarette. "Want one?"

In a daze, Elise shook her head.

Brigitta exhaled thick smoke. Then, "Look, if you're on the bus, you knew what you were getting into. Although it was hard for me the first time, too."

Elise again reached for the dead bolt, and Brigitta pulled her hand away. A cluster of the SS doctors looked over. "Is there a problem?" one asked.

"*Nein,*" Brigitta called. "She's new. It's her first time."

"A *Jungfrau!*" one said, and they all laughed. A virgin.

"What—what do you—we—tell their parents?" Elise demanded. Then, looking at the door, "The bodies . . ."

"Oh, there's one letter describing an illness—usually pneumonia. Or appendicitis. And the bodies are cremated, of course. Then the death certificate comes with a nice urn."

Elise turned away in a sickened daze. Hadamar. Death. Urns. Suddenly it was clear what had happened to Gretel.

"It gets better, after a while." Brigitta dropped her cigarette butt and ground it under her shoe. "It's the best thing we can do for these unfortunates. In the long run, it's better for them—more humane. A mercy death. And the pay is more than we make for our regular shifts." She put one hand to Elise's shoulder. "Look, do you want to get a cup of coffee in the lounge while we wait?"

"No!" Elise shrugged Brigitta's hand away, as if it burned.

"You're new—you'll get used to it." Brigitta spoke in gentler tones. "We all have. It's a kindness, really. You have to think of it like that." She turned and walked away.

Elise ran—as fast as she could, as long as her legs would hold up—to the grassy lawn. It was dark, and she ran blindly, not caring. When finally she fell, she vomited until she was unable to breathe, unable to see through her tears. *Oh, God, my God,* she prayed. *Oh, God, help me. Help us all.*

———

When it was time, Elise climbed back on the bus, feeling hollow and numb. Without the children, the bus seemed eerily empty and deafeningly quiet. Brigitta sat down next to her. "Remember— they're 'life unworthy of life.' 'Useless eaters.' They take places in hospitals needed for wounded soldiers. The best young men die in war, and then the *Volk* lose the best available genes. If we don't step in and do something, their genes will take over. The government *must* intervene, to save Germany."

"And what about the fifth commandment?" Elise asked, looking at the painted window, unable to see. " 'Thou shalt not kill'?"

Brigitta's brow furrowed. "That's no commandment of God's—just a Jewish lie, meant to keep us weak. We don't need to follow it anymore. Besides, it's not killing, it's euthanasia. *Kinder-Euthanasie*. Operation Compassionate Death."

"The doctors, the orderlies," Elise said. "They're all volunteers?"

"Yes."

"And what would happen if they wanted to stop?"

"They'd be sent to the Eastern Front, probably. Where the commander in charge of the unit would assign them to a suicide squad." She put her hand on Elise's arm. "If you're smart, you'll keep your mouth shut. As you know, this is a top-secret program. No reveals will be tolerated." Then, "I know, it's difficult to accept at first, but you must get past this. Complaining is only going to bring you trouble from above."

Elise's ears began to ring. She thought she might be losing her mind. She closed her eyes. "*I will lift up mine eyes unto the hills*," she prayed silently, "*from whence cometh my help. My help cometh from the Lord, which made heaven and earth. . . .*"

But where was God as the children of Charité were being murdered? Elise wondered. She said Hail Mary after Hail Mary, and still received no answers. And felt nothing but horror and despair. She must have dropped off to sleep, but woke with a start when the bus pulled back into the parking lot of Charité, in the midmorning.

And then the thought hit her. What if God were asking the exact same thing? *What if God is asking where are we?*

Back at Charité, Elise changed into her black funeral dress. She was walking out the doors of the hospital when she noticed Dr. Brandt striding from the main entrance. He was still in his white coat and SS armband.

Breaking into a run, she caught up with him on the sidewalk, her heels banging on the concrete. "Dr. Brandt," she said breathlessly, "I need to speak with you." The scent of car exhaust lingered in the sticky air.

Brandt looked annoyed, as though he'd heard a mosquito buzz. "I'm busy, Nurse . . ."

"Hess," she reminded him, "Nurse Hess."

"Yes, Nurse Hess." He looked at her, now recognizing her face. He smiled. "I'm going out to get a cup of decent coffee. That fake coffee they serve in the cafeteria isn't fit for man or beast."

"Dr. Brandt," Elise said, falling into step with him, "who is Nurse Aloïsa Herrmann?"

He stopped short and stared. "How do *you* know about Aloïsa Herrmann?"

Elise looked him full in the face. "It's she who sends letters to the parents of children being shipped off to Hadamar. Whoever 'she' is."

"And what do you know about Hadamar?" Dr. Brandt loomed over her.

"I know——" Elise took a shuddery breath. *God, give me strength.* "I know it's where you're sending children to be murdered."

Without warning, Dr. Brandt's hand shot out and slapped her across the face. The blow caught her off balance, sending pain rocketing through her cheekbone and skull. She staggered backward and put a hand up to her reddening skin.

"That is not for you to know! It does not concern you!"

"It *does* concern me! These are my patients! They're being murdered and their parents are being lied to!"

"Who have you told? Who knows?" Dr. Brandt gripped her arm.

"Stop!" Elise cried. "No one!"

"Don't interfere with what you don't understand. If we don't rid ourselves of these . . . *lice,* they will multiply and compromise the entire body. This isn't about morality—it's about delousing. Genetic hygiene. The mercy killing of the sick, weak, and deformed is far more decent, and in truth a thousand times more humane, than to support a race of degenerates."

Four SS officers approached. Two pulled out guns while the other two forced Elise up against a wall. The rough mortar between the bricks scraped her back. She heard the clicks of two safeties being released.

"Everything all right here, Herr Doktor?" one of the officers asked.

There was a beat, a curious moment in time, when all of them knew that life or death was hanging in the balance. It stretched on forever and yet passed in an instant.

"Yes, let her go," Dr. Brandt answered. "She is young—just a misunderstanding. Yes, Nurse Hess? I know who your mother is, and I would be most unhappy to tell her of your unprofessional behavior today."

"*Jawohl,*" she managed, her voice cracking.

The two officers released her and turned toward Brandt. "*Heil Hitler!*" they said, raising their arms in sharp salute.

"*Heil Hitler!*" Dr. Brandt replied, arm raised.

She slid down onto the pavement as her legs crumpled beneath her.

The officers continued along the sidewalk, and Dr. Brandt resumed his mission to find decent coffee without looking back.

I'm lifting my eyes to the hills now, Lord, Elise thought. *And I'll do everything in my power to make this stop, but I'd appreciate some help, all right?*

When she was finally able to stand and walk, Elise realized she didn't want to go home. And she couldn't bear to go back to the hospital. Then a word came to her—*sanctuary*. She began walking, across the Spree, and then to the church, not far from the Brandenburg Gate. She needed to talk to God.

Elise was no stranger to St. Hedwig's in Berlin-Mitte. It was where she had been baptized, made her first Communion, and was confirmed, thanks to her grandmother, who'd insisted over Clara's objections. And it was near the hospital, so she could easily go for morning Mass or evening vespers.

St. Hedwig's, modeled after the Pantheon in Rome, had an enormous verdigris dome. Inside, the dome rose to a single high window, looking down on the congregation like a great eye. An oversized, bloodred Nazi banner hung from each Corinthian column, and a gold-framed painting of Hitler presided over the altar. On a large wooden crucifix hanging from above, Jesus wept. Here and there, flickering candles from small altars pierced the darkness.

Elise entered and dabbed the fingers of her right hand into the basin of holy water, then made the sign of the cross, touching her hand to her forehead, heart, and both shoulders, whispering, *"In nomine Patris, et Filii, et Spiritus Sancti, Amen."* Then she walked down the aisle, knelt, and crossed herself again.

Looking around, Elise spotted an older woman, with thick white hair twisted into a bun, walking to a side chapel devoted to St. Michael the Archangel. In the Catholic tradition, St. Michael was considered "a great prince who stands up for the children of your people." Elise could think of no one more appropriate to whom to pray.

She dropped a coin into a small wooden box, then took a brown wax candle, lit it, and knelt on a low needlepoint-covered riser to pray, the golden-blue flames flickering in the dim light. She prayed and prayed, crossing herself again and again. When she was done, she crossed herself one last time and stood.

"Excuse me, Frau," she said to the other woman in the chapel, who had also finished her prayers, "have you seen Father Licht?"

"In his office, I should imagine," the woman said. "Why, child, you're trembling! Are you all right?"

But Elise had already walked past her, eyes unseeing. "I just need to find Father Licht."

Father Johann Licht, Provost of the Cathedral of St. Hedwig, was in his office in the brick building behind the church itself. He had an angular face and hawklike nose, skin stretched over his hollow cheekbones into straight planes, and fine, dark hair brushed back under a black skullcap. Worry lines carved through his forehead and between his brows. He'd grown up in Ohlau, the youngest of seven brothers and sisters, studied at Innsbruck, and become a priest. Since Kristallnacht, he prayed publicly for the Jews every day at evening prayer, and was under constant surveillance by the SS.

His small office was simply furnished, with a plain wooden crucifix, a framed picture of Albrecht Dürer's *Praying Hands* on the wall, and a yellowing Käthe Kollwitz "Never Again War!" poster tacked up next to it. Licht sat in the wan light as he went over his notes for Sunday's homily. Elise knocked softly on the open wooden door.

"Yes?" he said, starting. Then his gaunt features warmed into a smile. "Elise! You gave me a shock! How are you?" he said, rising. "Is everything all right? Come, sit down, child."

Elise slumped down in the straight-backed chair opposite his desk. "I fear you won't believe me if I tell you, Father."

"You'd be surprised at what I can believe these days." He contemplated her face for a moment: the pallor, the seriousness of intent, the sudden aging of her young features. "Why don't I get you a cold glass of water?" he suggested, "and then you can start at the beginning." He poured from a pitcher on his desk.

Elise accepted the glass and sipped. Then she told her story.

When she'd finished, Father Licht rubbed his thin hands together, then took off his spectacles. "I'm sorry to say, child, that I—we—already know about this. The Nazis refer to their eugenics program internally as Operation Compassionate Death or the Children's Euthanasia Program. It's run through the so-called Charitable Foundation for Curative and Institutional Care."

Elise was stunned. "You—you know already? The Church *knows?*"

"Yes, the program's headed by Reichsleiter Philipp Bouhler, head of Hitler's private chancellery, and your own Dr. Karl Brandt, who you must know is also Adolf Hitler's personal physician." Licht opened one of his desk drawers and pulled out a carbon copy of a letter from a folder. "Take a look at this."

Elise read: "*I, as a human being, a Christian, a priest, and a German demand of you, Chief Physician of the Reich, that you answer for the crimes that have been perpetrated at your bidding, and with your consent, and which will call forth the vengeance of the Lord on the heads of the German people.*" The letter was addressed to Dr. Brandt, and was from Father Johann Licht.

Elise was shocked. "And how—how did he respond?"

"He hasn't. Just as no one has responded to our letters and telephone calls about the fate of the Jews. We've fallen into the hands of 'criminals and fools,' as Bishop von Preysing says. We've heard of what you've described happening, but the problem for us is that it's never been substantiated. Most of the Catholic hospitals, as you know, have been closed. And the nuns who were nurses there have been sent to rural convents. Without absolute irrefutable proof . . ." He fell silent. "Elise—you are a nurse, yes?"

"Yes, that's what I've been telling you. At Charité-Mitte. I've also approached Dr. Brandt."

"What was his response?"

Elise shivered at the memory of being pressed up against the wall, guns trained on her heart and head. "Let's just say that he was not about to let a mere nurse ask questions about anything."

"But what about one nurse and a priest—and the Bishop of Berlin?"

"Bishop von Preysing would come forward?"

"The problem is, Elise, we in the Church have wanted to come forward, publicly, for some time. But the Concordat that the Vatican signed in 'thirty-three prevents any criticism of Hitler's regime by the Catholic Church. And, on top of that, we have no proof. And without uncontestable proof, there will only be denial and subterfuge." He rubbed his beaky nose. "You're a nurse. A nurse at a hospital where this is happening. With your access to files, you could—"

Elise gave a grim smile. "Get all the proof Bishop von Preysing would need."

"It's dangerous work, Elise," Father Licht warned. "If you're caught . . ." The warning hung in the air. "Not even your mother could save you."

Something crossed Elise's face. In that moment, she decided she would see this through to the end, no matter what her mother might think, no matter where it might lead. " 'Withhold not good from them to whom it is due, when it is in the power of thine hand to do it.' Proverbs three-twenty-seven, yes?"

Father Licht smiled. "I'm heartened to see that someone in our congregation not only has been listening but also remembers."

"Besides," Elise said, "Jesus was quite the troublemaker, after all."

The smile disappeared from the priest's haggard face. "But remember, my child—that's why He was crucified. You must be careful. Please."

Chapter Six

Early the next morning, Herr Karl pulled up to the entrance of the tile-roofed Hannover Hauptbahnhof station, the requisite red Nazi banners flying, Maggie in the seat beside him. He let the car idle as he pulled her suitcase from the back.

"Good luck, *Fräulein*," he said, handing Maggie her valise. "Let's not draw this out."

"Thank you for everything," Maggie said, shaking his hand. They parted ways.

Inside, the station was deserted, except for one lone ticket seller snoring, with a newspaper over his face, behind a glass window.

Maggie felt like an impostor. *Shouldn't the SS be here at any moment, to arrest me?* she thought, her heart thundering in her chest and palms damp. She made sure to think in German, to go over her request, to familiarize herself with the Reichsmarks in her purse. Then, she took a deep breath and, with her gloved hand, rapped at the window.

"Whaa—?" The newspaper fell to the floor as the man started, then blinked, then rubbed his eyes with two fists. "Yes, *Fräulein*. How may I help you?"

Maggie feigned nonchalance, even though her heart was beating rapidly. "Ticket to Lehrter Bahnhof in Berlin, please."

"One way or round trip?"

For a long moment, Maggie blanked. Despite her fluency in German, she wasn't expecting that question. Her jaw dropped, her cheeks turned red, and her eyes widened. She just couldn't think of what he could possibly mean. Was she going to be found out so quickly? Was it over even before it had begun? How long would it take the SS to arrest her?

"One way or round trip?" the man repeated.

Maggie swallowed, looking for escape routes.

Then he started to laugh, a deep and hearty chuckle. "*Gnädiges Fräulein,* you clearly need coffee as much as I do in the morning!"

Maggie forced her stiff lips to smile. "Yes, I *do* need coffee, too," she agreed. "One *one-way* ticket to Lehrter Bahnhof," she managed finally, fumbling for the Reichsmarks to pay.

"Five past six. Track two."

"Thank you."

"Here's a schedule." The man handed her a printed sheet. As he picked it up, it tore slightly. He reached down to get her a fresh one.

Maggie, used to rationing, including the rationing of paper, was incredulous. "It's all right. I don't mind. It's still perfectly usable."

"*Nein!*" the man snapped, crumpling up the torn sheet and throwing it into the garbage. "*Wenn schon, denn schon!*"

Maggie realized it was the old German expression "If something is worth doing at all, it is worth doing right." She was silent, absorbing his sudden intensity, and accepting the new and unblemished schedule sheet.

"*Heil Hitler!*" the man said, giving the salute.

"*Heil Hitler,*" she managed to reply.

By six A.M., a few more people had arrived, some with suitcases, some with rucksacks, waiting with Maggie on the waxed wooden benches. At exactly five minutes past six, the black train pulled up on the track behind the station with a puff of steam and screech of brakes.

Once she boarded, it wasn't hard to find a seat by herself. Maggie opened a copy of *Berliner Morganpost* she'd bought in the station and pretended to read, trying to calm herself.

She knew it was propaganda, but what she read was disturbing: 19 RAF AIRCRAFT SHOT DOWN OVER THE CHANNEL was the headline for one article. ENGLAND HAS LOST 12,432,000 TONS OF SHIPPING SINCE THE WAR STARTED, blared another. Maggie turned the page. GREEK FISHERMEN REPORT THAT ROYAL NAVY SAILORS SHOT AND KILLED SWIMMING AND HELPLESS GERMAN SAILORS. TWO SOVIET DIVISIONS AND 156 SOVIET TANKS DESTROYED IN TWO DAYS IN THE BATTLE OF DUBNO. She folded the paper up and looked out the window instead.

Maggie saw cows grazing in pastures lit by the golden light, interspersed with dark forests of ancient oaks. A man in uniform came by to punch her ticket. Her heart was pounding and her hands sweating inside her gloves; still, she feigned boredom, and the conductor didn't seem to notice anything amiss.

By the time the police officer reached her, to check her identity card, she felt a little less shaky, and his perfunctory examination of her papers went without incident.

Maggie took out *Mein Kampf* and tried to make sense of it. She had read it a few years ago, at her late grandmother's house in London, when Hitler had invaded Poland. It seemed like several lifetimes ago. *"The result of all racial crossing is therefore in brief always the following,"* Maggie read.

"(a) Lowering of the level of the higher race;

"(b) Physical and intellectual regression and hence the beginning of a slowly but surely progressing sickness.

"To bring about such a development is, then, nothing else but to sin against the will of the eternal creator. And as a sin this act is re-warded."

Maggie ground her teeth and put the book away. The day was getting warmer, the sunshine through the glass heating the stale air. She turned to the crossword puzzle near the back of the paper—good practice for her German—and had nearly finished it when she heard the train's whistle and the screech of the brakes, then felt the train slow down, and finally stop.

"Lehrter Bahnhof station!" a clipped voice over a loudspeaker announced. "We have arrived in Berlin!"

Hugh met with John Cecil Masterman. Not at his office, however.

Masterman had studied at the University of Freiburg and had the bad luck to be an exchange lecturer there in 1914, when the Great War had begun. He was interned as an "enemy alien" for four years in a prisoner-of-war camp in Ruhleben—which was why he hated to be indoors. And why he'd asked Hugh to meet him on the far side of Tower Bridge.

Hugh was there early, at a quarter to eight. It was a humid morning; gray skies above threatened rain. But in any weather, the scenery was spectacular—across the river Hugh could see the par-apets on the great stone walls of the Tower of London, as well as the dome of St. Paul's Cathedral, and the suspension bridge with its two Victorian Gothic towers and horizontal walkways.

And then there appeared Masterman, with his long sloping nose, thick brown hair, and propensity toward grim-humored smiles. He wore a black Anthony Eden hat on his head and carried a long umbrella under one arm. "You must be Hugh Thompson," he said without preamble. "Let's walk, shall we?"

Together, they began the trek over the bridge. They were

alone, except for the sound of intermittent traffic and the rush of the wind. Below them flowed the murky Thames.

"I'm assuming Frain's told you about us," Masterman began.

"Yes, sir," Hugh replied. "About how MI-Five has been capturing German agents and turning them to our side."

"There haven't been that many, but when we do pick them up, they're taken to the London Cage or Camp 020 at Latchmere House. Then we see if we can turn them." Masterman gave one of his dour smiles. "We even take their pay and put it toward the war effort."

"What about those who won't turn?" Hugh asked. He knew about one captured German spy in particular, Josef Jakobs, who had parachuted into Ramsey in Huntingdonshire in January. Jakobs had been picked up by the Home Guard, who found that he'd broken his ankle when he landed. When arrested, he was still wearing his flying suit and carrying forged papers, a radio, British pounds, and a German sausage.

"He was tried in camera and found guilty under the Treachery Act of 1940. He was sentenced and executed by firing squad in the Tower of London only a week or so ago."

"I see," Hugh said.

"One of the other captured spies, hearing of Jakobs's fate, has proved much more amenable. We've been able to persuade him to work as a double agent for us." Masterman grimaced. "The key word to remember with double agents is *disinformation*. We feed them disinformation to send back to their contacts at Abwehr in Berlin. However—and this is a big however—we must also include some true information, to make the false seem credible. So it's a game, really. A very, very high-stakes game."

A seagull flying overhead shrieked. "Yes, sir."

"Our prisoner's a German, name of Stefan Krueger. You'll be working with him."

"Sir?"

"Krueger was an Abwehr S-chain agent—parachuted into Britain at the end of 1940, with the task of blowing up a factory producing Spitfires. However, he was picked up immediately and turned himself over to MI-Five. He was sent to Latchmere House and interrogated at length by Lieutenant Colonel Robertson. Do you know Robertson?"

"I know of him, sir."

"Robertson's a good judge of character. And he pegged this one immediately. Called him vain—said he thought of himself as something of a 'prince of the underworld.'"

Hugh's lips twisted into a sardonic half smile.

"But he's more of a mercenary. Krueger has no scruples and will stop at nothing. He plays for high stakes and would like the whole world to know it. He himself knows nothing of fear, and no feeling at all of patriotism—which is all to the good, actually. He feels no loyalty to Hitler or the Nazis. Right now he works with us because it suits him and because he's getting perks and extras that he wouldn't normally get in prison, like being able to live under room arrest at the Queen's House at the Tower of London."

Hugh's gaze went to the medieval fortress they were heading toward. Now the meeting place made sense. "What's he involved with?"

"Krueger has duped the Germans into believing—with the help of faked photographs provided by MI-Five—that he carried out a successful sabotage attack on the Spitfire factory, at the Supermarine facility in Woolston, Southampton." Masterman gave a bark of a laugh and opened his large black umbrella as heavy drops of rain began to fall. "MI-Five agents dumped rubble around the site and we planted a story in the *Daily Express* about the so-called raid. His handlers at Abwehr bought everything."

"Fantastic, sir." Hugh had forgotten his own umbrella and was getting soaked. "That's quite a coup," he said, ignoring the water drops drenching his best suit.

"Glad you think so," Masterman replied. "Because you're going to be in charge of his next 'mission.' It's been sent via code." The older man pulled out a piece of paper. "This is what we intercepted."

Hugh accepted the scrap of paper, raindrops splattering it, making the ink bleed. The letters and numbers made no sense to him.

NAF9H20
51649900161
515700247
51604700350
51595000479
51588900466
51588480049782
5158165005055
515804570056176
515764560058494

He memorized it, then handed it back to Masterman, who tucked it into his breast pocket. "Code, sir?"

"Yes. And although we have his cipher disk, it hasn't helped at all. So we'll show it to Krueger, but we'll also need to have one of our best men at Bletchley working on it. I suggest Edmund Hope. He's done some work with Frain. You've worked with him, too, correct?"

"Uh, yes," Hugh said. He tried not to grimace.

"You'll need to get him on this." Masterman looked closely at Hugh's face. "I hope that won't pose a problem, Mr. Thompson?"

"No, sir," he lied. "Of course not, sir."

Just as the rain eased up, the two men arrived at the Tower of London.

A former Norman keep, surrounded by thick stone walls, the Tower wasn't actually a single tower but a cluster of buildings—Norman, medieval, Tudor—topped with ornate weathervanes and gruesome gargoyles. Over the centuries, it had been an infamous prison: Queen Elizabeth I, Sir Walter Raleigh, Samuel Pepys, and countless unknowns had been kept there; many of them—including Queen Elizabeth's own mother—had left minus their heads.

The Tower had been closed to the public in 1939, just before Parliament had declared war on Germany. It was now being used for military purposes under the name the Tower Prisoner of War Collection Center. It had sustained some bomb damage but was still basically intact.

Hugh and Masterman showed their identification to the Yeoman Warders at the East Drawbridge entrance, then were met and taken inside by the Constable of the Tower, Sir Claud William Jacob. "Welcome to His Majesty's Royal Palace and Fortress, gentlemen."

Together, the three men walked through the rain to the Queen's House, a row of Tudor buildings with their decorative half-timbering on a square green. A few ravens strutted through the lush grass.

They went to one of the Tudor doors, guarded by two Yeomen Warders, and were let in by yet another Yeoman. He led them up the narrow stairs to the top floor, and opened a multitude of locks. The men then walked inside the chamber.

The walls were thick and the windows narrow. There was an

empty fireplace built into one wall, and a sink and toilet on the other. An unmade bed stood on one end, and a makeshift desk piled high with papers and books sat near the windows.

A young man with a full head of dark hair and a small pencil mustache looked up from reading at his low desk. "To what do I owe this honor?" he asked in perfect English.

"Good morning, Krueger," the Constable said. "You know Masterman. And this is—"

Masterman took over the introduction. "This is Agent Hugh Thompson. Thompson, meet Mr. Stefan Krueger."

Hugh nodded, not quite sure what Tower etiquette was. The Constable withdrew, but the Yeoman kept guard with the door open.

"Please, gentlemen—sit down," Krueger said. Hugh and Masterman sat on the thin mattress of the bed.

"Time for another mission, Herr Krueger," Masterman said.

"Yes," Krueger said, looking pleased, glancing at Hugh. "I thought it might be. My handlers get nervous when I don't check in for a while."

"And they've been in contact." Masterman handed Krueger the piece of paper. "I assume you've tried using the disk?"

"Yes." Krueger shrugged. "It doesn't work, and these letters and numbers don't mean anything to me, I'm afraid." He handed the paper back.

"We're going to get our people on it," Masterman told him. "When we've broken it, we'll come back to you."

Hugh cocked his head. "Who's your handler at the Abwehr?"

"Why?" Krueger grinned. "You have friends in Germany?"

Hugh was silent.

"Mr. Krueger," Masterman said, warning in his voice.

"All right, all right," the German said. "I work with two agents, named Ritter and Krause." Hugh didn't recognize the names. Then Krueger continued. "They work under someone they call The Boss. Have you heard of *him*?"

A wave of hatred hit Hugh with full force. He nodded a silent yes, but he knew more than Krueger—that The Boss was actually a woman. That she was, in fact, Maggie's mother.

And yes, Hugh had heard of her, knew her all too well, in fact—because years ago she had assassinated his father.

He felt hate stir in him, hot and bitter. Hugh wasn't the kind of man who acted rashly. He didn't shout, he didn't slam, but what he did do was obsess in silence, until his anger grew to incandescence.

The train came to a stop at Lehrter Bahnhof in Berlin with the hiss of steam and the screech of brakes. Maggie grabbed her suitcase from the overhead luggage shelf. *I'm here!* she thought, her heart racing. *Berlin!*

Maggie's ideas of Germany had always been informed by the country's famous mathematicians—Friedrich Bessel, Bernhard Riemann, and David Hilbert—and its famous schools—the Universities of Göttingen, Munich, and Würzburg. And the Berlin of her imagination was the city of the golden thirties—a film directed by Ernst Lubitsch, starring Marlene Dietrich, with Bauhaus sets, and a score by Kurt Weill.

Of course, that Germany, that Berlin, was long gone—replaced by the Third Reich.

And her immediate mission? To find Gottlieb Lehrer. *Pretend you're in love, pretend you're in love,* she admonished herself, which only seemed to make her more nervous. Love was one thing she didn't want to think about. *And certainly not about Hugh. Or John. They told you at Beaulieu*—stay in the present. *Don't think of the past or the future—you'll just get in trouble that way.*

Lehrter Bahnhof was the largest railway station in Europe, called "the palace among stations." But all the terminal's neo-Renaissance grandeur was lost on Maggie as she sat on a hard wooden bench in the thick, humid heat. She resettled her hat, pulled at her gloves, and kept a close eye on the handbag on her lap and the suitcase at her feet. Gottlieb would be wearing a bouton-niere of blue forget-me-nots, she'd been told, to match the forget-me-nots on her own specially made hat. To give herself something distracting to do, she pulled out her knitting. *Better practice before meeting Berlin's Madame Defarge.*

As Maggie began a row of stockinet stitch, she was approached by two police officers. "Good morning, *gnädiges Fräulein,*" said the taller one, sporting a thick white mustache. He was older, too old for the army most likely, as was his shorter and leaner partner.

"Good morning, officers," Maggie said brightly, slipping the knitting back into her handbag. She'd hoped that, as a woman, she would pass through Berlin unobtrusively. *Apparently not.*

"Where are you coming from?"

"Hannover Hauptbahnhof," Maggie answered, forcing herself to smile.

"And what are you doing in Berlin?"

A few people stopped and watched her being questioned. There was too much attention on her. Maggie's heart began to beat faster. "I'm meeting a friend."

"A friend?"

She felt light-headed. The fluorescent overhead lights suddenly seemed blinding and the wooden bench beneath her very hard. *Well, here goes nothing.* "A *special* friend." Maggie tried her best to look coquettish.

The two officers exchanged a look. "And what do you have in your suitcase?"

If they opened her suitcase, they would find both the crystals and the transmitting device. Some instinct, raw, primal, and strong, took over.

"Explosives!" She cocked her head to one side, batted her eyelashes, and gave them a sparkling smile.

The two officers looked at her, then at each other for a long moment. And then they began to laugh. They laughed loudly, and so heartily that even some of the onlookers began to smile and chuckle, before turning to go about their business once again. The tension dissipated—crisis averted.

"Well, just make sure the timer's working, *gnädiges Fräulein,*" the taller one said, slapping his partner's back.

"Have a good visit in Berlin," added the other, dabbing at his forehead with his handkerchief. "He's a lucky fellow, your young man is."

As they walked away, she saw Gottlieb. She was as sure as she could be, given the description: medium height, athletic build, close-cropped blond hair—almost albino white—and green eyes, emerald like a stained-glass window. His face was long—too long to be handsome. It was the face of a knight on a medieval tombstone, and his ears stuck out. He was sporting an unmistakable sky-blue forget-me-not boutonniere and a fedora with a knife-sharp crease. His posture was impeccable.

Then he saw her and their eyes met. "My dearest Margareta!" he called, across the station's waiting room.

Maggie made herself jump up, careful to take the suitcase with her. She ran to him and threw her arms around him, banging him in the back with the case.

"Ooops." She laughed. "Sorry." *All right*, she thought, *at least he doesn't smell bad. More like shaving soap and 4711 cologne than anything else.* "Dearest Gottlieb!" she exclaimed.

"Let me take a look at you," he said, placing his hands on her shoulders and moving her back so he could see her. He studied her as though he were trying to absorb her all at once. "I've missed you so much," he said, using the more intimate form of you, *"du,"* as he kissed her hand.

Maggie looked back at him just as intently. He might have stepped off a German propaganda poster, she decided, ears notwithstanding. She felt hysterical laughter beginning to rise in her throat—the culmination of sleeplessness and nerves. She tried to turn it into a winsome smile.

When it seemed as though that might fail as well, and laughing was inevitable, she threw her arms around him and clamped her mouth onto his. After a few seconds of what looked like passion, but actually felt awkward and absurd, Maggie drew away. She felt ridiculous, but at least her urge to giggle had passed.

"Yes, just as beautiful as ever, my little *Schatzi,*" Gottlieb said finally, catching his breath. "You must be tired and hungry after your long train journey. Come, let me show you home to freshen up, and then you can have something to eat and rest. Sound good?" he asked, picking up her suitcase in one hand and offering his arm.

Maggie wrapped her arm around his and smiled. "Of course. Whatever you say—*Schatzi.*"

Maggie and Gottlieb left the Lehrter Bahnhof and took the trolley to his apartment in Berlin-Kreuzberg, passing by the massive buildings of Berlin-Mitte, the civic center. Unlike London, there was little bomb damage here, she noticed, although when she did see one bombed-out building, its façade blown off and interior curiously intact, like a doll's house, she couldn't help but think of John. *He might have done that. He, or Nigel, or one of our friends.* It was an unsettling thought—that after living through the Blitz in London, people she actually knew were dropping bombs on others.

Gottlieb's flat was on the seventh floor of an older building on a tree-lined street. On the door's handle perched a tiny wrought-iron mouse. Above the mouse, watching its prey intently, was an iron cat. "Charming," she remarked.

Gottlieb held open the door for Maggie and she stepped in.

Inside, the building smelled of floor polish and age. A worn tiled staircase wound around an elevator cage. "After you," he said, holding her suitcase in one hand while opening the elevator's outer door and then pulling aside the brass grate with the other.

"You're sure this is safe?" Maggie asked warily. She hadn't come all the way to Berlin to die in an elevator.

"Absolut sicher sein," he said, which Maggie roughly translated to the British expression "safe as houses." She smiled.

The elevator ground to a squeaky halt on the seventh floor. "This is ours." Gottlieb opened both doors, then led Maggie down the dim hallway. It smelled as though someone was cooking liver and onions and, from behind closed doors, she could hear a dog bark.

She followed him to black-painted double doors marked 7B. "And, here we are!"

Across the hallway, a door creaked open. A tiny, elderly German woman with piercing eyes appeared in the shadows.

"Good morning, Frau Keller," Gottlieb said. "May I introduce Margareta Hoffman? A good friend from Rome."

"How do you do?" Maggie said.

Behind the woman, a miniature schnauzer appeared, still yapping. "Quiet, Kaiser!" the old woman said, ignoring Maggie.

She spoke directly to Gottlieb. "I want you to know, Herr Lehrer, that I don't approve of unchaperoned female guests. I don't believe in these new morals, or these so-called Brides of Hitler."

Gottlieb gave her his most charming smile and took out his key. "Yes, Frau Keller."

"And I don't want any noise. Do you understand? No late-night drunken comings and goings. *Ordnung muß sein!*"

There must be order! Maggie translated.

"Yes, Frau Keller," he said, turning the key in the lock.

She gave a sigh. "When you took the apartment, they told me you were a quiet young man, studious. Wanted to be a priest some-day. Now you're bringing home"—she looked Maggie up and down—"*women.*"

"Just one woman, Frau Keller," he corrected serenely, opening the door. She was about to reply when he hurried Maggie inside.

"Intrusive old bat," he muttered.

"I'll report you!" they heard, as he closed the thick door.

Maggie's first impression was that the room was clean and al-most empty. Spartan, in fact. "You live here?"

"My humble abode," Gottlieb replied.

The walls were bare. The only furniture was an old, moth-eaten sofa and a brass floor lamp. Next to the sofa was a stack of newspapers. There was a card table with a VE 301 People's Re-ceiver radio. Plate-glass windows with ancient-looking blinds looked over Hannover Square.

She walked to the window and looked out. Sure enough, on a bench in the square sat a gray-haired woman, hunched over her knitting, silver needles flashing in the sun. *Ah, my Madame De-farge.*

"Get away from the window!" Gottlieb snapped.

"What? Why?" Maggie said, even as she stepped away from the glass and dropped the blind.

"We must be careful of *everything* these days. Always assume you're being watched. Don't trust anyone. Didn't you learn any-thing in your British spy school?"

"Yes, of course I did." Maggie felt her temper flare.

"This isn't your first mission, is it?" Gottlieb looked at her closely.

"No," Maggie answered. Then, hearing the defensive tone she used, she added, "I mean, I've done work in London, and also at Windsor . . ."

"But this is your first mission abroad?" Gottlieb was incredulous. "The first time you've ever dealt with Nazis?"

It's a yes-or-no question, Hope. "Yes."

"*Mein Gott,* what have you sent me?" Gottlieb exclaimed.

Maggie was tired. Her muscles ached from the parachute drop. She was alone and, she was starting to admit, scared. And now her contact, the only person she knew in Berlin, in all of Germany, was doubting her? "Don't judge me until you've seen me work," she snapped.

Gottlieb glared, then held up his hands in mock surrender. "Fine, fine."

An unused-looking galley kitchen was behind one door and a bathroom behind the other, with dark-green tiles, black and white trim, and a large salmon-pink tub. "No baths, except on Saturday and Sunday," Gottlieb instructed. "And please be frugal with the toilet paper. It's issued 'according to needs.'"

The sunny bedroom had a balcony overlooking a courtyard with a small burbling fountain. The only furniture was a twin bed and a small bedside table with a reading lamp. Over the bed hung a wooden crucifix. The books on the table were the Bible, Goethe's *Faust,* Ignatius of Loyola's *Spiritual Exercises,* and Dietrich Bonhoeffer's *The Cost of Discipleship* with a white-beaded rosary draped over them. A postcard of the German boxer Max Schmeling was tacked to the wall. Maggie opened the table drawer to search for listening devices. It was empty, except for a Walther pistol. She closed the drawer.

"You're a minimalist," she remarked.

"Before I joined the Abwehr, I was studying to be a priest."

"Ah." Maggie picked up the Loyola and paged through it. "Jesuit?"

"Of course."

"And you're a boxer?" she said, noting both the postcard and a pair of boxing gloves on the windowsill. "A *Jesuit* boxer? That seems like a contradiction."

"Not really. Boxing may be brutal, but at least it's fair. There are rules to follow, honor in fighting the good fight." He gave a tight smile. "And, despite what Goebbels would have us believe, everyone bleeds the same."

They stood together in the bedroom, awkward with each other. "You will sleep in here," Gottlieb ordered. "I will sleep on the couch." He turned back toward the living area.

"Oh no," Maggie said, "I couldn't possibly—"

"I will sleep on the couch," he called, in a voice that discouraged argument.

Slowly and methodically, Maggie continued to search the apartment for any hidden listening devices.

"It's clean," Gottlieb said.

"I just want to make sure."

"Suit yourself."

One good thing about Gottlieb's Spartan existence—it cut down on the places any listening devices could be hiding. She peered into his icebox. There was only yoghurt.

"Yoghurt is still unrationed," Gottlieb said. "I hope you like it."

"It's not as if I'm here for the fine German cuisine, *Schatzi*." When Maggie was satisfied that the apartment was clean, she moved to the blinds and lowered them. Then she turned on the light, went to her suitcase, and opened it. She took out the crystals, still intact. She returned to the living room and handed them to Gottlieb. "I hear you need these?"

"*Wunderbar,*" he said. "I hope they still work after their trip."

"I do, as well."

"I'll get them to our contact," Gottlieb said. "The SS can track radio transmissions, so we only use the radio in emergencies." He looked at her. "Stand up straight!"

Maggie, who already had good posture, was startled. "What?"

"You're supposed to be a German woman of rank—stand up *straight.*" Maggie noticed in private he'd lost the intimate *du* and was addressing her with the more formal *Sie.*

"I *am* standing up straight," she retorted.

"Straighter!"

Maggie remembered what the man in the ticket window had said: "*Wenn schon, denn schon.*" *Well,* she thought, *when in Berlin* . . . She raised her chin, sucked in her stomach, and threw her shoulders back.

"Better," Gottlieb conceded. "You must be hungry—"

"Starving!"

Gottlieb shook his head. "Not so enthusiastic. Germans are not as . . . animated. Some restraint, please."

Maggie tried hard not to roll her eyes. "I would very much enjoy lunch now," she said with as much decorum as she could muster.

"Good. Let us go."

Chapter Seven

Gottlieb wanted to take the S-Bahn to the Tiergarten, but Maggie persuaded him to take the bus. "I'm in Berlin for the first time—I want to see everything," she said, in character as Margareta, but also as Maggie, ever curious.

"If you wish," Gottlieb said.

They waited at the stop at the end of his block. When the yellow double-decker bus arrived, they stepped on, and Maggie slipped into a window seat. The bus pulled away from the curb and merged into traffic, making its way through Kreuzberg. It was a glorious day with a bright blue sky, hot breeze, chestnut trees in bloom lining the streets. The air was filled with noise—the clanging bells of streetcars, the steady clip-clop of hooves, sirens wailing in the distance. They passed city streets lined with shops. A horse-drawn ice cart was stopped in front of a greengrocer's, huge slabs of ice melting in the sun as wiry men with iron tongs unloaded them.

Like the shops of London, the store windows of Berlin showed little food and few goods to buy. Outside were long lines of *Hausfrauen* wearing head scarves and carrying baskets. There was some bomb damage, charred bricks and stones here and there. Sandbagged doorframes. And, of course, the omnipresent inferno-red Nazi flags and banners.

To Maggie's eye the people she saw seemed resolutely normal, with blunt features and sturdy frames, like caricatures by Heinrich Zille. There were also men in uniform, storm troopers in brown with swastika armbands, the SS in black, the regular police in dark blue. Everywhere Maggie saw people raising their hands in the *Hitlergruss* salute—comical, almost, in its frequency. Everyone walked with—not a swagger, no, but a strut of the comfortable, the convinced, the confident. And, yes, she had to admit their posture was impeccable.

"Eyes down," Gottlieb ordered under his breath.

But it was too late. Maggie had already caught a glimpse of the naked man, hanging from a rope around his neck, swinging from a branch of an ancient oak tree. His face was nearly black from blood, his eyes were glassy, and his tongue lolled out of his mouth. He was dead, or nearly so. He was surrounded by SS officers. The painted sign beneath him read: *I am a Jew who fornicated with an Aryan woman. I deserve to die.* In front of the soldiers, a woman was on her knees, weeping, wearing only her underwear. One of the men was cutting off her long golden braids with a straight razor, leaving her almost bald.

"Don't. Say. A. Word," Gottlieb whispered between clenched teeth.

Maggie, shocked, did as she was told. She looked around the bus. The few passengers on it were looking at their newspapers, or had their heads turned the other way.

Maggie fought the urge to vomit. She began the deep breathing she'd been taught at SOE training camp.

Finally, they reached the Tiergarten, a huge wooded park in the heart of Berlin. Gottlieb and Maggie stepped off the bus, then entered the park. On shady, graveled paths through oaks, maples, and birch trees, they strolled hand in hand, like the young lovers they were pretending to be. Sunlight could barely pierce through the thick foliage. "Are you ready for lunch?" Gottlieb asked.

"No," Maggie said curtly. "I'm not hungry—certainly not after witnessing that."

Gottlieb shook his head. "You must eat something. There's Café am Neuen See—let's get something there." Outside, a hand-painted sign read: NO DOGS, NO JEWS, NO GYPSIES.

Overwhelmed, Maggie sat on a bench at a picnic table, while Gottlieb went inside, to the counter. Overhead the sky was a deep blue, the lake sparkled in the sun, and the park air was perfumed. The air rang with the sound of children laughing and playing among the chestnut trees, while their nannies, sitting in deck chairs, chatted and gossiped. A few black-hooded crows pecked at fallen crumbs. *How can it be?* she wondered. *How can these two realities be going on simultaneously? Does no one see? Does no one want to see?*

Gottlieb returned with a tray. "It looks like Munich, doesn't it?"

Maggie had never been to Munich, but Margareta would have, so she smiled and nodded.

Gottlieb set down a glass of white wine, a glass of water, a plate of mussels, and a slice of brown bread. There were people nearby, but none close enough to hear their conversation. Still, they knew to be careful.

"Wine and mussels," Maggie said, surprised. *No pretzels and beer?*

"Wine's plentiful after the invasion of France. And shellfish still isn't rationed."

"Aren't you going to have any?"

"I'm in training," he replied. "No cigarettes, no alcohol, no bread."

"Boxing. Right." *St. Gottlieb the Ascetic.* Maggie pushed the food away. She was still nauseated.

"Hitler and this war have been terrible for our country," he said in a low voice, "and there are many of us who believe this. We're trying to reconcile loyalty to Germany with our opposition to the Nazis."

"But how did it get so far? Why did no one speak up?"

"It wasn't that easy."

"Well, I don't see why not!" Maggie suddenly sounded very young.

"You," Gottlieb said, leaning in and whispering in her ear, "are stupid. *Stupid*. At best, you are naïve. You know, I was at university, studying to be a priest, when this all happened. My mother and father were proud of me. All I wanted was to serve God. And then—I had to serve Hitler, instead."

"You didn't *have* to, though," Maggie shot back.

"You think I had a choice? There was no choice. I was lucky I was able to work for the Abwehr, not be a soldier, not kill. At the Abwehr, there are a few other like-minded people. We are doing what we can to help as many Jews escape as possible. To lay the framework for a new Germany, a non-Communist Germany, after Hitler."

Maggie took a small sip of wine. She couldn't hold Gottlieb personally responsible for everything, she realized. "So, you were studying to be a priest?" she asked, changing the subject. "Why didn't you take your vows?"

"Well, the war came along . . ." He gave her a significant look. "And then I met you, of course, *Schatzi*."

"Of course." *How could Gottlieb see what they had just witnessed and maintain his faith?* "I assume you still believe in God?"

"Yes," he said, taking a gulp of water.

Maggie reached over and stroked his cheek. Anyone looking would assume they were in love. "Well, I'm curious—how can a world, created by an all-powerful and all-knowing God, contain so much evil?"

Gottlieb pulled away from her. "God may have drawn back

from the world, to give us free will. The problem of evil may be helpful, perhaps even necessary, for our spiritual development. Just as Christ's Crucifixion was necessary for His resurrection." His face was bleak. "I do think evil and the suffering comes from God—but I think it's there to challenge us, and test us. How can we carry on believing in God's love, even when it's hidden from us? Even when everything we see around us refutes it?"

"If that's the case, then I can't see any good reason to believe in God, one who's left us to battle evil—what we just saw, for example—all alone. Is this helpful for our spiritual development? There was a man *hanged* back there! What about *his* 'moral development'?"

"If I knew that," Gottlieb conceded with a sad smile, "I'd be God."

Maggie and Gottlieb strolled the winding paths of the Tiergarten, under enormous trees with their mossy trunks, past banks of ferns, the clopping of horses' hooves from the riding paths mixing with birdsong and distant traffic. "This is one of the only places that Berliners still feel at ease," Gottlieb told her. "It used to be a hunting preserve for royalty. Now it's for the people." A siren wailed in the distance.

Maggie saw a sign: JUDISCHER BESUCH VERBOTEN. Jewish visits forbidden. She thought of *Plessy v. Ferguson*, Jim Crow laws, and the "separate but equal" segregation of Negroes and whites in the American South. The Nazis certainly weren't the first to segregate and deny basic rights to human beings. "Not for *all* people," she couldn't resist pointing out.

Gottlieb nodded. "True." They walked by the Victory Column, commemorating the Prussian victory in the Danish-Prussian War, topped by an enormous statue of winged Victory, looking like an angel. "We Berliners call her Goldelse." Gottlieb indicated the winged woman. "It translates into something along the lines of Golden Lizzy. A lot of our monuments and buildings have nicknames like that."

"Ah, the droll Berliner sense of humor," Maggie said. "And, of course, every city needs its own phallic symbol."

Gottlieb raised an eyebrow, then offered her his arm. "Come. As long as we are in the Tiergarten, you must see the rhododendrons. They're legendary."

They walked and walked through the ancient forest, Maggie's new pumps rubbing a throbbing blister on the back of her heel. It was hot in the sun; she was starting to feel sweat on her scalp and her neck.

"It's worth it, I promise," Gottlieb said.

Finally, they came upon a lake ringed with blooms—fluffy clusters of pink, cerise, and coral. Some were on small bushes, some on towering, overgrown hedges. The cumulative effect was overwhelming. Maggie inhaled sharply. "Gorgeous!" she exclaimed.

"Now," said Gottlieb, "how can you see this and *not* believe in God?"

"Because I'm a mathematician."

"I was a top student at university," Gottlieb said. "But I must confess, I was never all that interested in mathematics."

"What?" Maggie exclaimed in mock horror.

"I just can't see how mathematics relates to the real world."

"But mathematics *is* the real world. It's everywhere. See how those rhododendron petals spiral? Well, the number of petals in each row is the sum of the preceding two rows. It's expressed mathematically by the Fibonacci sequence, which can be seen in, well, almost everything—the formation of crystals, the spirals of galaxies, the pattern of sunflower seeds. Math is nature's language, its method of communicating directly with us."

Gottlieb cocked an eyebrow at her passionate response. "It could also be God's way of communicating with us, no?"

"The rules of mathematics don't necessarily imply the existence of a deity."

"Well," he countered, "they don't deny them, either. I choose to see the hand of God."

"And I see science—rather than an invisible old man in the sky who seems overly concerned with my personal life. And sporting events, apparently."

"Most people of the world, throughout history, have believed in God."

"Most people of the world, throughout history, also believed the earth was flat and the sun revolved around the earth," Maggie countered.

Gottlieb smiled. "I believe in God. And in Jesus. And the saints."

"And the Devil?" The air around them was still and strangely silent. Despite the heat of the day, Maggie shivered.

"The Devil," Gottlieb said, considering. "Well, I used to think the Devil was purely theoretical. Now . . ."

"Now?"

"Now, let's just say that I definitely believe that evil is a palpable force at work in the world." Gottlieb cleared his throat. "By the way, the big party, the Fire and Ice Ball, is Saturday night." As an older couple walked past them, he was quick to grab Maggie's hand to bring it to his lips for a kiss. The couple smiled and walked on. "A birthday party. It's in Grunewald. That's where you'll plant the microphone, in the study. You'll be going as my girlfriend, of course."

Clara Hess's study, she thought.

My mother's study.

"Can't wait," Maggie said.

Prime Minister Winston Churchill was laying bricks.

Cigar clenched between his teeth, straw boater hat on his head, clothes protected by a canvas jumpsuit, Prime Minister Winston Churchill stood in the afternoon sun at his home, Chartwell, spreading mortar with a trowel, then pressing red bricks, one by one, on top of the wall's new layer. Above him, the sky was milky with clouds, threatening a possible storm. An inquisitive robin looked on from the lower branches of an apple tree.

Bricklaying was his prayer, his meditation, his salvation. As was painting. Still, he wasn't so lost in his own thoughts that he couldn't hear the footsteps behind him. "Frain!" he barked.

"Good afternoon, Prime Minister," Frain responded.

"Hand me a brick."

Frain did as he was told and handed Churchill a red clay brick from the pile on the grass.

"What news?"

"Sir, Masterman's been working with Stefan Krueger, our double agent in the Tower—and has Hugh Thompson on the case now. Going well, but we still haven't deciphered the latest code. Masterman says Thompson's taking it to Bletchley—letting Edmund Hope have a crack at it."

"Brick!" The P.M. scraped off excess mortar. "And, speaking of the Hope family, how's my former secretary faring?"

"We have confirmation Miss Hope has made it to Berlin, sir, with radio crystals and microphone intact. She's set to plant the microphone tomorrow night. Although I'm still not sure it was a good idea to send her, specifically."

With his trowel, Churchill scooped another glob of mortar from the wheelbarrow. "Of *course* it's a good idea, Frain," he growled, the cigar still clenched in his teeth. "It's *my* idea. Clara Hess is what you in the intelligence business call 'a human asset with strategic importance.' She'll be vulnerable after her failure at Windsor. If we didn't send Miss Hope on this particular mission, how on earth could Clara Hess figure out that our Maggie is her daughter? How else could we reel that woman in?"

"If Miss Hope ever finds out she's being used as bait . . ."

"Miss Hope won't. And even if she does, if it works, it's worth it."

"And you really think Clara will jump ship? She's in a very high position in the Abwehr."

"A high position, yes, but her time is up. One more failure and she'll be out. And one thing I know about Clara Hess is that she's a survivor. Like a cockroach."

The two men heard footsteps and looked up. It was Clementine Churchill, the Prime Minister's wife, wearing a flowered dress and wide-brimmed hat. "It's time for lunch, gentlemen."

"Mrs. Churchill," Frain said, doffing his hat.

"Oh, not now, Clemmie—I'm just getting started."

"Well, Cook has been at work all morning and will be cross if you're not dressed and at the table for luncheon on time. Lord Beaverbrook and Mr. Attlee have already arrived."

Mr. Churchill wiped his hands on his jumpsuit. "All right, my dear."

"And are you talking about our Miss Hope?" Clemmie asked as the trio made its way back to the house.

"Why, you know I can't tell you anything of that nature!" the P.M. grumbled.

"Winston, these are people and not chess pieces. I trust you and Mr. Frain remember that."

Chapter Eight

Hugh left his office at MI-5 and took the crowded, noxious, fly-infested Tube to Euston Station. From there, he took the train to Bletchley.

Hugh had no desire to meet with Edmund Hope. However, they were both professionals, and Hugh hoped that the work would take precedence over any possible grudges. But he still found the idea of the upcoming meeting disconcerting.

After passing green fields dotted with white spring lambs and stopping at the Tring, Cheddington, and Leighton Buzzard stations, Hugh finally reached Bletchley, a small town about forty miles northwest of London. It was the home of the Government Code and Cipher School, known as Station X—but more commonly called Bletchley or the Park.

It was located on the Bletchley estate, an ugly red-brick Victorian mansion now overrun with both military and academics found to be good at crossword puzzles. But the real business of those who worked at Bletchley was breaking Nazi military code.

At the high front gate, Hugh presented his papers and was waved inside. He walked the long distance through the front lawn. Although it was hot, young men and women—code breakers and staff—were playing the childhood game of rounders with a broomstick and an old tennis ball, their laughter echoing in the distance. Finally, he reached the grand neogothic entrance of the Great House, guarded by two men in uniform, holding rifles. Again, he presented his identification and was waved in.

In the airless, high-ceilinged main hall, covered in dark wood paneling and held up by pink marble columns, he asked for Edmund Hope.

"He's expecting you?" asked a shrunken elderly man in a seersucker suit, sitting at a small metal desk. He was smoking a pipe; the tobacco smelled sweet.

"Yes, we have an appointment," Hugh answered.

"One minute." The man put the pipe down in a glass ashtray and picked up the telephone receiver. He dialed four numbers. "An Agent Hugh Thompson to see you, sir?" A pause. "Yes, yes, of course, sir."

The man looked up at Hugh with watery blue eyes. "He says he's in the middle of something, and he'll be with you as soon as he's able." He nodded to a hard wooden bench along the wall, underneath a stained-glass window and a poster for the Bletchley Park Orchestra's performance of Purcell's *Dido and Aeneas*. "Why don't you take a seat?"

More than three hours later, Hugh was still waiting. He'd paced, sat down, tried to break the code himself and failed miserably, tried again, only to resume pacing. His stomach rumbled. He looked over at the older man. "Is there somewhere where I can get something to eat?" Hugh asked.

"There's a canteen," the man replied, "near Hut Four. Behind the main house and take the path to your left. Ask anyone and they'll point it out for you."

"If Professor Hope comes while I'm gone—"

"I'll tell him where you've gone." The man winked. "Don't worry lad."

But Hugh did worry. He was worried about his new job with Masterman and the Twenty Committee. He was worried about breaking the code. He was worried about working with Edmund Hope. He was worried about being able to work with Krueger. He was worried about making sure Clara Hess thought her plans were succeeding, when in fact they weren't. And, in the back of his mind, as always, he was deeply worried about Maggie.

After a few wrong turns, he reached the canteen, smelling of cooking grease and dirty dishwater, papered with propaganda posters. A close-up of a man's face with a black *X* over the mouth, captioned, *Closed for the duration—loose lips sink ships.* Another, with an image of a dying soldier: *Careless talk got there first.*

As he pulled out a few coins to pay for his tea and buttered roll, he heard laughter and turned. A few men in rumpled suits were finishing up dinner together—shepherd's pie by the looks of it. And one of them was, unmistakably, Edmund Hope.

If Edmund was embarrassed at being caught going to dinner while leaving Hugh waiting, he didn't reveal it. "Mr. Thompson!" he called, arm in the air. "Come join us!"

Hugh took his tea and roll and made his way over. One of the men moved so that he could sit down. "Hello."

"This is Hugh Thompson," Edmund told those who remained. "Mr. Thompson, these rapscallions are Josh Cooper and Alan Turing," he said, pointing to each one in turn.

The men said hello, then turned back to their conversation, an animated discussion on the Collatz Conjecture. "I hear Paul Erdös has posted a reward for anyone solving it," Cooper said. "Five hundred U.S. dollars."

Edmund whistled through his teeth. "Nice. Where is Erdös these days?"

"Princeton, I believe," Turing said through a bite of shepherd's pie. "He doesn't stay in one place for long."

"He's a Hungarian Jew, can you blame him?" Edmund said. "He's lucky to have escaped in time. I hear—"

Hugh had no time to waste. "Edmund," he said, "I don't mean to interrupt your dinner, but may we talk privately?"

Edmund looked to the other code breakers. "Do you mind, gentlemen?"

"Not at all," Turing said, as he and Cooper rose to leave. "Long night ahead of us. Cheers, Mr. Thompson."

Hugh looked around, noting the empty dining room, then cleared his throat. "Professor Hope," he began, "as you may know, I'm now working with John Masterman."

"The Twenty Committee."

"Yes, well, the thing is that we have a German agent in custody, who's acting as a double agent. He's received some new information in code, but he refuses to tell us anything about it."

"So, Masterman wants a boffin to take a stab at it." Edmund sighed. "All right, I accept."

"Thank you, sir. Do you have a piece of paper?"

Edmund pulled out a crumpled paper and an old fountain pen from his jacket pocket.

Hugh wrote down the numbers and letters that he'd memorized. When he was done, he handed it to Edmund, who squinted at the sequence. Then he took out a lighter from his jacket pocket and hit the roller, so that sparks flew. He set the piece of paper on fire. Together, the men watched it burn until only ash remained.

"He had a cipher disk, as well," Hugh said. "Standard German issue. No one at the Twenty Committee found any correlation between the code and the cipher disk."

Edmund gave a grim smile. "I'll have a look at it—and be in touch," he said. The meeting was over. He stood and turned to go.

After a few steps, however, the professor turned back to Hugh. "Have you heard anything from—"

Hugh knew exactly whom he meant. Maggie. "Not since she was last in London. She's . . . away now."

"Right, right," Edmund muttered to himself as he turned again to leave, shoulders stooped. "All right then."

"But you should probably know . . ."

"What?"

Hugh blurted it out. "The code for this mission was sent by your—by Clara Hess."

"I see," Edmund said. Then he waved Hugh away. "That will be all."

Once Edmund had left the canteen, he leaned against the wall of Hut 5, his legs shaky. From his back pocket, he took out a silver flask and drank.

David Greene wasn't used to going on dates with women.

Which was why he was disconcerted to be sitting across a white linen–swathed table at the Savoy Grill for dinner with Rosamund Moser. In the background, the band played under the hushed tones of conversations and the soft clinks of china and crystal.

Rosamund was lovely. Stunning really, in David's opinion, in her sharp FANY uniform. She was young, well educated—St. Hilda's at Oxford—and possessed a delicate beauty, with chestnut hair, pale skin, luminous eyes, and full lips. He had known her growing up, for her parents were friends of his parents, but he was enough years older that he'd mostly been able to ignore her. However, when he'd telephoned and asked her if she'd like to have dinner sometime, she'd accepted so coldly that he was surprised his ear wasn't frostbitten.

Sitting across the table from each other was proving even more awkward.

"So," David said. "You're looking well."

"Yes," Rosamund replied curtly. "I believe you've mentioned that already." It was true, David had already complimented her on her looks. Three times.

He cleared his throat. "How are—and how are your parents?" he asked, trying again.

"They're fine," she said. "Mummy is at the house in the country, while Daddy's working for the Admiralty. I don't know what he does and he doesn't tell us. All very top secret, hush-hush."

After another silence, she asked, in obligatory tones, "And how are *your* parents?"

"They're well," David said. "Yes, well—quite well." Inwardly, he cursed himself for being tongue-tied. Normally he was charming with women, gallant, even. But that was when he was free and easy, a man-about-town—not on a *date*, with a *woman* who could tell her parents everything, and who would then tell *his* parents everything. His parents, who were ordering him to marry, or else he'd forfeit his trust and inheritance.

And certainly he couldn't tell Rosamund that he'd asked her out to see, just see, if it was even remotely possible for him to feel enough of a spark with a kindred soul, a Jewess, someone from his exact background, that they might—might, that is—have enough in common to perhaps—someday—settle down together and raise a family. Still, that was unlikely to happen, especially as she wouldn't even meet his eyes.

The band launched into a cover of "Blue Champagne."

"You seem uncomfortable," David remarked, finally.

"'Uncomfortable'?" Rosamund hissed. She met his eyes. "I know who—what—you are, David. I know all about you, you know. You were the talk of Oxford while we were there. You're a family friend—and it was humiliating for me. Absolute mortification. It was difficult enough being Jewish, but then you had to go and act—like that. It reflected poorly on me, David. And it cost me friends."

She knew, David realized. But he needed her to say it. "What, exactly, did you find humiliating?"

"That you're a . . . friend of Dorothy's. And, just for the record, I think it's absolutely shameful. Disgusting, too." She folded her arms over her chest and pressed her pink lips together.

David took a breath. "Yes, I did have the pleasure of meeting Miss Dorothy Parker once, but that's not—"

Rosamund raised a hand. "Leviticus twenty-thirteen: *If a man lies with a man as one lies with a woman, both of them have committed an abomination; they shall surely be put to death; their blood shall be upon them.*"

David stared. He knew that "gross indecency" was illegal. If his actions were found out, he could be arrested and imprisoned, even do hard labor. Since "friends of Dorothy" were widely diagnosed as diseased, they were often "cured" with castration, lobotomies, pudendal nerve surgery, and electroshock treatment. And while at Oxford most looked away, in London, especially working in government, one had to be careful. Extremely careful. "I'm sorry if . . . I've offended you. Truly."

"*You* don't offend me," Rosamund clarified. "But your behavior does. Color-coded pocket squares to signal interest to absolute strangers. Foot positions in public lavatories. It's disgusting. It's unnatural. An abomination in the eyes of God."

David recoiled as if struck. "You've heard from God on this, then?"

"I've heard from the Rabbi. God expects us to be chaste and reserve . . . that sort of thing . . . for marriage. Within the context of marriage, it's a *mitzvah*. And marriage can only be between a man and a woman."

"So why did you say yes to my dinner invitation? Why subject yourself to my company, if it's so distasteful to you?"

Rosamund looked across the room to summon their waiter. "First of all, because my parents asked me to, and I didn't want to tell them why I didn't want to. They don't know anything about your . . . proclivities, and I don't want to be the one to shatter their illusions. Second, because I wanted a chance to tell you how I felt, after all those years of humiliation at Oxford. And third, because I'm absolutely sick of rationing." She looked up at the hovering waiter. "I'll have the roast, please. Rare."

The next morning, Elise did as she had promised Father Licht, and snuck into the record-keeping rooms of Charité Hospital. There, she found drawer upon drawer of records of Charité's patients deemed "unfit for life." All had been dispatched to Hadamar.

Within each file was abundant paperwork. Notification of admission to the Hadamar Institute. A letter to the parents, reporting a fake illness, such as pneumonia. Then the real death report, for Nazi eyes only. A death notification with the false reasons. The death certificate. Letter to the parents about the dispatch of the urn. And often, correspondence, sometimes tearstained and written with a shaky hand, from the parents, pleading for more information about what had happened.

In the files, Elise also found a letter from the Führer—the official letter, which gave Dr. Brandt and the other doctors their go-ahead for the mass murders. It was dated—backdated?—from the day Germany declared war.

> *BERLIN, 1.Sept.1939.*
>
> *Reichsleiter Bouhler and Dr. Karl Brandt are instructed to broaden the powers of physicians designated by name, who will decide whether those who have—as far as can be humanly determined—incurable illnesses can, after the most careful evaluation, be granted a mercy death.*
>
> *Signed, A. Hitler*

God help me, Elise prayed. With shaking hands, heart thudding, she made copies of the papers, wrinkling her nose at the stench of the sulfur used to make reverse-image photocopies.

As she was copying, the door opened. "Nurse Hess!" she heard. "What are you doing in here?"

Elise startled and tried not to panic at the sight of Nurse Flint. "Oh, um, Dr. Brandt asked me if I could try to fix the photocopy machine. He said it was broken."

Nurse Flint cocked one eyebrow. "There are protocols for handling a broken photocopy machine and you know that. And we must follow them. *Ordnung muß sein!*"

Elise smiled her brightest. "I think I almost have it, Nurse Flint."

"How would you feel if one of the technicians tried to perform a nurse's duties?" She clapped her hands. "Step away from the machine, Nurse Hess."

Before she did so, Elise tried to gather up the papers she had been copying.

"Hand them to me," Nurse Flint ordered. She was taller than Elise and outweighed her by at least sixty pounds. It suddenly seemed close and hot in the room.

Elise handed over the files.

"Nurse Hess, these are confidential records. Why on earth would you be making copies?"

"As I said, I was fixing the photocopy machine."

Nurse Flint's eyes narrowed. "There seems to be nothing wrong with it."

Elise tried to pull up the corners of her mouth into a smile. "Well, of course there isn't—I fixed it."

Nurse Flint threw the papers into a nearby bin. "Don't do it again."

"Yes, ma'am."

Nurse Flint seized Elise by the elbow and steered her out of the records room. Elise knew that her mission—or at least this particular attempt—had failed.

In another wing of Charité, Herr Mystery, also known as Patient No. 1564, was lying silently, staring up at the whitewashed ceiling.

The most pertinent thing about his case now was that he seemed to be unable to speak—even though there was no damage to his vocal cords that any of the doctors could find. "Shell shock," Dr. Brandt called it. "Battle trauma." It could be permanent, the doctors said—or it could go away at any moment.

Elise believed that all Herr Mystery needed was someone to talk to. And so, when she checked on his vital signs, she made sure to keep speaking to him. "It's a beautiful day today," she said, as she took his pulse with warm, steady hands. "You wouldn't know it in here, but the rhododendrons in the Tiergarten are blooming."

She opened the dressing on his wound. "Ah, that's healing nicely," she soothed as she removed the gauze and taped on fresh. "You'll begin to feel like your old self in no time." As she said the words, she watched his eyes, his pupils. He understood her; she was certain of it. She could tell by his reactions, even though he pretended to ignore her. Even though he looked afraid.

She lifted his head and plumped his pillow. "There now," she said, settling him back down. "I'll ask the doctor when we can have you sit up. Once you can do that, we can get you into a chair and I'll push you outside. Fresh air and sunshine—won't that be nice? Certainly nicer than in here."

Herr Mystery reached out and put his hand on her forearm. He looked into her eyes. Elise could see his gratitude.

"You're welcome." She patted his hand. "I'll be back to take your vitals again in a few hours."

After work, Elise went straight to visit Father Licht in his office at St. Hedwig's.

"I'm so sorry I couldn't get the files. I was so close. I was actually making the copies—and then I was caught." She shuddered at the memory.

"I don't want you to put yourself in danger," Father Licht said.

"Well, I'm the one who has to see that bus leave, filled with children, every day," Elise countered, crossing herself, "knowing full well where it's going and what's going to happen."

Father Licht nodded grimly. "But if you suspect they're on to you . . . I know your mother is quite high up in the party, but even she might not be able to help you . . ."

"My mother has nothing to do with this," Elise said. "I'm the one who has to live with my knowledge. I'm the one who chooses to do something. I believe it's what God would want."

"Then, may God be with you, my child." He rose and put on his jacket. "And now I'm afraid I must leave."

"Where are you going?" Elise asked.

He smiled. "Bible study group."

Father Licht's weekly Bible study was held at the home of the widow Hannah von Solf.

Secretly, however, it comprised a Berlin-based Nazi resistance circle. They came from all walks of life: barons and shopkeepers, Catholic priests and Lutheran pastors and Communist atheists, factory owners and trade unionists. The disparate men were united by their hatred of Nazism and their desire to end Hitler's regime. Their membership, which had begun with only a few in 1936, had grown to more than twenty. And they all knew that if they were ever discovered, they would be murdered by the Gestapo—no questions asked.

Father Licht sat down next to Gottlieb Lehrer in Frau von Solf's salon. The furniture and décor were art deco, all angles and symmetry. Most of the men were substantial, and it looked as if the delicate chairs they sat on would give way at any moment.

There were twelve members present. Frau von Solf motioned for a young maid to put down a tray of *Pfannkuchen,* dusted with powdered sugar. "I'll pour the tea, Helga," the Frau von Solf said to the maid. "You may go."

After she had served the caraway tea and the men had helped themselves to pastry, she called the meeting to order. "Herr Lehrer," she said to Gottlieb, "would you please begin?"

Gottlieb looked at the pale faces surrounding him. "I am pleased to say that our friend from Britain arrived safely."

There was a round of applause.

"And our radio operator now has the crystals he needs."

"Excellent," Frau von Solf said, clapping her ring-laden hands together.

"However, we still have to plant the bug in Frau Hess's study."

"Isn't her Fire and Ice Ball tomorrow night?" asked Frau von Solf.

"Yes," Gottlieb answered. "And I have concerns. She's inexperienced—"

"*She?*" said Herr Zunder, a Lutheran minister at the Berliner Dom. "A *woman?*"

"That was my reaction, too," Gottlieb replied.

"A *woman,*" Frau von Solf said drily. "My word."

The men didn't pick up on her sarcasm.

"According to our plan," continued Gottlieb, "she'll plant a bug in the study at Frau Hess's villa, then return to Britain the following night. Although, as I've said, I have concerns. She's done one or two minor things in Britain—but this is her first foreign mission. If anything goes wrong, I'll be there to make sure the microphone is set."

"I will pray for her," Licht said. "And you, too—that your mission is successful."

"I will pray as well," said Herr Zunder.

Frau von Solf wiped powdered sugar off her lip with a linen napkin. "And Father Licht, what do you have to report?"

"I have a source at Charité Hospital. This person may be able to gain access to some of Dr. Brandt's files."

"You're sure Bishop von Preysing will speak out?"

"If we have irrefutable proof, yes, Frau von Solf," Licht replied. "As well as Bishop Michael von Faulhaber of Munich, Bishop Clemens August Graf von Galen of Münster, and Dietrich Bonhoeffer of the Confessing Church."

"Excellent. And Herr Zunder, what news have you?" And so they talked, drinking tea, long into the night.

———

When Elise returned home to Grunewald, she knew what she had to do. Maybe she couldn't get the files—or couldn't *yet* get the files—but she might be able to save a life or two.

The attic of her home was large and unused, except for storage. No one ever went up there—only the maids, once a year, to retrieve the Christmas decorations. But Christmas seemed a lifetime away. The room could easily be cleaned out and the old trunks and broken furniture moved to one side, in order to make a habitable living space.

When her mother was out of the house and the maids thought she was at the hospital, Elise snuck back upstairs, where she scrubbed and straightened—careful, though, of every footstep. The attic had trapped the heat of the summer days and the air was difficult to breathe. *How many can I hide?* she wondered as she leaned on her mop. She was tired and dusty, her dress covered by a filthy apron and a kerchief covering her hair.

There was one bed up in the attic already, a double, which Elise made sure no mice were nesting in. So that was room for two. But maybe one more?

She found an old roll-up mattress with navy-blue ticking stripes she'd once used for a camping trip with the Bund Deutscher Mädel. It was thin, and the floor was hard, but still . . .

There were a few chamber pots, left over from the old days. *Well, they're going to have to do,* Elise decided. *The children will need fresh sheets and towels. A change of clothes. A supply of water and food . . .*

Am I insane? She remembered all too well how it felt to have the SS men pin her against the wall, while the other two aimed their weapons at her. But then she thought of Gretel. And Friedrich. And the others.

Satisfied the attic was at last habitable, she tiptoed out.

It was late in the evening, but Ernst Klein hadn't yet finished his appointed rounds. He knocked on the door of Esther Mandelbaum. There was silence, and then he heard slowly shuffling feet. After an interminable pause, several dead bolts were turned with loud clicks.

"Who is it?" came a quavering voice.

"It is I, Frau Mandelbaum—Ernst Klein."

He heard the scrape of a chair being removed. Then the door opened. "Herr Klein." The woman who stood before him wore her still-thick hair in a silver chignon. "How lovely to see you. Please do come in. Would you like a cup of what passes for coffee these days?"

Ernst hated himself for what he was going to do.

"I'm afraid no, Frau Mandelbaum," he replied. "I have—I have a letter for you." He took it out of his rucksack and handed it to her hastily, as though it burned his fingers.

It was a standard-sized business envelope, bone-white, with her name and correct address spelled out in neat black type. The return address was the Reich Association of the Jews.

"So," Frau Mandelbaum said impassively, "it has finally arrived." She opened the envelope and took out the letter and read: *"The arrested are to gather at the synagogue on Wednesday, 9 A.M. Wear working clothes and bring hand luggage that is easily carried. Also, bring food for two to three days. In addition, take with you your valuables and cash. No matches or candles."*

"It's not property confiscation, just a work assignment," Ernst said.

"A work assignment? At my age?" Frau Mandelbaum gave a sniff. "It's a death sentence. And you and I both know it."

He was silent a moment, then asked, "What will you do?"

She shrugged. "What can I do?"

They both stood there, at an impasse. Then Ernst dug a clipboard and pen from his bag. "I'm sorry to have to ask you this, Frau Mandelbaum, but you are required to sign here."

"Of course," she said, accepting the pen and signing her name in neat script. "If God lived on earth, people would break His windows."

Ernst gave a bitter laugh.

"At least *you're* still safe," she told him. "With that shiksa wife of yours."

Ernst pulled out another letter from his breast pocket. When she saw his name typed in the same black letters and the return address, Frau Mandelbaum's eyes widened.

Ernst nodded. "Apparently not."

"Will I see you at the synagogue?"

"Perhaps, Frau Mandelbaum. Perhaps."

Chapter Nine

David and Freddie lay together in David's bed, their heads on thick, goose-down-stuffed pillows, staring up at the ceiling, passing one cigarette back and forth, a crystal ashtray between them.

"You know that what you did was wrong," Freddie began.

"On the contrary—you seemed to like it quite a bit!"

"No, no, I mean asking Rosamund Moser to dinner—*that* was wrong."

"I know," David sighed. "But she didn't have to be so waspish about it."

"Well, it's understandable, no? But, in all seriousness, marrying some poor innocent young girl—that's wrong. Rosamund—any girl—deserves a man who will love her. *Really* love her."

"I know, I know." David covered his eyes with his hands. "But I was desperate. What else can I do?"

Freddie turned over to face him. "Be honest. Everything aboveboard. Marry someone who knows."

"Who *knows?*" David laughed, a short, bitter laugh. "Then no one would marry me."

"What about Daphne Brooks?"

"Daphne? She's a lesbian!"

Freddie smiled. "Exactly. And I can't help but think her parents must want *her* married."

"Oh," said David. Freddie watched him, waiting for all the

cogs to click into place. Finally, they did. "*Oh!* Right! And then we could each go about our business—"

"With no one interfering."

"Well, she's not Jewish—"

"Surely she can convert."

"And I'm not sure she'd want to have children."

Freddie took David's hand. "Let's not get ahead of ourselves. I'll set up a dinner party, with her and her girlfriend. We'll all have a little wine . . ."

"Wizard!" David exclaimed. "You're brilliant, my love."

Freddie smiled. "Well, I can think of a number of ways for you to reward me . . ."

It was Frieda's day off.

Since she was married to a Jew, there wasn't much she could do. She wasn't permitted to stroll in the Tiergarten. She wasn't allowed to go to the movies. And she wasn't even allowed to queue up for food until four o'clock—by which time all the shops would be sold out of rations.

So, Frieda tied an apron around her waist and began to clean the apartment. She swept, washed the floors, scrubbed the windows. And she dusted. Which was why she moved the papers on Ernst's desk.

It was then that she saw the envelope.

"*Mein Gott,*" she murmured, her fingers trembling as she picked it up. The typed *Doktor Ernst Klein* and their address burned her eyes.

Still, Ernst delivered mail for the Jewish Reich Organization. This letter could be anything. It could be nothing. Frieda hesitated, then, with hands shaking, opened the envelope and took out the sheet of paper inside. What she saw made her feel faint, so faint she had to sink down on the threadbare sofa.

Only two days away.

Was Ernst even going to tell her? Or tell her only at the last minute?

A work camp. She held out no hope for decent treatment at any Nazi-run so-called work camp.

Not knowing what else to do, she waited, cold and stone-still on the sofa, as the light changed, the sun went down. And then she sat in the darkness.

When Ernst returned to the apartment, he didn't realize anyone was home. He flipped on the light switch for the bulb overhead, then gasped.

"What are you doing, sitting here in the dark?" he demanded. Then he saw the letter in her hand. He realized what she had done, what she had seen, what she now knew.

He sat beside her and took her hand.

"I want you"—his voice broke, but he pressed on—"to help me die."

"What?" It was not what Frieda was expecting him to say. Help him to escape, to go into hiding, to rob a bank and bribe someone—yes. But help her husband commit suicide? No. "I'm a nurse—I'm supposed to help heal people. I can't help you—or anyone—die. That's insane. *Insane*."

Ernst rose and ran both hands through his hair until it stood up on end. "This whole situation is insane, Frieda! Either way I'm going to die. I'd rather do it myself than let those Nazi bastards get the satisfaction. Do you think what I will face is going to be any better?"

"They're using that argument to euthanize people. Children from the hospital who are mentally, developmentally ill . . ." Frieda was trembling. "Elise still doesn't know, but it's becoming less of a secret every day."

"It's not the same argument! I'm not a child!" Ernst began to pace in the small room. "I'm a grown man, in control of all my faculties. This is *my* decision. I want to die now, at home, with you. I want to die with my dignity intact. I saw the film *Ich klage an*. We both did."

"Suicide is a sin. A mortal sin."

"I'm a Jew," he said. "I don't believe in sin, at least not the way you do. And I don't believe in hell—unless it's where we're living now."

Frieda put her head in her hands and sobbed. "I can't do it!"

"Then I will."

"You?" Frieda looked up. "You don't have the medicine."

"It doesn't take medicine to jump from a roof. It doesn't take medicine to hang yourself with a cord and kick out the chair. It doesn't take medicine to—"

"Stop!" Frieda screamed. Then, in a quieter voice, "Stop." She covered her eyes with her hands. "I need to think about it. I need time to think."

"Think as much as you want," Ernst told his wife. "We—or rather, I—have two days."

It was five P.M. and the corridors of Charité were crowded with staff changing shifts.

Elise needed to leave soon to get back home and dress for her mother's party. She made her rounds swiftly and efficiently, taking temperatures, blood pressures, listening to pulses. All was well.

Until she reached Herr Mystery. The patient was thrashing in his sleep, moaning. Elise put a hand to his forehead. Fever—he was burning up. No wonder he was having nightmares. *"Verdammt,"* she muttered. She'd hoped that he was over the worst of the postsurgery infections. Apparently not. She turned him on his back, then began to insert a hollow IV needle into the vein of his inner elbow.

"No!" he moaned suddenly, in English. "No! Don't! Stop it!" He struggled, then suddenly went limp, back to deep sleep, lashes dark against his pale skin.

Elise recoiled in shock. *English?* she thought, bewildered. *Finally he speaks—and he speaks in English?* She looked around—no one else had heard him.

She knew that if he'd been overheard, he'd be reported. Taken in for questioning. Most likely hanged.

Another death. And for what? Then she remembered the attic. It was already fixed up to hide someone. And an adult might be easier to conceal than a child . . . Elise gave a crooked half smile. Plus there was the distinct satisfaction of hiding a British refugee right under her mother's nose—on the very night of her party, no less. *Not that it's about me, God,* she prayed. *But if I do get a little bit of enjoyment, that's not horrible, yes? Will you forgive me?*

She hung the IV on the frame of his bed. "Come, Herr Mystery," she whispered as she wheeled the bed out of the room, looking straight ahead, trying to appear as though what she was doing was perfectly normal. Her heart raced. "Let's find you somewhere more private to convalesce."

"It's an emergency," Elise said into the receiver, her hands worrying at the thick metal cord.

"I'm a priest, not a taxi service," Father Licht objected. "And I'm celebrating Mass tonight."

"It's—it's important. I'd rather not say more over the phone. But it's life and death."

"The paperwork?"

"Something else. But similar."

Father Licht took off his wire-rimmed glasses and rubbed the bridge of his nose, where there was a red indentation from their weight. "All right. When do you need me?"

Elise looked out the window, cursing the summer, which brought with it longer days and more sunlight. She would prefer to wait until dusk. But she needed to get back for her mother's birthday party. She was supposed to accompany Clara on the piano. If she didn't show up on time . . .

"Meet me at seven—at Charité's service entrance. And, Father—please bring a change of priest's clothing."

Maggie and Gottlieb were getting dressed for the Fire and Ice Ball. *"Feuer und Eis?"* Maggie asked, dabbing on perfume in Gottlieb's bedroom. "You know, there's a Robert Frost poem about fire and ice:

"Some say the world will end in fire—"

Gottlieb, trying to tie his bow tie in the bathroom mirror, quoted back:

"Some say in ice. . . ."

"You read American poetry?" Maggie was shocked.

Gottlieb gave up on his tie. "Surprised the brutish Hun has read something besides Goethe?"

"Because—oh, never mind. Do I look all right?" Noreen had anticipated Maggie's needing a formal dress when she'd packed her case, but it was blue—and according to Gottlieb, for this particular party young women were supposed to dress in white, older women in black.

Luckily Noreen had also thought to give Maggie clothing rations. During the day, Maggie had gone to the KaDeWe department store in Wittenbergplatz. There she bought, with most of her coupons—and a lot of her cash—a white chiffon evening dress.

"Would you mind helping me with my tie?"

"Of course." Maggie retied his bow tie, deliberately looking away from the swastika pins in his lapel.

"Do you have the microphone?"

"It's in my handbag."

"Not loose, I hope."

Even though she was nervous, Maggie bit her lip. Gottlieb and his attitude were getting on her already stretched nerves. "I have it wrapped in two handkerchiefs."

"Good, good." He walked to the front door and opened it, giving her a courtly bow. "After you."

Maggie breezed through. "Thank you, *Schatzi.*"

Elise waited for Father Licht in the shadows of Charité's service entrance, emerging only when the priest's battered car pulled up. She had transferred Herr Mystery from the bed to a wheelchair.

"Gott sei Dank," she said, looking both ways to make sure no one was around. "I'm going to need your help."

Father Licht left the car with the engine idling, and looked at the young man in the wheelchair, who managed to give him a crooked smile. "I can see why you didn't want to discuss this over the telephone," he muttered.

"Father Licht, please meet Herr Mystery. Herr Mystery— Father Johann Licht."

"*Freut mich,*" Father Licht said as he opened the back door, then helped Elise lift the man out of the chair.

Herr Mystery nodded at Father Licht, then grimaced from the pain of moving.

"He's not a big talker," Elise explained to the priest. Then, to Herr Mystery, "Are you all right?" She leaned in to push his curly dark hair out of his eyes and feel his forehead. He was feverish. She pulled the priest's garb Father Licht had brought over his head, then tucked a blanket around him.

"Look," she whispered in English in the injured man's ear. "I know you're British—you were talking in your sleep. If you get caught, you'll . . . be in a lot of trouble. So, I'm taking you some-where safe."

Herr Mystery closed his eyes. Elise realized he had too much morphine in his system to be aware of much.

"Your friend's the silent type," Father Licht observed as he and Elise slid into the front seats.

"The less you know, the better," she retorted.

"I understand. Where to, *gnädiges Fräulein?*"

"Grunewald."

"Grunewald?"

"It's where I live." Elise rolled down the window, breathing in the warm evening air. "Where I fixed up the attic to hide the chil-dren. He's no child, but it looks as though it's going to come in handy now."

As Father Licht drove through the streets of Berlin-Mitte, Elise began to drum her fingers on her lap. "I know you're nervous," the priest said, "but you're going to have to hide it better than that."

Elise stopped her hands. "Terrified."

Father Licht flicked his eyes up to the rearview mirror, taking in the silent man. "About hiding your taciturn friend?"

Elise gave a nervous bark of laughter in response. "No, about being late. My mother's having a party. And if I don't get there soon, she's going to *kill* me."

A driver took Maggie and Gottlieb to Grunewald. In his lap, Gottlieb held an enormous bunch of orchids wrapped in tissue and tied with silver ribbons for their hostess. In the car, they were silent for most of the ride, holding hands and looking at the scenery. Finally, Maggie spoke. "Is the party at"—she struggled with the name—"Clara Hess's home?"

"Yes," Gottlieb replied. "Grunewald is a well-to-do suburb of Berlin. Just a bit past Charlottenburg, near the Olympic Stadium."

"I see."

"We can't just go in and go out," Gottlieb said.

"No, *really*?" Maggie snapped. *Does he think I'm an idiot?*

"I know you're anxious," he said, keenly aware that the driver could be listening to them, "but don't worry."

"Don't worry," she echoed. "Of course not."

Eventually, the long black car began to wind through the tree-lined streets of Grunewald, stopping when the driver pulled up to a high, ornate gate. One guard checked Maggie's and Gottlieb's papers, while another peered suspiciously inside the car and the trunk. Maggie feared both men could hear her heart thundering in her chest, but apparently they didn't, because ultimately they waved them through.

The car pulled into the circular gravel drive of a white neoclassical villa, and they waited in line, behind gleaming Brennabors, Mercedes-Benzes, and Maybachs. They inched their way past a fountain and strutting peacocks, and up to the grand front entranceway, hung with long red Nazi flags and bunting. *Is this a party or a rally?* Maggie wondered.

A doorman in black livery opened Maggie's car door and offered a white-gloved hand to help her out.

"Danke schön," she said. Gottlieb walked around to meet her, bent low to press his lips to her hand, and then offered his arm. *He might be pompous*, Maggie decided, *and have ridiculously big ears, but his manners are impeccable*. She took his arm, as well as a deep breath, and together they walked up the marble stairs and through the double doors, into Clara Hess's home.

"Here!" Elise said, pointing to a large white villa. "But not the front. Pull into the servants' entrance—there, yes, that's it."

Father Licht did as he was told, pulling around the gleaming dark cars waiting in line to be admitted to the front, and going through a different security check—where Elise did all the talking. "Yes," she said, showing her papers, "I'm Clara Hess's daughter."

"Who are these two?" The guard frowned.

Elise gave an impatient exhale. "Well, they're priests. Obviously."

"What are they doing here?"

"They're going to bless the food, of course."

The guard looked dubious.

"Look, we're running late, and I really don't want to tell my mother—Clara Hess—that it was because of a holdup for security . . ."

"All right," the man said, waving them through. "Have a good evening."

Father Licht looked impressed and not a little relieved.

"Park here," Elise said, pointing. "All the servants will be busy getting ready for the party," she said. "At least that's what I'm counting on. Come on, you're going to help me get him to the door and then up the back stairs. Then you *can* bless the food."

She gave the priest a half smile. "After all, I wouldn't want to tell a lie."

It's big, Maggie had to admit when she walked through the doors, looking around as Gottlieb handed the orchids to a maid. They entered a marble great room with a circular stairway. Servants circulated with silver trays holding crystal champagne coupes etched with small swastikas. Hanging over the fireplace was an enormous oil painting of Adolf Hitler by Conrad Hommel—the Führer in full dress uniform under a foreboding sky, gazing over a battlefield. Gottlieb reached for two glasses. "Here you go, *Schatzi*," he said, offering her one.

Maggie accepted the glass and took a tiny sip. She forced a smile, fixing her lips in an approximate curve of merriment. "Thank you."

The next room was even grander, with Ionic columns and a marble fireplace large enough to roast a wild boar. Partygoers milled about—men in dress uniform or white tie with Nazi pins and medals, women in long gowns of black or white silk, with long buttoned gloves. The room was scented with beeswax candles and vases and vases of flowers—white roses and greenery dotted with tiny white blooms. A string quartet played Bach. Gottlieb remarked, "Edelweiss is the Führer's favorite flower."

"How lovely." Maggie's tone was flat.

They passed through room after room, each with its presiding painting or bust of Hitler. They came to a library, where Maggie was confronted with a massive portrait of a young Clara as Elsa in Wagner's *Lohengrin*. Suddenly, she was overwhelmed; she needed to clear her head and stop her hands from shaking. "Let's go outside for a moment," she said to Gottlieb, gesturing to the French doors that opened to the villa's gardens.

He took their empty glasses and gave them to a servant. Then he clicked his heels together and offered his arm. "Your wish is my command."

The gardens were extensive, grand and symmetrical, with marble statues of gods and goddesses and burbling fountains. Blue-green peacocks with iridescent tails strutted over the velvety grass, their imitation eyes keeping careful watch. Wide paths wound through banks of roses, and the entire space was ringed with birch trees, glowing white in the setting sun.

"*Bosco sacro,*" Maggie said.

"Sacred wood?" Gottlieb said.

"Yes, a grove of trees in an Italianate garden, inspired by groves where pagans worshipped."

He leaned in and whispered in her ear, "We have company."

Maggie turned to see another couple strolling toward them. Gottlieb obviously recognized them. He stopped and gave a smart salute. "*Heil Hitler!*"

The man responded with a salute, as did the woman with him. Maggie recognized them from photographs—Reich Minister of Propaganda Joseph Goebbels and his wife, Magda. Goebbels was a tiny man, cadaverously thin, with a long, pinched face and a clubfoot. Yet there was a strange appeal to him: dark, shining eyes, graceful hands, a deep baritone voice. Magda Goebbels was handsome, not beautiful, and wore glittering swastikas fashioned from diamonds, jet, and rubies.

"You remember Gottlieb Lehrer, from the Abwehr?" Goebbels looked to his wife. "He works with Clara Hess."

"*Guten Abend*, Herr Lehrer," Magda said.

"*Abend, gnädige* Frau Goebbels," he responded, kissing her gloved hand.

Goebbels looked at Maggie. She felt a tremor of fear. "And who is this?"

"Dr. Goebbels, *gnädige* Frau Goebbels," Gottlieb responded, "may I present Fräulein Margareta Hoffman, *mein feste Freundin*." Maggie noted that he called her the equivalent of "my serious girlfriend."

"Delighted to meet you, *gnädiges Fräulein*," said Goebbels, kissing Maggie's hand. "What a beautiful creature," he remarked to Gottlieb. "How did you two meet?"

Despite the warm evening breeze, Maggie began to shiver.

"In Rome, Dr. Goebbels," Gottlieb said without hesitation. "I was there for the Abwehr conference with the Vatican. Fräulein Hoffman was assigned to me for various secretarial duties. When the conference was over, she graciously agreed to have dinner with me. By the end of my stay, I had not only fallen in love but convinced Fräulein Hoffman to visit me in Berlin."

"But you *are* German, yes?" Goebbels probed. His eyes locked on Maggie's.

"Yes, sir," Maggie said, her palms damp in her long gloves. She remembered her cover story. "I grew up in Frankfurt, and went to school in Switzerland, at Château Mont-Choisi."

"Ah, that explains your accent." Goebbels nodded.

"And how are your little ones, madame?" Gottlieb asked

Magda, changing the subject—the Goebbels had six adorable blond children.

"All are quite well, thank you."

At the French doors, a butler rang a silver bell for everyone to come inside. Both couples made their way through the garden, allowing for Goebbels's limp.

As the older couple went inside, Gottlieb and Maggie lingered for a moment. "There's a joke," Gottlieb whispered in Maggie's ear, "about the Aryans."

Maggie was pale. "Really," she managed.

"The Aryans—athletic like Goebbels, slim like Göring, and blond like Hitler."

Maggie gave a grim smile. "Shall we?"

Gottlieb offered his arm. "We shall."

Agonizing over every footfall on the stairs and each creak of the floorboards, Elise and Father Licht managed to get Herr Mystery up to the attic and onto the bed. She carefully opened the window a crack, peeking out to see a young couple walking in the garden below.

She turned back to her patient and tucked him in, then put a hand to his forehead. "You're still warm," she murmured. She reached into a bag she'd brought from the hospital that contained needles and tubes, bags of saline and bottles of antibiotics. "I'm going to start you on another round." She cleaned her hands with a cotton pad soaked in alcohol, then inserted the IV line into his inner elbow. As she hung the bag from the bed's headboard, Herr Mystery closed his eyes and began breathing deeply.

"What now?" whispered Father Licht.

Elise checked the hands on her tiny gold watch in the light from the setting sun. "Now I need to get dressed." She looked at the sleeping body in the bed, then tiptoed to the priest and flung her arms around him impulsively. "Thank you so much for your help, Father," she whispered. She let go; the priest's face was red.

"Shhhhh," he reminded her. *"Wände haben Ohren."* Walls have ears.

"You're right—we must go. I will take you to the kitchen, where you can bless the food. If anyone asks, it's a personal favor for me." She winked. "That way I don't have to say I lied in confession."

All of the party guests were crowding around the grand staircase. Maggie overheard snatches of conversation: *"I really don't see why the British don't come to their senses—it's not like they can win, after all . . ."*

Goebbels went partway up the stairs, then turned to face his enraptured audience, mesmerizing them with his black eyes.

"Ladies and gentlemen," he cried, *"Heil Hitler!"*

"Heil Hitler!"

"I'm pleased—no, delighted—to be here to celebrate the birthday of the eternally young, eternally beautiful, *gnädige Frau* Clara Hess."

Maggie, braced for her first sight of her mother, noticed the sour look on Magda Goebbels's face. Was Herr Goebbels just a bit too enthusiastic for his wife's taste?

Goebbels continued, "Who is not only the epitome of Aryan womanhood but an integral and important part of the Third Reich. I am proud to present . . . *Clara Hess!*" With a flourish, he gestured to the top of the stairs.

A figure emerged on the landing, tall and slim with white-blond hair and the regal posture of a Valkyrie. Unlike the rest of the women at the party, she wore a gown of gleaming crimson. It was impossible to look away from her.

Maggie began to tremble. *No—no, this can't be happening . . .* Gottlieb noticed and put his arm protectively around her shoulders. *This can't be happening. I can't believe this is happening.* Maggie had known this moment would come, she'd gone over it countless times in her head. But no rehearsals could have prepared her for the reality. She swayed, unsteady on her feet, as Clara descended.

Chapter Ten

Clara Hess swept down the curving marble stairs to join Goebbels, a Mona Lisa smile touching her crimson-painted lips. When she reached him, he bent and kissed her black-gloved hand.

"Thank you, Joseph," she said, turning to the assembled throng. "And thank you, everyone. How kind of you all to come here, to celebrate my birthday. I ask for no present but your presence." Her smile widened. "As some of you may remember, I used to be an opera singer, a lyric soprano. Of course, I have more important work to do now, but I do like to remember my roots, as well as celebrate our shared Germanic culture. Tonight, I beg your humble indulgence, while I sing. I may be more of a mezzo now, but my passion for music remains the same."

The crowd parted before her as she walked through the vestibule and into the great room amid another swell of applause. In front of the marble fireplace was a grand piano. Clara stood in its wing and turned, her crimson train swirling about her feet.

She gestured to the piano bench. "Ladies and gentlemen, my accompanist—my daughter, the beautiful and accomplished Elise Hess."

A sister? I have a half sister? Maggie gave an involuntary gasp.

But the bench was empty.

Then, red-faced and breathless, a young woman in white

dashed in through a side door and slid into place in the glow of the silver candelabra. She took a shaky breath, then opened the score to *Lohengrin* as Clara glared her disapproval.

There was polite applause as Elise raised her hands, poised over the keyboard.

Maggie bit the inside of her lip and tasted blood. She heard a faint buzzing in her head. *No, this can't be happening. It really can't. It's like a nightmare. I'll wake up soon, yes, I'm sure of it . . .*

Elise lowered her hands to the keys and began to play the minor-key opening chords. Clara took a breath and sang Ortrud's aria:

> *Entweihte Götter! Helft jetzt meiner Rache!*
> *Bestraft die Schmach, die hier euch angetan!*

The room seemed to swim in front of Maggie. "Are you all right?" Gottlieb whispered, leaning closer.

"Fine, just fine," she said. The Jicky perfume she'd put on earlier was too heavy for the hot weather. Maggie thought the spiciness of it might suffocate her. To distract herself, she translated in her head:

> *Desecrated gods! Now help my vengeance!*
> *Punish the shame that was done to you here!*

Gottlieb whispered, "I knew Elise Hess was a nurse, and I thought her piano playing was just a hobby. But she's actually quite good."

Maggie deliberately swayed on her feet and made a distressed sound. "*Schatzi?*"

Clara sang on:

Odin! I call upon you, Strong One!
Freya! Exalted One, hear me!
Bless my deceit and dissimulation,
so that my vengeance may be successful!

And, with that, in a heap of chiffon, Maggie crumpled to the hard black-and-white marble tiled floor. "Air, she needs air!" Gottlieb called.

"I'm a nurse!" Elise called, jumping up from the piano bench and making her way through the crowd to Maggie. She knelt at Maggie's side, then paused and looked up at Gottlieb, who was cradling Maggie's head in his hands. "She's fainted—probably just too much excitement. Let's get her away from the crowd. Please take the *gnädiges Fräulein* to my room," she said to two hovering footmen.

"It's all right." Gottlieb picked up Maggie's evening clutch and tucked it under his arm, then bent to sweep her up in his arms. "I have her."

Elise led the way, back to the vestibule, then up the grand staircase, to a wide red-carpeted hallway. "This way," she said, walking past gilt-framed oil paintings and tables with marble statues of Roman gods and goddesses. "In here."

Gottlieb laid Maggie down gently on the bed while Elise went to the bathroom and soaked a cloth in cold water. "Here," she told Gottlieb, handing him the cloth. "Put this on her temples." She went to the window and opened it wider. "I'll get some smelling salts," she said.

The moment she was gone, Gottlieb went through Maggie's clutch. The microphone was still there. As Elise returned, he closed the little purse with a snap. "Just looking to see if she had any herself," he lied. "I have no idea what you ladies keep in these tiny handbags of yours."

"A Reich secret," Elise said. "We'll never tell." She wafted the tiny glass bottle of smelling salts under Maggie's nose. "This should do the trick."

Maggie reacted with a start. She looked around, taking in the bedroom of a young girl, then Gottlieb, then Elise. *My half sister*, she remembered. The faint might not have been real, but she was still light-headed from the shock.

"How are you feeling?" Elise asked in the same soothing tones she used with her patients at Charité. The same voice she had used on the patient she had hidden upstairs in the attic.

"I'm . . . fine," Maggie croaked. "Just embarrassed."

"It's such a lovely party," Gottlieb told Elise. "And we're honored to be here. But I'm afraid the excitement—all the famous people—may have been too much for *mein feste Freundin*."

"Probably no dinner and then a glass of champagne on an empty stomach." Elise grinned. "Or, perhaps you're not an opera aficionado. I'm not a big admirer of Wagner's myself." She winked at Maggie.

Maggie smiled back, in spite of herself. She and Elise looked nothing alike—while Maggie was pale and slim and red-haired, Elise was rosy and curvy and brunette. But there was something about the set of their mouths and the line of their jaws that betrayed their connection.

"Let me run down and get you something to eat," Elise suggested.

"No, no, I'm fine—" Maggie protested, trying to sit up.

"I insist," Elise said. "In my real life, I'm a nurse—so I know these things." She smiled up at Gottlieb. "Would you make sure our patient stays in bed until I can bring up a sandwich and something to drink?"

"Of course," he said, sitting down next to Maggie and clasping her hand.

The moment Elise was gone, Maggie whispered, "My clutch—"

"—is fine." His lips were pursed, disapproving. "A weak thing to do," he hissed. "Why on earth did they send me someone so green?" He shook his head.

"Gottlieb—"

He held up one hand. "Still, as far as I can tell, nothing is broken."

"Thank God," Maggie breathed.

"I thought you didn't believe in God?"

"It's an expression."

"So, what happened?" He sounded exasperated.

Maggie felt a flash of annoyance. Gottlieb didn't trust her. He didn't think she was competent. *If you were any good yourself, Schatzi, you'd at least have considered the possibility that I faked that faint. It's not my fault you can't think on your feet as fast as I can. And my shoes are a lot less comfortable than yours.* "I did it on purpose. To get away from the crowd."

Gottlieb's eyebrows raised in an expression approximating respect. "Well, we now have an excuse to leave early. Do you want me to do it?"

"You'd look rather conspicuous carrying a handbag."

Gottlieb was not amused. "I can put it in my pocket."

Maggie wanted to show the arrogant albino that she was no rank amateur. "Really, I can do it. I *want* to do it." She sat up and looked around the room. It was beautiful, with robin's-egg-blue wallpaper and a silk coverlet. In the corner was a Victorian-looking cage holding a dove, who stared at Maggie with inquisitive eyes.

"Fine," Gottlieb told her. "It's your head on the block."

There was a dressing table, with a yellowing Palm Sunday frond tucked behind the mirror, along with several photographs of Elise, Clara, and Herr Hess together—ice skating, skiing, in bathing suits by a sparkling lake. Maggie tried not to feel jealous that

Elise had grown up with a mother, even a terrifying Nazi one, not to mention a father. *It's not her fault, after all.*

"Here we go . . ." she heard Elise say as she reentered the room. She was holding a heavy silver tray, which she set down on the bed. "Just like room service! I didn't know what you'd feel like eating, so I brought up a few different things." Elise put her hand on Maggie's shoulder and laid a linen napkin across her lap. The tray held a plate of hors d'oeuvres, a glass of water, and a delicate porcelain cup rimmed with swastikas, that contained steaming coffee. "Eat!" Elise urged.

Maggie was suddenly ravenous. "Thank you, Fräulein Hess," she said, through a small cheese-filled gougère. "This is perfect." She patted Gottlieb's hand. "In fact, I'm feeling much, much better now."

"Shall we go back to the party, *Schatzi*?" he asked.

"Why don't *you* go?" Maggie suggested, taking a sip of the coffee. After days of ersatz rationed brew, she'd never tasted anything so wonderful.

"If you're sure . . ."

"I am." Maggie nodded, then reached for another flaky gougère. "Go! Enjoy yourself!"

Gottlieb blinked. Maggie had a feeling of smug satisfaction. He finally understood what she was up to. He left.

"Herr Lehrer is quite gallant," Elise noted, turning toward the mirror and picking up a tube of lipstick.

Maggie smiled at Elise, who was painting her mouth. "Want to try?" the other girl asked, holding out a golden tube.

Maggie blotted her lips with the napkin, set aside the tray and rose. Standing next to Elise, she applied the lipstick, which smelled of violets. The pigmented wax was still warm from Elise's lips; the act felt dizzyingly intimate.

"Now, let's see," Elise said. "You've eaten, that's good. You have lipstick on, excellent. Let me fix your hair." She picked up a boar-bristle hairbrush. "Here you go," she said, brushing the coppery strands into place. "Perfect."

Maggie's heart was racing. She had a sister. A sister who was sweet. A sister who was fixing her hair—a quintessentially sisterly thing to do in Maggie's opinion, based on books and films. Her sister, who was the daughter of the traitor Clara Hess. Her sister, who was probably a Nazi, too. Maggie took a tremulous breath to clear her head. *I have a mission. I will not be distracted.*

She smiled at Elise. "Fräulein Hess, if you don't think it's too much of an imposition—especially after all of your kindnesses—I'd love to tour your beautiful home. If you don't mind."

"And here we have Mother's conservatory," Elise said, her mind on Herr Mystery. It was a huge room, with a grand piano and an oversized painting of Clara as Brünnhilde in Wagner's *Siegfried*. *What if his temperature's still elevated? What if one of the maids needs something from the attic? What if he cries out and someone hears him?*

There were many silver-framed photographs of Clara over the years, including her as a young girl. Maggie picked up one. Clara, perhaps two years old, dressed for snow, perched in an ornate carriage with oversized, spindly wheels. From the clothes she realized it was probably from before the turn of the century. She was struck by how innocent Clara looked. How angelic. What had happened to change her?

"Oh, it's lovely," Maggie exclaimed, a lump in her throat.

"If you're feeling better now, we should probably be getting back to the party."

"You know, I've heard so much about your mother—from Herr Lehrer, of course—I'd love to see where she works. She's such an inspiring woman and has accomplished so much." She smiled. "If it's not too much trouble."

Elise hesitated, not wanting to continue the tour but unwilling to displease a guest. "Follow me," she said, and Maggie did, through an interior door into a library with built-in bookcases and silk-covered walls, dominated by a desk. Here, too, were paintings of Hitler, as well as a reproduction of Rubens's *Council of the Gods*.

Maggie knew what she had to do. "Oh," she said, stopping abruptly and putting one hand to her forehead.

"Are you ill?" Elise asked.

"Oh, I'm sure I'm fine . . ." Maggie stumbled. "Oh, dear—I'm afraid I'm feeling a trifle faint again."

"Sit down," commanded Elise. "I'll run and fetch the smelling salts."

"And a glass of water?" Maggie asked, sitting on the tufted black leather sofa. *That will buy me a few extra minutes.*

"Of course. Just relax—take deep breaths—I'll be right back," said Elise before she left the room.

Not right *back, I hope.* Maggie dug in her purse for the microphone.

Nearest to the desk was the optimal place to conceal it; they'd taught her at Beaulieu. There was a photograph behind the desk, of a younger Clara, taking a curtain call with her conductor. *Her husband?* Maggie thought as she pulled over the desk chair. *Well, technically, he would be her* second *husband, I suppose.*

Still, her hands were shaking as she tried to secure the microphone and it fell. *"Damn,"* Maggie muttered, kneeling down to search for it. It must have bounced under the desk. She crawled on her hands and knees, trying to find where it had gone. She spotted

a "Feldfu.f" field transmitter–receiver radio. Was Clara eaves-
dropping on military conversations?

She heard Elise's voice. "Margareta?"

Mein Gott, Maggie thought.

"Margareta?"

"Here," Maggie called weakly.

"Oh, my goodness!" Elise said, putting the smelling salts and
water on the desk, then bending to help Maggie up.

"So sorry . . . I wanted to get a look at this beautiful photograph, and then I had another dizzy spell . . ."

She stood with Elise's help, thinking when their hands touched
that although they were strangers, they shared more or less fifty
percent of their DNA. *How very, very strange.*

"Here," Elise said, holding out the water glass. "Drink this."

Maggie took a noisy gulp. "Thank you."

Elise watched her face, then nodded. "Good, your color's coming back."

Maggie picked up a framed photograph. "Who's that?"

"That's my father. He's a conductor for the Berlin State Opera.
In this picture, he's just conducted my mother's first leading role,
in Gounod's *Faust.* She's retired now, but he's still a conductor.
Quite famous, actually, if you follow opera."

"Why did she retire?"

"She developed nodes on her vocal cords—lost part of her
higher register. When she sings now, she picks her repertory very
carefully, so that the ragged edges don't show. The piece she picked
for tonight is fairly low, and she can manage it, as long as she's not
projecting to an opera house." Elise gave a crooked half smile.
"And Ortrud's perfect for her."

Ortrud, in Wagner's *Lohengrin,* was incapable of love. *What's
Elise saying?*

There were voices in the hall. Loud voices. A man and a woman. They were arguing. "I *know* I'm late!" the male voice boomed. "I told you I would come after the performance!"

"And so you've missed everything!" the female voice screeched back.

"Well, I'm here now, aren't I, kitten?"

"Miles, I was humiliated. You deliberately missed my party, because you hate my friends."

"Your Nazi cronies? Those common criminals? I *despise* them—that's no secret."

"We're high-ranking members of the party."

"*You're* a high-ranking member of the party. I just happen to be married to you."

"*Papa und Mutti* are fighting again," Elise whispered to Maggie. Maggie looked at Elise, who seemed to be accustomed to the harsh words. She felt a sudden stab of pity for her half sister. Elise might have grown up with a mother and father—but was her life really any better than Maggie's with Aunt Edith? From the sound of the shouting, Maggie thought perhaps not. But before she had time to respond, she heard, "What on earth are *you* two doing in here?"

Up close, Clara's face had more fine lines than Maggie had noticed during the performance; more indents around the mouth from pursed lips than around the eyes from smiling. Herr Miles Hess was tall and broad, with thick gray hair and a bushy mustache.

"Father, Mother, allow me to present—"

"Margareta Hoffman," Maggie interrupted, willing her paralyzed legs to move, walking toward them. The microphone would have to wait, at least for the moment. She could only hope that someone didn't accidentally step on it. "I truly enjoyed your performance, *gnädige* Frau Hess. And it's an honor to meet you, Herr Hess."

Herr Hess kissed Maggie's hand. "Likewise, Fräulein Hoffman."

"Thank you," Clara said. "I'm glad you enjoyed it . . . while you could. Although, I suppose, a fainting spell can't be helped." She glared at Elise. "Unlike tardiness." Then she asked, "What are you two doing in here? Why aren't you at the party?"

"Fräulein Hoffman wasn't feeling well," Elise interposed hastily, "so we brought her to my room to recover. When she was feeling better, I took her on a tour of the house."

"This room is off-limits. In fact, it should have been locked."

"Clara—" Miles said.

"It *was* locked. We used the door from the conservatory," Elise said.

"I see." Clara looked Maggie up and down; then her beautiful eyes narrowed. "Have we met before?"

Oh, the things I could say. "No, no—I don't think so."

"Hoffman . . . I don't remember your name on the guest list," Clara continued, taking a step closer, head tilted to one side in contemplation.

"Mother!" Elise exclaimed.

"I'm Gottlieb Lehrer's girlfriend," Maggie said evenly, although her heart was racing. Her hands were starting to shake; she clasped them behind her back. "He also works at the Abwehr."

"Gottlieb Lehrer? Oh, yes, one of Canaris's men," Clara said absently. She kept staring at Maggie. "Red hair—it's rather unusual, isn't it?"

Yes, I inherited it from my father—the man you betrayed, Maggie thought. "Oh, it's darker now, but when I was younger it was bright red—almost orange. I was teased horribly."

Clara reached out a hand to touch one of Maggie's locks. Maggie fought the urge to slap the beringed fingers away. But Clara dropped her hand before it made contact, shaking it as though she'd received an electric shock. "Are you sure we haven't met?" she asked again. "You look so familiar. But I can't quite place your face."

Maggie felt her cheeks flush. "No, no, I don't think so, Frau Hess."

Clara gave a dazzling smile. "Well, let's all get back to the party then, shall we? I still need to cut the cake."

"Cake!" enthused Miles. He winked at Elise. "Guess I came just in time." He offered his arms, and Elise and Maggie each took one. The three walked out of the study together. Clara used her key to lock the conservatory door, then returned to the hall door and locked that, too.

Conversation drifted past Maggie's ears: "*After all, our segregation of the Jews is inspired by the United States and her segregation of Negroes . . .*" "*Racial hygiene, you know—social Darwinism . . .*" "*It all started in Cold Spring Harbor—that's near New York City . . .*"

A general, apparently drunk, was shouting, "Blood must flow! Blood must flow!" as he was escorted out to his waiting car by two of the liveried servants. Behind him, a woman in diamonds patted him on the back, saying in soothing tones, "Of course, darling. Of course it must."

"Elise, come with me—there are some people I want you to meet," Clara said, sweeping her daughter in her wake.

"Let's talk more later," Elise whispered back to Maggie.

"Ah, Fräulein Hoffman," Goebbels said, walking over to her. "I trust you're feeling better?"

"Yes, Herr Goebbels," Maggie managed. "Thank you."

"Excellent! Let me introduce you to a few people."

Maggie smiled her brightest, fakest smile, and walked with him. She spotted Gottlieb, but he was in an animated conversation with two men. One was the bloated Hermann Göring, Hitler's *Reichsmarschall* and successor, his uniform straining at ostentatious golden buttons. The other was a distinguished-looking white-haired man with bushy eyebrows—Admiral Wilhelm Canaris from the Abwehr, Gottlieb's superior officer. Maggie recognized them both from pictures she'd studied at Beaulieu. Gottlieb didn't see her; she was on her own.

Goebbels led her to a cluster of people sipping champagne and chatting. A thirty-something man with golden hair was at the beginning of a story, blue eyes dancing with mirth. "I saw Wolff Gondrell, the cabaret performer, in the *That Speaks Volumes* revue last week."

"Tell us!" insisted one of the tipsy ladies. Maggie forced herself to continue to smile.

"Well," he said, "a young man applies for a job as a salesman. The bookseller shows the young man his sales methods and explains, 'The most important thing in the bookshop is the window display, yes? You must *never* pile up books of the same kind there. No, the customer likes to see relationships among the books.'"

He gestured to one of the servants for another glass of champagne, then drained it. "And he says, 'Well, here I have *Maid of Orleans*, next to *Casanova*. And here is Martitt's *The Frigid Woman*, next to the *Guide to Hot Food*!' That's brilliant, isn't it? Having the subject next to the instructions . . .'"

"My, my," Emmy Göring said, pressing a gloved hand to her heart.

The man waited, eyes twinkling, teasing his audience. Then, the punch line. "*The Eternal Jew* next to *Gone With the Wind*. Understand? Gone with the wind!"

The group laughed heartily. Maggie tried to join in, but her jaws and face felt frozen.

"Gone with the wind to Poland," Göring said. "And from there . . ."

"I hear they're going to live on reservations—like the U.S. government did with the American Indians."

"I hear they're going to be shipped to Madagascar."

"Just as soon as we take Russia, and then Britain falls in line." Goebbels turned to Maggie. "Fräulein Hoffman, do you think Churchill will ever surrender?"

Oh, my. "Unfortunately, I don't think so, Dr. Goebbels."

"And why is that?" His eyes glittered.

Were they somehow on to her? She had to be more careful. As a German, even one who'd been in Rome, she wouldn't be privy to much information about Churchill or the British, and what there was would be propaganda. "From what I've read in the papers, Herr Churchill seems to be a stubborn man." She took a sip of the icy champagne. "And I also hear he's rarely sober."

"A stubborn man and a drunken fool!" The golden-haired man chortled. "Exactly!" He eyed Maggie appraisingly. Inside, she shuddered.

"Fräulein Hoffman, you said you worked as a typist, yes?" asked Goebbels.

For Winston Churchill, Maggie thought. "Yes, sir. I worked for Gottlieb Lehrer in Rome, for the Abwehr's conference with the Vatican."

"Lucky Herr Lehrer," the golden-haired man said, with a grin. "Herr Goebbels was just telling us that Göring there is looking for a new girl—a new typist, that is." He gestured to the overweight man talking with Gottlieb.

"Oh, really?" Maggie managed. She just wanted to meet up with Gottlieb and get out. Surely he knew what danger they were in . . .

"What are you doing now, Fräulein Hoffman?" Goebbels's dark eyes bored into hers.

"N-now?" Maggie managed.

"What are your future plans? Are things serious with this young Lehrer?" He leaned closer. "Do you want an excuse to stay in Berlin? This job with Göring would kill two birds with one stone."

"Not to mention serve the Führer and the Reich," the golden-haired man added with another wink.

"Ah, and that, too," Goebbels agreed with a thin smile.

Frau Goebbels cut in. "Although you realize that there will be any number of young women interviewing for the position."

Maggie thought desperately. She was supposed to go back to England the next day. But working for Göring—it could be an amazing opportunity. The secrets she might uncover . . . And Gottlieb could transmit them back to SOE. She at least had to try.

"And there's no guarantee you'll get it," Frau Goebbels continued. "You'll have to take a typing test."

"Of course," Maggie said. Her thoughts were racing.

"Here's my card," said Goebbels, ignoring the disapproving stare of his wife. "Come on Monday, eight A.M. sharp. The Reich Chancellery."

Maggie smiled. "*Danke schön*, Dr. Goebbels." She slipped the card into her handbag. "I'll be there."

Elise and her father sat together on a bench on the perimeter of the room, away from the guests. "I missed you, Papa," Elise said as they shared a slice of cake decorated with fondant roses and silver dragées.

"And I missed you, too, *Engelchen*."

"How long will you be home this time?"

"Not long. We're rehearsing for a new production of *Lohengrin*. We'll be performing it here, then taking it to Zürich next week, leaving on Sunday." He kissed her forehead. "Want to get away with your old papa?"

Elise loved traveling with her father and the opera company. But now she had work. Not to mention her houseguest upstairs. Then she had an inspiration. "A trip to Zürich sounds perfect, Papa." She smiled. "Absolutely perfect."

Gottlieb and Maggie were conferring in a corner. The party had gone on long into the night. They'd taken cautious sips from their champagne, careful not to drink too much, smiling broadly and fatuously at each other as they did so. "I'll do it," he said.

"No, I'll do it!"

"You're not up for it."

"I am! And I'll be less conspicuous than you."

"I can't wait to get you on that plane and away from here!" Gottlieb whispered, furious.

"Believe me, I can't wait to leave this hell, either."

Maggie headed back to Clara's study, and this time—using a hairpin to pick the door's lock—she planted the bug without incident behind the gold-framed portrait of Hitler. *There you have it, Gottlieb,* Maggie thought triumphantly as she slipped out of the room.

After another glass of champagne, they threaded their way through the room to thank their hosts. Now that the bug had been planted, Maggie wanted desperately to go. The last thing she wanted to do was have another interaction with Clara.

"Ah, leaving so soon, Herr Lehrer?"

"I'm afraid so. As you saw, Frau Hess, Fräulein Hoffman is not feeling well."

Clara appraised Maggie's face. "Well, you look much better now," she said. Her eyes didn't waver, and Maggie felt them burning into hers. She realized that, although beautiful, one of Clara's eyes wandered slightly.

Clara smiled, a cold smile. "Good night, then."

Maggie sought out Elise, on the periphery of the party, an onlooker as the others danced. "Thank you again—for all your help."

"Oh, it was nothing," Elise responded cheerfully. "I'm a nurse. It's what I do. And I'm so glad you're feeling better."

"Well, I appreciate the care."

"Of course." The girls stared at each other. Maggie braced herself. She was certain that Elise would notice their resemblance.

And maybe she did, at least on a subconscious level, for she grasped Maggie's hand. "I know you're new to Berlin, so if you ever need anything—and I mean *anything*—just let me know." She took a pen and piece of paper from the drawer of an ornate end table and scribbled down some numbers. "This is how to reach me, here at home and also at the hospital."

"Thank you." Maggie accepted the slip of paper, surprisingly touched. "Thank you so much, Fräulein Hess."

Elise embraced her and whispered in her ear, "You're not one of *them*, I can tell, Fräulein Hoffman."

"No, I'm not," Maggie whispered back.

"Good for you. Neither am I."

The two new friends kissed goodbye.

On the ride back to Charlottenburg, Maggie and Gottlieb remained silent, but once they entered his apartment and closed and locked the door behind them, Maggie spoke. "The microphone was planted successfully."

"Congratulations," Gottlieb said scathingly. "Although you

might have warned me about your plan to faint like a Victorian maiden."

Maggie realized that was the closest she was going to get to an apology, so she took it and moved on. "And I wasn't idle the rest of the night, either. I'm in! Or, at least, I have a typing test."

"In? In where?" Gottlieb, his eyes shadowed from exhaustion, was slumped on the sofa.

Maggie sat next to him and kicked off her evening sandals. "Ouch," she said. "High heels are brutal." She pointed and flexed her blistered feet.

"And what exactly were you talking about with Goebbels?"

"I told them we met when I worked as your temporary secretary in Rome," she replied. "And then Goebbels said that Göring is looking for a new typist. The interview's on Monday. Göring's the *Reichsmarschall*! Just think of the memos and papers I could get my hands on . . ."

"Who cares?" Gottlieb interrupted, tugging at one end of his bow tie so that it loosened. "By then you'll be long gone."

"But—what if I'm not?" Maggie countered. "Can you imagine what would happen if I were assigned the job? The information I could get my hands on? Pass on? To you!"

Gottlieb looked shocked that she'd even raise the possibility of changing her itinerary. "That is not part of your assignment."

Maggie tried not to grind her teeth in frustration. "Gottlieb, an amazing opportunity has presented itself. I'd be a fool not to follow up on it."

"You'd be an even bigger fool not to leave precisely as scheduled." He turned to her, green eyes serious. "Spies in the field don't have a long life. The only way to keep you alive is to get you in and then get you out as quickly as possible. A long-term situation—"

"Would provide invaluable information. People always underestimate their secretaries—believe me, I know. They say and do things in front of us that they'd never do in public. I used to hate that part of the job—but now I see that it can work to our advantage."

"And I say *nein*," Gottlieb insisted. "You'd be in one of the most dangerous spots in all of Germany. If you somehow betrayed yourself, if you were discovered, you would be shot at once. Or hanged—a bullet would be considered too good for you. And perhaps the group I'm working with would be exposed." He shook his head. "No. It's too dangerous."

"I realize that it's dangerous. But it's a calculated risk."

"Which you will not take."

Who are you to give me orders? "Look, Gottlieb—I just came from London. Do you realize how horrible things are there? The Luftwaffe's destroying the city. People have been buried alive. There are children without parents, parents without limbs, homes destroyed, invasion imminent. It's absolutely desperate."

"No."

"Well," Maggie said in clipped tones, picking up her sandals, "it's not up to you, is it?"

He rose. "You will be at the pickup point tomorrow night, as planned, for your flight back to London. We will not deviate from the plan." He stared at her, a muscle in his jaw twitching. His pale face was mottled red with anger.

Maggie yawned, a big yawn, and stretched. "I'm exhausted— I'm going to go to sleep," she said, closing the bedroom door.

"And you are leaving tomorrow!"

Maggie called through the closed door, "Good night, *Schatzi*."

Later that night, at the party, more and more champagne was consumed from crystal coupes. The orchestra played a Strauss waltz, and the guests' voices rose louder and louder, and the dancing grew wilder as the violins sounded their high notes verging on hysteria.

"Where's your husband, Clara?" Goebbels asked the blonde as they sat out the dance; his clubfoot made it hard to waltz.

"He went to bed, I think. He'll be off to Zürich soon, to conduct *Lohengrin*."

"*Lohengrin*—one of my favorites."

Clara rested one arm on the back of the settee and leaned closer. "Joseph, what do you know about that girl? The one with the red hair?"

"Oh, Margareta something-or-other? She came with Gottlieb Lehrer."

"Have they known each other long?"

"I don't know about that, but they certainly seemed quite infatuated. I believe they met in Rome." He looked at her quizzically. "Why do you ask, darling?"

Clara smiled and patted his knee. "Let's just say I'm curious is all. Please have your people run a thorough background check."

Goebbels looked around. "I think she and young Lehrer left an hour or so ago. If you'd like, I can have my men follow them . . ."

"No, no—not tonight." Clara shook her head. "But soon. Monday morning. I just want to make certain everything's in order. Now come," she urged, standing and extending her hand, "dance with me. Let's not waste this gorgeous music."

Chapter Eleven

Maggie had a restless night, full of half-realized nightmares and memories from the evening before, of spiders with teeth, and sticky webs tangled in her hair. However, the next morning, she woke early, dressed, and put on her hat and gloves. It was Sunday morning, and Gottlieb had left her a note that he had gone to Mass. She grabbed her knitting and hurried down to the square.

There, on a wooden bench, surrounded by hooded crows pecking at her feet, sat the woman Maggie called Madame Defarge, needles clicking away. She nodded to Maggie when she sat down beside her. *"Guten Morgen, gnädiges Fräulein."*

"Guten Morgen, gnädige Frau," Maggie replied. She took her knitting out of her bag. She already had a good few inches started in the black wool. Now she called upon her memory of Morse code to alternate knitted stitches with purls and dropped stitches. Translated, it read, *Mission accomplished. Staying in Berlin. Great opportunity. Will know more by Monday night.*

"Excuse me, *Frau,*" Maggie said. "Would you mind taking a look at my knitting? I'm afraid my stitches aren't as smooth as yours."

"Of course, dear," the woman said. "Let me see."

Maggie handed over the needles and yarn. The woman studied the stitches, then pursed her lips. "Let me show you a different kind of stitch, dear," she said.

A pair of SS officers in black stopped in front of them. They doffed their skull-and-crossbones hats to the two women. "Knitting for the soldiers?" asked one.

"Of course," said Madame Defarge.

"*Viel Erfolg!*" said the other. Maggie smiled. What he'd said translated to "Good luck with your work." *Ha*, she thought. *Good luck indeed.*

The woman finished her row. "Take a look at the stitches, dear."

Maggie did, reading the knitted code. "*Affirmative,*" it read.

"Thank you," she said. The older woman pulled out her coded stitches. Maggie did the same with hers. There was no trace of the messages that had been exchanged.

"Any time." The older woman continued to knit.

"I hope to see you on Tuesday," Maggie said, putting her knitting away in her bag and rising. *Because by Tuesday I'll know if I have the job.*

"I hope so, too, dear."

Elise also woke early. She tiptoed up the servants' stairs to the attic, to check on Herr Mystery.

He was awake, she saw, lying in the bed, his eyes raised to the early morning sunlight streaming in the high round windows, glass panes tilted to let in fresh air. The only sounds were the occasional coos and wing flaps of a mourning dove, along with the chime of church bells.

"Good morning, Herr Mystery," she whispered in faintly accented English. "How was your night?" She reached for his wrist and took his pulse. It was strong.

He looked at her but made no reply.

"It's all right." She tucked a thermometer between his lips and checked his IV. "I know you speak English. That's what tipped me off, by the way—you were talking in your sleep. That's why you're here. I thought it was best to get you somewhere safe before you incriminated yourself."

Herr Mystery blinked. Elise took out the thermometer. "It's one hundred. Just slightly elevated. We'll keep an eye on it, but it looks like you beat the infection." She smiled.

"Where am I?" He spoke the way the British usually spoke German: without any accent, the vowel sounds just a touch too long.

"You're in Grunewald. A suburb of Berlin. This is my home—the attic of my home, that is. My mother would not be . . . pleased . . . to find out we are hosting you, so you must be as quiet as possible. You must stay here, in hiding, until we find somewhere safer for you."

"You can't do this," he said, reverting to English, clearly realizing there was no use in keeping up the pretense. "You could be arrested—killed. Charges of 'aid and succor to the enemy.' "

"Well, you can't go back to the hospital—you were calling out in your sleep. In *English*. They'd hang you for sure."

There was an electric silence as each contemplated the enormous risk inherent in the rescue.

"Thank you," he said finally.

Elise rose to her feet. "You must be starving. Let me get you some breakfast."

Before she could leave, however, Herr Mystery grasped her small hand, gripping it tightly. "No, really. Thank you."

They held each other's gaze for a long moment. "I feel like I know you," he told her. "But that's not possible, is it?"

"No," Elise answered briskly, in her best nurse voice. "I'm quite sure we've never met. Now you lie back and rest. I'll bring up some rolls and coffee, and also a few books, if you're up for reading. There's a chamber pot under the bed, unless you don't think you can manage . . ."

"I'll manage," he mumbled.

To smooth over his embarrassment, Elise said, "We'll have you back on your feet in no time."

"And then what?"

"Well . . ." She still had to work out the details of her plan. "Let's cross one bridge at a time, shall we?"

"What's your name?" he asked, obviously reluctant for her to go.

"Elise Hess. And yours?"

"John," he replied. "John Sterling."

Frieda was in Charité's medical supply room, looking for both morphine and phenobarbital. She took a bottle of each down from the shelves.

Elise came in, looking for insulin. "What do you have there?" she said, looking over Frieda's shoulder. "*Mein Gott*, that's enough to kill an ox. What do you need that for?" Her stomach lurched. She grabbed her friend's arm. "It's not Dr. Brandt, is it? Has he asked you to . . . you know . . ."

"No," Frieda whispered, her voice shaking. "It's for Ernst. Ernst has asked me to . . . help him die."

"What? You can't!"

"What choice do I have? If I don't, he'll do it himself. Elise, you know that because I'm a nurse, I can do it for him with far less pain than he ever could."

"No," Elise insisted. "No. There has to be another way."

Frieda looked close to death herself, her face drawn. Her eyes were dull and unseeing.

"I need to do something right now," Elise told her, "but meet me on the roof in ten minutes, all right?"

Frieda gave a reluctant sigh. "All right."

Satisfied that no one was around, Elise went to the medical records room. But the door was locked. Not just locked but triple pad-locked. She said a silent prayer to St. Jude, the patron of lost causes.

Another nurse in gray and white passed. "What happened here?" Elise asked her.

The nurse stopped, frowning. "Another of Dr. Brandt's rules."

"But how are we supposed to get to patient files when we need them?"

"There's a new form—it must be signed by Dr. Brandt before you can be let in. And even then, you'll be supervised by Nurse Flint."

"I see," Elise said. The other nurse walked away. *Great, just great,* Elise thought, realizing that three iron locks would be impossible to pick. She needed to find out where Dr. Brandt kept the keys.

But first, there was Frieda.

Up on the roof of the hospital, in the harsh midday light, Elise and Frieda shared a cigarette.

"Maybe it really is a work camp," Elise said, inhaling. "Maybe it's just for the war, and then, after, he'll be able to come home . . ." She stopped, realizing how inane she sounded.

"I know the propaganda films all show the Germans marching unopposed into Poland." Frieda frowned. "All the Jews looking happy and healthy in their ghettos. Everyone thrilled to be there, before being shipped off to Madagascar, or whatever final destination they're talking about this week . . ." She brushed hot tears from her cheeks. "But do you seriously think that the Nazis, who are willing to murder children—Christian children, Nazi children, for God's sake—are really going to waste their time and money taking care of *Jews?*"

Elise was silent, remembering the gas chamber at Hadamar. "No," she said, dropping her cigarette and crushing it under the heel of her shoe. "No, you're right." She crossed herself.

"And Ernst would rather kill himself than die at their hands."

Elise knew that Frieda would know how to administer the correct dosages of morphine and phenobarbital. Ernst could die in his own bed. With dignity. Without pain.

No! something inside of Elise screamed. *No, we haven't come to that—not yet, at least.* Not only was suicide a mortal sin but it would somehow signify that they were lost, that Germany was lost, that their humanity was lost.

"Frieda," Elise said, thinking fast, "telephone Ernst—have him meet us at the hospital after work."

"But the curfew laws . . ."

"He's just going to have to make sure not to get caught."

"Bastards took our telephone."

"Then go!" Elise gestured toward the stairwell. "I'll cover for you. Bring him back here."

"What then?"

Elise put her arm around her friend. "I have a plan. Now *go!*"

Elise and Frieda set Ernst up as a corpse for the day, draped in a sheet to hide him, in Charité's basement morgue. His instructions were to lie as still as possible, hour after hour, until they came to get him.

When it was finally time, the two nurses had him sit in a wheel-chair. They made their way to the back entrance, where Father Licht was waiting in his car. It was late afternoon, with sunshine slanting and burning. A hot breeze had picked up. The air smelled of spilled oil and car exhaust.

Two doctors appeared, their white coats flapping around their legs in the wind, red and black bands around their arms. "What's going on here?" demanded the first one, squat with gray hair and glasses.

"Special day pass," Elise lied. Frieda looked as though she might faint, while Ernst gritted his teeth.

"On whose orders?" said the other, also gray, but tall and thin, with a beakish nose.

"Dr. Brandt's," Elise replied without hesitation.

Father Licht opened the door of the car and stepped out. With his priest's collar and wide-brimmed *cappello romano*, he carried a quiet authority. "It's for a special religious service, *Herr Doktors*."

"Really," the second doctor said. "And which service would that be?"

"The feast of St. Drithelm."

"And which church?"

"St. Hedwig's. I'm the priest there."

The first doctor turned to Elise. "And who are you?"

"Nurse Aloïsa Herrmann."

"And where is the patient's paperwork?"

"Ach du lieber Himmel!" Frieda said, finally recovering her voice. She clapped one hand to her forehead. "I must have left it back at the nurses' station. Shall I get it?"

"Nein, nein," the first doctor said, waving a careless hand.

"Enjoy your saint's day," the other said.

"Thank you, *Herr Doktors*," Father Licht called, getting back into his car.

Elise and Frieda helped Ernst into the backseat. "No time for a long goodbye," Elise warned.

Frieda kissed her husband's lips, then pulled herself away. He leaned back and she raised the blanket up over his head, covering his face. She stepped back, hand over her mouth, as though trying to force down screams. "I love you."

"I love you, too, darling," Ernst whispered.

"It's the only way," Elise said to her, slamming the door shut and slipping into the passenger seat. "We'll keep him safe."

Father Licht turned the key in the ignition, pressed down on the clutch, and shifted into reverse.

"I'll find you . . ." Frieda whispered as the car rolled away. Then she doubled over, clutching her abdomen in pain, willing herself not to cry.

David and Freddie were at the Ritz Hotel for dinner, with Daphne Brooks and her girlfriend, Kay McQuire. David and Freddie looked dapper in their dinner jackets and black tie, Daphne in a sunny yellow gown that set off her blond ringlets, and Kay in trousers with a white silk blouse with the collar open at the throat and cuff links at the wrists. Her short brown hair was glossed back with Brylcreem.

"Another bottle of fizz, if you please," David called to one of the waiters hovering nearby, as yet another cleared their dishes.

The waiter removed the empty bottle from the stand, dripping with the melted ice. "Yes, sir."

"A girl could get used to this." Daphne leaned back in her velvet chair and sighed with contentment. In the formal dining room of the Ritz, with its thick carpets, heavy draperies, and glittering chandeliers reflected in panels of mirrors, the war seemed—at least for the moment—worlds away.

David and Freddie exchanged glances. "Well," David said, as the waiter returned with a newly opened bottle of champagne and began refilling their glasses, "that's actually one of the things we wanted to talk to you about."

Kay raised an eyebrow and took out a cigarette. Freddie reached for his Evans lighter and lit it for her. "Thanks, darling," she said, taking a long drag.

David cleared his throat. He reached for his champagne, raising the glass to his dry lips and taking a nervous swallow. "We . . . have a business proposition for you."

The two women looked at each other. "Well, you certainly have our attention," Daphne said.

"You see," David continued, "there now seems to be a little issue about my trust and my inheritance. Where once everything seemed quite straightforward, now there are . . . strings attached."

Kay shrugged. "How could that possibly have anything to do with us?" Daphne asked.

"Good question! Here's the thing—"

Freddie sighed. "Would you get to the point, please?"

"Oh, merciful Minerva!" David glared at him. "In a nutshell, ladies, unless I get married, I'll forfeit my trust and my inheritance. As you well know, the blessed state of holy matrimony was never something I ever aspired to—" He stopped, looking over at Freddie.

"Stay on topic," Freddie admonished.

"And so I was wondering—hoping, that is—that one of you two ladies might consent to enter into it—as a business arrangement—with me." David took a deep breath. "Wherein one of you would agree to marry me and pose as my wife. All the while free to live her own life, of course. Just as I would mine."

Daphne giggled. "And did you have one of us in particular in mind?"

David gave an impish smile. "The choice would be like poor Paris's—a man surrounded by goddesses."

"And the golden apple at stake," Kay said. She thought for a moment, her ruby lips pursed, then reached over for Daphne's hand. "We're in a good place, David. We have a two-bedroom flat in Bloomsbury—of course, one bedroom's just for show. Our landlady thinks we're old maids, who are also the best of friends. We have our tribe of like-minded women, go to the theater, go to dinner parties, write, support candidates. We're ARP street wardens, for goodness' sake. We have made, against all odds, a life together. A *good* life."

"Of course," David agreed. "And Freddie and I hope to do the same. This . . . marriage . . . would be in name only. A few family functions to attend."

"That's all?" Kay asked skeptically.

"Well, there would be the conversion, of course . . ."

"Convert?" Daphne gasped. "To Judaism?" She shook her head. "I'm sorry, but I'm an Anglican."

"There's also the small matter of"—David paused delicately—"an heir."

Kay and Daphne met eyes, shocked. Without words, the two women came to an understanding. "No," Kay said finally, turning a cold stare to David. "No. We're not about to sell our integrity— not to mention even *think* about bringing another human life into the world—merely to save your precious pocket money."

She stood and threw her linen napkin on the table. Daphne stood, too. "We may not be as rich as you, but we work for a living, and we're able to support ourselves," she said. "We live as we want—more or less. I'd rather have toast and beans at home, with the woman I love, than all the champagne at the Ritz. Come on, Kay—we're going."

The two women swept out, leaving whispers and stares in their wake. David and Freddie looked at each other. "Well," Freddie deadpanned, lifting his champagne coupe to his lips. "That went well."

David looked up and caught their waiter's eye. "The bill, please," he said glumly.

"You have company," Elise said to John when she and Ernst reached the attic.

John sat up in his bed, taking in both Elise and Ernst. Ernst spoke first. "Ernst Klein. Rogue Jew. Pleased to meet you."

"John Sterling, injured British pilot. Pleased to meet you, too," he said in broken German.

"Well then," Elise said. "Ernst, you take the roll-up mattress on the floor there. I'll get you some clean sheets and blankets. I'll also bring up a washbasin and then some dinner."

"You're taking too great a risk, Elise," Ernst warned.

"Mother's rarely home, and doesn't pay much attention to me when she is. Neither do the servants. There's always a lot of food around—most of it goes to waste anyway. You two just rest. I'll set everything up, and then we can make plans tonight."

Ernst's eyes filled with tears. "I can never thank you enough . . ."

"Yes," John said, "how can we ever repay you?"

"Let's just focus on getting you both out," Elise whispered firmly. "And Ernst, would you please take a look at John's incision? It seems to be healing well, but you're the surgeon, after all. And for heaven's sake—be quiet."

Frieda was unable to think, unable to breathe. Ernst was at Clara Hess's home. This was no game; his life was on the line. She loved

Elise, but she also thought her friend was naïve, spoiled, and un-
aware of the terrible danger Jews were in. He would be safe for
what—a few days, maybe? And then what? What if a servant
heard a footstep, or wondered where all the bread was going?
What would happen to Ernst then?

Frieda changed out of her nurse's uniform in the locker room
and dressed quickly, pinning on her hat in the mirror by the door.
It wasn't as if she had a plan in mind. She just walked out of the
hospital and then kept walking.

"I'm here to see Frau Hess," Frieda announced at the Abwehr,
after showing her identity card to the guards at the entrance.

"Do you have an appointment?" the receptionist asked.

"Frau Hess will want to see me."

"What is this concerning?"

Frieda's voice didn't waver. "Her daughter. Elise."

"And who are you again?" Clara Hess was at her desk, going over
reports. She looked up as Frieda entered, taking in the younger
woman's worn dress and scuffed shoes. "How do you know my
daughter?"

"Frau Hess, my name is Frieda Klein, and I work with your
daughter, Elise, at Charité Hospital."

"I'm an extremely busy woman, Fräulein Klein—what is this
about?"

Frieda took a tremulous breath. "Has Elise ever . . . ever spoken about me? Or my husband?"

Clara blinked. She put down her silver pen and looked Frieda in
the eye. "You're the nurse who married the Jew," she said, putting

the pieces together. "I'm sorry, but I work in Intelligence—I have nothing to do with deportations."

"I'm not here to talk about my husband," Frieda insisted. "Or, at least not directly. I'm here to talk about Elise. What she's been doing."

Clara's eyes narrowed. "My daughter? What *has* she been doing?"

"Something that—if it were found out—would bring great embarrassment to the Abwehr. And to you, in particular."

Clara leaned back in her leather chair. Her gaze was cold. "I'm listening."

"I will tell you everything I know," Frieda continued. "But only on the condition that Ernst won't be hurt in any way. That he won't be sent away. Save him—and I'll tell you everything."

"My dear," Clara said with an icy smile. "Why don't you sit down?"

That night, Maggie and Gottlieb had another argument.

"You're still here?" he asked, coming back to the apartment at the end of the day. He'd been to Mass at St. Hedwig's and then to the Berlin Boxing Club, to take his anger out on their heavy bags and several unfortunate sparring partners.

Maggie met his gaze. "Yes, I'm staying to do the interview. And if I get the job, I'll be staying indefinitely."

"You," he said, stabbing a finger at her, "are a reckless fool!" His rising temper caused his face to turn red. Even his oversized ears were red.

Maggie was stunned by his intensity. "No, I'm not," she countered. "It's exactly what I was trained to do. Appraise a situation and act accordingly."

"Those are not your orders!" Gottlieb exploded. "You're supposed to follow orders!"

Maggie was becoming frightened, but knew she couldn't show it. If she showed any fear or uncertainty, she'd be on the next SOE plane to England. "My orders have room for improvisation," she retorted. "I've already given word I won't need a pickup tomorrow, and that I'll send word on Tuesday."

"Every day you stay here, every message we transmit, puts us all in danger!"

Maggie's temper finally snapped. She'd had it with Gottlieb, with the Nazis, with all of Germany, with its stupid protocols, cruel rigidity, and endless rules. How could anyone with any sense have let it get this bad? "It wouldn't be necessary for me to be here at all if you people had stood up to Hitler in 'thirty-three." There, it was ugly, and she'd said it. It was out.

Gottlieb looked as stunned as if she had slapped him. "They wouldn't just hurt us, you know. They'd hurt our families first. I have a mother and three sisters. Do you think I want to see them questioned by the Gestapo? Tortured? Beheaded?"

Maggie instantly regretted her impulsive outburst. Of course it wasn't just Gottlieb at risk. She was jeopardizing all the people he cared for, the people he loved. "I'm sorry, Gottlieb. I'm sorry that your family's in danger. I'm sorry your country has been led astray by these monsters."

"Germany's not the only country with monsters," he countered, enunciating each word furiously. "You in America have the Ku Klux Klan, Henry Ford, and Father Coughlin—it's not as if the United States is a utopia of any sort. And let's not forget the MS *St. Louis*."

Maggie flushed. He was right, of course. "But that's why we need to act—why *I* need to act. I'll let you in on a little secret, Gottlieb. To the men in those positions, we secretaries, janitors, cleaning ladies, receptionists—we're all invisible. They simply don't see us. We're there to be used, no more human than a telephone, or a typewriter. And because they think we're the same as furniture, they let slip all kinds of things around us."

"Not Germans."

"Germans, too," Maggie countered.

Gottlieb stood and went to the kitchen cupboard. He reached for a bottle and two glasses. "You are *not* doing this. You're not putting yourself, and the few members of the resistance we have, in danger."

"Gottlieb—I'm smart, I'm trained, and I have the courage to do this."

He sat down on the sofa and poured brown liquid into both of the glasses. "Brandy," he said, holding one glass out to her.

Maggie accepted it. She and Gottlieb both swallowed. Maggie's throat burned. But she did feel a tiny bit better.

"Sit down," he ordered.

"No."

Gottlieb finished his own drink, then poured another. "Sit down. Please."

Maggie sat, but as far away from him as the sofa would allow.

"You asked me, in the Tiergarten, if I believed in evil," he continued. "Ten years ago, I would have said no—that there's no such thing as 'evil,' just the absence of God's love. However, since then, I've changed my mind. I do believe in evil. I do believe in Satan. I believe that we all are in hell here—in Berlin, in Germany—and the reason we are is that we didn't speak up sooner. There are things going on . . . It's not just the invasions, the conquering."

"The Jews," Maggie said. "Yes, we all know. We heard about Kristallnacht."

Gottlieb winced. "No, you don't, or at least you don't know the half of it. Back in the early thirties, many people saw Nazism as an answer to Communism, to atheism—and thought that, with the Nazis, we could fix the economy and keep our churches. Well, they've let us hang on to our churches, but as soon as the war is over, they'll demolish them, too. They want a pagan, warrior society. With no room for love, for empathy, for compassion."

"Yes, I *know* that." Maggie swallowed more brandy.

"No, you still don't know the full extent of the horror. They're killing children. They've started killing large numbers of German children who are mad or deaf or dumb. Or missing an arm or a leg. Or drooling. Or 'disruptive.' They're sending them to special hospitals and gassing them."

"What?" Maggie blinked. She heard the words but couldn't comprehend them.

"I'm telling you—they're killing children. And now they have all these Jews out of Germany, in concentration camps in Poland. What do you think they're going to do with them? They can barely feed them now—what about this winter?"

Maggie was silent.

"There are stories about the Nazis setting up a Jewish colony in Madagascar—more like a police state. But I've heard about what's going on, in the ghettos, in the camps. They're working them to exhaustion. Then they're shooting them, rounding them up and shooting them, and dumping the bodies into mass graves. But—if they're willing to gas children—how long do you think it will take them to start gassing the Jews?"

"They're killing . . ." Maggie finally managed to say, "children?" Her brain felt paralyzed. "Why?" was the only word she could find.

"Do you know anything about art?" Gottlieb asked.

"Art?" Maggie made her frozen head nod. *What on earth does art have to do with killing children?*

"When the Nazis came into power, they had an enormous exhibit of the so-called degenerate art of the Jews and Communists. It was ugly. The painting, the sculptures were about war, and the brutality of war. The wounds of the injured. The pain of death. About the agony of the living. It was the art of the avant-garde. This art was seen as the violence of the Jews and Bolsheviks— often considered one and the same—against the German people.

"In the place of real art, they put neoclassical statues, because the Greeks and Romans were untouched by Jews. Sentimental 'blood and soil' paintings touting the glories of war, the bravery of soldiers, the valor of wives and mothers, and the value of racial purity and obedience."

"Propaganda, in other words."

"Bad art." He spat. *"Kitsch."*

"And who gave them the right to decide for everyone? Who are they to decide?"

"They see themselves as gods on Mt. Olympus. Protectors of a racial utopia."

Maggie gasped. "The hubris! But what does all of this have to do with the children? And the Jews?"

"What Hitler did to our art, he wants to do with our people. The disfigured, the blind, the Gypsies, the Jews—they're all parts of our society that he finds ugly. Hitler's determined to make over Germany in his own vision—a pagan warrior culture, where everyone is racially pure, everyone is strong, everyone is *perfect*. He's doing 'aesthetic' cleansing, but not just with art and architecture—with human beings."

Maggie shuddered. "But," she said, thinking the metaphor through to its ultimate conclusion, "everyone ultimately gets old. What happens then?"

"A warrior state doesn't have room for compassion or pity."

"And what about compassion for its warriors? What about the soldiers coming home, maimed and disfigured?"

Chapter Twelve

Berlin-Mitte, Monday morning, nine A.M. The New Reich Chancellery was on Vosstrasse, just off Wilhelmstraße.

It's designed to intimidate, Maggie realized, looking up at the authoritarian and disproportionately high marble columns of the entrance. Albert Speer's oversized architecture lacked any relation to the humans who passed through its gigantic doors. It was stern and sterile, pretentious and preposterous. And, for the Thousand Year Reich, perfect.

After showing her papers to the armed guards, Maggie walked through the marble reception room, also designed to make any and all visitors feel small. There she was met by a stern-faced SS officer, whose loud hobnailed boots heralded his arrival. He was young, with a cleft chin and pale eyes.

"Heil Hitler!" he cried, clicking his polished black heels together and raising his arm.

Maggie knew that succeeding in her mission was worth more than her hatred for saluting. *"Heil Hitler!"* she responded. Her voice echoed in the vast space.

"You are Margareta Hoffman?" he asked.

"Ja," Maggie replied, heart thudding in her throat.

"Please, *gnädiges Fräulein,* follow me down the corridor to the third door on the right." She walked through double doors, almost seventeen feet high, into a seemingly endless mirrored gallery, the thick carpet muffling her footsteps. The air was fragrant from the enormous formal bouquets dotting each gilded side table.

Maggie found the waiting area. A number of other women were already there, some young, some older, all nervous-looking. She took an empty seat, crossed her ankles, and folded her gloved hands over her pocketbook.

"Ladies. I am Captain Hocken." Hocken, white-blond with an unfortunately small chin, cleared his throat and looked down at the assembled candidates. "There are a few things you should know before you begin your typing test. First, you will *not* be meeting Herr Göring today. Only the top three from today will have that honor. You will compete by taking dictation. But not on a notepad, no—you will type directly. Herr Göring likes to hear the sounds of the typewriter as he speaks—says it helps him think better." He sniffed. "Second, Herr Göring prefers all typing to be double-spaced, so that he can make notes easily."

The women all nodded. Maggie was relieved that she wouldn't have to interview with Göring yet. She was also relieved when she heard the task. *Just like Mr. Churchill,* she noted, *except he likes a silent typewriter. At least I have plenty of experience typing dictation. Although certainly not on a German machine . . .*

One by one, the women went into the large office to take dictation. When Maggie's turn came she made a few mistakes at first, because of some of the unfamiliar German symbols. It soon turned into a complete and utter disaster.

When she was done, she went back to her seat, cheeks burning. *So much for all your grand plans, Hope. Piece of cake, huh?*

"How was it for you?" a young girl asked. Her feet were too fat for her pumps and excess flesh encased in silk squeezed out from her shoes.

"Terrible," Maggie replied. "I was nervous. You?"

"Terrified!" The girl tittered, which turned into a hiccup.

Hocken reappeared at the door. Everyone waited, on tenter-hooks, to see if she were one of the chosen. "Ladies," he said, "I want to thank you on Herr Göring's behalf for your time. Frau Kohlheim, Frau Krueger, Fräulein Oster, Fräulein Hoffman.

"You may be excused." Maggie didn't know whether to be re-lieved or disappointed. The women named rose to their feet, pock-etbooks in hand, dissatisfied looks creasing their faces.

"The rest of you, we will put your paperwork through security check as you progress to the next level of the interview."

He looked back to Maggie and the three other women. "I'm sorry, *gnädige Fraus.*"

"Not at all," Maggie managed.

She walked back through the long corridors of the Chancellery, blind to the marble and mirrors. She was angry with herself for such a poor showing—and on typing, of all things! And yet, part of her was relieved that she was finished, that she would be going back to England. She'd be able to see her friends again, sleep in her own bed, leave the hell of Berlin . . .

"Fräulein Hoffman!" she heard echo in the high-ceilinged hall-way. Maggie turned. It was the golden-haired man from the party. *"Guten tag, gnädiges Fräulein.* I am Gustav Oberg. We met at Frau Hess's birthday celebration."

"Oh! Of course. Lovely to see you again, Herr Oberg."

"I see you took Goebbels up on his offer. How did it go?"

"Not well." Maggie shrugged. "Nerves."

"Well, that's good news—for me, at least."

"Really? And why is that?"

"I'm looking for a— Well, let me start at the beginning. May I take you out for a cup of coffee, Fräulein Hoffman? *Real* coffee, I promise."

Maggie was wary, but still intrigued. She had only one day left in Berlin—what did she have to lose? "Of course, Herr Oberg."

Gustav Oberg took Maggie to a café not far from the Chancellery. He ordered for them both, then looked at her with appraising eyes.

"So, Göring's loss may be my gain," he said, as the waiter put down their cups.

"What do you mean, Herr Oberg?"

"I'm looking for a . . . companion."

"Herr Oberg!" Maggie rose to leave.

"No, no!" Herr Oberg said. "No, you misunderstand." He gestured for her to sit back down, and, after a moment, she did. "Not for me—for my daughter."

Ah, thought Maggie. "What's your daughter's name? And why does she need a companion?"

"Her name is Alexandra. Her mother died five years ago. And right now she is . . . not herself. Nothing contagious, never fear. But she must stay inside the house, in bed or on the sofa, and it's wearing on her, I can tell. She needs a companion, a young woman, who will read with her, knit with her"—he waved his hands dismissively—"do whatever it is you young ladies do together."

"I see." Maggie's mind was spinning. Surely she could do that. And if she were hired, she could stay here, in Berlin; maybe she could learn something.

"Since I am a widower and my daughter is indisposed, I would also ask you to take on some hostess duties. At dinner parties and the like. Just sit at the foot of the table and smile, that sort of thing."

And who are your dinner guests, Herr Oberg? And what, exactly, would I be in a position to overhear?

He took another sip of coffee. "Of course, it's perfect—because you've already been through security."

He thinks that I was cleared before *the typing test* . . . "Yes, of course, Herr Oberg."

"All that red tape with security . . . I understand the need for it, but I'd hate to have to go through it with someone." He paused. "I understand you have a boyfriend? The man you came to the party with?"

She thought of Gottlieb, of his mother and three sisters. If it were at all possible, she must leave him out of this. The dangers were incalculable. "No, Herr Oberg. Not anymore. Things . . . Well, they didn't work out."

"Good!" Oberg exclaimed. "Er, not good, I mean, I'm sorry—but we are now living in Wannsee, a little outside of Berlin, and it makes things easier. Our house is beautiful—right on the lake. What do you say?" He gave her a wide grin. "You will come and work for me? I will provide room and board and Tuesdays off."

"And the pay?"

"Forty Reichsmarks per week."

Maggie didn't want it to seem too easy. "Forty-five."

Oberg sighed. "You drive a hard bargain, Fräulein Hoffman. All right. Forty-five per week."

Maggie smiled, a Cheshire cat smile. "Yes, Herr Oberg. I would be delighted to come and work for you, to be a companion to your daughter."

"Excellent." He motioned for the waiter. "And now let's order some oysters and champagne, to celebrate!"

In a daze, Maggie walked back to Gottlieb's flat to pack her things.

"This is lunacy!" he shouted as she threw everything she'd

brought to Berlin into her valise. "Absolute lunacy! You *do* understand that, yes?"

"I do." Maggie looked up at him calmly. "It's a calculated risk. And one I'm willing to take in order to get into the inner circle."

"It was dangerous enough for you as a courier!" Gottlieb started to pace, ears flaming red. "If you stay, you'll be completely on your own! I wash my hands of you."

"Are you breaking up with me, *Schatzi?*" Maggie snapped the catches on her suitcase shut. "I'm devastated. But I have my proof of Aryan identity card. As long as they think I'm a fellow Nazi, it will be fine. I don't need you."

"*Fine?* Your paperwork will be under intense scrutiny. *Intense.* SOE does a decent enough job, but I'm not sure that what you have could stand up to it. What will you do then? They'll hang you, you know—won't even bother with the guillotine or a bullet. But not before the Gestapo will have tortured you, and you've told them everything you know. About *everyone* you know!"

"First of all, Herr Oberg is under the assumption that I've already been through the background check. And, I have a cyanide capsule. *Not* that I have any intention of using it." She pinned on her hat and tugged on her gloves.

"It's far too dangerous for a woman," Gottlieb raged. "And not only are you risking your own life but you're risking mine as well. Even if we've 'broken things off,' I'm still the one who brought you to Berlin. I'll be under a microscope. My entire group will be under intense scrutiny."

"I know, and for that I am sorry, truly." Maggie knew too well what a terrible risk Gottlieb had taken to pose as her boyfriend, to have her in his flat. "But there's a war on, you know—as we say at home." The two, face-to-face, were silent for a moment. "Would *you* do it?" she asked, softly. "If you had the chance?"

"That's not a fair question!" Gottlieb spluttered.

Maggie was losing patience. "Of *course* it's a fair question!" She grabbed her bag and headed for the door. "And that's why I *have* to do it!"

"No," Gottlieb said. "What I would do is use my head. I would follow orders. What you are doing is grossly irresponsible. The rules apply to everyone."

"One thing I learned from SOE is that rules are meant to be broken."

"SOE? 'Churchill's gangsters' is more like it. I'd thought more highly of you."

"We're taught to think on our feet, to press our advantages."

"Which might get us both killed!"

"Now, look," Maggie snapped. "Blindly following orders is what brought your country into this nightmare in the first place." She reached the door, then turned and took a breath, meeting his furious gaze resolutely. "I'm afraid this is goodbye—for now." She extended her hand.

But Gottlieb refused to take it. "I hope you'll be back, *Schatzi,* " he said, shaking his head as she stepped through the door. "I'll pray for you."

Maggie arrived at Herr Oberg's summer villa in Wannsee by train that afternoon, carrying her suitcase. It was a lovely stone house, set on the lake, protected by tall iron gates.

She trudged to the servants' entrance and rang the bell. She was met by the housekeeper, Frau Berta Graf, who had gray-blond hair and a bulbous nose red with rosacea. "We've been expecting you, Fräulein Hoffman," she said, as she led Maggie through the kitchen and then the house.

"It's beautiful," Maggie exclaimed. It wasn't to her taste, but she wanted to make conversation.

"Oh, Herr Oberg has only recently acquired this house. It belonged to a Jewish department store owner and his family."

"What happened to them?" Maggie asked, dreading the answer.

"Oh, they emigrated. And they'd left all the original furnishings—isn't it lovely? All of the antlers are Herr Oberg's, though. He's quite the hunter and outdoorsman, you know."

Maggie found out a great deal from the voluble Frau Graf. That Herr Oberg was married to his work and rarely came home at all. That his seventeen-year-old son, Lutz, had done extremely well in the Hitler Youth, and was now studying at the National Political Academy. And that Oberg's daughter, Alexandra, was, well, having some problems adjusting to life without her mother.

"What kinds of problems?" Maggie asked, as they made their way to the top floor, where she was shown to a tiny room with a sloped ceiling and a round window. It was furnished simply, with a twin bed and a worn rug. A framed portrait of Hitler was displayed on a lace doily on the dresser, next to a candlestick in a green glass holder and a box of matches.

"Oh, you know—young girls. Hormones, boyfriends, and the like. She's just been unhappy—you certainly have your work cut out for you . . ." Frau Graf clapped a hand over her mouth. "I've done it again! I've said too much. You must excuse me, *Fräulein* . . ."

"Of course," Maggie said, reassuringly. "I heard nothing."

"The candle and matches are in case of a power outage—they're more frequent here these days, with the bombing. And you'll be taking dinner in the kitchen with the rest of the staff. I will see you at six."

Jawohl. "Thank you, Frau Graf."

Maggie unpacked, but in the way she was trained—so that

she'd be able to leave at a moment's notice. She looked out the window. No drainage pipe, and it was a long, long way down.

At dinner, in the servants' dining room with Frau Graf and Herr Mayer, the gardener and all-around workman, Maggie learned even more about her new employer and his family. She learned that Oberg loved his new summer house in Wannsee. She learned that since his wife had died, he'd had numerous affairs with various actresses and cabaret singers, but never anything serious. She learned that, before the war, he'd been a lawyer and his main love was his work. And that when he returned home after a long day, he'd often spend hours in his study, poring over his files and papers.

Now that's *a useful bit of information,* Maggie decided, taking a bite of herring salad.

She also learned that, because he was deaf in one ear, Oberg couldn't serve in the military. And because of his fanatical party loyalty he had risen high in the ranks. He wasn't just ambitious—he believed, truly believed in what the Nazi party stood for—the Master Race and Aryan superiority. Moreover, he was a huge favorite of Hitler's, who considered him an example of all that was German: intelligent, cultured, and refined, as well as a proponent of *Lebensraum,* anti-Semitism, *Führerprinzip,* and *Weltanschauung.*

Herr Mayer explained that Herr Oberg was one of the financial managers in Hitler's private department, the Chancellery of the Führer.

"What sorts of projects does he work on?" Maggie asked.

"He works under the auspices of State and Party Affairs," Herr Mayer answered, mouth full of herring, proud of his employer. "He's extremely important—has a big office near the Tiergarten."

"Really?" Maggie said. "What's the project?"

Frau Graf helped herself to more bread. *"Geheime Reichs-sache,"* she added, putting a finger to her lips.

Secret Reich Matters? Maggie thought. *Interesting . . .*

"It's an important project, is all we know," Herr Mayer added.

"Impressive." *And good to know, indeed.*

David and Freddie walked out of the Piccadilly Theatre on Denman Street in the West End.

"It's wonderful to get out and do something fun for a change," David remarked, as they made their way through the crowd.

"Agreed," Freddie said. "It was good of Noël Coward to give us all something as light and frothy as *Blithe Spirit*—although it's getting some criticism."

"What?" David said, aghast, as they took a right on a shadowy side street. Their evening shoes smacked against the cobblestones. "What was it Emmet Fox said? 'Criticism is an indirect form of self-boasting.'"

"Oh, they're saying, 'How horrible to be making fun of the dead in the midst of war,' et cetera, et cetera. . . ." They walked farther down the street, people becoming less frequent, the only light from a half-moon and the stars.

"Nonsense!" David replied, voice booming with post-theater enthusiasm. "I loved it, especially Margaret Rutherford. Now *that's* what I call stage presence."

"Shall we go to the White Swan, old thing?" Freddie said, clapping a hand on the other man's shoulder. "Nightcap?"

A shadow moved behind them, and a voice called out, "Bloody pansies!"

David and Freddie whipped around. From the shadows emerged three men, beer bottles in their hands.

"Yeah, because you look like pansies to me. Right, Bill?"

"They dress like pansies, they walk like pansies, they're going to the White Swan like the pansies all do . . ."

"So they must be *pansies*," the first one finished. "Bloody arse bandits." He broke his bottle against the wall. The smashed pieces rained to the ground. He stood there in the darkness, moonlight glinting off the jagged broken glass.

David and Freddie locked eyes. They were outnumbered. "Look, we don't want any trouble—" David began.

"You might not want it, but trouble's here for you, cottager," said the first man. "Get 'em, boys."

The two others grabbed David and Freddie and threw them against a brick wall. The man with the bottle inched closer. *"The righteous shall rejoice when he seeth the vengeance: he shall wash his feet in the blood of the wicked."*

Freddie kneed the man who was restraining him, hard, in the groin. "Ooooowww!" As the man howled in pain, he dropped his hands from around Freddie's neck.

"Run!" David cried.

Freddie punched the other man, and he, too, fell to the ground, whimpering and clutching his face. "No," Freddie managed. "I'm not leaving you."

"Think you're a big man, do you?" the first man sneered. With that he took the broken beer bottle and turned toward Freddie. But when David stepped in front of Freddie, the man thrust it into David's abdomen.

"Ah!" David screamed. "Jesus!" The man pulled out the bottle, now glistening black with blood. David's eyes rolled back in his head and he crumpled against the wall.

There was a noise, and a group from the theater approached. One of the women screamed, a gloved hand to her mouth. "What's going on here?" a man shouted.

The two attackers who'd fallen scrambled to their feet. They ran.

Freddie sank to his knees beside David. "Help him." He glanced up at the approaching people looking down in shock at all the blood. "Call an ambulance! Someone! Please—help him!" He cradled David's head in his hands. *"Breathe—breathe, damn it!"*

It was after midnight at Bletchley Park. In his office, lit by a single green banker's lamp, windows blinded by thick blackout curtains, Edmund Hope again wrote the numbers Hugh had given him on the green chalkboard on the wall.

He sat back in his chair and put his feet up on his desk, sipping from a mug he'd filled from his flask of gin. The letters and numbers danced in front of his eyes, mocking him.

```
NAF9H20
51649900161
515700247
51604700350
51595000479
51588900466
51588480049782
5158165005055
515804570056176
515764560058494
```

He'd already run statistical analyses on the numbers, and had come up with nothing. "Damned onetime pad cipher," Edmund said. He put one hand over his eyes and massaged his temples.

There was a shadow in the doorway. "Can't be that bad—can it?" Alan Turing entered, rumpled but still bright-eyed and alert.

"I've tried everything," Edmund admitted. "*Everything*. But it's no use—without anything more to go on . . ."

Turing turned to the chalkboard. Then he looked at Edmund, his brown eyes dancing. "That's because you're looking at it all wrong. It's not a code."

Edmund looked up, shocked. "What?"

"I said, old boy, 'It's not a code.' It's a message—and a pretty straightforward one at that."

Edmund looked back at the letters and numbers on the chalkboard. Turing took a sniff. "Maybe you should go easier on the gin?" Edmund looked down at his mug, then made a pretense of pushing it away. "Look, it's simple, really," Turing said. "What stands out in the first line?" He jabbed at it with a finger.

Edmund threw up his hands. "I don't know. And at this point I'm starting not to care."

"H two O!" Turing chortled. "*Water!*" He walked over to the chalkboard. "And what is NaF?"

"Sodium fluoride," Edmund said, blinking. He sat up, starting to rally. "But what about the nine, then?"

"Nine stashes of the fluoride set to go into water. Look at the nine numbers below—they're not in code—they're latitude and longitude symbols. Nine of them."

Edmund was pulling out a map from his desk. "If that's so, they'd all be pretty close together . . ."

"Exactly!" Turing said, clapping Edmund on the back.

Edmund, reading the symbols on the map, said, "They're all locations close to London."

"I'm sure you'd have figured this out on your own, but, let me guess—they're all reservoirs, hence the H two O."

"My God." Edmund whistled through his teeth. "So, someone is planning—"

"To drop unknown amounts of fluoride into nine different London water reservoirs."

"But what would that do? Poison us?"

Turing bit his lip as he thought. "Depends. On how much fluoride and how much water—our two variables. I'm a mathematician, not a chemist—and not God, after all." He walked out, calling over his shoulder as he left, "And do bathe, Edmund—you smell like a distillery."

Clara and Cook were in her study, going over dinner plans for the week. "No, no need for anything on Friday or Saturday—I'll be at the ballet and then the opera."

"Ma'am . . ." Cook began. She was a slight woman, with a beakish nose and gray hair covered by a starched white linen cap.

"What?" Clara snapped. "I don't have all day."

"I've noticed—well, I've noticed some food missing. Bread, mostly, but some meat and cheese, too. Some fruit. Just a little here and there, but I wanted to let you know. I don't want me or the staff to be accused of stealing . . ."

Clara looked up from her menus. "It's nothing you need concern yourself with," she said to the older woman. Then, "You may go."

When the heavy door clicked shut behind Cook, Clara allowed herself a smile. "Oh, *Mausi,*" she said. "Stealing crumbs now, are we? But not as clever as you think. And certainly not as clever as I am."

She picked up the black phone's receiver and dialed. "Hello, Joseph," she purred.

On the other end of the line, static cracked and then a man's voice said, "*Liebling*—how wonderful to hear from you!"

"I just wanted to check in, to see what you've learned about our Margareta Hoffman."

"She left Berlin."

"What do you mean, she's left Berlin?"

The line crackled and Goebbels cleared his throat. "The last we know is that she took a typing test for Göring. Wasn't hired."

"And then?"

"Then she . . . vanished. She's probably left the country by now."

"What about Gottlieb Lehrer? Surely he must know her whereabouts?"

"A 'lover's quarrel,'" Goebbels said. "They fought and she left. He allegedly hasn't heard from her since."

Clara was silent, her hands snaking around the metal telephone cord.

"Clara? Are you there?"

"She could still be here, in Berlin."

"Why's this girl so important to you?"

"Let's call it a hunch. I don't believe she is who she says she is."

"Well, I hope you have more than a 'hunch' about Operation Aegir."

Clara took a sharp breath. The truth was that she hadn't heard from her contact in some time, and she had no news. "Going well, quite well, of course."

"Because if it starts to go south—like that Windsor affair— well, Clara, I don't need to tell you that you're on thin ice with Canaris, especially these days. . . . Even I might not be able to save you this time."

"Of *course* it will go as planned," Clara snapped. Then, in silkier tones, "Now, about the opera tonight—you'll be there, yes?"

———

"What's the first thing you're going to do when the war ends?" John whispered to Ernst.

The doctor inspected the incision. "You're healing nicely," Ernst said, pulling John's shirt back down. "After the war is over, I will find my wife, Frieda. And then we will find somewhere to live. Somewhere safe."

John sat up. Ernst looked over at him. "Are you married?"

"Not married, but as soon as I get home, I'm going to remedy that. My girl—Maggie—she's the only thing that's getting me through this mess."

"Good for you. We're in the same boat, then."

"I know she's back home, waiting for me, praying for me. That's what keeps me going."

That night, in her small, tidy room on the top floor of the villa at Wannsee, Maggie finally had a chance to think.

Since she'd returned to London from training, everything had happened so quickly—the mission, the jump, coming to Berlin, meeting up with Gottlieb . . . Not to mention meeting her mother and learning she had a half sister.

Maggie brushed her hair, turned out the light, and crawled into bed. Although the bed was soft and the linen pillowcases smelled like lavender, it was hard to feel sleepy as she lay wondering who'd slept there before, where that person was now.

But they'd warned her against that. Think in German, breathe in German, sleep in German, *be* German. . . . It was sweltering and the room was stuffy. Maggie tossed and turned. *It would be easier if I wasn't sleeping in a bed I suspect belonged to a deported Jew*, Maggie thought. *SOE didn't cover this.*

She realized she wasn't angry with Gottlieb. No, Gottlieb was one of the brave few working against the Nazis. He'd taken an enormous risk in taking her in, and even though she was gone, her association with him did put him, and his group, in continued danger. *It will be worth it, Gottlieb,* Maggie thought. *I know it.* Then, *It will be worth it—right?*

The room was dark, blackout curtains pulled tightly shut. All Maggie could hear was the wind in the birch trees near the window and, distantly, the drone of planes. She remembered Princess Lilibet and Princess Margaret at Windsor Castle—they'd been able to identify each plane by the sound of its engine, saying "theirs" or "ours" as the aircraft passed overhead.

What if I should have gone back? Maggie thought, starting to doubt herself. What was it she'd said to Noreen before she'd left? *"Piece of cake." Ha! What a fool I was,* Maggie thought. *This is no game.*

She turned and pulled the sheet over her head, braced for nightmares.

Chapter Thirteen

Maggie was unprepared for the sight of Alexandra Oberg the next morning in the sunroom.

Alexandra was slender, with blond braids and enormous sea-blue eyes. She also had an unmistakably burgeoning belly underneath her loose-fitting tea gown. She ran her hands over her bump possessively. Maggie guessed that the girl was at least in her third trimester, if not close to her due date, and suddenly realized why she might need a "companion."

"*Guten morgen*, Fräulein Oberg," Maggie said, "it's a pleasure to meet you."

Alexandra carefully lowered herself into one of the parlor chairs. "So, how is Papa treating you?" she asked.

"I haven't had too much to do with your father, actually."

"He's worried about me," Alexandra said, matter-of-factly. "And about the baby. Sit down, please."

Maggie did. "How far along are you?"

"Thirty-five weeks. Feels like thirty-five months at this point."

Alexandra's face was pale and bloated, and her ankles were swollen. But she had a lovely smile. "I was making packages for the front, for a while," she told Maggie. "But now my doctor wants me to stay at home. Bed rest."

Maggie had heard of such things in late-stage pregnancy. "High blood pressure?"

"Yes."

"Then why don't you lie down on the sofa and we'll put your feet up. That will help the swelling."

With a grunt, the girl raised herself, then waddled to the sofa, slipped off her shoes, and slowly lowered herself. Maggie took a number of needlepoint cushions and slid them under her charge's feet to elevate them. "I'm supposed to be like this all day, but I get so bored," Alexandra said. "Still, I know I'm lucky."

"Oh?" Maggie said, trying to sound neutral. She'd never heard of an unwed mother refer to herself as "lucky."

"I'm a 'bride of Hitler'—carrying a baby for the Fatherland. It's the greatest honor a racially pure woman can have." Alexandra's face fell slightly. "Even if my father doesn't quite see it that way. But it's every German woman's duty—to bear as many children as possible for the Führer." She patted her belly. "His father is Aryan—Nordic, of course. And after I've delivered I will give the child up to the *Lebensborn*." The girl's eyes shone with resolve.

"And the father?"

"He's in the East, at the Russian front. An officer," she said proudly. "He is doing his duty, and I am doing mine."

"Were you . . . in love with him?"

"Gods, no!" Alexandra laughed. "We were at *Mädchen* camp and there was a party, a big bonfire with the Hitler Youth . . . Well," she said, finally blushing, "you can imagine what happened."

Maggie blinked, trying to take it all in. "Would you like anything to drink? Eat? Do you need a blanket?"

"Oh, I'm fine now that you're here." Alexandra closed her eyes. "Maybe you could read to me? There's a copy of the *Frauen Warte* on the table there—would you read one of the articles?"

Maggie picked it up, a weekly Nazi magazine for women. On the cover was a drawing of massive German artillery, taking aim at a map of Great Britain. The cover caption read, *The Rhythm of Labor Resounds Again in Our Nation's Factories! We Have Clenched the Fist That Will Force England to the Ground!*

Maggie fought a shudder. "Perhaps something lighter?"

"There's a piece about German women," Alexandra said, laying her arm over her eyes and settling in. "I'd like to hear that again."

"Of course, *gnädiges Fräulein.*" And so Maggie read aloud, *"We Women in the Struggle for Germany's Renewal"*—and tried to keep herself from screaming.

Evening Mass at St. Hedwig's ended with Father Licht's daily final blessing: *"I pray for the priests in the concentration camps, for the Jews, for the non-Aryans. What happened yesterday, we know. What will happen tomorrow, we don't. But what happened today, we lived through. Outside, the Synagogue is burning. It, too, is a house of God . . ."*

Afterward, Father Licht found Elise. "And how are our friends doing?" the priest asked.

"Not too badly, considering," she replied.

"Come, child," Licht said. "Let's go to my office. We can talk in private."

Gottlieb Lehrer was already there. He stood as soon as he saw Elise.

"Elise, this is Gottlieb Lehrer. Gottlieb, Nurse Elise Hess."

"Guten tag," Elise said. She looked at him closely. "Haven't we—"

"—we met at the party," Gottlieb said. "Yes—Clara Hess's party. You assisted my girlfriend when she fainted. I'm grateful for your help, *gnädiges Fräulein.*"

"Of course," Elise said, taking a seat.

"You're Clara Hess's daughter?" Gottlieb shook his head. "I don't envy you."

"And your escort that night, Margareta Hoffman—is she really your girlfriend, or one of us?"

Gottlieb smiled thinly. "The less you know, Fräulein Hess, the safer you are."

Father Licht put his elbows on his desk and made a steeple of his hands. "Elise, Gottlieb is one of the people I work with on various projects, including transporting Jews to safety in Switzerland."

"Really?" Elise said, leaning forward. "How have you been able to manage that?"

"I've been working with Dietrich Bonhoeffer at the Abwehr," Gottlieb replied. "In short, the German reputation for mistreating Jews has started to get out and Goebbels wants to control Germany's image. And so, to counteract this, we select some Jews to go to Switzerland, talk about how wonderfully they're treated, how excited they are to go to Poland and then Madagascar—and then, well, somehow they just disappear."

"Disappear?" Elise frowned.

"Of course we make sure they're provided with money, papers, safe houses, and so on," Gottlieb assured her. "We've been able to get a number of Jews out this way but not enough. And we can't keep it up forever."

"Well, I have two men I need to get out—what assistance can you offer?"

"We're aware of the great sacrifice you're making, Elise, and we're looking into different safe houses. A more secure solution than Clara Hess's attic," Licht said.

Gottlieb whistled through his teeth. "You have two hideaways staying with you? Were they there during the party?"

"One was," Elise admitted. "Hide in plain sight, as they say. What can you do for them?"

"We're looking into various options, Elise. But I also want to talk to you both about the so-called children's euthanasia program at Charité. Gottlieb," the priest said. "Nurse Hess has worked with some of the patients at Charité murdered at Hadamar as part of that program. She is an eyewitness."

"Ah," Gottlieb said. He crossed himself.

Elise did as well. "The horrors I've witnessed are burned into my brain and my heart," she said. "I will never forget—never. And as long as I have breath, I will make sure what these child murderers are doing will come to light."

"You saw the actual crime—did you see any of the paperwork?"

"Some," Elise said. "They're quite cagey about it—using the names of fake staff members for letters, lying directly to the parents. I tried to copy some of the more incriminating files, but they're now under lock and key."

"What about the administrative offices?"

"The administrative offices?"

"Yes, all the higher-ups are at the Chancellery, part of the so-called State and Party Affairs, located at Tiergartenstrasse Four."

"I work at Charité," Elise said and shrugged. "I think that's my best bet for access to paperwork. Although now the file rooms are triple-padlocked. The administrators in charge of records seem to have caught on to me. Now they're going to great lengths to conceal evidence."

Licht closed his eyes in silent prayer.

"I'll keep trying," Elise said, realizing that every day that passed, more children would be bused to Hadamar.

"And I'll pray to St. Jude," Gottlieb said.

"Why, thank you so much for your vote of confidence," she replied, hoping her sarcastic tone was not lost on him.

"Elise, did you know that, before the war, Gottlieb was studying to be a priest?" Father Licht intervened, before the young man could answer.

"And I was going to be a nun! Still plan on taking my vows after the war is over."

Gottlieb scowled. Elise, with her Rhine maiden curves and dancing blue eyes, didn't strike him as someone likely to become a nun. But she was used to such looks. "Let me guess," she said to him. "Jesuit?"

Father Licht permitted himself a small smile, which he hid behind his hand.

"Why, yes," Gottlieb said, surprised. "How did you know?"

"You seem very . . ." Elise considered her words. "Intense."

"Hmpf," Gottlieb said, not sure whether to be pleased or insulted.

In the Hesses' attic, with assistance from Ernst, John's health continued to improve.

Every day, he dressed himself in some of Elise's father's old summer clothes: linen trousers and soft, frayed shirts. Day after day, in sock-clad feet, he walked the perimeter of the space, first with assistance from Ernst, then on his own, getting stronger and faster. Ernst read the books Elise brought for them from her father's library—Franz Kafka's *The Trial,* Thomas Mann's *The Magic Mountain,* Alfred Delp's *Tragic Existence*—and tried to help John with the German translations.

Every morning, before the house was awake or the servants arrived, Elise tiptoed upstairs with a picnic basket of food to last all

day—sandwiches, mostly, and fruit and a large Thermos of coffee
and a carafe of water. She brought wooden bowls of shaving soap
and blades, and pitchers of fresh water and a basin for washing.

She also procured a wireless radio, which—ear pressed to the
speaker—John used to find the BBC. He might be far from home
and in enemy territory, but he loved hearing English after so many
months, and was heartened that Britain was holding on. And he
listened in shock, hearing the voice of Winston Churchill himself,
giving his latest speech.

"We live in a terrible epoch of the human story," the Prime Minister announced, in sonorous tones, *"but we believe there is a broad
and sure justice running through its theme. It is time that the enemy
should be made to suffer in their own homelands something of the tor-
ment they have let loose upon their neighbors and upon the world. We
believe it to be in our power to keep this process going, on a steadily
rising tide, month after month, year after year, until they are either
extirpated by us or, better still, torn to pieces by their own people."*

John and Ernst looked at each other. *"It is for this reason that I
must ask you to be prepared for vehement counteraction by the enemy.
Our methods of dealing with them have steadily improved. They no
longer relish their trips to our shores. . . .*

*"We do not expect to hit without being hit back, and we intend with
every week that passes to hit harder. Prepare yourselves, then, my
friends and comrades, for this renewal of your exertions. We shall
never turn from our purpose, however somber the road, however griev-
ous the cost, because we know that out of this time of trial and tribula-
tion will be born a new freedom and glory for all mankind."*

John stood, tears pricking his eyes, as the BBC played "God
Save the King."

Only when the broadcast was over did Ernst speak. "So the
Germans have bombed British civilians. Now Britain's going to
bomb more German civilians."

The Englishman looked at the German. "Yes."

"Do you think those bombings will have anything to do with the eventual outcome of the war?"

"Maybe." John shrugged. "Maybe not."

"An eye for an eye, yes?"

John looked uncomfortable.

Ernst slumped back on his roll-up mattress. "All I can tell you as a doctor is—everyone bleeds the same."

As August passed, Maggie learned Alexandra's schedule. In the mornings, she would read to the girl, in the sunroom. They would have lunch together. Then Alexandra would take a nap. In the evenings, they would knit for the soldiers.

To the casual observer, Maggie and her young charge seemed like friends. They often laughed together, shared *Kaffee und Kuchen*, confided girlish secrets. All the while, Maggie was hiding her dismay at the way Alexandra, a healthy and intelligent girl, had been brainwashed into becoming some kind of breeding machine for the Reich, her own talents secondary to her capacity to produce future Nazi warriors.

But Alexandra believed that Maggie was Margareta Hoffman, originally from Frankfurt, who'd gone to school in Switzerland and then met Gottlieb Lehrer in Rome. She thought it was unbelievably romantic that Margareta had given up so much for her lover, to follow him to Berlin.

"And then he just—threw you over?" Alexandra said one day as they knitted soldiers' socks.

"It's . . . complicated," Maggie said. *Oh, you have no idea exactly how complicated.*

"Too bad you didn't have his baby!"

Maggie looked up.

"I'm joking! I can tell you're the type who wants a proper wedding. But, were you in love with him?"

St. Gottlieb? Not likely! Maggie exclaimed inwardly. But then she thought of Hugh. "I do miss him," she confessed. "I do."

"Hmmm," said Alexandra, who had clearly been hoping for more drama.

"Sorry it's not romantic enough for you. I should have drowned myself in the Spree instead?"

"Well, that's more dramatic. Wagnerian, even!"

Maggie had to laugh. "I prefer to stay dry."

"What was it like in Rome?"

Maggie had been prepared for this question. "Very hot, very dusty. But we just worked and worked, all the time. We barely had any chance to see the city."

"Do you speak Italian?"

"Not much—they just wanted German girls, to speak and type in German."

"And that's where you met Gottlieb?"

"And that's where I met Gottlieb, who was there with the Abwehr."

"Was he"—Alexandra looked so young—"your first love?"

Maggie stared out the window, at the garden and the sparkling lake beyond. "No," she answered. "Not Gottlieb."

"Who was your first love, then?"

"He was a pilot."

"Was?"

"He—he died. On a mission."

"A pilot—I'm sorry for your loss." Alexandra pressed a hand to her heart. "One of our brave Luftwaffe, defending the Fatherland. Do you miss him?"

"Very much."

The two women knitted together in silence.

"Have you ever thought . . ." Alexandra began.

"Yes?"

The girl had the grace to blush. "My father?"

Maggie didn't see Herr Oberg much, but she was aware of the way he looked at her. "Nonsense!" She smiled, determined to change the subject. "What do you say we play some records while we knit? Bach? Or today, perhaps, Beethoven?"

Maggie's effort to get into Oberg's study was proving difficult. He often didn't get home until late, and then spent hours and hours working, leaving only a short window between the time he went to bed and when he woke up in the morning.

Finally, one day late in August, Herr Oberg arrived home early from work and went to bed early. Maggie catnapped, then woke at two. In order not to make any noise on the stairs, she slid down on her bottom, using her hands, one stair at a time. She then crept quietly in stocking-clad feet over the thick carpets on the floor where Herr Oberg's and Alexandra's bedrooms were, holding her breath and listening for any sounds.

Finally, she reached the study. She'd been eyeing the lock and didn't think it would take much to open. She pulled out a hairpin from her bun and gently inserted it. If it were the type she thought, a gentle push with the pin would release the mechanism and open the door.

It was not that kind of lock.

Damn, damn, damn, Maggie raged. *All right, I've spent enough time in the hallway,* she decided, looking around, listening, making sure she was alone. Time to painstakingly make her way back to the safety of her bed, to plan her next attempt.

———

On Maggie's day off, she toyed with what to do. And then, impulsively, knowing it was against all SOE rules, she decided to call Elise. *She's my sister,* she rationalized as she picked up the handset of the telephone. *And the world's at war. Who knows if we'll ever see each other again?*

Maggie felt she couldn't have a guest to Herr Oberg's, and she certainly didn't want to go back to Clara's house, so she suggested meeting at the beach at Wannsee.

Elise took the S-Bahn from Grunewald to Wannsee and met Maggie near the sparkling blue lake. She spread out a blanket on the sand, and Maggie opened a large umbrella she had borrowed from the Oberg villa. The air smelled of spicy pine needles. There were a few other people—mothers and their children, building elaborate sand castles under striped umbrellas or splashing in the shallow water. Boys played in sand forts, brandishing toy guns. Birds sang from nearby chestnut trees. The two young women kicked off their sandals and stripped down to their bathing suits.

"Are you feeling any better?" Elise asked as she slipped on sunglasses and lay back.

Maggie was pretending to be still mourning after her breakup with Gottlieb. "Every day, it's a little better," she said with a smile. The warm sand under the blanket felt good, the sound of the water lapping against the sand was relaxing, and Maggie felt her shoulders drop just the slightest bit for the first time since she'd arrived in Germany. "And how's Fritz?" Elise had told Maggie about Fritz, her dance partner.

Elise sighed. "I adore Fritz, but in the same way I adore puppies and kittens. It's not serious. And he doesn't believe that, when the war is over, I want to take my vows to become a nun."

"Oh, come now, Elise—I find that hard to believe."

"It's true! I want to dedicate my life to Jesus."

"What about, you know, waiting until you're older? After you've lived a little. Fallen in love."

Elise shook her head. "I know what I want."

"Do you think it's a kind of rebellion?" Maggie cocked an eyebrow over the tortoiseshell frames of her sunglasses. "Against your mother?"

Elise's eyes followed the flight of a black heron. "I never thought of that. It's possible, I suppose. But it doesn't change the fact I love God and want to devote my life to Him. And, of course, I'll still be a nurse. Maybe even a doctor, someday. After this horrible war."

"And how does your father feel about your donning a habit?"

"He doesn't seem to mind. He's away so much, with the opera. . . . But you're right—my mother, she despises the idea." Elise fingered the tiny cross on the thin chain around her neck. "It even bothers her that I wear this. She'd rather I wear a swastika." Her tone was bitter.

"She's, um, quite important in the party, I gather?"

Elise gave a snort. "Once upon a time, Mutti had everything— beauty, fame, glamour, handsome men, including my father. He was her conductor, you know. Their love affair made them famous. He divorced his first wife for her. Oh, the scandal!"

Maggie bit her lip.

"But then she had the surgery. And, as a result, she lost her upper range and retired from singing. As you heard, at the party— although she's not too bad as a mezzo, as long as she isn't projecting to a large hall. But one of her greatest admirers was Herr Goebbels. Who brought her to the Abwehr, where she's become a sort of star. I think working in Intelligence has replaced opera for her."

"I see," Maggie responded. *Substituting one stage for another.*

Although Clara must have been working for German Intelligence long before she officially went to the Abwehr . . .

"And she definitely bought into all the propaganda about Hitler. 'Hitler will save us from the Communists!' she said. 'He will restore the glory of Germany!' I do believe she pictures everything in Wagnerian terms. And she was a favorite of Hitler's—he adored her in the role of Elsa. Göring and Himmler did, too. Goebbels—well, I've always suspected there was, or still is, something between them. They can be loyal and generous friends to people in their inner circle. And they admired her—she brought the Nazi party glamour and culture. Do you think she could"— Elise lowered her voice—"find anything monstrous in such a party, in such men, when they adore her so? Absolutely not. She thinks they're brilliant and has swallowed their politics whole."

Maggie felt she had to tread carefully. She and Elise hadn't talked about politics. "And what about you?"

Elise gave a short, sour laugh. "Well, since my parents ignored me for the most part, I was free to read, free to think, free to make up my own mind."

As her companion went on, Maggie gleaned the impression of a beautiful but distant and narcissistic mother, who knew very little about her own daughter. And a preoccupied and famous father. It sounded lonely, and far different from the childhood she'd imagined Elise had enjoyed. Yes, she was a smart and capable young woman with high ideals and morals, but she was also the solemn child, who, despite worldly and wealthy parents, grew up very much alone. Maggie felt a warm rush of love and appreciation for her own Aunt Edith.

"What do *you* think of all this?" Elise asked suddenly.

"I'm . . . an optimistic agnostic," Maggie said, knowing she had to be careful. "A secular humanist. And not at all political." She smiled. "Shall we swim?"

The next night, Maggie tried the study door again, this time with a long, thin knitting needle. Again, she'd failed. Maggie bit her lip and stopped herself from pounding at the door in frustration.

There was a noise in the hall. Maggie whipped around, hiding the needle behind her back. She knew she could talk herself out of almost any situation, but if not, she knew how to kill with a knitting needle—through the eyeball and deep into the brain, the same technique that could be used with a pen or pencil.

"Mein Gott," she heard a deep male voice whisper. "Are you a ghost?"

Maggie took a ragged breath. "No ghost, Herr Oberg. It is I— Fräulein Hoffman."

Herr Oberg, still wearing his uniform, took a few steps closer and appraised her, in her nightgown and robe. The appraisal lasted too long for Maggie's taste.

"What are you doing here, Fräulein Hoffman?"

"I—I couldn't sleep," Maggie lied. "I thought I'd come downstairs for some cooler air."

Herr Oberg looked down on her. "I couldn't sleep, either," he said at last. "We seem to suffer from the same affliction."

He put his hand on her shoulder. In the darkness, given her state of undress, it seemed a forward, even possessive, gesture. The touch of his hand on her shoulder burned. Maggie kept completely still, not meeting his eyes. "Get some sleep, Fräulein Hoffman," he said finally. "I'm having a few important guests over on Saturday night. I would like you to sit at the foot of my dinner table and be hostess."

Maggie's mind raced. She remembered that he'd mentioned the possibility earlier. "Wouldn't that honor fall to your daughter?"

"Alexandra is in no condition to be seen," he said. "You—you will be splendid."

She had to get away. "Yes, Herr Oberg," she said, making her way back to the door to the servants' staircase.

"Wear something pretty," he called. "If you don't have anything suitable, my daughter surely has something. And there are gowns and jewels that belonged to my late wife—have my Alexandra show you those. They would suit you well."

"Yes, Herr Oberg. Good night," Maggie said as she reached the door and opened it, bolting up the stairs, her heart in her throat. Play hostess at a Nazi dinner? Wear a dead woman's jewels? *Oh, which ring of hell are we in now?*

Maggie went back to her room, her head spinning. She felt as if her cover might be approaching its expiration date.

Chapter Fourteen

Freddie knelt by David's still body until the ambulance arrived. One of the onlookers found David's wire-rimmed eyeglasses, which had fallen during the attack, miraculously unbroken. He handed them to Freddie, who slipped them inside his breast pocket. Without his spectacles, David's face looked young and intensely vulnerable.

The ambulance finally arrived. "You know, we have bombs falling almost every night," one of the medics grumbled, adjusting his steel helmet. "It's not like you lads need to go out looking for trouble."

Freddie looked up with a grim face. "Trouble found us."

The other medic was examining David's wounds. "Stab wounds to the abdomen. Can't tell how deep, but he's lost a lot of blood. Let's take him in."

"Where?" Freddie asked.

"Guy's Hospital has a few open beds last I heard. We'll try there."

"You'll *try* there?"

"Lots injured this week—all the beds are full." The medic and his partner lifted David onto a stretcher and moved him to the back of the ambulance. "But we'll make sure he's all right and they get all the glass out, of course."

The low, forlorn wail of the air-raid siren sounded. "Oh, hell," the first man grumbled. "Damned Blitz—come on."

Freddie prepared to board, too. "Wait—are you family?" the first medic asked.

"I'm—I'm a . . . friend," Freddie said.

"Look, sir—if you're not immediate family, the best thing you can do is go home and contact his next of kin. Then come to the hospital."

The ambulance door slammed closed in Freddie's face.

Freddie knew he had to call David's parents.

He took a taxi, infuriatingly slow in the blackout, back to David's flat in Knightsbridge. He could hear planes overhead and bombs dropping in the distance—the East End, most likely. But there was no time to think. Freddie took the stairs two at a time, opened the door with the spare key David always left on the transom, then ran to David's study. His desk was a mess, with papers, files, books, and letters everywhere. Freddie turned on the desk light.

"Address book . . . address book," he muttered. Finally, he found it, a tiny leather volume, pages filled with David's flourish-marked script. Hands shaking, Freddie flipped through it, looking for *Greene*. Finally, he found it: Benjamin and Ruth Greene's country house in the Lake District.

He picked up the receiver. "Yes, Operator," Freddie said. "Please connect me." He gave the number.

A bomb dropped on a building down the street. There was a shattering explosion, which knocked Freddie to the floor. The power failed, but he managed to hold on to the receiver. Freddie tested his limbs—nothing seemed to be broken. Miraculously, the connection was completed.

"Yes, is this Mr. Benjamin Greene?" Freddie said. "Sir, this is Freddie Wright, your son's . . . friend. I'm so sorry to tell you this, but David's had an accident. He's been taken to Guy's Hospital, in London."

Trying to sit up, Freddie held his hand over his other ear. Another bomb was dropped somewhere else on the block, creating earthquake-like tremors. Now, Freddie could hear the wail of ambulances. His body was sore and his ears were ringing.

"Yes, we're being bombed right now, I'm afraid, sir. From what I understand he's lost some blood." Another pause. "No, sir, he was . . . mugged." Then, "Right. Yes, sir. See you as soon as you can get here, then." He hung up the receiver.

He knew he had to get to the hospital.

Freddie made his way through London in the blackout. He could hear the bombing raid had moved on to another part of the city, but as he traveled through the streets, tripping over debris in the dark, orange fires still smoldered.

David was in surgery when Freddie finally arrived at Guy's Hospital. "Are you a family member?" asked a nurse with a white, winged cap.

This time Freddie was prepared. "His brother."

"All I can tell you, sir, is that your brother is still in surgery," she said. "He's had a lot of bleeding. One wound penetrated to his liver—what we call liver laceration. The doctor is ascertaining the damage and then doing the best he can to repair it."

"Is he going to be all right?"

"Dr. Marland is one of our best surgeons, sir, and I know—"

Freddie put his hand on her forearm and bent to look into her eyes. "Please. Tell me. Is he going to be all right?"

The nurse clasped her hand over his. "It's touch and go, dear. He's very slight after all—there wasn't much protection for him. There's a chapel on the first floor, if you'd like to pray."

Dr. Marland, in blood-spattered scrubs, found Freddie kneeling on a pew in the small chapel of the hospital. "Mr. Greene?"

Freddie didn't respond.

"You're David Greene's brother?"

Freddie looked up. "Yes."

"He's out of surgery," the doctor reported without preamble. "We were able to repair the liver. It's going to take him some time to recover, but he'll be fine."

"Fine?" Freddie couldn't comprehend the word.

"He'll be fine," the doctor repeated. "Is he married?"

"What?"

"He's going to need some help while he's recovering. If he's not married, it's best if he stays with someone."

"Oh—I'll, I'll look after him, of course."

"Good. That's settled then. Good luck to you both."

And with that, the doctor left.

Freddie was in David's room when he opened his eyes.

"You look terrible, old thing," David managed to croak.

Freddie gave him a look of pure joy. "Not as wretched as you, I admit." He poured David a glass of water from a nearby pitcher. "The nurse said you could have a few sips when you woke up."

"So," David said, "am I going to die?"

"Not for a long, long time," Freddie said as he held the glass while David took a sip. He lay back, exhausted.

"You were lucky," Freddie said, interlacing his fingers with David's. "Looks like you'll be with me until you recover."

"He'll be with us, of course." It was David's mother, swooping in on a cloud of Arpège. Ruth Greene was a petite, slender woman with bleached platinum hair and the sparkling green eyes David had inherited. "Oh, my darling, darling boy," she said, sweeping up to the bed, nudging Freddie aside, and stroking David's fair hair. "How are you, my love?" She kissed his forehead. "We were so worried about you. Weren't we, dear?" she called to her husband, a few steps behind her. Benjamin was the same height as his wife, with a long, thin face and silver spectacles, much like his son's.

David blanched. "Oh, merciful Minerva—you're all here. Together. I really *am* about to die, aren't I?"

"Of course not, darling," David's mother crooned, kissing his forehead, then rubbing off the lipstick smear.

Mr. Greene stepped up to David, setting down his briefcase on the floor by the bed. "Good to see you, Son," he managed, before turning away and wiping his eyes.

A nurse, young and very pretty, peered in and smiled at the assembled group. "I'm sorry, but family time is over," she announced cheerfully. "Time for Mr. Greene's morphine."

"Sleep well, dearest," David's mother said, giving him one last kiss. "We'll be back to check on you later."

Freddie smiled up at Mr. and Mrs. Greene. "I'd like to sit with him, until he falls asleep, if that's all right with you."

"Of course, darling." Mrs. Greene patted his cheek with a gloved hand. "How sweet of you—what a good friend you are," she said, and then Mr. and Mrs. Greene departed.

Freddie bent down to David. "You gave me the scare of my life," he whispered.

"Sorry," David said, already drowsy from the morphine.

"I just want to tell you—that I love you."

"I . . . love . . . you . . . too . . ." David replied.

Their lips touched just as Mr. Greene returned for his briefcase. The older man stared at the two young ones in shocked disbelief, which turned to anger. His cheeks turned red and his hands started to shake. "Get! Out!" he shouted at Freddie.

"Sir, I—"

"Get out! Don't make me throw you out!"

Head down, Freddie left.

"David . . ." his father began.

But David had turned his head away. He let his father believe that morphine had done the trick and he was fast asleep, oblivious to what had just happened.

Generally, Herr Oberg ate an elaborate dinner alone, in the dining room. He didn't eat with his daughter and, in fact, seemed to want as little to do with her as possible. When Maggie saw them interact, his face was crimson and his manner was stiff. Maggie's own interactions with her employer were limited to "Good morning, sir," and "Good evening, sir."

Maggie bided her time until Oberg was out at the ballet. This time, she'd found a larding needle—used to poke lardoons of seasoned pork fat into roasts—in the kitchen. She took a flashlight she found there as well. She made sure Alexandra was tucked safely in her bedroom, snoring loudly, then crept, for the third time, to her employer's locked office.

She held the flashlight in her teeth as she worked at the lock with the larding needle. It was the perfect size and shape. *Finally,* Maggie thought, as the lock clicked open. She pushed open the heavy oak door, slipped in, then closed the door softly behind her.

Oberg's study was dark, and smelled of smoke and leather. Her heart was pounding. While she didn't think anyone at the villa suspected her of being anything more than Fräulein Oberg's companion, she'd been taught to anticipate the worst.

Flashlight in hand, Maggie walked over the carpeting to the

massive desk. Without touching a thing, she looked for hairs, pow-der—some secret way that Oberg might be using to see if his things had been rifled.

She didn't see anything. Not only that, but the desk itself was immaculate—no papers, no files. Just a photograph in a silver frame of a woman Maggie assumed was his late wife.

By the desk chair stood his briefcase—standard, black leather. Was it rigged to explode? Any special locks?

It appeared not. Maggie breathed a sigh of relief, the knot in her gut unclenching just the slightest bit.

With a hairpin, she was able to pick the locks open.

She sat down on the carpet and opened the briefcase in front of her.

There, flashlight still in her teeth, she went through the papers. Most of them were letters and memos from the Kraft durch Freude's Central Office II, Division IV—Health and Social Wel-fare—of the Reich Interior Ministry, and Office IIb.

There were some from the Reich Committee for the Scientific Registration of Serious Hereditary and Congenital Illnesses, as well as memoranda from the various medical departments, trans-port department, inspections department, and calculations office, talking about "units" and delineating the various costs of "treat-ment." Still more memos and letters that Oberg was carbon-copied on from other departments—bus drivers' salary, bus repairs, cost of gasoline, cost of film, doctor and nurse salaries. Notices of in-spection of various facilities. A special budget for staff parties and alcohol.

Numbers swarmed in front of her, calculations of costs. Histo-ries of costs. Projections of future costs. *Costs of what?*

Maggie tried to figure out where the main office was located, but the best she could find was a postbox address: Berlin W 9, P.O. Box 101. *That's odd.*

Maggie shook her head, confused. The language meant nothing. Only the mention of hospitals, like Charité, and institutions, such as the Hadamar Institute, and mention of the "Reich's community and nursing homes" gave any indication they were talking about people. But this had nothing to do with the war—with soldiers, supplies, munitions factories, troop movements—nothing. Just internal German bureaucracy.

Damn! Maggie felt a hot flush of disappointment and anger. She'd risked so much for so little. Oberg, so important in his own mind, was a midlevel bureaucrat—a paper pusher—and none of the papers he was pushing were the least bit useful.

Still, with her tiny SOE-issued camera, the one Noreen had given her in London so long ago, Maggie photographed as many documents as she could, each click intensifying her disappointment. She stopped short when she came to a packet of mathematics problems awaiting Oberg's approval. The first question, obviously for children, read: *If it costs 15,000 marks to build one house per working-class family and it costs 6,000,000 marks to build and run an insane asylum, how many working-class houses can you build for the cost of one insane asylum?*

Excellent, Oberg had written in red pen. *APPROVED.*

Maggie shook her head. *It's time to go home, Hope,* she thought as she put the papers back, exactly as she'd found them, closed the locks, and replaced the briefcase as it had been.

Maggie slipped out of Oberg's study and up to her room, silent as a ghost.

The next morning, when David awoke, the young nurse was at his bedside. "Just need to take your vitals," she said, checking his pulse and sticking a thermometer under his tongue. "Your pulse is strong, that's good," she added briskly. Then she pulled out the thermometer. "And your temperature's normal. You're doing quite well, considering."

David stared off into space.

"You know," the nurse continued, "it's none of my business, but your brother—that is, your brother who your parents now tell me isn't really your brother—is still in the waiting room. He slept here last night. Don't think he's eaten a thing."

David wouldn't meet her eyes. "He should go."

The nurse put a hand on his shoulder. "I can fetch him."

"My father . . ." David finally looked at her. "I can't . . ." She didn't look away. "I know what you're thinking—here I am, a grown man—and I can't even stand up to my own father."

"That's not what I was thinking at all," she said. "What I was thinking is that it's hard."

"Hard?" David repeated. "What's hard, exactly? Being stabbed? Living through the Blitz? Fighting a losing war? Having parents who love you—but only conditionally? Or"—he lowered his voice and she leaned in to hear him—"being *like that.*'"

"I was just thinking that *life* is hard," she replied. "Life is hard—for all of us, luv. And maybe it's just a bit easier if you have someone by your side. I'll check in on you again in a bit."

The cafeteria at Guy's Hospital was crowded. After Freddie paid the cashier for his cup of tea and toast, he looked for somewhere to sit. There was an empty chair at Benjamin Greene's table.

Freddie decided to bite the proverbial bullet. "May I sit down?" he asked Mr. Greene, who was pretending to read *The Times* with shadowed eyes.

There was no reply.

Freddie sat and stirred his tea. Mr. Greene ignored him.

"I know my being here makes you uncomfortable," Freddie said, "and for that I'm sorry."

"Let's get one thing straight," Mr. Greene said, laying down the newspaper and taking off his reading glasses. "I don't have any feelings about your being here. You're nothing to me. No one."

"We all love him," Freddie persisted gently. "And I just want to know how he's doing."

"You *love* him? Then get out of his life," Benjamin Greene snapped and folded his paper shut. "Leave. Him. Alone."

"No." Freddie was resolute.

"No?" Mr. Greene shoved back his chair and stood. "If you think you're going to get your hands on my fortune, now or later, you are sadly, sadly mistaken."

"You can't buy his love," Freddie countered. "And if you hold it over him, he's going to hate you for it. David's better than that. And, sir, I think that deep down you're better than that, too."

"I could have you arrested for gross indecency," Mr. Greene whispered. "You'd be put in jail. Chemically castrated."

"Then you'd have to do that to your son, too."

Mr. Greene was going to retort, then stopped himself, put on his hat, and stalked out.

Freddie pulled over the *Times* Mr. Greene had left and scanned the articles. Most were about the meeting between Winston Churchill and Franklin D. Roosevelt, the eight points of their Atlantic Charter, and if and when the United States would finally commit to war. "Well, well, well," Freddie muttered, tossing the paper aside. "Close, but no cigar, eh, Winnie?"

Chapter Fifteen

Edmund Hope took the train from Bletchley to London the next day, to go to MI-5 and speak with Hugh Thompson.

They sat down together on a bench in Hyde Park, watching a group of boys dressed in white with straw boaters playing cricket with a red leather ball and a willow bat. The clouds were dark and sullen. "As it turns out," Edmund said, "the sequence of numbers and letters you gave me wasn't actually a code. It was a numeric description."

Hugh cocked an eyebrow.

"Translated, it tells us that Hess wants Stefan Krueger to obtain a large supply of fluoride and dump it into nine of London's water reservoirs."

"To what effect, Professor Hope?"

"Well, back in the day, the Russians used sodium fluoride in the gulags' water supply to control their prisoners. They thought that ingesting repeated small doses of fluoride would, in time, poison certain areas of the brain—making the prisoners easier to control. My guess is that they shared this information with the Nazis. And now Commandant Hess"—he spat the name—"wants to use sodium fluoride to poison our water, most likely to make the British population easier to control during an invasion."

Hugh ran his hand through his hair until it was standing on end. "Is it true? Would it really do that?"

Edmund watched the boys at cricket, undeterred by the heat. Their shouts rang through the humid air. "It's unclear. I spoke to Professor Ingold at University College London—one of the most brilliant chemists we have. I asked him if, in a hypothetical situation, an enemy dropped a significant amount of sodium fluoride into one of London's water reservoirs—what would happen."

"What did he say?" Hugh asked, mopping his face with a handkerchief.

"More or less that it would do nothing, nothing at all. Well, it might kill any plants that it came in contact with at full strength— plants and perhaps fish. The person doing the dropping would have to wear goggles, a breathing mask, and gloves. But Ingold said the effect on London's drinking water would be minimal, if any."

"What did he think about the evidence from the gulags—and from the Nazis?"

"Laughed, actually. Said he'd heard about the research done at I.G. Farben in Germany with sodium fluoride, but he didn't think they were the most impartial of scientists—maybe even were working with a chemical company who wanted to get rid of the fluoride, make a little money off the deal. But from the double-blind studies Ingold's seen, small amounts of sodium fluoride have no effect on the human brain—and may even have the added benefit of preventing tooth decay." Edmund smiled, a rare sight. "According to Ingold, some fluoride in the drinking water might be doing Britons a favor in terms of dental health. If, of course, such a drop were to take place."

He pulled out a silver hip flask and opened it. He offered it to Hugh, who shook his head. Edmund took a large swallow and contemplated the clouds. Then he asked, "Any word from our girl in Berlin?"

"Still there," Hugh said, a stone in his throat.

"*Still* there? But—why?"

"I honestly don't know, sir."

"Has she been captured?"

"I don't believe so. Although, as you know, I'm not in the loop on this one."

"Well."

"Yes." Hugh folded his newspaper. "If that's all then?"

"That's all. Just curious—what are you going to do about the fluoride and the reservoir?"

"You mean, how will I prove to"—Hugh stumbled—"to Clara Hess that Krueger dropped fluoride in the water?" His eyes darkened. He jutted his chin at the flask. "Professor Hope, do you mind if I have a sip of whatever you're having there?"

Edmund nodded and passed the flask.

This time Hugh took a pull, then passed it back, smiling a grim smile. "Let's just say I have a few ideas."

"You know"—Edmund took a drink himself—"in the midst of everything that went on at Windsor, I never had a chance to say how sorry I am. For your father. His death. His murder."

Hugh was shocked. "Th-thank you, sir."

"And, of course, how dreadfully sorry I am for my former wife's part in it." Edmund passed the flask back to Hugh.

"It had nothing to do with you, sir." Hugh took a long swallow and passed the flask back.

"No," Edmund said, taking the flask. "But still."

"Thank you for that."

"And about the accusation of my being a double agent?"

Hugh braced himself.

"Don't ever do that again."

Hugh didn't know what to say until he saw Edmund's face crease into another smile. "No—no, sir. I promise. I'll never do that again."

The men sat in silence, passing the flask back and forth, watching the boys play.

Herr Oberg's dining room had more mounted antlers than art, and even the few oil paintings framed in gold were of hunting scenes. Glass eyes stared down at the guests assembled below, high-ranking Nazis and their wives. Rows of servants lined the walls.

Maggie, dressed in the gown she'd worn to the Fire and Ice Ball and wearing the late Frau Oberg's jewels, was sitting at the foot of the long table where the guests included, Maggie noted with a frisson of fear, Dr. Goebbels and his wife. During all of her time in Germany, she'd never been more afraid. Her knees were shaking under the table, and she grasped her hands tightly so they wouldn't tremble.

Still, no one seemed to expect much from her, certainly not coherent conversation, and for once she was grateful. She pushed roast pork around her plate, trying to smile and laugh at the appropriate times. There was a small commotion at the head of the table as Herr Oberg stood to propose a toast. "To *Judenrein!*" he proclaimed, lifting his glass of champagne.

The rest raised their glasses in response. "To *Judenrein!*" they intoned.

Maggie, too, raised her glass. She forced herself to say the words, which she knew meant "Jew-free." She set her face in a smile and took a sip.

"And yet," Goebbels said, "according to Himmler there are still more than four thousand Jews left in Berlin, and many of them are in hiding. We have a long way until we will perfect the Reich."

Herr Oberg, flushed with wine, was in a jovial mood. "Like rats, we will flush them out!"

Goebbels nodded. "Those ghettos in Poland are getting

crowded, I hear. And winter is coming. . . . That would take care of quite a few, I think."

"I'd thought Britain would have surrendered by now," Oberg grumbled.

"We all did. But Britain's still fighting. And with her navy still on patrol, we can't afford to take any of our ships out of commission to use for transportation. We'd counted on using Britain's fleet." Goebbels sighed. "If we only knew where to put several million Jews, there would not be so many after all." Then, *"Nach Russland abkarren . . . am Bestan wäre es, diese überhaupt."*

It took Maggie a moment to translate. *The rest of the Berlin Jews should be carted off to Russia, but best of all would be to kill them.*

Her stomach knotted as they once again clinked glasses and laughed.

"Your work is also vitally important, Herr Oberg," Goebbels remarked as the dishes were cleared.

"Thank you, sir," Oberg replied, flushing with pleasure.

"You've dealt with plenty of *Mischlinge* in your line of work, yes?"

"Of course," Oberg replied. "And we are ever becoming more efficient."

"Efficient, yes." Goebbels turned to Maggie, his dark eyes piercing hers. "Fräulein Hoffman, you seem to be making the social rounds these days. First I see you at Clara Hess's party, now at Herr Oberg's table. Tell me—is Gottlieb Lehrer's loss Herr Oberg's gain?"

That brought roars of laughter from the men and some uncomfortable looks from the women.

Maggie knew she had to tread carefully. "It's lovely to see you and your beautiful wife again, Dr. Goebbels," she answered. "I work for Herr Oberg now, as a companion to his daughter. He most graciously asked me to take part in this dinner party."

Goebbels's eyes narrowed. "Last time we spoke, you were with young Lehrer, and going to interview for a secretarial position with Göring."

Maggie made her lips twist into a smile. "Neither seemed to work out, sir," she replied.

"And then you vanished into thin air!"

Maggie dabbed at her mouth with a napkin, to hide the shaking of her hands. "Hardly, sir. I'm certainly enjoying my time with Fräulein Oberg and the wonderful lake air."

"Do you happen to be in touch with Frau Hess?" Goebbels asked, as the servants began to carry in *Birnentorte,* a chocolate and pear cake. "She seems to be quite taken with you."

Maggie nearly dropped her napkin. "N-no, sir."

He waited for the plate to be set down in front of him before saying, "She's been trying to find you."

"R-really," Maggie managed.

"Yes." Goebbels smiled. "You should send her a note when you have a chance. I think she'd appreciate that." He motioned to one of the servants to take his empty glass away. "I'll probably see her later tonight—I'll give her your regards and let her know where you're staying."

Maggie sat, frozen, at her end of the table. Why would Clara want to find her—a woman who was the date of a low-level Abwehr agent? Did she suspect something? What did she know?

Seeing Oberg look at her with concern, Maggie forced herself to pick up her knife and fork and join in the conversation once again. Once Goebbels told Clara that Maggie was working for Oberg, it would be over. The Gestapo would come.

When the last guest had left, Oberg smiled at Maggie. "You were magnificent, my dear."

Maggie, who felt as though she might lose her mind at any second, was feeling less than magnificent. All she wanted to do was get away. If her cover hadn't been compromised yet, it would be by morning. She had only a few hours in which to run. Every second counted. "Thank you, Herr Oberg," she replied evenly.

"Please," he said, "after such a wonderful evening, why don't you call me Gustav? And may I call you Margareta?"

"Of course," Maggie answered, even though her heart was hammering treacherously. Was Goebbels on the telephone now, telling Clara that she was working for Herr Oberg? And then what would happen? Would the Gestapo bang on the door and take her to headquarters for interrogation? Certainly in the morning. . . . But what if he called Clara tonight? Would there be SS officers pounding on the door during the night?

"Would you like a drink, my dear?" Oberg suggested. "In my study? Some cognac, perhaps?"

Maggie forced a yawn. "I'm afraid it's late and I'm tired," she said, moving away from him.

He pressed closer, pinning her against the wall, hot breath scented with chocolate. "You have such beautiful hair," he murmured, running a hand along her cheek. "What I wouldn't do to see it down . . ."

Maggie pulled away. "I'm sorry, I have"—it took her a moment to think of the word in German for menstrual pain—"*Krämpfe*. It's not the best time."

She was relieved to see his look of ardor dim. She walked to the door to the servants' stairs. "Good night, Gustav."

"Good night, Margareta," he replied regretfully.

Maggie forced herself to walk in a sedate fashion up the stairs to her room.

However, as soon as she'd closed the door and locked it behind her, she set to work with feverish intensity. She tore off the borrowed jewelry, stepped out of her evening gown, and slipped on a nondescript cotton dress. Over it, she put on a cardigan. And then, as she'd rehearsed at training camp, she rolled up a blouse and stuffed it under the sweater, creating the illusion of a dowager's hump.

From the secret pocket in the hem of her skirt, she took out the slip of silk with her codes. Then she lit a match and let the silk burn on the green-glass candle stand. When only ashes remained, she mixed the ash with water from the basin, then used her fingers to paint the gray through her hair, hide the coppery red of her curls. She used some of the dry ash as powder, and darkened the circles under her eyes and below her cheekbones. She pinned on her hat and pulled on her gloves, then picked up the bag with knitting and the false bottom with the camera. She knew what she'd captured on film in Oberg's office didn't amount to much. Should she risk taking it and being discovered?

In for a penny, in for a pound, she decided, and threw it in.

Then, looping the handbag around her neck, she opened the window and crawled out, leaping down to the lower-floor roof—an insane distance, but she had no choice. When she'd recovered from the impact, she climbed down a trellis. She hit the ground, looked around her, and then began to run. In the yard next door, a chained dog began to bark.

Only when she reached the U-Bahn station did she slow, affecting a shuffle and limp, as though her joints were arthritic. She kept her eyes down and tried to focus on her breath. *In and out, Hope— in and out—just like Thorny taught you . . .*

Her train pulled away from the station just as an SS van pulled into Herr Oberg's drive.

Chapter Sixteen

The Berlin-Mitte that Maggie returned to had changed. The RAF had been making nightly raids—there were more bombed-out buildings, some completely leveled, others decimated. The hot morning sun shone red through the haze of dust and destruction. The acrid stench of smoke wafted on the breeze as air-raid sirens throbbed in the distance.

Maggie glanced surreptitiously at the people on the street and realized that the Berliner invincibility she'd noted when she first arrived had been punctured. She could see it in the people's eyes—a flicker of realization, of panic, of the knowledge that the war wasn't just something happening in the abstract but was now coming home to them.

On the one hand, she felt sorry for them. She knew, all too well, what it was like to mourn civilian deaths, to spend nights in a bomb shelter, to see a beloved city attacked.

And yet, these were the same people who had given Hitler his absolute power, who didn't question the Nuremberg Laws, who turned a blind eye to the horrors of Kristallnacht. Some—many?—were people like Herr Oberg, who wanted Berlin to be *"Judenrein."* And his daughter, who'd been brainwashed into becoming a soldier-making machine for the Reich. As terrifying as it was to be on the run, there was relief in leaving the Obergs' stolen villa. She longed to be home in London.

Maggie shook her head. *Focus,* she scolded herself. By now the SS must be looking for her. And she had to make contact with Madame Defarge before she was spotted. *Gottlieb,* she thought, heart pounding, *Gottlieb will be able to help me.*

When she reached his apartment, however, she pressed the buzzer again and again. Nothing. She leaned on it for a full fifteen seconds. Still, no response. Then she went to the street and threw a pebble at his window.

Above her, a window opened. "Go away!" she heard Gottlieb's voice call down.

"Let me in!" Maggie called back. "You must—"

"I don't know you." The window slammed shut.

Hot, red anger welled up inside her, and all the German profanity she'd ever heard came unbidden to her lips. But his window did not reopen.

Maggie saw the knitting woman on the bench, took a calming breath, and crossed the street. She sat down near, but not too near, her.

The woman moved closer. "Your young man's tough," she said under her breath. "I saw him once in a boxing match—he has a technique of tiring his opponent out but not throwing any punches, and then, in the tenth round, scoring a knockout. Don't take it personally."

"He's not my young man. And if I don't make it back," Maggie said, taking it quite personally, "you have to tell them that I've been found out and I'm on the run. I don't suppose . . . that you . . ."

Could hide me? The unasked question hung in the air.

"No, child." The woman shook her head. "I'm sorry. I can't."

"One of your associates?"

"Nein."

"I understand." *Splendid,* Maggie thought, *here I am risking my neck, and before the cock's crow, they've denied me thrice.* She saw a man in a black trench coat walking closer to them. And it wasn't the usual quick, eyes-down Berliner walk. He was looking at everyone. Taking everyone's measure. *Looking for me?*

"Goodbye," she said, getting up slowly, in character.

The old woman kept her eyes on her knitting and nodded. *"Viel Glück."*

In her office at the Abwehr, Clara Hess was seething. "What do you mean, they *lost* her?"

On the other end of the telephone line, Goebbels was unflustered. "She must have suspected something when I mentioned your name. By the time we reached Oberg's, she was gone. We sent men by Gottlieb Lehrer's flat, and one of them thought he spotted her, but she gave him the slip."

Clara drummed her long red-painted nails on her desk. "Then she *has* to be a spy."

"Oberg said all her paperwork was in order, that it had been checked when she interviewed for the position with Göring. But I dug a little deeper—since she didn't get an interview, they actually never *did* check her papers."

Clara wrapped the silver telephone cord around her fingers so tightly that they became white. "Bring in Gottlieb Lehrer for questioning."

"Questioning by you, or by the SS?"

"Me. Immediately."

It didn't take long for Maggie to realize the man in the black trench coat was following her.

She began walking slightly faster, but still limping and not fast enough to draw attention to herself. It took every ounce of self-control she had not to break into a run. She stopped in front of a butcher's window to see if he was still following behind.

He was.

Walking faster, she went to the entrance of the Gleisdreieck U-Bahn. The man followed, relentless. Maggie stood waiting on the platform, heart in mouth, for the train. When it pulled into the station, she stepped aside to let the passengers off, then stepped on.

The man stepped on, too, into the car behind her.

Then, moments before the train left the station, Maggie muttered, "Oh no! I've forgotten my ration card!" and pushed her way through the crowd. Just as the train pulled out, she slipped through the doors and jumped back onto the platform.

She turned to look at him—and saw the rage burn in the man's eyes as he realized she'd given him the slip. Maggie looked across the tracks. Nazi guards were shouting at people to leave their luggage on one end of the platform, and line up on the other. The uniformed men held large dogs on leather leashes; the barking echoed off the station's tiled walls. The people being herded were men and women, young and old, some rich, some poor, some alone and some in family groups. A few of the smaller children wailed.

"I'm thirsty, Mama," a little girl with dark curls cried. "I'm so thirsty!"

The woman turned to one of the guards. "May I get my daughter some water?"

"Nein!" he shouted, and struck her in the face with the butt of his gun.

The woman fell, then put one hand to her face. Blood ran from her nose. "It's all right, Mama," the little girl said. She had stopped crying. She had forgotten about the water. In that instant their roles had been reversed, and it was her job to comfort her mother. "It's all right."

They're Jews, Maggie realized. She had heard about the deportations of Berlin's Jews to ghettos and work camps, of course. Still, that was nothing, absolutely nothing, compared to seeing it for herself.

Another train pulled up. It was rust red and boxy. Not a passenger train at all but one used for transporting cattle.

Maggie watched in horror as the people boarded, trying to catch a last glimpse of the little girl before she got on the train. It seemed as though hundreds were being packed into each car.

"Don't look," a young woman said softly to Maggie. She was blond and awkward, with fat braids and pink cheeks.

There were no toilet facilities on that train, Maggie realized, no water. If they were going to one of the ghettos in Poland, it would be days before they reached their destination. . . . She couldn't look away.

Another train pulled up on the track in front of her with a shriek of brakes and a cloud of steam. She must put miles between her and the man in black, she realized. She stepped on, letting the doors slam behind her.

Gottlieb knew he had to get out, and fast.

Stopping only to put his papers, his wallet, and his rosary in his pockets, tugging his black hat's brim low over his face, he opened the door to leave.

The SS officers had already reached his floor. Their commander pulled out his gun. "Get back inside," he ordered Gottlieb.

Across the hallway, Frau Keller shuffled to her own front door, opened it a crack, and peeked out. Her dog started to yap. "Shhhh—quiet, Kaiser!" she admonished. She watched as the SS soldiers followed Gottlieb into his apartment. Then there was a single gunshot.

After a few moments of silence, Frau Keller could hear profanity, and then furniture being smashed. She saw one of the men take Gottlieb's crucifix and throw it into the hall. At her feet Kaiser lowered his head and whined in fear.

That was when Frau Keller closed the door softly, bolting and then chaining it. "Come, Kaiser," she whispered, reaching down to pat the dog's head. "Let's get you something to eat now, shall we?"

Maggie didn't know what to do. She sat, paralyzed, as stop after stop passed by, hunched over, her hat hiding her face. She knew it was insane to stay on the train—at any minute the Gestapo could enter the car and demand to see her identification.

Pull yourself together. You can have a nice big breakdown after you get back to London. . . . She looked up at the S-Bahn map and realized that she was heading north, into Berlin. Two stations away, at Potsdamer Platz, not far from the Brandenburg Gate, there would be an intersection of four subway lines. It seemed like her best option for throwing the agent off her scent.

At Potsdamer Platz, she kept her head down and walked swiftly. She boarded the first train that pulled in. At Brandenburger Tor, she realized she was in Mitte-Berlin, the city's center.

Charité was in Mitte.

Charité was where Elise worked.

Could she get there without being followed? *There's only one way to find out. And, since I'm running out of options* . . . She took yet another train to Lehrter Bahnhof and then stepped off, exiting from the ceramic-tiled station into the punishing midday sun. There was a telephone booth outside the station marked OEFFENTLICHER FERNSPRECHER. Maggie opened the door and then slammed it closed behind her. She searched through her handbag for the correct change with trembling hands. Then she picked up

the black and silver receiver, slipped a coin into the slot, and dialed
Elise's work number, which she'd memorized from the slip of
paper her half sister had given her at Clara's birthday party.

"Charité Hospital in Mitte," she told the operator. *Pick up, pick
up, pick up!* Maggie urged as she heard the shrill, metallic rings.

Finally, someone did. "*Guten Tag*. Charité Hospital."

"*Hallo,*" Maggie said. "May I speak with Elise Hess? She's a
nurse."

"Please hold. I will transfer your call."

There was a silence, then a voice answered, "*Hallo*, fourth-
floor nurses' station."

"Hello, I'm trying to reach a nurse named Elise Hess."

"I'm not sure if she's working today."

"Would you be able to check, please? It's a family emergency."
Oh, it really is a "family" emergency, Elise.

There was an interminable wait, and then Maggie heard a voice
that made her weak with relief. "*Hallo?*"

"Elise! This is Margareta—Margareta Hoffman?"

"Of course!"

"You remember how you said I could call if I needed anything?"

"*Mein Gott!* Are you hurt?" Elise's voice, warm and reassuring, poured from the receiver.

"No. But I need you to get me inside the hospital. I can explain
later."

There was a silence so long that Maggie feared the other woman
had hung up. The line crackled. "Meet me at the delivery entrance," Elise said finally. "I'll be there as soon as I can."

As Maggie crossed Hannoversche Straße in the nearly unbearable
heat, she heard a voice. "Stop!"

Slowly, as though she were achy and arthritic, she turned around.

It was a police officer. He was young, blond, pockmarked. Could he be older than fourteen? Too young for the Eastern Front, Maggie realized. "Show me your papers!" he ordered.

Maggie kept her head down. She prayed her limp, gray hair and humpback fooled him, but she knew her face would betray her. Still, do young people ever really look in the eyes of the old? Her breath came faster.

With gloved hands, she pulled up her purse and fumbled at the catch. Maggie hoped it looked like tremors from old age. She knew the SS had been alerted. But the local police? Was this a random stop, or were they actually looking for her specifically?

It seemed to take forever to get the catch open. "Oh, never mind," the officer said, finally, watching her struggle. "Sorry, *gnädige Frau*. Have a good day."

"Danke," Maggie managed without looking up, grateful for the wide brim of her hat.

She took several shaky breaths to compose herself, and then shuffled on.

Exactly as she'd promised, Elise arrived at Charité's delivery entrance, out of breath from running.

"Mein Gott!" she murmured, and put one hand over her heart. Maggie knew how she must look—ashen, shaken, wild-eyed. Not to mention gray-haired and humpbacked.

"I'm sorry, but I'm afraid I'm in a bit of trouble . . ."

Elise looked around to see that no one was watching them. She put her arm around Maggie's shoulders, as though to help the old woman. "Come with me. For God's sake, keep your head down."

Maggie shuffled with Elise through back corridors until they reached an emergency stairwell. The two women climbed to the door that Elise and Frieda had propped open to the roof.

"We'll stay here, out of sight," Elise told her. Exhausted, Maggie sank down to sit, back against the wall, finding momentary relief in a small rectangle of shade. Elise followed suit.

"I would never have come here if I didn't feel I had no other option," Maggie said. "But the truth is, I need somewhere to hide. And I thought that, maybe, you could hide me—and perhaps help me find a way out of Germany."

"What's wrong?" Elise's once round and rosy face was now all shadowed angles and planes.

Maggie felt the stabbing pain of guilt. How many innocent people would she entangle in her trouble? "The less you know about it, the better. Again, I never would have come here if I felt there were any other choice—"

"Did Father Licht send you?" Elise interrupted.

"Who?" Maggie was confused. *Who was Father Licht?* "No." She shook her head. "I just thought that— Well, you've been so kind to me . . ." *And you're my half sister . . .*

"Did Frieda tell you about me?"

Maggie's brows furrowed. "Frieda?"

"It doesn't matter. All right, I don't know if I can get you out, but I can certainly hide you. We can cut and dye your hair—"

"No," Maggie insisted. "I must leave Germany, but not because I'm a Jew." In English, she added, "You see, I don't actually belong here. I'm British."

Elise gaped at Maggie. *"Nein,"* she exclaimed. *"Nein!"* Her face had gone pale.

"It's true," Maggie insisted.

Then, to Maggie's astonishment, Elise started to laugh, golden and sweet, punctuated with hiccups. "No!" she gasped, trying to catch her breath. "*No!* This is a joke! Surely one of the girls at the hospital sent you, as some kind of prank . . ."

"I'm sorry," Maggie said. "But it's true. I know it sounds crazy, but . . ."

Else's giggles had turned to laughter, hysterical laughter. "You—*you* are a spy?"

Half sister. "Yes."

"No, it can't be, it's like a dream," Elise said. "I'm going to wake up any minute."

"It's a lot to take in," Maggie said. *Believe me, I know.*

Elise reached out and clasped Maggie's hand. "I will do everything I can to get you out."

"So, will you hide me? Help find a radio?"

"Of course." Elise wiped her eyes as her haggard face bloomed into a smile. "Of course. Now, let me get you somewhere safe before anyone sees us."

The door to the roof opened. Both women tensed until Elise saw that it was Frieda.

"*Was ʒum Geier?*" Frieda exclaimed. *What the vulture?* Maggie translated literally. Meaning, were the vultures circling already?

"It's all right," Elise reassured Maggie. "She's one of us." Then, to Frieda, "She's a friend. A friend who needs help."

Frieda scowled. "And you're going to take her home with you, too? Yet another lost kitten?"

The tension Elise lived with day and night began to break through. "I'd like to remind you that your husband is one of my 'lost kittens,' Frieda!"

"But you don't think things through, Elise! The pilot—people eventually assumed he ran away because he's a deserter, but you never even gave a second thought to what an empty bed would mean. And I'm being harassed day and night by SS, wanting to know where Ernst has disappeared to. Do you even have a plan for smuggling them out of your attic? And then—you want to add"— she sniffed at Maggie—"*her* to the mix?"

Maggie's heart quickened.

"What would you have me do, Frieda? Deny her shelter? She's as good as dead out there!"

Frieda smiled. A strange smile. "Well, I'm glad then that I made my *Pakt mit dem Teufel.*"

"What do you mean—pact with the Devil?"

"Giving my husband, my beloved, to you," Frieda snapped. "Trusting him to your care."

"Frieda—"

"Nein!" The blonde put a thin, blue-veined hand up in the air. "We are done." She went to the exit, then slammed the door shut behind her.

Elise and Maggie stared at each other.

Maggie could see the strain in Elise's eyes. "No room at the inn?" She felt her last chance dying. "I don't want to put you, or anyone else, in any danger."

Elise put her hand on Maggie's. *"Nein,"* she said, "there is always room for one more."

At St. Hedwig's, Elise led Maggie directly to Father Licht's office. He looked up from the paperwork on his desk.

"I thought I might see you today, Elise," the priest said. "Please close the door."

"Father, this is Fräulein Margareta Hoffman—"

His eyebrows rose, and behind his glasses his eyes opened wide. "*You* are Margareta Hoffman?"

Maggie stiffened, ready to bolt. Who was this man? How did he recognize her name? Just because he was wearing a priest's collar and skullcap didn't mean he was on their side . . .

"Yes, why?" Elise said.

Father Licht rose. "I am very glad to see you, Fräulein Hoffman. Elise, how did you know to bring her here?"

"I just thought maybe I could hide her, the way I did with—" She stopped abruptly. "But once again, Father, I'll need your help."

"My children, we have much to discuss," he said, rubbing his thin hands together. "But before we begin, I suggest we all take a moment to say a prayer." He bowed his head and closed his eyes. Maggie and Elise did the same.

> Lord, make me an instrument of your peace.
> Where there is hatred, let me sow love . . .

"Now," said the priest, when the prayer was ended, "let's discuss how we're going to handle this, shall we say, rather *unusual* situation."

The final part of Hugh's assignment was to let Clara Hess know that Operation Aegir had succeeded. Masterman's plan was that Hugh carry out the mission Krueger would have. Or at least make it *seem* as if the mission had been carried out.

Hugh's orders were to stencil large wooden crates with a skull-and-crossbones symbol plus the stern warning

SODIUM FLUORIDE

DANGER! TOXIC BY INGESTION

Do not get in eyes or on skin. Do not ingest. Wear proper mask.

Then he was to take photographs of the crates. These he would send to Hess in Berlin, to prove the mission's triumphant success.

However, Hugh had a few other plans.

And for those, he'd need a partner. He picked up the green Bakelite receiver and dialed Mark Standish, his friend at MI-5. "I need a favor, old thing," he said. "Can you get away from the wife and little one tonight?"

"Why?" Mark replied instantly. "Do you actually want to go out and have some fun, instead of moping after your girlfriend?" Mark had worked with Hugh on the IRA bomb case and the Windsor case—and knew all about his relationship with Maggie. "Meet at the Rose and Crown for a pint?"

"Rose and Crown, first—and then have some fun, yes," Hugh replied. "Lots of fun."

By the time Hugh and Mark had downed innumerable pints at the Rose and Crown, and reached the designated storage building with the crates Hugh was supposed to paint, both young men were well and truly drunk.

The warehouse was massive and stuffy. Hugh found the light switch and turned on the overhead fluorescents. Mark had the camera from the XX Committee slung around his neck and an open can of Barkley's stout in each hand. Hugh carried the stencils, black paint, and a paintbrush.

"So, what now?" Mark demanded, wobbling from all the beer he'd consumed. "We stencil the crates and get a few shots for Hess?"

Hugh grinned. He was staggering as well. "I have something a bit more . . . interesting in mind."

He set the paint can down and pried off the lid. Inside, the paint was glossy and black, and smelled of linseed oil. He dipped his paintbrush into the thick liquid. "And here, my dear friend Mark, is where we're going to—as Maggie likes to say—wing it."

Mark stood back and watched as Hugh painted each box, eyes growing wider with each one. "You can't be serious," he protested. "Surely we're going to turn them around and paint with the stencils now, yes?"

"No." Hugh's eyes were dark with suppressed anger. "We are not."

Mark held up his hands. "You must be joking. This is career suicide."

"She killed my father," Hugh said. "She nearly assassinated the King and kidnapped the Princess."

"She's Maggie's mother," Mark stammered.

"Yes, and she left her. *Left her*. Believe me, if Maggie knew what I'm doing, she'd approve. My father—may he rest in peace— would, too." He dipped the paintbrush into the paint, then pulled it out, splattering himself inadvertently with tiny black drops. "Get the camera!"

"You're a madman!" Mark said, taking a swig and handing the other beer to his friend. "You'll give the film to Masterman, he'll somehow get it to Clara Hess in Berlin, and then—"

"And then I'll finally have my revenge. Or at least a tiny sliver of it."

Mark gave a gust of a sigh. He was too drunk to argue. "Well, it's your arse on the line, my friend."

"And that, my friend"—Hugh smiled, a wild and dangerous smile—"gives me a *fantastic* idea."

Chapter Seventeen

Admiral Wilhelm Cánaris, Head of the Abwehr, lifted the handset of his telephone and dialed 1 for his secretary. "Tell *gnädige* Frau Hess I need to see her. *Now!*"

Canaris was an enigma to most. A distinguished-looking man with white hair and shaggy white eyebrows, he was ostensibly head of the military intelligence organization, yet distrusted by Hitler and most of the high-ranking Nazis, including his former protégé SS-Obergruppenführer Reinhard Heydrich; the German Foreign Minister, Joachim von Ribbentrop; and the Abwehr's own Clara Hess.

The truth was that Canaris was part of the undercover German resistance movement. In September 1939, the Admiral had visited Poland and seen the atrocities committed by the SS Eisengruppen. He learned, through Abwehr agents, about other incidents of mass murder throughout Poland. These murders weren't the actions of a rogue Nazi squadron but actions on orders from Hitler himself.

Shocked and horrified, Canaris began working covertly to overthrow Hitler, posing as a loyal Nazi and trusted friend. He climbed the political ladder at the Abwehr and was instrumental in recruiting like-minded men, all determined to work against the Nazis and for the enemy for a Germany free from Hitler.

He used his position in the vipers' nest of the Abwehr to control both the information and the so-called disinformation the

Nazis received. Although he was technically Clara Hess's boss, because of her connections with Hitler and Goebbels, she was beyond his sphere of power. Today, however, even they couldn't help her.

And he took a moment to rejoice in the fact that he would soon be rid of her.

Clara Hess was not used to being summoned. She'd always sided with Ribbentrop, usually against Canaris, in Abwehr politics and policies—and knew the Admiral was no admirer of hers. After powdering her face and applying a fresh coat of scarlet lipstick, she strode reluctantly into his office, leaving behind her a trail of Chanel No. 5.

As a former stage performer, she knew not to let any fear show, and held her head high. Canaris stood up behind his massive desk when she entered. *"Heil Hitler!"*

"Heil Hitler!"

"Please have a seat, Frau Hess."

Clara did so, displaying her silk-covered legs in spectator pumps to their best advantage. Canaris sat as well. He picked up a file. "We've received the photos from your man in Britain," he said.

Clara smiled. She'd been in touch with Krueger and knew things were on track. "Fantastic," she said. "May I see them?"

Canaris passed the folder to Clara, and she opened it to look at the glossy photographs. When she saw the first, of a crate emblazoned with the sloppy challenge IN LONDON IN 1914, YOU MURDERED HUGH THOMPSON, SR., she blinked, and became very still.

One photograph after another showed wooden crates, painted with personal messages: I GREW UP TO TAKE HIS PLACE.

WE OUTWITTED YOU AT WINDSOR & WE HAVE OUTWITTED YOU AGAIN. She paged through them, one by one, her face betraying nothing.

And then, in stark black and white, was a picture of Hugh, from behind, trousers pulled down, displaying his lean and pale buttocks to the camera.

Clara closed the folder and swallowed hard. She slid the folder across the desk, back to Canaris. He took it and slipped on a pair of glasses. "I'm afraid, Clara, in light of the Windsor situation and now, this botched mission—"

"My spy was turned," Clara interrupted. "He was weak, susceptible . . ."

"You were in charge. You must take responsibility."

"I hope they hanged him," she spat. "Bullets would be wasted on him."

"Clara—" Canaris put the folder into a desk drawer and locked it. "I'm sorry to have to be the one to tell you this, but there have been too many mistakes. It's hard enough that you're a woman, working in a man's world—"

"You won't get away with this!" Clara raged, standing. "Wait until Goebbels hears about this!"

Canaris spoke gently but firmly, the way he would have with a child or dog. "It's over, Clara. I'm sorry. I've spoken with Goebbels—he's the one who interceded for you, actually." He pressed a button on his telephone.

Two SS guards appeared at the door. Canaris nodded. "Please escort Frau Hess to the car we have waiting to take her home."

"I need to go back to my office," she insisted. "I'm going to the opera tonight and I have to change."

"Still playing the part." Canaris sighed. "All right, you may go back to your office." He nodded at the waiting guards. "Tell the driver to take her directly to the Berlin Opera House when she's finished." He looked back to Clara. "Any personal effects you have in your office will be packed and sent to your home."

She looked down at him with a cryptic, almost pitying smile. *"Jawohl,"* she said, and swept out.

At St. Hedwig's, Elise and Father Licht decided that Maggie would go to Elise's. "I know I prepared those rooms for the children . . ."

"Children?" Maggie asked.

"The children of the euthanasia program," Elise explained. "Operation Compassionate Death."

"What?" Maggie was bewildered. *Children? Euthanasia?*

"I'm being selfish, telling you any of this—but I can't bear to keep the secret any longer. Nazi doctors are murdering children. 'Life unfit for life' they call them—blind, deaf, epileptic, schizophrenic . . ."

"Wait—" Maggie was still trying to wrap her mind around the terrible things Elise was telling her. "Yes, Gottlieb told me—the blind, the deaf. But—how are *you* involved?"

"I've seen the children at the hospital," Elise said. "I've seen how they're evaluated. And I've seen them put on the black buses and taken to places such as Hadamar, where they're—" Elise swallowed. "I'm a witness. And I'm trying to get the paperwork the resistance needs to publicly denounce this program, which was approved by the Führer himself."

Maggie shuddered. Suddenly, the papers in Oberg's office made sense. Those weren't "units."

The "units" were children.

It clicked, the way numbers did when she was solving a maths equation. "And Herr Oberg is in charge," she said slowly, putting the pieces together. "At least of the financial side of the operation."

"Herr Oberg?" Elise said.

"Yes," Maggie said thoughtfully. "He ostensibly works for the State and Party Affairs office. I looked at his papers—they deal in what they're calling 'units.' Units being sent, by bus, to places like Hadamar. He's in charge of the"—a chill went through Maggie—"the business end of the operation, the bus drivers' salaries, the buses, the fuel . . ." Maggie pulled out her handbag and started to unlock the fake bottom.

"There are some of us"—Elise looked at Father Licht, who nodded—"who want to expose these monsters. Father Licht and some of the Bishops have already gone to the Pope. But because the German Catholics signed the Reichskonkordat, we can't protest. Or at least, we can't protest without absolute proof. They'll deny and cover up anything and everything. But if we had proof . . ."

If they, Germans, could actually expose such atrocities to their own people, the film she had would be far more important to these people than to the British. If the British told people about it, it could be dismissed as war propaganda. But if it came from Germans themselves—and from the *clergy* . . .

Maggie made her decision. "Here," she said, taking the camera out of her bag and popping out the film cartridge. "I was able to photograph some of Oberg's papers, about the costs and the 'units.' I think they might be of use to you."

Father Licht accepted the film. "Thank God," he said. "And, thank you."

Elise took Maggie's arm. "Now let's get you into hiding. We need to work on an escape plan."

Clara Hess returned to her office in a daze. She closed the door and then locked it, shutting out the guards escorting her.

It was time to face facts. Her marriage had long been over. She had only a distant relationship with her daughter. Her looks were fading. And now, the only things she could count on—her work and her status in the Nazi party—were gone. Still, she had friends—powerful friends. And there was the opera tonight . . .

She poured some schnapps, downed it, and then poured some more. Her lipstick had migrated to her teeth, and her mascara had run, leaving smudges under her eyes. In the haze of alcohol drunk too quickly on an empty stomach, she placed a call to Goebbels's office. "I'll see you at the opera tonight, won't I, darling? Miles is conducting—it's *Lohengrin,* after all—your favorite . . ."

Goebbels cleared his throat. "Clara, I know what happened with Canaris today. And I think it would be best"—he paused, trying to think of a delicate way to phrase it—"if you kept a low profile for a time. Take a holiday. Leave Berlin."

"What?"

"Please, Clara . . ."

Her eyes narrowed. "Tell me."

"You are—how shall I phrase this?—out of favor with the Führer at the moment. I think the less you're in the spotlight, the better. You know how capricious he can be."

He went on. "Your best bet is to be quiet, stay at home. It may be too late for you to have any more children of your own, but you could be of use. Perhaps adopt one of the *Liebensborn?*"

Clara, who'd always been the beloved, the admired, the feared, was speechless with fury. But she hadn't risen to where she was by showing her cards too soon. "Well, thank you for your advice, Joseph," she purred into the phone. "You've given me quite a bit to think about. Oh, one more thing—any word on the whereabouts of Margareta Hoffman?"

"Nein," Goebbels answered. "She disappeared from Oberg's

house sometime in the night. We have our men looking for her. Don't worry, we'll find her."

"And Lehrer?"

"He resisted arrest. Then shot himself."

"You mean he's *dead*?"

"Yes—why so upset?"

"Because he might have been our connection to a larger resistance ring, that's why!" And, with that, Clara banged down the phone.

She would not hang her head in shame, she would not disappear. She would not adopt a child and chase after the *Ehrenkreuz der Deutschen Mutter,* the cross-shaped medal Hitler awarded to dutiful German mothers.

She opened her desk drawer and pulled out a small mother-of-pearl-handled gun. Before she left, she had to take care of the unfinished business in the attic.

Elise snuck Maggie, still with her gray hair and humpback, up the servants' staircase of her home.

"How long have you been hiding people here?" Maggie whispered as they tiptoed up the stairs.

"Only since the party. I snuck the first man in that night, actually."

Maggie raised an eyebrow. "You snuck someone into your house the night of Clara Hess's party—with all those Nazis around?" She whistled through her teeth. "As they say in Britain, you have stones, Elise. Big stones."

"Do I even *want* to know what that means?"

"I'll explain when we get out of here." She stopped and grabbed Elise's hand. "You are coming with us, yes? We *are* all going together?"

"I'm not sure," the other girl said. "My biggest concern is getting the three of you out. As for myself . . . Well, I love my country, even though things are horrible right now. If I leave . . ."

"Who'd be left to pick up the pieces?" Maggie finished for her, realizing that Elise was going to stay, regardless of the danger. "I understand." Then, "Do you still want to become a nun? Even after witnessing all this?"

"I'm trying to keep in mind what Thomas Aquinas said in his *Summa Theologica*."

"Sorry," Maggie said. "I'm not familiar with it."

"St. Thomas said that there can be both an all-powerful God and evil in the world—because an all-powerful God is powerful enough to turn evil into good—even if we don't know exactly how or when He does it."

Maggie shrugged. "If an all-powerful God is going to turn evil into good, I really wish He'd hurry up."

In the attic, John was sitting up in the armchair while Ernst was sprawled on the mattress on the floor, reading a book.

Elise gave the secret knock at the door, and then opened it. "Gentlemen, we have a new guest," she said. Maggie followed her into the room.

Maggie saw a man in a chair, head raised from the book he'd been reading. "John?" she managed finally.

He blinked.

"My God." She unpinned her hat and dropped it to the floor, then took down her hair. As it spilled out, the red became visible against the gray.

His eyes widened. And then he said, "Maggie?"

"John." She took a step forward. "Are—are you all right?"

He rose. "I'm . . . How did you find me?"

Maggie and John continued to stare at each other. Finally, she moved toward him, tentatively traversing what seemed to be an enormous, perilous distance. Right before she reached him, she tripped on the edge of the carpet and stumbled, falling on one knee.

"Ouch," she said, and then found she couldn't move.

"Easy there." John knelt and held out his hand. It was thinner than she remembered, she could see the blue veins through translucent skin, but she took it, fighting back hot tears.

"You look absolutely terrible," John said, helping her to her feet and brushing the ash off her cheeks with his fingertips.

"You look pretty awful yourself," Maggie found herself retorting. He did. His hair was streaked with gray, his eyes were shadowed, his shoulders held so much tension they looked hunched. "Like you've been through a war or something."

"Or something."

Maggie reached up, putting her arms around him. He smelled like John, her memory of John—warm and soapy. His muscles were still lean and wiry. He held her so tightly she could barely breathe. Neither of them said a word, but there was enough electricity between them to make Maggie tremble.

They sat down on the bed, holding hands, faces wet with tears. "We all thought— I thought—" Maggie began.

"That I was dead?" John wouldn't let go of her hand. "Almost. But I never stopped loving you. I never gave up on you. And thanks to Elise . . ."

"My God," Maggie moaned, and buried her face in his neck, holding on tight. He was there, he was real, he wasn't an apparition.

"I love you, Maggie," he whispered, stroking her hair. "I never stopped loving you."

Tears stung Maggie's eyes. She thought of the memorial service they'd had for John.

"I love you, too. And we need to talk. But first, we need to get out of here."

Ernst grinned. "At the risk of stating the obvious, I'd say you two know each other."

Elise wiped at her wet face, then cleared her throat. "I'm sorry to interrupt, but we must get moving. I have a plan—it's something I've been thinking about for a while, but I was waiting for John to recover fully before I suggested it."

"What is it?" John asked.

"My father, you see, is the conductor of the Deutsche Oper Berlin—the Berlin Opera," she said. "He travels quite a bit, usually in Germany, but also sometimes to Austria. He's about to go to Switzerland."

"We'd need papers," Maggie said.

"Not necessarily." Elise took a deep breath. "I'm going to get you out of Berlin—out of Germany—and to Switzerland."

"Yes, but how?" Maggie said.

"My idea—and bear with me—is to hide you in the Berlin Opera's musical instrument cases—the double bass, the timpani—when they travel to Zürich."

Ernst, John, and Maggie looked stunned by the suggestion. "Would we fit?" Maggie asked, after a moment.

"Oh yes." Elise nodded. "My friends and I used to hide in cases all the time when we were younger. It's absolutely possible for an adult to hide in a number of instrument cases."

"And could we breathe?" Ernst asked.

"We'll have to make some holes."

Maggie frowned. "Do you really think your father would do it? Isn't your mother a high-ranking Nazi?"

"Yes," Elise said, "but surely you remember their argument, the night of her birthday? Her party membership put quite a strain on their marriage. It's one of the reasons my father's never around anymore—he can't stand what she's turned into. He's been here for the last few weeks, but sleeping in one of the guest rooms. Besides," she continued resolutely, "he doesn't need to know what we've done until after you've arrived safely in Switzerland. What other options do we have?"

Maggie was impressed—her half sister's plan was good. Impossibly dangerous, but good. She smiled. "I love it. Let's do it."

Clara Hess stood in the adjoining attic room, her ear pressed to the thin wall. This new information, she realized, called for a change in plans.

She tiptoed to the staircase, then made her way down. It was time to get ready for the opera.

Chapter Eighteen

The Staatsoper Unter den Linden, or Berlin Opera House, was an enormous building with soaring columns and red Nazi banners snapping in hot gusts of wind. But to Elise, the massive structure was like a second home; she'd been coming here to see her father rehearse or conduct ever since she was old enough to walk.

Elise bypassed the grand entrance and went in through the stage door around back. "*Hallo*, Herr Benz," she called to the guard on duty, a bald man, squinting through his pince-nez, reading *Der Stürmer*, the weekly Nazi party newspaper.

"*Guten Tag, gnädiges Fräulein,*" Martin Benz called back, tipping an imaginary hat. "You're here to see your papa? They're rehearsing now—room one oh eight B."

"Thank you, Herr Benz," she said, with a mock curtsey, something they'd been doing for years. "It's nice to see you again."

Elise walked quickly through the long corridors of the opera house until she reached the rehearsal room. She could see her father standing on a small apple box, baton in hand, behind a music stand that held a thick, pencil-marked score.

The orchestra was just finishing the overture to Wagner's *Lohengrin*, the violins almost angelic in their high fermate. Hess lowered his baton and observed a moment of silence, like a prayer. Coming back to reality, he spied his daughter. "Elise!" he said, opening his arms.

"Papa!" She ran to him, like a little girl.

"Have you come to join me for lunch, *mein Engel*?" he asked, packing up his score. Around them, violinists were chatting and joking, putting their instruments back into their cases.

"*Nein*, Papa—I have a request for you. A few requests, really."

"Anything, *Engel*."

"First, I would like to come see tonight's performance."

He flourished his baton like a magic wand and gently tapped it on her head. "Your wish is my command!"

"And I would like to bring three friends."

"Of course. I will have four tickets waiting for you. Box seats."

"And I would like to come with you to Zürich."

"What?" Hess was surprised. "You mean tonight?"

"Yes, tonight," Elise replied. "I need—" How much should she tell him? "Well, let's just say I need a little distance from Mutti. And the hospital. I think the change of scene and mountain air would do me a world of good."

"Of course, *Engel*. I'll arrange for your train ticket. You will come with me in first class—very fancy. Nothing but the best for my little girl." He kissed her on the top of her head.

"Thank you!" Elise's mind was whirling with all she had to do. "See you tonight—you're the best papa ever!"

Once back at the Hess villa in Grunewald, Elise worked quickly and efficiently.

She called the hospital. She was deathly ill and could not possibly come in for the next few days. Then she went through her father's closet, picking out two formal suits. She did the same in her mother's enormous wardrobe, choosing one of her gowns, and also a blond wig.

Then, making sure the coast was clear, she went up to the attic and gave the secret knock. Ernst opened the door. "We're going to the opera!" she announced gaily, passing out clothing. "And then we're going to Switzerland."

"What? Tonight?" Maggie asked.

"Now?" added John.

"Yes," Elise declared. "Are you ready?"

It was dangerous to go, but it was even more dangerous to stay. Maggie considered for a moment. "First we'll need to find a radio."

Elise grew pale. That was one thing she'd never bargained for.

"It's all right," Maggie reassured her. "Just look for the one under your mother's desk."

Elise found the transmitter-receiver and carried it to the attic. Maggie took it from her, set it gently on the floor, and opened it. Even though it was German-issued and different from the ones she was used to, it had the same parts: receiver, transmitter, and power-supply unit. She screwed in the miniature Morse key, plugged in the appropriate wires, and then hung the transmitter out the window.

"My goodness," John said, impressed. "You really are a spy."

She patted his cheek and sat down behind the machine. "I *told* you." She turned on the power and the bulbs glowed. She put on the headphones and took a deep breath. She thought back to her time with Noreen, at Baker Street, and the "poem" she'd been given, the Declaration of Independence: "equalrightslifeliberty-happ," and the corresponding alphabet.

The concept of life and liberty, and protected rights for all—let alone the pursuit of happiness—seemed almost impossible to imagine after having spent time in the ring of hell that was wartime Berlin. Still, Maggie tapped out her code, asking for a pickup for three at the Zürich train station in Switzerland the following noon.

"Do you think they received it?" Elise asked. Her face was very pale.

"I hope so," Maggie said, unplugging everything and putting it away neatly.

"How will we know?"

"The BBC song list. They'll play 'A Nightingale Sang in Berkeley Square,' to acknowledge receipt."

"I always did like Vera Lynn," John said, grinning sweetly as he took Maggie's hand and helped her to her feet.

"I'm glad," Maggie said, taking his hand and pressing it to her lips. "Because I think now it's officially our song."

"You have similar figures," Elise remarked to Maggie in her bathroom, handing her one of Clara's gowns, a draped and flowing white silk Madame Grès. She gave a crooked smile, as she'd always been a bit too curvy to borrow any of Clara's couture. "You could be sisters," Elise said approvingly.

Oh, so close, Elise, Maggie thought. *So close and yet so far.*

Giving Maggie some privacy to wash the ash out of her hair and get dressed, Elise dressed in her own room, in a pink taffeta gown. When she was done, she went to Marthe's gilded cage. "I don't know when I'm going to be back, little one," she told the dove, who regarded her, head cocked.

She opened her bedroom window. "But just in case I don't make it, it's time for you to be free." She unhinged the cage door. "There you go—*fly!*"

There was an anticlimactic moment as Frieda's bird continued to sit on her perch, tilting her head to one side, regarding Elise with shining jet eyes.

Then, Marthe hopped down to the cage's open door. She gave Elise one last, long quizzical look, before flapping her wings and flying off. She landed on a branch of a nearby apple tree and sang a series of trills back to Elise before taking off again, shrinking to a dark speck against the oppressive gray sky.

"Good luck, little bird," Elise whispered, knowing that Frieda wouldn't mind, as long as Ernst was safe.

Up in the attic, they tuned the radio to the BBC and pressed their ears against the speaker. Finally, they heard their dedication, thin and crackly, letting them know the message had been received in London. "And this song is dedicated to His Majesty's Hope." The flute made its trilling introduction, and then Vera Lynn's voice sang out: *"And a nightingale sang in Berkeley Square."*

Maggie and John turned to each other. "Our song?" he whispered in her ear, grinning.

Maggie closed her eyes, swaying in his arms. "Yes."

"Then we'll have to play it at our wedding, darling."

She smiled and pressed her lips to his neck. "We're almost home," she said. They kissed.

The door clicked open. "The servants are here," Elise whispered, "so we must pretend that they missed seeing you come in, and that we've been in my room the whole time. Now," she said in her best nurse voice, "you are all German aristocrats, having a bit of champagne before the opera. John, you will be silent—and if anyone asks, I'll tell him or her that you're a Luftwaffe pilot, suffering from shell shock, which has affected your speech.

"When we're done, we'll go downstairs and our driver will take us to the opera. There will be tickets waiting for us at the box office." She looked at all their faces. "Ready?"

"Jawohl," Ernst replied.

Chapter Nineteen

Together in the neo-Baroque theater of crimson, cream, and gold, they sat in box seats and watched and listened to Wagner's ethereal overture to *Lohengrin*, the story of the Swan Knight. Or, at least, tried to watch. The legions of Nazi SS officers in their dress uniforms proved distracting, as did the armed guards stationed at each exit.

Backstage, Clara paced. If she could not be a singer anymore, if she could not be one of the top Nazis, beloved by the Führer, she would be a turncoat, for the British. They would welcome her and all of the secrets she knew. She would still be a diva. She would be a legend. History would laud her.

"They'll miss me when I'm gone," she muttered. "Joseph will regret pushing me out. They'll all see."

As a child, she'd been caught between two parents: an abusive lawyer father and an overindulgent former ballerina mother. When they divorced—a scandal—she chose, in court, to live with her mother. Little did she know her mother would soon die from syphilis. With her mother dead and her father refusing to take her in, Clara had been sent to her grandmother's farm in Austria, where she had barely enough to eat. It was only her voice, her golden voice, that lifted her out of her bleak circumstances, and only her voice that led her to fame and fortune.

When she'd been approached by Sektion during the Great

War, of course she had accepted. They needed her. The need to be needed, the need for approval, the need to belong—these thirsts drove her. Spying, plus music, was the drug she needed to put her past behind her. But the past, unconfronted, is never really forgotten.

Backstage, because she was the conductor's wife, her presence was not commented on, even if it didn't go unnoticed. "May I get you a chair, *gnädige Frau?*" the stage manager asked.

"Nein, " she replied absently, waving him off, lost in her own thoughts.

Clara looked through the wings at the audience. There, in her usual box seats, was Elise. And the Jew. And the pilot. Clara's eyes narrowed. Who was that blonde? It could be Clara's own doppelgänger—tall, slim, and blond. Clara felt faint, as if she had seen a ghost. And was that her gown? Was that . . . Margareta? Could it be?

And sitting next to Margareta was Elise. Elise knew Margareta? Who else did Elise know? What else was that foolish, stupid daughter of hers involved with? She'd found the two in her study . . . Maybe Elise was doing more than Frieda had either let on or knew about. Despite herself, she began to feel a wave of grudging respect for her daughter.

She felt for her gun in her handbag. It was nestled there, ready for the last act.

When, finally, the last notes of the opera faded away, and the house erupted in thunderous applause, Elise whispered, "Come with me." Together, they followed her down the fire escape stairs until they reached a door. Elise opened it. A ramp led to the backstage area. The cast was there in their costumes and makeup, sweating from the exertion under the hot lights, chatting animatedly, fueled by leftover adrenaline.

Elise spotted one of the stage managers, dressed in black from head to toe. "*Hallo*, Herr Shultz, do you know where my father is?" she asked. He pointed back toward a closed door. "Come," Elise told the group.

They reached the rehearsal room, filled with musicians. "What are we doing here?" Maggie whispered.

"They're packing because they're taking the train to Zürich tonight. You'll see," Elise whispered back. "Trust me."

And Maggie found that she did.

Elise saw her father, in animated discussion with the first violinist. "Excuse me," she said, putting a hand on Miles's arm. "May we use your office for a moment? One of my friends has to make a telephone call." She indicated Maggie, Ernst, and John.

"Of course, *mein Engel*," Miles answered, distracted. "Here's the key."

"Thank you, Papa." Elise gestured to the three. "Come!"

Miles Hess's office in the opera house was opulent, with thick carpets, oil paintings, and velvet-covered furniture. A window overlooked the Gendarmenmarkt. Elise turned on the light, then went straight to his desk. "Ah, it's here!" she exclaimed.

Maggie, John, and Ernst exchanged looks.

Elise sank to her knees, opening a large leather Rimowa trunk with strips of molded wood, covered in colorful travel stickers: LANGHAM HOTEL, LONDON; MENA HOUSE HOTEL, CAIRO; HÔTEL TRIANON, PARIS.

"It's where he keeps his orchestral scores when he's traveling," she explained, lifting the heavy lid, taking out bundled scores and piling them under the desk. "It's a big trunk, because he always wants the score for every single instrument's part, in case he needs to look something up. Well, come on—help me take all these out!"

"But this trunk will fit only one of us," Maggie objected.

"You, to be specific," Elise said to Maggie, "as you're the smallest."

It took a few precious minutes, but the trunk was finally empty. "Wait," Maggie said. She took a pen from her handbag and punched a number of holes in the side of the trunk. Then she took a bunch of newspapers and dropped them inside. She colored. "At spy camp they said I had an iron bladder. Let's hope they were right."

Elise studied Maggie. "Are you ready?"

"As I'll ever be," Maggie replied resolutely. "If—when—we get to Zürich, I want to talk to you. We need to talk."

"About what?" Elise looked confused.

As much as Maggie wanted to tell Elise the truth, this wasn't the time. "Nothing that can't wait—we all have enough to think of now." She and John kissed, and then she folded her body inside the trunk.

Elise's lip touched her cheek. "Good luck, dearest Maggie. I'm going, too, so as soon as we're all onboard the train and moving, I'll check on you."

And with that, she closed the lid.

Back in the empty rehearsal room, Elise repeated the process with John and Ernst. The two men opened the cases, punched airholes in them, then placed the instruments in a supply closet. Elise locked the door. She had John fit himself into the harp case, and Ernst into a timpani case. Both cases had wheels.

The first part of the mission accomplished, Elise went to see her father, now chatting with a man she recognized. Herr Wallfrid Bauer was a prominent arms manufacturer. Elise slipped up beside her father, smiling brightly.

"Ah!" said Herr Bauer. "And here is your charming daughter, all grown up now!"

"Yes." Miles nodded with pride. "And I'm pleased to say she is a nurse, at Charité."

"If I ever have a medical emergency, I know who to call!" Herr Bauer chortled at his own cleverness. Elise didn't join in. Then there was the sillage of Chanel No. 5 perfume, and Elise turned to see her mother appear.

"Hello, kitten," Miles said, kissing one of his wife's gloved hands. "I wasn't expecting you tonight."

"Frau Hess, you look as beautiful as always," Herr Bauer said as he bent to kiss her other hand. "I only wish it had been you to-night, singing the part of Elsa. Although you were wonderful as Ortrud, at your party."

"Thank you." Clara's scarlet-painted lips twisted into a smile.

"*Hallo, Mutti.*" The color had drained from Elise's face. She hadn't counted on her mother being there.

"*Mausi.*" Clara turned to her husband. "And now, my darling, shall we go?"

"Go?" Elise's breath caught in her throat. "You're coming with us?"

"Of course, *Mausi,*" she crooned, reaching out a hand to stroke the younger woman's cheek. "I wouldn't miss this trip for the world."

Chapter Twenty

The Hess family sat in the first-class train compartment on red velvet seats. Over the door was an SS Death's Head insignia. Clara pulled down the window shade and turned on the dim light.

Elise had seen soldiers patrolling outside; now she swallowed hard. She folded her gloved hands in her lap and concentrated on holding them still as the train started its engines, then pulled away from the station with a screech of wheels and hiss of steam. She crossed herself and closed her eyes to pray for the three hidden in the baggage compartment. She hoped the porters had been gentle with the cases. She thought that the odds were good that the cases had been moved carefully—while they might not necessarily treat human beings well, Germans could be counted on to care for the instruments used to play Wagner with respect.

"I see you're still wearing your cross, *Mausi*," Clara said over the rumble of the engine, pushing back the veil of her hat. The blackout curtains made the air in the compartment feel stifling. "Where's your swastika necklace? I paid a fortune for it, you know."

"It didn't go with the dress," Elise managed. Why was her mother smiling that Mona Lisa smile? Why was she here?

"Pity," Clara murmured.

There was a knock at the compartment door. "Maestro! *Gnädige* Frau Hess! *Gnädiges* Fräulein Hess!" The conductor bowed. "I am at your service. May I bring you something to drink?"

"I would like brandy," Clara decided.

Miles considered. "Coffee."

"A bottle of Fanta, please," Elise said, thinking of the three in the luggage compartment and how they must be thirsty.

When the conductor left, Clara said with a wicked smile, "You'd better watch yourself. Soda can get you in trouble."

"What?" Elise said, startled. Was her mother reading her thoughts?

"Relax, *Mausi,* " Clara said, patting the girl's knee and smiling. "I mean your waistline. All that sugar in soda . . . Don't you think that dress is fitting a bit snugly? I think a little slimming is in order."

Elise found she could breathe again. "Of course, Mutti."

Trapped in the silk-lined trunk, Maggie tried to relax and breathe slowly. At Beaulieu, they'd been taught to count when they needed to calm down in a dangerous situation. And so she counted, to a hundred, to a thousand, then started over again at one. She tried not to think about her legs cramping up, or her lips getting dry. She tried not to think about the increasing pressure on her bladder. *Why did I have to drink so much water today?* She calculated pi— getting up to almost a hundred decimal places before her memory gave out, and then began to reiterate Fermat's theorem.

The porters had been rough with the case, but she hadn't been injured, and for that she was grateful. And although she couldn't hear much, she could feel the train's engines start up. *Next stop, Switzerland,* she thought. *I hope John and Ernst are all right—didn't get too banged up in the move. Or worse.*

It was dark and close in her trunk, which felt disconcertingly like a small coffin. *Stop it, Hope. Back to Fermat for you. Let's see, no three positive integers—a, b, and c—can satisfy the equation $a^n + b^n = c^n$ for any integer value of n greater than 2. So . . .*

Second by second, minute by minute, the hours ticked away and the miles flew by as the train rolled on through the German countryside in the dark.

Miles had soon leaned his head back against the white lace headrest and begun snoring softly.

Clara had removed her hat and shoes and tucked her stocking-clad legs up under her, like a cat. "Try to get some sleep, *Mausi*," she urged, closing her eyes. "Lots of shopping to do in Switzerland, after all."

Elise obeyed but secretly stayed awake, waiting until she heard her mother's breathing change. Then she rose silently, grabbed the bottle of Fanta and the bottle opener, and eased her way out of the compartment. She walked the train's corridors hurriedly, holding on to the wall with one hand to keep her balance. It was late. Most of the other passengers were sleeping; the conductors paid her no mind.

Just as she was about to exit the last car before the luggage car, someone stepped in front of her. A man, dressed in a conductor's uniform. A young man, a boy really. Scarcely old enough to shave. He was looking down at his feet, counting and practicing dance steps. She recognized the steps he'd been doing—the most basic move in swing dance. *Rock-step, step-hold, step-hold. Rock-step, step-hold, step-hold.* In his arms, he held an imaginary girl.

He looked up, his face blushing furiously at being caught. "What are you doing back here?"

"You dance well," Elise said. "I—I'm one of the musicians. And I left something in my case."

He turned even pinker. "You still can't go in there. It is forbidden. Most of the musicians have their instruments with them," he added. It was true; those with smaller instruments always carried them by hand. The Berlin Opera even bought each of their cellists an extra ticket for a seat for his instrument.

"But, you see," Elise said, trying her best to bat her eyelashes, "I play the harp. It's too big to travel with me. And that's why it's back there."

"And why are you carrying a soda?"

Elise wasn't prepared for this one. She blinked. "Performing tonight's made me very thirsty."

The boy didn't look convinced. "Show me your papers."

Elise smiled. "I'll show you how to do that step properly," she said, putting down the bottle. She grabbed one of his hands and put it around her waist, then took her arm and encircled his back. "Five six seven eight . . ." she counted.

They began to dance. The boy was awkward. "Now, it's not as hard as you're making it out to be," Elise said. "When you do your rock step, don't twist out as much. There—there you go—good." They moved together in harmony for a few moments. "All right, now don't drop your shoulders. That's it—yes!" They danced together, beautifully now, to imaginary music. Finally, the boy twirled her and tried for a dip. She slipped slightly in his arms and they lost the beat.

"That's a whole other lesson," Elise said, laughing. "I'm assuming I can go in now?"

The boy gave her a rapturous grin. "Don't be too long," he said, voice cracking on the last syllable.

"Keep practicing," Elise said, picking up her soda. "You'll be doing lifts and backflips in no time."

She eased open the door to the baggage car. Inside was shadowy, the gloom punctured by only a single blue fluorescent light overhead. Elise picked her way through the piled luggage until she reached her father's trunk. She rapped on it with her knuckles, then opened the brass clasps and raised the lid.

"Oh, thank goodness it's you," Maggie whispered, sitting up and looking around. She rolled her neck to undo the kinks. "How are John and Ernst?"

"I'm about to get them now," Elise replied. "Are you all right?"

Maggie stretched her arms and then rose tentatively to her feet, grimacing. "I'll live. Let's get the boys."

Together they searched for the harp and the timpani cases. After a battle with the clasps, both John and Ernst were released. Like Maggie, they stretched and shook out their limbs.

"How are you?" Elise asked.

"I admit I could use some water," John said. He looked ghostly in the shadows.

"It's not water." Elise pulled out the bottle of Fanta and the opener. "But it's all I could carry here without being conspicuous."

She opened it and handed it to Maggie, who handed it to John. "You're the one who's injured," she reminded him.

"But you're the one who's been on the run," he said lightly, handing it back to her.

Ernst grumbled, "Oh, why don't you just kiss each other and get it over with," and, grabbing the bottle, put it up to his lips and took a greedy swig.

John and Maggie drank in turn. They sat on trunks and looked at each other, smiling foolishly. They were on their way home, after all.

"How much longer?" John asked.

Elise peered at her watch. "About six more hours," she answered. "You're going to have to go back in the cases now, I'm afraid. But the next time I see you, we'll all be free." She grinned. "It's rather like a movie, isn't it?"

"They always edit the boring bits, the embarrassing bits, out, don't they?" Maggie said, climbing back into her trunk.

Ernst stepped into his case. "Still, I'd rather be here, in a timpani case, en route to Zürich, than on a train bound for Buchenwald."

That brought them all up short.

"Well, when this is a movie, and Hedy Lamarr is playing Maggie and Gene Tierney is playing me, we can make sure they only show glamorous things," Elise said lightly. "But for now, let's just concentrate on getting to Switzerland."

Clara, only pretending to be asleep, knew exactly when Elise left the compartment.

She trailed her daughter, staying just far enough behind to remain out of sight. She watched Elise dance with the guard, horrified at the *verboten* swing dance moves. And she waited, in the shadows, until Elise left the luggage compartment and made her way back down the corridor. She realized what her daughter must have done—hidden the three in instrument cases. Lord knows as a child, Elise had delighted in hiding in them herself!

Clara had no time to dance with the guard. "Here," she said, looking past his wide blue eyes, and crumpling a wad of Reichsmarks into his hand. "Stay out." He watched her in mute bewilderment as she let herself inside.

Instrument cases, everywhere.

She started at the left, opening cases, then flipping the lids shut in frustration.

From inside her case, Maggie could hear the commotion. Someone was looking through the cases. And it wasn't Elise. It was just a matter of time until whoever it was reached her case. She had a sudden flashback to her training at Arisaig. *Keep it together, lass!* she remembered a Scottish instructor yelling. *No matter what they throw at you, keep it together! Don't you dare fall apart!*

Staying still and waiting seemed like too passive a move. Whoever was there would inevitably find her. Her only advantage was surprise. She waited until she heard the person get close. Then she banged the lid open with all her might. The searcher staggered backward and fell heavily against a pyramid of Rimowa luggage.

"Frau Hess?" Maggie whispered. "Clara?" Then, seeing Clara's expression, "Mother?"

"Margaret Hope." One corner of Clara's mouth turned up in a smile. "You must have many questions. But, first, know this—I never meant to hurt you."

"I do have a question," Maggie said, desperately trying to still her racing mind. *She must not be allowed to find John and Ernst. Think, Maggie, think! Keep her talking.* "Why me? Why did you have a child?"

Clara shook her head. "Sektion demanded it of me. They thought it would cement my relationship with your father, in a way not even marriage could."

"My very existence is due to Sektion?"

"It was part of my mission, yes." Clara put one hand to her temple."

"But you left England."

"If I stayed, you'd always have been in danger. And I knew your father would take good care of you."

Maggie gave a bitter laugh. "Well, that's debatable. And the accident—how did you convince everyone you'd died?"

Clara chortled. "I bribed a morgue attendant. He falsified the paperwork, substituted another young blonde, a prostitute, with no family or friends. From there I left London, went to Grimsby, where—"

"Where a U-boat picked you up."

"Why, yes," Clara said.

"You planned the same route for Princess Elizabeth," Maggie realized.

"How did you know that?"

"Because I was there with her."

Clara raised one eyebrow, then opened her purse. There, glinting in the blue light, was the mother-of-pearl-handled gun. "I'm through with that life now. With those people." She picked the gun up.

"You're going to shoot me?" Maggie asked.

Clara studied her, then shook her head.

"Take me with you," she said, handing the gun over to Maggie. "To London. I can be extremely useful."

Mind spinning, Maggie accepted the gun. "You want to go to London?" she asked, incredulously. "They'll hang you there."

"No," Clara said firmly. "I possess too much information that they want. I'll be invaluable."

There was a soft sound. It was the young guard. His gun drawn, he entered the car. "*Was—?*" He stared at the two women.

"*Mein Gott,*" he whispered, clicking the safety off his Walther pistol.

"Put your gun down," Maggie said evenly.

"*Nein,*" the boy said, eyes blank with fear. He began to back out of the compartment. Maggie knew exactly what he intended to do—close the door and bolt it, then call for help. They would all be captured just hours before they reached the border.

"Stop!" she cried. "Please, stop." She took a step forward. "I don't want to have to shoot you. I don't want to hurt you."

He aimed the gun at Maggie's heart and fired. A stain, like a dark red rose, bloomed through the silk of her dress. And in that instant, she focused, aimed, and squeezed the trigger three times. As she'd been trained to do, she shot the boy once through the forehead, then twice through the heart.

He staggered from the impact of the shots. Life left his eyes. Then he fell to the floor.

Maggie's once-white dress was now stained red—with her blood, and with his, which had sprayed her. There was so much blood. Who knew humans contained so much blood?

Elise, aware her mother was no longer in their compartment, opened the door. She stood frozen in shock.

"Brava, darling. Perhaps you are your mother's daughter, after all," Clara said to Maggie. "Ah, Elise, how good of you to join us."

"You killed him," Elise accused Maggie shrilly. "You *killed* him." Then, to Clara, "And what are *you* doing here?"

"You didn't know? Your friend Frieda betrayed you. She let me know of your little nest of rats in the attic."

Maggie fell to her knees, gasping from pain. Her dress was soaked with blood. It was puddling under her, sticky and red.

Maggie had killed him. She'd killed a man. A boy, really. It was what she'd been trained to do, what Thorny had told her to do. "Kill the Kraut!" he'd thundered at Beaulieu. But she hadn't ever pictured "the Kraut" looking so young, so small, so vulnerable. "Elise," she said to the horrified girl, her voice weak now, "I'm . . ."

Still in shock, Elise released Ernst and then John from their cases. Swiftly appraising the situation, Ernst scrambled to Maggie and tugged off his jacket. "You can't die on me," he said firmly, pressing it against her wound. "I'm a doctor. We've come too far." John knelt, taking Maggie's hand in his.

"What are you doing here?" Elise repeated to Clara.

"Going to London with your half sister, *Mausi*. It's time for Mutti's third act."

Maggie looked up at Elise, whose mouth had fallen open in an expression of horror, as if she'd seen a monster. Their eyes met, then Maggie crumpled to the floor.

Chapter Twenty-one

Maggie opened her eyes. She saw nothing but blinding white. For a blissful moment, she didn't know where she was, or even who she was. Then the memories flooded through her.

She looked around and saw white sheets, a white enamel bed frame, white walls, white curtains, and, in a sky of dazzling blue outside the window, puffy white clouds. It was quiet. The air smelled of freshly laundered sheets. Through a haze of morphine, she saw an older woman, plump, with a kind face, dressed all in white, come toward her. "Mademoiselle Hope?" the nurse asked gently.

Maggie nodded. The slight movement set off a chain reaction of pain, which seemed centered in her abdomen.

The woman stood by her bed, her gray hair and eyes framed by a white, winged nurse's cap. "Mademoiselle Hope," she said in French, "you are in Universitätsspital Zürich—the University Hospital of Zürich. You sustained a gunshot wound to your right ribs. You will need to rest, but the doctors anticipate a full recovery."

"What about the others?" Maggie asked weakly.

"They survived. Monsieur Sterling and Dr. Klein have returned to London. And Mademoiselle Hess has returned to Berlin."

Elise! Maggie thought. A picture flashed of Elise's face—her

horror and disgust—when she'd seen Maggie shoot the boy. And
then when she learned they were sisters—

Maggie turned her face away. "And Madame Hess?"

The nurse shook her head. "A gentleman is here from Britain—
he will tell you the rest."

"How—how long have I been here?"

"You were brought in yesterday."

The events on the train came coursing back, horrific images she
could not obliterate. *What have I become?* Maggie wondered. She
looked down at her hands, remembering. They were clean now,
but she could still feel the blood, sticky and hot. Then she grabbed
the enamel basin on the bedside table and vomited. There was
nothing in her stomach, so she brought up bile, black and bitter.

The nurse held her shoulders as Maggie vomited, then brought
her cool water to drink, wiped her face with a cloth, and laid her
back against the pillow. "The bullet is still in you," the nurse
warned. Maggie touched her wound, probed it gently with her fingers. Yes, there, embedded in flesh, she could feel the hard outline
of the bullet. "The doctor will remove it later today," the nurse
continued. "It's a minor procedure."

"No."

The nurse looked surprised. "No?"

Maggie's face hardened. "I said no—leave it in."

A shadow appeared at the door. It was Sir Frank Nelson, Director of the SOE. "Leave us, please," he said to the nurse as he
removed his knife-creased hat. "May I get you anything, Miss
Hope? Water? Tea from the hospital cafeteria?"

Maggie's lips twisted as she remembered his asking her to make
him tea back in London, which now felt like an eternity ago. *My,
how the worm has turned,* she thought. But instead of feeling joy,
she felt nothing but numb.

Nelson closed the door. They were alone in the room. "Father Licht was able to get the film developed and the resulting information to Bishop von Preysing and Bishop von Galen."

"And what did the Bishops do with it?"

"They're going to speak out at High Mass today. By tonight, German resistance groups will have flyers of the homilies distributed all through Germany, and dropped on German troops. Hitler and his cronies will be exposed for the child murderers that they are."

"What about Gottlieb Lehrer?" Somehow, her own safety meant so little, knowing how much peril those two valiant men were in.

"Lehrer, I'm sorry to say, was killed by the SS. Or, rather, he committed suicide rather than be taken prisoner and have secrets tortured out of him. Father Licht is still safe, as far as we know."

Gottlieb? Dead? "But he's a Catholic. He would *never* commit suicide. He'd consider it a mortal sin."

"He saved the resistance group."

"But according to Catholic doctrine, he'll go to hell."

Nelson shrugged. "Maybe his version of hell wasn't as bad as what he was experiencing in Berlin. At any rate, surely God would take his motives for the greater good into consideration?"

Maggie said nothing. Gottlieb was dead. The German boy was dead. The little girl and her mother on the train were probably dead. Elise . . . She felt numb inside. Nelson reached for the enamel pitcher and poured her a cup of water. She waved it away.

"Miss Hope," Nelson said. "You were right to obtain that information and get it to Lehrer and his group. It wouldn't have done much good to us in Britain, and in fact might have backfired if we'd tried to use it—dismissed as mere propaganda. But directing the information into the hands of the German resistance movement, and letting a German Bishop expose what the Reich was doing . . . that's a coup. Against the rules, of course. But still, a coup. Brava."

"I don't give a flying fig about any coup." Maggie was fighting back tears. "What about the murders? Operation Compassionate Death? Has it been shut down?"

"Not yet," Nelson answered. "But it's only a matter of time now. The program will be officially shut down within days. But unofficially . . ." He shrugged again. "Hitler and his goons are capable of anything, as you now well know." He graced her with a sad smile.

Maggie stared up at the ceiling, eyes unseeing. The "units"— the children. Gottlieb, Elise. John, alive. The escape. Clara . . .

"How is"—Maggie didn't know what to call her—"Frau Hess?"

Nelson pulled up a metal chair, its legs scraping against the spotless linoleum. "Frau Hess is fine," he answered. "And she's an important Nazi official with any number of ties in Berlin. She could have returned to Germany. Instead, she deliberately surrendered herself to us."

"She did what?" Maggie wasn't sure if something had happened to her ears or if she'd been administered too much morphine.

"We were surprised as well. After all, she was on Churchill's most-wanted list. But after her plot with the London water supply failed—"

"Plot with the water supply?"

Nelson smiled. "Classified information, I'm afraid, Miss Hope. But I assure you that Clara Hess is in British custody. She's been transferred to the Tower of London, where she will be interrogated."

"What will happen to her?"

"She'll be imprisoned. If she's willing to work for us, she'll live. If not . . ."

Clara's unspoken fate hung in the air between them. Nelson pulled out a silver cigarette case and a lighter. "Do you mind?"

"Not at all."

He lit it, then watched the tip smolder before saying, "She had an unusual request."

"And what is that?"

"She wants to be interrogated by you, Miss Hope."

"Me?"

"You."

Maggie was silent.

"I suspect a game of some sort, quite frankly," Nelson continued. "As does Mr. Churchill. But we're not going to know what she has up her sleeve until you talk to her."

"I am *not* talking to her," Maggie spat. "I will never lay eyes on that woman, ever, ever again. Do you understand me?"

Nelson dropped his cigarette in the cup on Maggie's bedside. It hissed as it hit the water. He rose. "I'll leave you to get some rest, Miss Hope. You should be released today, and we've chartered a flight for you back to Britain tonight." He turned.

"I'm not going to talk to her! Never!"

"Feel better, Miss Hope," he said at the doorway.

"Wait!" she called. "What about John?"

"Mr. Sterling is fine. In fact, he's back in London now."

"And Ernst?"

"We were able to get him to London as well."

"And Elise?" Maggie asked in a small voice. "Did she really go back to Berlin?" If Elise had gone back to Germany, there would be no chance to talk to her, to explain . . .

Nelson nodded. "Yes, she decided she was needed in Berlin."

Maggie wished tears would fill her eyes, but they remained hot and dry. "Just go," she said. Nelson hesitated. Maggie threw the cup at him, splattering him with water and ashes. *"Go!"*

———

Elise sat in one of the pews at St. Hedwig's Cathedral for High Mass.

The cathedral was crowded—women in their best dresses and hats, men in suits, small children being shushed. The air was scented with candle wax and incense, and shafts of light pierced the edges of the boarded-up windows. The light danced over the floor, the pews, and the faces of the congregation.

There was a murmur in the crowd as Bishop von Preysing rose to give the homily.

And in the soaring space, the Bishop spoke. Within moments, Elise realized what he was talking about—that he had received the information about Charité and Hadamar from Father Licht, and had decided to publicly denounce Operation Compassionate Death.

He didn't mince words—and ended with "Woe to mankind and woe to our German nation if God's Holy Commandment 'Thou shalt not kill' is not only deliberately broken, and if this act of mass murder is not only tolerated, but allowed to continue."

Throughout the cathedral, there was stunned silence.

Women had tears running down their cheeks, while men looked on with pale faces and set jaws. In the back, one older woman fainted. She was helped up by two ushers and taken outside for air.

Bishop von Preysing put his hands together. "Let us pray."

Elise knelt and bent her head. She prayed for Gretel. She prayed for the deaf boy on the train. She prayed for all the murdered children.

She tried to pray for Maggie, and for her mother, but the words wouldn't come.

———

Copies of Bishop von Preysing's homily were distributed through-out Berlin. Bishop von Galen and other higher-ups in the Catholic Church also spoke out against Operation Compassionate Death, and copies of their homilies, too, were circulated.

Through the Solf Circle, the resistance group Father Licht belonged to, the British propaganda office obtained copies of the homilies and dropped flyers of them over German cities and German-occupied territories, to let the people know that their government was murdering children. There was rioting in Hadamar and Ansberg, and the other sites where Operation Compassionate Death was being carried out.

Adolf Hitler was about to give a speech at the Staatliches Hofbräuhaus in Munich, where in 1920 he had once proclaimed the twenty-five theses of the National Socialist program. Then, the assembled crowds had cheered and applauded. Now, two decades later, the people waited, stony-faced and silent, for their Führer.

Inside the Hofbräuhaus, the mood of the top Nazis was subdued. *"Mein Führer,"* Goebbels said. "Are you sure you want to do this—now?" Goebbels was keenly aware of the disposition of the crowd. They had heard or read the homilies. Many of them had relatives and friends who had "disappeared" to Hadamar, or one of the other institutes, only to be returned as ashes in a black urn.

"My people need me," Hitler replied, pushing back a limp lock of hair. "They may not know it, but they need me."

Goebbels knew better than to object. *"Ja, mein Führer,"* he answered, head bowed.

Hitler stepped out onto the balcony.

There was complete silence. Then, from the back, came one soft call of "Boo!"

Soon, the call was picked up by others in the crowd. "Boo! Boo!" they shouted. *"Boo!"* Hitler glared at his audience, daring them to continue—and yet they did. His composure began to melt.

He glared into the mass of people with his hypnotic silver eyes, but this time no one was mesmerized, no one was afraid.

They met his eyes, and still they called "Boo!"

The Führer opened his mouth to say something—then closed it. The booing continued, becoming louder and stronger. Abruptly, Hitler turned on his heel and left the balcony.

Once they realized what had happened, the crowd burst into applause. They applauded von Preysing, they applauded von Galen, and they applauded themselves. They had stood their ground. They had saved their friends and relatives. They congratulated themselves as they left the Hof: "Now the euthanasia program will end. Now our children are safe."

Inside, Hitler met with Goebbels, Bormann, Heydrich, and Himmler. "I want von Preysing arrested and executed!" the Führer screamed, pacing with his hands behind him, clasped so hard the knuckles were white. He was furious, forehead crawling with veins of rage.

He swept all of the items off the desktop in sudden, wrathful petulance—lamps and bronze figurines and teacups falling to the floor with an ominous crash. He flung open cabinet doors, just to slam them—hard. It was a temper tantrum of the worst kind, that of an adult.

"*Mein Führer,*" Goebbels soothed. "Would you like some tea?"

"*Nein!* I want von Galen and the rest of the clergy in handcuffs, *immediately*!"

"I say this as both a colleague and a friend. I don't think that would be prudent—at this time, that is." Goebbels was white with fear.

Hitler threw himself into a chair, head in hands. His uncanny understanding of mass psychology had failed him, and he was both enraged and hurt, as a favored child disciplined for the first time.

"They booed me," he muttered. "My people—my *volk*—they *booed* me. Me! Do you understand? That has never happened. Ever! How could they do that to *me*?" His metallic eyes darkened and flashed with hatred and hurt. "I am their *Führer*!"

"If we arrest von Preysing, von Galen, Delp, and the other high-ranking clergy," Goebbels said, "they become martyrs. Bavaria, especially, has a strong Catholic base. By taking the Bishops into custody, you risk alienating a huge source of your support. And we risk alienating the Pope. So far he's held his tongue, but . . ."

Hitler sat up. "The Pope will stay quiet, he always does. What do you suggest, then?"

"Publicly dismantle the Operation Compassionate Death program. But continue it in secret, of course. The clergy don't know a thing about eugenics. Or racial hygiene. Or economics, for that matter. But—for now—we need to appease them."

Hitler smiled. "We will give them some lessons . . ."

"Yes, *mein Führer*, when we've won the war, there will be time for lessons."

"In a generation or two, the clergy will all be dead and Jesus will be forgotten." Hitler's body, so taut before, started to relax. He looked to Goebbels. "That priest at St. Hedwig's—the one working with von Preysing—what's his name?"

"Father Johann Licht, *mein Führer*."

Hitler made a steeple of his fingers. "Someone must pay, and if it's not a Bishop—yet—it shall be a priest. Arrest him."

Reinhard Heydrich held many titles: SS-Obergruppenführer and General der Polizei, chief of the Reich Main Security Office and Stellvertretender Reichsprotektor of Bohemia and Moravia. He was also a consummate athlete—fencer, boxer, cross-country skier. Whenever possible, he preferred to be moving. This need, plus the demand for utter secrecy, was why he often conducted meetings on horseback.

It was early, well before the start of the workday, but the air was already shimmering with heat. Dew-covered spiderwebs glittered on the grass. Heydrich rode through the lime and chestnut trees in the Tiergarten with Adolf Eichmann, the "Czar of the Jews." Both men were dressed in traditional riding garb: black velvet–covered helmets, jackets, breeches, leather gloves, tall black boots, and riding crops. Their horses were proud and noble stallions.

"I spoke with Göring yesterday," Heydrich said. His seat was impeccable. "He wants to know where we are with the Jewish question." He pursed his lips. "As you know, it's complicated. No country wants them, even Britain. Even the mighty United States of America won't take any more than her usual quota. Don't forget about the MS *St. Louis*."

Eichmann put his heels into the horse's flanks to keep up. "I was able to get three thousand smuggled into Britain, but, as you know, that's a drop in the proverbial bucket."

"Where are we with the Madagaskar Projekt?" Heydrich asked.

"The Madagascar Project was an option when we thought we could take Britain easily. No one expected her to hold out this long. But as long as the British navy is still fighting, we can't afford the risk to our own ships." The horse whinnied and twitched his ears but increased his pace.

"What of the cleansings in Poland?"

"They're proving to be inefficient—shooting is too time-consuming, too hard on the morale of the soldiers involved. There are just too many Jews. If we can't get the Jews out, we'll have to deal with them. Somehow."

Heydrich pulled on his horse's reins, to slow down. The horse, unhappy, flicked his tail, but obeyed. "Tell me about Operation Compassionate Death."

Eichmann shrugged. "It's officially been closed down. Of course, unofficially, it still exists. 'Life unfit for life' is now being poisoned or starved in secret—instead of gassed."

Heydrich considered. "What if we look to Operation Compassionate Death as an inspiration? We might be able to improve upon its efficiency."

"Go on."

"If we used a faster-acting and more powerful poison, for example, we could speed up the process of extermination."

"We could get Mennecke on that," Eichmann said. "I hear they've done experiments with something called Zyklon B gas on Gypsies at Buchenwald. But what about disposal? Disposal of the units was the real issue with Operation Compassionate Death."

Heydrich whipped the flank of his horse. "Well, isn't that why we have *Lebensraum?*"

"What do you mean?"

"Most of the concentration camps are in Poland, under our control and well away from the German population, unlike Hadamar and the rest. We will have enough room and privacy to dispose of as many units as we need to. No moralistic Germans to interfere out there. It's like America's Wild West."

"Excellent, excellent idea!" Heydrich slapped Eichmann on the back, and gave one of his winning grins. "Of course, we'll need to discuss it with the Führer and the others. In the meantime, get plans from Kurt Gerstein and some of the other Reich scientists. I want numbers. How fast can we actually do this? How many units can we process per day?"

They dug the heels of their riding boots into their horses' flanks and turned back toward the stables. "Once I get those figures and have the Führer's approval, I can call a meeting—the official villa in Wannsee would be perfect, don't you think?" Eichmann said.

"We could make a weekend of it." He smiled. "And when the war is over, I've already made sure that the villa will be mine."

The SS arrested Father Licht and took him to Gestapo headquarters at No. 8 Prinz-Albrecht-Strasse. "Look at the parson in the Easter bonnet!" one of the SS officers called, referring to Licht's black biretta, as the handcuffed priest walked in.

The Gestapo was a law unto itself, free from condemnation by the German legal system. Licht was interrogated, then taken to Columbia-Haus, the Gestapo prison center in Berlin, notorious for the screaming that could be heard coming from its windows.

All of this and worse Father Licht endured, without giving up any information on the von Solf Circle. Returning to his cell, naked, bruised, and bloody, he would drop to his knees and pray.

When they realized they would get nothing from him, the SS decided he should be sent to Dachau. At least twenty prisoners were being dispatched that day, taken by the SS to the Grunewald train station.

"Come on, come on," one of the SS officers grumbled as the prisoners scrambled out of the back of the van. He hit the men with his nightstick to get them to move faster.

Father Licht kept his eyes down as they waited in line to march to the train platform. "Off with the hat! Take off your hat, Father!"

Father Licht continued to look down into the tracks, unmoving.

With his nightstick, the SS officer poked at the priest's black biretta, knocking it off. The hat fell, turning over and over in the air, until it came to rest on the tracks below.

The train pulled into the station, crushing the felt hat beneath its wheels. Licht turned to the SS officer. "God be with you, my son."

The man blinked, years of Catholic school and Masses bringing the words to his lips out of habit. "And also with you, Father."

Chapter Twenty-two

David's parents collected him at Guy's Hospital and took him back to his flat in Knightsbridge. Mr. Greene helped him into his freshly made bed while Mrs. Greene hovered. "Are you all right, darling? Do you want one of your pain tablets? Some water? A cup of tea?"

"A cup of tea would be lovely, Mother, thank you," David said, as he lay back against the pillows. That left him alone with his father.

"By the way, do you have my glasses, Father?"

Mr. Greene reached into his breast pocket and handed the wire-framed spectacles to David. "Your—Mr. Wright, that is—held on to them for you. He gave them to me to give to you."

David settled them on his nose. "Yes, that's better. I can see clearly now."

The two men sat in silence until Mrs. Greene returned with the tea tray. "Here you go, darling," she said, pouring a cup and handing it to David.

"Thank you, Mother."

Mrs. Greene seemed nervous and Mr. Greene uncomfortable. "We'd better let you rest now, darling."

David put down the cup. "There's one thing I want to say to you. To both of you." His parents stood very still.

"A bad thing happened to me. A very bad thing. But I lived

through it, and came out the other side. And now, I have a better idea of what's important to me. As we know all too well these days, life is finite. A random German bomb—or an angry stranger—can change things in an instant."

"David—" Mr. Greene began.

"No, I want to say this. I need to say this. My life, until now— even with the war—has been a series of parties and dances and good times. I thought a certain, shall we say, *standard* of life was imperative. But then, I believed I was lost, about to die. And do you know what I thought about? You and Mother. My friends. And, yes—Freddie."

"Oh, for heaven's sake," Mr. Greene said, turning to go.

"Wait, Benjamin," Mrs. Greene said. "Let him finish."

"Thanks, Mother." David took a breath. "And so, while I've definitely enjoyed my flat and my car and my trips and my par- ties—I now realize that's not what really matters in life. People matter. And to me, Freddie matters most of all. I love him. And he loves me. And if that means I forfeit my trust fund, my inheri- tance, so be it. I have a job, I can support myself. And I can live the kind of life I want to live."

Mr. Greene couldn't take any more of this. "You'll be arrested! And worse . . ."

"I appreciate your concern, Papa, I really do. But Freddie and I are careful. There are a lot of us in London, who are very, very careful. And we can live good lives, productive lives." He thought of Kay and Daphne. "Happy lives."

"Oh, David . . ." Mrs. Greene wept, reaching out to stroke his hair.

"I'm sorry, but this is the kind of life I choose for myself, no matter what the consequences." He turned over. "And now I'd like to get some sleep, please."

———

Back in London, after being debriefed and taking a few days to recover, Maggie knew what she had to do. There was no question who she wanted: John. And there was no question that the proper thing to do, before things with John proceeded any further, was to break things off with Hugh.

She called and asked him to meet her at a neutral spot—the Caxton Bar at St. Ermin's, a Queen Anne–style hotel in Westminster. She arrived early and sat at a small table. Hugh came up behind her and placed his hands on her shoulders. "Hello, Maggie," he said in her ear.

In one movement, she stood and turned—ready to take him down. The other patrons in the bar looked up and fell silent.

"It's just me." Hugh held up his hands and smiled. "Sorry to startle you."

"Of course," Maggie said, relaxing and embracing him. They kissed cheeks and sat. A waiter came by, and they ordered pink gins. As the silence between them grew, Maggie took a cigarette and lighter from her purse.

"Since when do you smoke?" Hugh asked.

"Since I returned from Berlin," she said, lighting up.

The silence turned uncomfortable. "I'm glad to see you, Hugh," Maggie said finally, resting her cigarette in the ashtray. Her wound ached and she was struggling not to cry. This would not be easy.

The waiter set down their drinks. "Thanks," Hugh told him. "And I'm glad to see you, too. I was worried."

"I was doing"—Maggie picked up the cigarette again and tapped ashes into the lead-crystal ashtray—"my job. It just happened to take a bit longer than expected."

Another awkward silence. Hugh sipped his drink. "So," he said. "I hear John's alive. Good for him."

"Yes. Finding that out was quite a shock. Along with many, many shocks."

"I heard about that, too. You met your half sister. And now Clara Hess is in British custody."

Maggie smiled wanly. "And I hear you had a little something to do with that. I didn't realize you were quite so . . . photogenic. I would love to have seen the look on her face when she saw those photos you sent."

Hugh cleared his throat and loosened his tie. "Er, yes, well—" He picked up his pink gin. "Probably not my 'finest hour.' "

"I don't know," Maggie disagreed. "You didn't exactly follow protocol, but it was immensely satisfying, I'm sure." She smiled. "I wish I could have been there."

"Me, too." Hugh grinned. "It was amazing. Of course, now I'm unemployed. Masterman very nearly sent me to the Tower of London to be beheaded. He was apoplectic."

"What about Frain—surely he'll take you back? You and Mark could be together again—I'm sure he's missed you."

"Alas, no—I can't go back to MI-Five. My 'reckless behavior' and 'letting the personal get in the way of the professional' has me blacklisted in Intelligence now."

"I'm sorry."

"It's not your fault."

"What will you do?"

"Join the army, most likely." Hugh arched an eyebrow. "Or maybe the Royal Air Force. Pilots are popular with the ladies these days, you know."

Maggie bit her lip. She'd forgotten how handsome he was. But she couldn't falter now . . . "That's something we need to talk about—"

"Look, Maggie," Hugh said, taking her hand. "Do what you need to do. I don't want to stand in your way."

Maggie's eyes swam with tears. "You were *never* in the way, Hugh."

"You need to see where things are with John. If you didn't, I'd always feel like your second choice."

"You could never, ever, be second anything, Hugh," she protested fervently. "I want you to know that." She crushed out her cigarette and downed the rest of her drink. She stood up, kissed his cheek, and left.

Hugh opened his mouth, as if to say more, then closed it. He sat back, then shook his head, swallowing hard. "First no job, and now no girl. Perfect," he muttered. "Bloody perfect."

From behind him a voice asked, "Is this seat taken?" The man the voice belonged to was young and very tall, with a sharp part in his wavy brown hair, a crimson bow tie, and matching, double-point pocket square.

Hugh looked up and shrugged. "It's all yours."

The man joined him at the little table. "Let me buy you a drink," he said. "You look like you could use one."

"I could." Hugh took the man's measure: a confident Oxbridge graduate, probably rich, most likely well-connected. "And you are?"

The man held out his hand. "Kim Philby."

As John had been presumed dead, his parents had let go of the lease on his apartment. He had nowhere to live. Until a fellow RAF pilot offered up his second-floor efficiency on a tree-lined street in Notting Hill.

Late that night, Maggie rang the buzzer, then climbed three flights of stairs.

John opened the door. He was unshaven, eyes sunken with weariness and a deep sadness. Then his face lit up. "Well, hello there."

Maggie smiled back. "Hello there, yourself."

He took her hand and pulled her inside. The apartment was clublike, with tufted leather furniture, wide plank oak floors covered by worn Persian carpets, thick drapes, and clutter—books and gilt-framed etchings and blue and white Chinese urns. But Maggie was oblivious to her surroundings.

They kissed with a longing so deep it made her knees wobble. John wrapped her in his arms. "Finally . . ."

Somehow they maneuvered down the narrow hallway to the bedroom, where they ended up on his bed, kissing hard, clothing discarded piece by piece.

John leaned over her and, with a fingertip, slowly traced the curve of her cheek. Maggie tried to speak, but couldn't. She wrapped her arms around him, taking the hardness of his body into her arms.

A clock ticked on the mantel and a breeze from a half-opened window blew over them. John's hand grazed Maggie's ribs. "Ow!" she yelped.

He pulled back instantly. "Oh, sorry—did I hurt you?"

"The bullet's still there," she said, propping herself up on her elbows. "I've decided to leave it in."

"Why on earth would you do that?"

"It's my . . . Berlin souvenir," she answered lightly.

"Since we're doing show-and-tell, here are my stitches," he told her, raising his vest. "Surgery from a lacerated kidney. I'm sure it will fade in time, but I'll always have a scar."

They lay back on the bed, silenced by the enormity of their memories, their scars. What had happened in Berlin, what had happened on the train. In a low voice John said, "I don't want to be alone."

"You don't ever have to be alone ever again," Maggie said softly. "I'm not going anywhere."

"I want you to know," he said, "that everything is, ahem, in working order."

"What?"

"That my injuries from the crash landing—nothing was damaged beyond repair. Everything is . . . fully functional."

"Ah," Maggie said, "good to know."

They were both young, but they were both exhausted. "I'm glad to know all is in working order," she said. "So why don't we sleep now and test everything out tomorrow?"

"Oh, thank God," John said. "I want our first time to be special." He turned over, put his arm around her, buried his face in her hair, and fell asleep instantly. He was restless in his sleep and called out in nightmares, but kept his arm around her. Maggie stayed awake a bit longer, listening for planes overhead, unable to relax.

In the morning John rolled over and kissed her on the lips. "Before we, you know, there's something I need to tell you," Maggie murmured.

"What's that?" he said, kissing her shoulder blade.

"While you were . . . gone, I saw someone. We . . . stepped out together."

"What?" John said, distracted.

"His name is Hugh Thompson. He was my handler at Windsor. Last night I'd just come from breaking up with him."

"*What?*" John repeated. He stood and started to pace. He spun to face her. "Are you—are you joking?"

"I'm sorry, John. But it's the truth. And I wanted to tell you earlier, but there was never the right time. And I've broken things off with him."

"The fact that you were with him in the first place—" His face was mottled with anger. "I was in hell in Berlin. Literally *in hell*. Only the thought of you kept me sane—and barely, at that. And there you were, safe and sound in England, off frolicking with some . . ."

Maggie got off the bed and went to him. "I'm sorry, John."

"Did you sleep with him?"

Maggie saw no reason to lie. "Yes."

He jerked as if she'd struck him. "Your first time was with *him*?"

Wait, why am I being treated as if I've done something wrong? "We all thought you were *dead*, John!"

He went to the fireplace and picked up the poker by the key handle. He took it and swung it against the wall. The plaster cracked. He swung again. This time a large chunk of plaster crumbled to the floor, leaving bare bricks exposed. He turned to face her. "And it took you, what, all of five minutes to get over me?"

"I *never* stopped loving you," Maggie said, eyes swimming with tears.

"It was the thought of you—*you*—that kept me going in that hell. That kept me fighting."

He stayed true to me, against unbearable odds, while I had just . . . moved on. "I'm sorry. I'm so sorry. All I can say, again, is that we thought you were dead."

John continued to pace, both hands running through his hair until it was standing on end. "And you killed someone! You shot a man, in cold blood! I don't know you anymore."

Now it was her turn for anger. "How *dare* you judge me? You've killed any number of people. But you were up in a plane, so you didn't have to see it. And it's not as if you're some sort of blushing virgin yourself—"

John took another swing at the wall with the poker. There was a terrible noise, and more plaster rained down, revealing the brick wall beneath. "I'd appreciate it if you left," he said, turning.

Maggie was suddenly frightened of him, frightened of the strange look on his face. The humor, the joy, the *life*, had vanished from his eyes. She wanted the old John back, arrogant, infuriating, mocking. And she wanted, more than anything, to be the girl she used to be. But they had both seen too much, done too much. They knew too much about each other.

She wiped tears from her eyes, then straightened. "Of course," she said.

Chapter Twenty-three

Chuck, almost nine months pregnant, her handsome face plump and glowing with good health, bustled about the kitchen in her flat with her usual mix of cheer and pragmatism. "Sit down, sit down, Maggie," she clucked, trying to tie an apron around her middle and then giving up. "Nothing fits anymore," she groaned. "Now you sit down and we'll talk."

"I wish we could talk. But I'm not allowed to say anything. About anything."

"Well," Chuck said, cheerfully rattling the tea things, "why don't you start with telling me how you feel. No state secrets there, right?"

"May I help? Really, in your condition—"

"Oh, in my condition—that's just silly. I actually feel better up and moving. It's when I sit down that I start to feel overwhelmed." Chuck poured hot water from the kettle into the teapot and then brought the tray to the table. "Now, tell your old flatmate what's on your mind." She handed Maggie a cup and saw how raw her friend's face was with hurt and anger.

"I don't feel like myself anymore," Maggie confessed. "All I want to do is cry. And sleep. I don't want to talk, I don't want to eat, I don't want to leave my room. I'm a stranger in my own mind."

"You've seen things you wish you hadn't," Chuck said bluntly, taking a sip of tea. "Of course you have demons."

Maggie laugh-snorted. "Of a sort."

"We all have demons, you know." Chuck was a pediatric nurse at Great Ormond Street Hospital. Of course she had her own demons.

"Not the simple girls." Maggie shook her head. "Simple girls don't have demons. Simple girls want to have fun, whatever that is. My whole life I've been an overachiever—and what has it done for me? Nowhere. Nothing. Remember the twins?" The twins Clarabelle and Annabell had lived with Maggie and Chuck last summer. She laughed, a harsh laugh. "The twins were simple girls. Flat as paper dolls. Only worried about boys and clothes . . ."

"Perhaps," Chuck agreed. "But you don't know what was really in their hearts and minds."

"I wish I were a simple girl," Maggie said. "That I could amputate all my ambition. But I can't. It's too late now. And now, because I tried for too much, I'm ruined inside. I'm broken."

"I've seen soldiers come back like this, Maggie," Chuck said, reaching out a hand. "Shell shock is what we call it. Father Time is your best healer."

"Maybe there's something to be found in literature. After all, Dickens believed that both Scrooge and Tiny Tim could be saved. In Nazi Germany, they'd gas Tiny Tim dead, burn his body, and send his ashes up and out a chimney. They'd send Scrooge to a concentration camp in Poland."

"A little bird told me you still have that bullet in your body. As a friend and a nurse, darling, I have to tell you, it has no business being there." Chuck pointed her finger.

Maggie's hand went to her side. She could feel the bullet under the skin. "It stays."

"For heaven's sake, why?"

"Chuck, it has everything to do with everything I'm not allowed to say. Horrible things. Things that I'll feel guilty over for the rest of my life, and then take to my grave. Because of what I've seen, what I've done, I'm a walking corpse now. I'm dead inside. I can't feel anything anymore. I'm trying to hold myself together with glue and it's not working. I'm falling apart. My center, as they say, will not hold."

"What about your studies? Maths?"

"Math. I used to be able to count on math! Two and two made four, and so on. There was always an answer. Nietzsche says that God is dead—but for me now, science is dead, too. Or at least contaminated and perverted."

Even math and science have betrayed me, Maggie thought. *The arrogance of those people, using science, misusing science . . .* She remembered the problem about the working families and the asylum and buried her head in her hands and began to cry, shoulders shuddering with choked-back sobs. Now she didn't even have math and science to believe in.

Chuck let Maggie cry. Then she asked, "So what are you going to do?"

"Mope," Maggie said, wiping at her face. "I've discovered I'm quite talented at moping. And napping. And listening to *It's That Man Again* on the wireless. A bit of whining thrown in for good measure."

"What about your job?"

"What about my job?" Maggie shrugged. "I'm no good to anyone like this."

"Well, they can't kick you out for being traumatized on one of their own missions."

Maggie shook her head. "I've gone on too much about myself. I'm sorry."

"It's all right, darling," Chuck said. "We're old friends, after all."

Maggie looked down at Chuck's baby bump. "And now you and Nigel have added a new person to the historical line."

Chuck rubbed her hands over her abdomen protectively. "It's exciting. A bit terrifying, too."

"Nonsense," Maggie said. "You and Nigel will be wonderful parents."

"Maggie," Chuck said, "I'd understand if it's too much. . . . But, after the baby's born, we'd like to have a christening, and then a little party afterward. I know you're not feeling yourself again yet. . . . But you're invited, and very much wanted."

Maggie reached over impulsively to hug her friend. "I'll do everything I can to be there, dear Chuck."

Chapter Twenty-four

Six underground stops away from Westminster Cathedral was Postman's Park. Which was where Maggie went, instead of Nigel and Chuck's baby's christening.

It was a tiny green plot in central London, just a short walk from St. Paul's Cathedral, where the churchyards of St. Leonard, St. Botolph, and Aldersgate, and the graveyard of Christ Church, Newgate Street, converged. Everyone called it Postman's Park because so many of the nearby postal workers had their lunch there, but officially it was known as George Frederic Watts's Memorial to Heroic Self Sacrifice. It was a small spot, humble, and easy to miss in the midst of the City's rushing self-importance.

In a corner of the park, hidden under a canopy, were beautiful handmade painted tiles by William De Morgan, a contemporary of William Morris's. Each tile was a memorial to someone who sacrificed his or her life to save another.

This was where Frain proposed that he and Maggie meet. Despite being so close to Fleet Street, it was quiet in Postman's Park. And although the air was cool, it smelled of grass and soil warmed by the sun. Frain, who'd been sitting on one of the benches and reading *The Times*, stood when Maggie appeared. He looked as he always did, like an aging matinee idol—his hair sleek, his suit pressed perfectly, and his handmade Italian shoes impeccably shined. His eyes were the same, too: gray and hard as slate.

"This had better be good," Maggie said, sitting and taking out a cigarette.

Frain sat back down and took out his lighter for her. The wheel struck the flint, producing a blue and yellow flame. "Thank you," she said as she inhaled, both of them watching the tip ignite into red.

"Since when do you smoke?" Frain asked.

"Since when are you so curious about my personal habits?" she retorted. Then, "Since I returned from Berlin."

"I see," Frain said. Then, "Thank you for agreeing to meet me here."

"Did I have a choice?" Maggie was exhausted—her face was drawn, with smudges of purple under her eyes. She had lost the plushness of youth.

"Of course you do. But since I was the one who originally brought you into the spy game, I do feel a certain amount of responsibility to you." Frain lit his own cigarette. "How are you?"

"I'm getting through, one hour at a time. No, let me rephrase that—one minute at a time."

She wouldn't look Frain in the eye, and instead glanced over at the painted tiles. *"William Donald of Bayswater aged nineteen, railway clerk, was drowned in the Lea trying to save a lad from a dangerous entanglement of weed. July sixteenth, 1876,"* she read aloud. *"George Lee, fireman. At a fire in Clerkenwell carried an unconscious girl to the escape falling six times and died of his injuries. July twenty-sixth, 1876. Elizabeth Boxall aged seventeen, of Bethnal Green who died of injuries received in trying to save a child from a runaway horse. June twentieth, 1888."* Maggie gave a delicate snort. "It's a bit macabre, no?"

"Actually," disagreed Frain, "I think it's rather beautiful."

"Didn't realize you had a ghoulish streak, Peter."

"Unlike these poor souls, you didn't die, Maggie. But I want you to know that I understand the sacrifice you made. That you're still making. That you will continue to make."

She finally fixed her gaze on him. "You knew all along, didn't you? You and Churchill."

There was no "Mr. Churchill" anymore.

"About my father and my mother. *That's* why I was hired for the secretary job in the first place. *That's* why I was able to become a spy. *That's* why I was sent to Berlin. I was bait to bring Clara in." She stared at the tiles, no longer seeing the litany of heroics. "You both used me. And, worst of all, I let you. I was an ambitious young thing and I believed in the cause. I wanted to be a patriot." Her lips twisted in a smile. "Ha!"

"Maggie." Frain searched for the right words. "I was hoping that you'd never learn the truth, but it was inevitable, I see now. Now you know. And now you have to deal with what's been uncovered."

"Well, I have a fantastic way to 'deal with it,' as you so ambiguously say—I quit." She threw her half-smoked cigarette down and ground it savagely under her heel.

Frain sighed. "It's not that simple, Maggie."

"Well, let me make it that simple for you. I quit. I resign. I'm walking away. You can find someone else to get information out of that woman. Because I'm never going to speak to her, ever again."

"I'm not sure that anyone else can. She'll only talk to you. And if she doesn't talk, she'll be executed."

"That's not my problem—I quit, remember?"

"You can't quit, Maggie," Frain said. "You're a spook now. You're part of a family."

"Don't you *dare* talk to me about 'family'!"

"When you first started with Churchill you were certainly smart, but unfocused, a bit unformed. Frankly, I didn't know if you had what it takes to work in Intelligence—whether you had the skills, the cunning to survive. But the way you handled yourself in Berlin shows us that you're the whole package now. Look at yourself. You're strong, capable, and yes, even ruthless. You should be proud of how far you've come."

"I don't want to be ruthless," Maggie shot back. "I never wanted to be ruthless. I want to be ruthful. Full of ruth, in fact."

"I understand that you're upset. But it will be worth it when we win this war."

"Look, Peter," Maggie said bitterly. "I've changed. I've done things I never thought I was capable of doing. I killed a man. A boy, really. He's dead now—because of me. Me! His blood is on my hands, and I'll think of him for as long as I live."

"He was the enemy."

"That's nonsense! He was a boy. A boy! A scared little boy, with the rest of his life ahead of him."

"A boy who was willing to kill you."

"Because he *had* to. Because that's what he was brainwashed to do. That's the world we live in now. Just a few years ago, we might have been friends."

"And that's the world we're fighting for," Frain argued. "But, for now, you must . . . turn your heart to stone. We don't have time right now for guilt or empathy or compassion. You must set aside your moral compass—and do whatever it takes—to win."

"'*Battle not with monsters, lest ye become a monster.*'" Maggie stood and smoothed her skirt. "If I set aside my moral compass, doesn't that mean we've already lost?" She blinked back hot tears. "Just as I've lost a sister. She thinks I'm a monster, you know. And then there's Gottlieb—" Her voice broke. "Gottlieb is dead now. Because of me."

"No." Frain shook his head. "Gottlieb is dead because he was a German resistance fighter who, unfortunately, was caught."

"He didn't want me to stay. He didn't want me to work for Oberg."

"If you hadn't worked for Oberg, you'd never have found the files that you were able to pass on to the resistance circle."

"He's dead," Maggie insisted dully. "Just like that boy is dead."

Frain leaned back, studying the tip of his cigarette. "We're part of the same club now, Maggie. It's the club no one realizes exists before they're in it. And it's the club no one with any sanity would want to be a part of. But now we're in it. Together."

"The murderers' club. Yes, I'm a card-carrying member now. How absolutely wonderful for us. Is there a secret handshake? A certificate? A medal, perhaps?"

"You need some time. You need to heal."

"I'm just so tired." She slumped down on the bench. "Can't you understand that? I'm tired—exhausted—in the very marrow of my bones." Then, "That boy's face haunts me."

"I know," he said. "I know. But we need *you*."

She stabbed a finger at him. "You need my access to Clara."

"We need you."

"But I don't need you. I've already spoken with Lord Nelson, and I'm going back to Arisaig, to the training camp. It was peaceful there. I can teach the new recruits. Get them into shape. Run along the Scottish coast. That's all I can handle right now."

"Of course. Run the beaches, get your head together. But I'll be in touch."

"Don't be. I'm serious."

"Listen to me, Maggie Hope. I'm older than you. I've seen things you can't even begin to imagine. I've done things that make me want to smash my head against a wall and howl. I know I have the reputation for being cold and calculating—ruth*less*, if you will. I follow my brain, not my heart—and certainly not my conscience. But one thing I'm sure of in this war is *you*."

Maggie gave a harsh laugh. "Flattering words, Peter, and a few months ago, they would have done the trick. But I don't want to be a 'warrior' anymore. So—no. Thank you."

Frain rose and held out his hand. "And I don't want to be this dashing and debonair. But we all have our crosses to bear."

Maggie smiled, finally. She grasped his hand. It was strong and warm. She rose as well.

"Go to Scotland," Frain said, clapping her on the back. "Whip those trainees into shape, get your head together. In a few months, I'll give you a call and we'll see where you are. Oh—and get that bullet removed."

Maggie put her hand to her side instinctively. "How do you know about my bullet?"

Frain crushed his cigarette beneath the sole of his shoe. "I'm in Intelligence—it's my job to know everything. And it's damned stupid to keep that thing inside of you."

"I'm quite fond of it now."

"You're plucky, Maggie—I'll give you that."

"Oh, Peter, please don't call me plucky. I *hate* being called plucky. Plucky is for Pollyanna heroines who stomp their feet, and toss their hair, and put their hands on their hips. Even if I ever used to be like that, I'm far too damaged now."

"Give it time." He tipped his hat. She nodded. After a long, hard look at each other, they turned and walked in opposite directions.

Chapter Twenty-five

The christening supper was held at Chuck and Nigel's flat. It was a simple affair—weak tea, Lord Woolton pie, and victory buns. There was a knock at the door. When Nigel went to open it, Maggie stood there.

"Sorry I'm late," she apologized, raising on tiptoe to kiss Nigel on the cheek. She took off her gloves and unpinned her hat, which he took. "And sorry I missed the ceremony."

"We're glad you could make it, Maggie," Chuck said as she hugged her friend.

"Of course!" Maggie said, a little too brightly, handing Chuck a gift wrapped in gilt paper. "Congratulations on Griffin's baptism. Where's the darling boy?"

"The little bunny's napping right now." Chuck led Maggie inside. "Poor thing's completely knackered from his big day. May I get you something? Tea?" Around the table were John, David, Freddie, and Ernst, as well as Mr. and Mrs. Greene. The men rose at her arrival.

"How lovely to see you all again," Maggie said stiffly. She spotted an open champagne bottle. "Fizz?"

"Coming right up, darling!" Nigel said.

"Sit down, darling," Chuck said. Maggie obeyed, sitting next to Ernst at the linen-swathed table, across from David and Freddie.

John had a blank look on his face, hard and cold, the kind of look Maggie imagined he'd had as he flew into battle.

"We were just talking about Ernst's next move," David said, realizing Maggie's discomfort and trying to smooth things over. "Since he's a doctor, a surgeon at that, he's volunteered for active medic duty. He'll be working on the front lines."

"Ernst, you're a Jew, yes?" Mr. Greene asked.

"Yes, sir," Ernst answered. "And if not for Elise and Maggie, I'd be in a concentration camp by now. Or worse. And, because of your son, and his connections with Number Ten, I'll be able to use my skills to help save British soldiers."

"David," Mr. Greene said, "is that true? Did you arrange that?"

"I see no reason why Ernst should be stuck in an internment camp. So I put in a word with the P.M."

The Greenes exchanged a significant look. "You've saved a Jew," his father said.

His mother put a hand over her heart. "It's a *mitzvah*."

"That's wonderful, Ernst," Maggie said, accepting the glass of champagne Nigel offered.

"You must have left family behind in Berlin?" Mr. Greene said.

"Benjamin," Mrs. Greene warned. "He might not want to talk about it."

"I did," Ernst replied. "My beautiful and brave wife, Frieda."

"Frieda?" Mrs. Greene's forehead creased. "Surely that's not a Jewish name?"

"No," Ernst said. "Frieda is Lutheran. And blond and blue-eyed at that. Which is why I think—I pray—she will be safe. David even arranged for her to know that I'm safe."

"Well," Mrs. Greene said, giving her husband a significant look, "it's a brave new world, isn't it?"

David grinned. "And John's coming back to Number Ten, right, old boy?"

"My plans are . . . uncertain." He refused to meet Maggie's eyes. "But yes, at least for the present, I'll be back working at Number Ten."

David broke the awkward silence. "And what are you doing, Mags? Can you tell us?"

"I'm going to Scotland. Really and truly," Maggie answered, draining the rest of her glass. "Taking a bit of a working sabbatical."

"Well, you've earned it, certainly." Chuck reached over to squeeze her hand.

"Please," Maggie said, desperate to change the subject, "open Griffin's gift."

The gold paper fell away to reveal a tiny blue hat and scarf. "Oh, how lovely!" Chuck exclaimed. "Did you knit it yourself?"

Maggie nodded.

David leaned over to take a look. "A few off stitches there, Mags. Not that I could do better, of course."

"Not off stitches, David—it's code, actually. Morse code."

"Ooooh!" Chuck said. "How fantastic! What does it say?"

"Well," Maggie said, "on the hat is *Griffin Nigel Ludlow, first of September 1941*. And, on the scarf—where I had a bit more room— is a Christina Rossetti poem." Maggie recited. "*Who has seen the wind? Neither I nor you: But when the leaves hang trembling, The wind is passing through. Who has seen the wind? Neither you nor I: But when the trees bow down their heads, The wind is passing by.*"

Chuck nodded, pleased. "You may become a believer yet!"

"Maybe." Maggie gave a rueful smile. "I am, perhaps, more like our Prime Minister—who says that while he's not a pillar of the Church, he *is* a flying buttress."

Nigel cleared his throat. "Today, we celebrate young Griffin's joining the Catholic faith. But let us also celebrate the fact that we're together—Christian, Jew, and agnostic. British and German."

Maggie looked over at David and Freddie and winked. *"Like that" and not "like that,"* she thought. David winked back. After all, Chuck and Nigel, not to mention Ernst, didn't know David's secret.

Nigel refilled everyone's champagne, and Chuck served bread and apple pudding, with mock cream. When the plates were cleared, Chuck smothered a prodigious yawn.

"I think," suggested Mrs. Greene, "we should leave the young parents now. I'll take care of the dishes, my dear," she told Chuck. "You go and lie down while you can."

"Miss Hope," John said to Maggie, rising.

Oh, so we're back to "Miss Hope" now. Maggie nodded. "Mr. Sterling." *Well, at least that's over with,* she thought, her heart thudding.

She realized that the champagne, on an empty stomach with only a few bites of cake, had gone to her head. The room was tilting at an odd angle. *Stop it, room.*

In the foyer, everyone kissed Chuck and Nigel goodbye. "Here are your things, Maggie," Chuck said, handing Maggie her hat and gloves.

The group made it through the front door, and then with more goodbyes, to David's parents and Ernst, it was just David and Freddie, and Maggie and John, left standing on the pavement. "Rose and Crown, anyone?" David asked, to break the silence.

"Why, David Greene, I do believe you're trying to get me drunk!" Maggie said with forced gaiety. She sounded like a tipsy Scarlett O'Hara.

"Since I can't drink for a while, due to my still-healing liver, someone should do the honors for me." David offered her his arm. "Shall we?"

At the Rose and Crown, their haunt when they'd all worked together at Number Ten, David ordered drinks. Maggie downed her half-pint, then reached over for David's and downed that as well. She set the glass down with a thump. Her head was spinning. "Get me another, love?" she said to David. Then, to the group, "I think I'll just step out for a moment—get a little fresh air." Freddie, David, and John all rose as she stumbled to her feet.

"Would you like some company, Maggie?" Freddie asked.

"Oh, no, Freddie darling, I'll be fine. Just need a minute or two. A bit stuffy in here is all." She put her arm on his. "Have I ever told you how happy I am for you, Freddie?" she slurred. "Love—it's so lovely to see people in love. I love *love*." She kissed him noisily and then, carefully, made her way to the entrance.

There, on the bench outside, sat Hugh.

"You!" Maggie exclaimed, managing to sit beside him without falling. "What are *you* doing here?"

"It's my business to find people, remember?" he replied. "And I wanted to talk to you before you left. I heard about Scotland— wanted to say goodbye is all."

"Well, well—it seems that everyone in London now knows I smoke, have a bullet lodged somewhere inside me, and that I'm going to Scotland."

He studied her closely. "Are you all right?"

"I've just had a bit much to drink. Not enough food . . ."

"A deadly combination," Hugh said, putting his arm around her and pulling her close.

Maggie knew his having his arm around her was wrong. It was

also wonderful. She didn't know how she felt about him anymore. If she encouraged Hugh, it would give him the wrong idea. She still had feelings for Hugh, but she didn't want to use him to feel better about John's breaking things off with her. She was, in a word, confused.

"Maggie, please," he whispered in her ear.

He smelled good, like bay rum. And it felt good to be held. But, still, it wasn't fair to him. She was broken. She was damaged. She was of no use to anyone.

"Please," Hugh repeated, his arms around her, holding her closer.

"No, Hugh," Maggie said clearly. She was beginning to feel nauseous. The edges of her vision began to blur. *My mother, Elise, Gottlieb, that German boy, the little Jewish girl . . .*

"I love you, Maggie." Hugh's lips touched her cheek, then moved to her throat. Maggie felt a sudden panic. She realized how drunk she was, how out of control the situation was getting. This was not going to end well.

"Hugh, I said *no!*" Maggie pushed him away.

Suddenly, there was a tall figure standing beside her. "The lady isn't interested."

It was John, glowering. Hugh stood and met his gaze.

Maggie couldn't take any more. "I think I'm going to throw up," she announced. Her stomach contracted sharply, and she doubled over. She stayed leaned over, not sure if she could right herself without passing out. Not sure if she ever wanted to right herself. Then her stomach contracted again.

When there seemed to be a pause, John gently gripped Maggie's arm, helped her up, and led her to the adjacent alley. "If you're going to be sick, at least do it here," he murmured, one arm around her shoulders, fingers gripping the bare skin of her arm, the other hand holding back her hair. Hugh followed behind.

Maggie vomited again. And again. When there was absolutely nothing left to expel, she slid down against the brick wall.

"Here," John said, taking out his handkerchief and handing it to her.

"Thanks," Maggie muttered, wiping her lips and chin, exhausted. Too exhausted to feel shame, but not too exhausted to realize that shame would eventually come. She noticed Hugh was still there. *And both of my former beaux witnessed this display? Perfect. Absolutely perfect.*

Maggie groaned, then looked up at John. His face was impassive, dark eyes staring down. Hugh was pacing. She let her hot, throbbing head fall to her hands. "I'm sorry," she moaned.

"I'll take it from here," John told Hugh.

"No, I'll take care of her," Hugh countered.

"I *said* I would do it."

"Who the hell are you?" Hugh demanded.

John's nostrils flared. "John Sterling."

Hugh's jaw dropped. "The . . ." He gathered his wits. "You're the one we thought—you were dead."

John gave a grim smile. "Reports of my demise were greatly exaggerated."

"And you two are back together now?"

"No!" Maggie managed from the pavement. "No. We are *not* together."

"Well, then *I'll* get her home," Hugh said.

"No." John's teeth clenched. "As I said, I'll take it from here."

"Please, please, both of you—just leave me alone . . ."

"Watch her, while I get her things," John told Hugh.

Maggie wasn't conscious of much, but she was coherent enough to be glad her growing headache eclipsed her humiliation. "So, that's John," Hugh said, finally.

"Yes," Maggie managed.

"I see."

Finally, John returned with her hat and gloves and a glass of water. "Drink this," he admonished. Maggie shook her head. She much preferred to be in pain. Being in pain meant she didn't have to think. "Come on now," John demanded.

Maggie took the glass, but it slipped from her hand, spilling water into her lap. She heard voices, as though from far away. "So is this what you do now? Get drunk and make a spectacle of yourself? Is this what you and Hugh did together, while I nearly died in Berlin?"

Maggie moaned, "No . . ."

"Watch it," Hugh countered. "It's only since you've broken her heart that she's been like this."

"I?" John spat. "I broke *her* heart?"

"Yes, and now she's broken mine. Are you happy now?"

"Happy? Who the hell is happy these days?"

John grabbed Hugh by his tie and punched him in the face. Hugh staggered back against the wall, then regained his footing. Suddenly the two men were grappling with each other in the alley, like boxers in a clinch.

"Boys!" Maggie tried to rise. "*Really* now. This is getting ridicu——"

It felt warm in the alley, so very warm, and the yelling and punches were very loud. Her head hurt. She felt her stomach lurch again, and the alley started to tilt. She knew she was about to faint, and sure enough, she was back on the ground, this time with her cheek pressed to the pavement.

Before blackness closed over her, she heard John—or was it Hugh?—say, "Bloody hell!"

Chapter Twenty-six

Maggie opened her eyes. This time it was dark. And hot, and stuffy. But at least she was clean, in her nightgown, and in her own bed.

The blackout curtains were in place, but her door was open, and she could see the light infiltrating the rest of the flat. She had no idea how much time had passed.

Her head hurt. Her body hurt. Her soul hurt. She tried to sit up, groaned, and sank back down again. A voice said, "Drink this." She squinted and focused enough to see David perched on the striped armchair, holding out a glass of water for her to drink. Obedient and weak, she took the water, drinking it all down.

"Good girl," David said.

She handed the glass back to him, exhausted by the effort. He had a pot with a cozy over it, next to a mug. He took off the cozy and poured, then handed the steaming, fragrant tea to her.

Maggie swore never to mock the British penchant for tea again. "Thank you, David," she croaked. Her voice sounded like she hadn't used it in years.

"Of course," he said.

Freddie appeared in the doorway and leaned on the frame. "Does it live?"

Maggie tried to smile. "It does," she replied hoarsely. "I assume

I have you two gentlemen to thank for getting me back here in one piece? Thank you."

Freddie blew a kiss and walked on.

"I must admit, Mags, you gave us quite a scare there," David told her. "I don't think I've ever seen you that drunk. To be candid, I don't think I've *ever* seen you squiffy."

"I know, I know . . ."

"Well, you won't get a lecture from me, although, in future, I do advise lining your stomach first and then alternating your drinks with glasses of water." They listened to the faint noises of Freddie rattling dishes in the kitchen. Finally, David said: "Do you want to talk about it?"

"Talk about what?"

"What happened? John? Hugh? Your mother? Berlin? Your AWOL father? Schrödinger's cat? Any of it?" He smiled. "Pick one—dealer's choice."

Maggie sank back down into the pillows and pulled the sheet over her head. "No," she moaned. "I don't want to talk. I *never* want to talk."

"When you're ready, then," David said. "And I think a loud cry would do you a world of good, too."

She poked her head back out from under the sheet. "I can't—I can't cry."

"Maybe not now," David said, rising and moving to the door. "But you will. And John, however pigheaded and obtuse he might be, isn't angry with you. He's just—well, he's just angry. He'll calm down in time. He'll be able to see your side of things, too."

"David?" Maggie called, as he left the room. "How did things work out for you? With your parents and Freddie and the apartment and all that?"

"It appears there's one happy ending, at least for now. While all

my schemes and ideas came to naught, and my parents still disap-
prove of my relationship—they refer to it as a 'friendship'—with
Freddie, they've decided to turn a blind eye, and let things go on as
before."

"Really?" Maggie said, pulling the sheet down and propping
herself up on her elbows. "What changed their minds?"

"Ernst, actually," David said, smiling. "As you know, it's a trifle difficult to get Jewish immigrants into Britain, let alone German
Jews. But I was able to pull a few strings—and since Ernst is a
surgeon and wants to be an army doctor, the Government has
cleared him for medical duties."

"But you're still not married," Maggie pointed out. "And not in
any position to have a child."

"Talmud, Sanhedrin 37a states—*For this reason was man created
alone, to teach thee that whosoever destroys a single soul . . . Scripture
imputes guilt to him as though he had destroyed a complete world. And
whosoever preserves a single soul . . . , Scripture applies merit to him
as though he had preserved a complete world.*"

"So, in other words, you saved the world."

David shrugged. "I do what I can." He sat down on the edge of
her bed. "You know, Maggie, I'm never going to love women. And
while I realize it's the road less traveled, it's a great relief to know
who I am. And to be who I am. And while it's still dangerous, at
least, as long as I mind my own business in public, Freddie and I
should be all right." He stood. "Oh, and your father rang."

"You mean the always-ambiguous father I scarcely know?"

"That's the one! I assured him you were recovering."

"I don't want to talk to him. About anything. He warned me
not to go—and would just love to be able to say I told you so." She
gave David a grim smile. "I used to think I knew everything. I
don't know anything anymore."

"It's been a crazy few years, that's for sure. With more crazy to come. But we'll keep buggering on, as the Boss says. And maybe, someday, things will be all right again."

"What is it your people say? 'From your lips, to God's ears.' "

"When you're well enough to come out, I'll make you some toast."

"Thank you, David—for, well, for everything."

That evening, Maggie took the Tube to Euston Station, where she would catch the overnight train to Fort William, and then on to Arisaig, a small town on the western coast of Scotland. Arisaig was the home of one of the SOE training camps. This time, however, Maggie was returning to be an instructor, not a student.

The train platform itself was dark, illuminated only by a few blue bulbs of blackout lights. It was a hot, sullen night. The sky lit up every few minutes with flashes of lightning, and she could hear the distant rumble of thunder. Finally, the train pulled up in a cloud of steam and shriek of brakes. She handed her two tagged suitcases to a uniformed porter and climbed aboard.

The train was crowded—full of new recruits, both men and women, soldiers and civilians, on their way to various training camps. They were loud and their laughter was raucous. She walked the smoke-filled corridors looking for an empty seat, ignoring the occasional whistle or catcall from a man in uniform.

She found an empty compartment and sat down on the dusty velvet seat cushion. Then, with a screaming whistle, the train began to lurch forward, on its way to Scotland.

Maggie startled when the conductor knocked on the door, asking for her ticket, her heart beating wildly, her brain full of images of train journeys in Berlin. But she gave it to him, and he moved on without noticing her trembling hands.

She blinked, as though to clear the memories, took off her

gloves, and rummaged in her handbag for the book she'd brought, one she'd once read in an English class at Wellesley College. She'd memorized the words then, but she hadn't understood them. But the poem haunted her, and she wanted to give it another chance now. She opened the yellowing pages.

> *Turning and turning in the widening gyre*
> *The falcon cannot hear the falconer;*
> *Things fall apart; the centre cannot hold;*
> *Mere anarchy is loosed upon the world,*
> *The blood-dimmed tide is loosed, and everywhere*
> *The ceremony of innocence is drowned;*
> *The best lack all conviction, while the worst*
> *Are full of passionate intensity.*

As the urban landscape slipped away into the darkness, she read and reread the words. English class had always scared her. Unlike math, there was never a right answer. Words always seemed slippery, with multiple meanings—impossible to pin down. But now there was an odd relief in that very property.

Although the words of the poem were bleak, she felt a strange comfort in them. Yeats himself, who'd survived the Great War, had felt as she did. Through the years, through the centuries, many, many people had felt the same way.

Absently, her hand went to her side, feeling the outline of the bullet there, just beneath her skin. And she braced herself for whatever lay ahead.

Clara Hess was the new occupant of the Queen's House at the Tower of London, billeted next door to Stefan Krueger.

With no makeup on her face, her long hair loose, and wearing her prison-issued jumpsuit, she looked years younger than she had in Berlin, girlish even. She sat at a small wooden desk, writing in a journal.

When the two guards at her door announced that Edmund Hope had arrived to see her, she didn't seem surprised in the least. When Edmund entered, Clara smiled, a warm and generous smile.

One he did not return. He took off his hat but did not sit down.

"Hello, Edmund," Clara said, rising and walking over to him, her feet bare on the cold stone floor.

He did not respond but stared, as if unable to fuse together the pictures in his mind of his late wife with the woman in front of him.

"Don't stare, darling," she said finally. "Or at least blink once in a while. Otherwise it's rude."

Finally, finally, Edmund spoke, almost in a whisper. "There are people here, people in charge, who believe you have turned to our side now, and that you're willing to work for us. They hold the Machiavellian, and I say cynical, belief that they can use you."

Clara opened her mouth to reply, but Edmund put up a hand. "You'll never see her again. I'll make sure of that."

"Oh, Edmund," Clara said, stretching like a cat. "She'll return. Wait and see."

Biting back unsaid words, Edmund strode out of the room, calling "Guard!" The door closed behind him, and then she heard the series of locks click, one by one, fifteen in all.

Clara turned back to the window, staring out over the Thames and Tower Bridge, a small smile playing on her lips.

Historical Notes

As with *Mr. Churchill's Secretary* and *Princess Elizabeth's Spy*, *His Majesty's Hope* is not a history, nor is it meant to be—it's a novel, an imaginary tale.

However, I used many historical sources. Instrumental to writing about Berlin in 1941 were the books *Hitler's Spy Chief: The Wilhelm Canaris Mystery*, by Richard Bassett; *Berlin: The Downfall, 1945*, by Anthony Beevor; *Moral Combat: Good and Evil in World War II* and *Sacred Causes: The Clash of Religion and Politics, from the Great War to the War on Terror*, by Michael Burleigh; *The Perfect Nazi: Uncovering My Grandfather's Secret Past*, by Martin Davidson; *The Ghosts of Berlin: Confronting German History in the Urban Landscape*, by Brian Ladd; *In the Garden of the Beasts: Love, Terror, and an American Family in Hitler's Berlin*, by Eric Larson; *Bonhoeffer: Pastor, Martyr, Prophet, Spy*, by Eric Metaxas; *Berlin at War*, by Roger Moorhouse; and *Hitlerland: American Eyewitnesses to the Nazi Rise to Power*, by Andrew Nagorski.

To research the Children's Euthanasia Program, also known as Operation Compassionate Death (renamed Aktion T4 after the war), I relied on *War Against the Weak: Eugenics and America's Campaign to Create a Master Race*, by Edwin Black; *The Origins of the Final Solution: The Evolution of Nazi Jewish Policy, September 1939–March 1942*, by Christopher R. Browning; *Eugenics and Other Evils*, by G. K. Chesterton; *Forgotten Crimes: The Holocaust and People with Disabilities,* by Suzanne E. Evans; *The Origins of Nazi Genocide: From Euthanasia to the Final Solution,* by Henry Friedlander; *A Moral Reckoning: The Role of the Catholic Church in the Holocaust and Its Unfulfilled Duty of Repair,* by Daniel Jonah Goldhagen; *The Catholic Church and the Holocaust 1930–1965,* by Michael Phayer; *Masters of Death: The SS-Einsatzgruppen and the Invention of the Holocaust,* by Richard Rhodes; and *Into That Darkness: An Examination of Conscience,* by Gitta Sereny.

In researching the Special Operations Executive's spies and the XX Committee, I relied on the following: *Secret Agent's Handbook: The Top Secret Manual of Wartime Weapons, Gadgets, Disguises and Devices,* introduction by Roderick Bailey; *The Insider's Guide to 150 Spy Sites in London,* by Mark Birdsall, Deborah Plisko, and Peter Thompson; *SOE Agent: Churchill's Secret Warriors,* by Terry Crowdy; *A Life in Secrets: Vera Atkins and the Missing Agents of WWII,* by Sarah Helm; *Sisterhood of Spies, The Women of the OSS,* by Elizabeth P. McIntosh; *Agent ZigZag: The True Story of Espionage, Love and Betrayal,* by Ben Macintyre; *Between Silk and Cyanide: A Codemaker's War, 1941–1945,* by Leo Marks; *Christine: SOE Agent and Churchill's Favorite Spy,* by Madeleine Masson; *Operatives, Spies and Saboteurs,* by Patrick K. O'Donnell; and *How to Be a Spy: The World War II SOE Training Manual,* introduction by Denis Rigden.

To research Bletchley Park, I'm indebted to *Bletchley Park People: Churchill's Geese That Never Cackled,* by Marion Hill; and *Codebreakers: The Inside Story of Bletchley Park,* edited by F. H. Hinsley and Alan Stripp. For an overview of code breaking, I cannot speak highly enough of *The Code Book: The Science of Secrecy from Ancient Egypt to Quantum Cryptography,* by Simon Singh.

Many films and documentaries were also helpful with research, including *Operation Barbarossa; Legendary Sin Cities: Berlin;* Leni Riefenstahl's *Triumph of the Will; Bonhoeffer: Hanged on a Twisted*

Cross: The Life, Conviction and Martyrdom of Dietrich Bonhoeffer; and *The Ninth Day.*

Father Jean Licht is a fictional character but inspired by a real priest, Father Bernhard Lichtenberg. Father Lichtenberg was a German Roman Catholic priest at St. Hedwig's Cathedral in Berlin during World War II. After Kristallnacht, he was known for praying publicly for the Jews every evening: *I pray for the priests in the concentration camps, for the Jews, for the non-Aryans. What happened yesterday, we know. What will happen tomorrow, we don't. But what happened today, we lived through. Outside, the Synagogue is burning. It, too, is a house of God.*

Lichtenberg protested against the Aktion T4 by writing a letter to the chief physician of the Reich: *I, as a human being, a Christian, a priest, and a German demand of you, Chief Physician of the Reich, that you answer for the crimes that have been perpetrated at your bidding, and with your consent, and which will call forth the vengeance of the Lord on the heads of the German people.* He was arrested, tried, sentenced, and sent to Dachau. He died in transit.

In June 1996, Pope John Paul II, during his visit to Germany, beatified Lichtenberg (meaning that, in the eyes of the Catholic Church, he has entered into Heaven and has the capacity to intercede on behalf of individuals who pray in his name). The process of Bernhard Lichtenberg's canonization (to declare him officially a saint by the Catholic Church) is still pending. His tomb is in the crypt of St. Hedwig's in Berlin.

Cardinal Konrad von Preysing and Cardinal Clemens August Graf von Galen (bishops during the war and elevated to cardinals after) were also real people, who both spoke out against the Nazis'

Aktion T4 program, despite intense pressure to stay silent. Cardinal von Preysing was the Bishop of Berlin during World War II and was an outspoken critic of the Nazi regime, saying: "We have fallen into the hands of criminals and fools." In a homily in March 1941, Bishop von Preysing reaffirmed his opposition to the killing of the sick or infirm.

Cardinal August Graf von Galen was the Bishop of Münster during the war, and an outspoken critic of Hitler and the Nazis. He also spoke publicly against the Aktion T4 program. In his homily on August 3, 1941, von Galen spoke against the deportation and murder of the mentally ill. *These are people, our brothers and sisters,* he said. *Maybe their life is unproductive, but productivity is not a justification for killing.*

It is a fact that Adolf Hitler was booed by Germans at the Hofbräuhaus, by people enraged by what they'd learned from German bishops, such as von Preysing and von Galen. According to Gitta Sereny in *Into That Darkness,* it was the only time Hitler was ever booed. He ostensibly shut the Aktion T4 program down soon after the incident, but it continued in secret, with doctors using starvation and overdoses of medicine instead of gas chambers to kill children. The last of the children were killed in a hospital in Bavaria, three weeks after the Germans had surrendered, in an area already occupied by U.S. forces.

According to evidence presented at the Nuremberg Trials, 275,000 people died because of the Aktion T4 program. It began with killing young children, then expanded to include older children, then the elderly. It also included *Mischlinge*—mixed Jewish and Aryan children.

Hitler gave his approval to the Aktion T4 program in 1939, signing a "euthanasia decree" backdated to September 1, 1939 (the official outbreak of war), which authorized Drs. Philipp Bouhler and Karl Brandt to carry out a program of "euthanasia." The letter states: *Reich Leader Bouhler and Dr. med. Brandt are charged with the responsibility of enlarging the competence of certain physicians, designated by name, so that patients who, on the basis of human judgment are considered incurable, can be granted mercy death after a discerning diagnosis.*

In the United States, I am grateful to the traveling exhibition from the U.S. Holocaust Memorial Museum, "Deadly Medicine: Creating the Master Race," which I was able to see in Philadelphia. Curated by Dr. Susan Bachrach, the exhibition shows how the Nazi regime aimed to change the genetic makeup of the population through measures known as "racial hygiene." I was also able to visit the U.S. Holocaust Memorial Museum in Washington, D.C., and was particularly moved by the exhibition "State of Deception: The Power of Nazi Propaganda."

In Berlin, I was privileged to visit the House of the Wannsee Conference Memorial and Educational Site, the Liebermann-Villa at Wannsee, the Käthe Kollwitz Museum, the German Historical Museum, the Holocaust Memorial, and the Topography of Terror museum.

Tiergartenstrasse 4 still exists, but the building that housed the T4 offices was bombed during the war. However, there is a plaque on the sidewalk at the address, reading:

Tiergartenstraße 4—In honour of the forgotten victims. The first mass-murder by the Nazis was organized from 1940 onwards on this spot, the Tiergartenstraße 4 and named "Aktion T4" after this address.

From 1939 to 1945 almost 200,000 helpless people were killed.

Their lives were termed "unworthy of living," their murder called "euthanasia." They died in the gas chambers of Grafeneck, Brandenburg, Hartheim, Pirna, Bernburg, and Hadamar; they died by execution squad, by planned hunger and poisoning.

The perpetrators were scholars, doctors, nurses, justice officials, the police, and the health and workers' administration. The victims were poor, desperate, rebellious, or in need of help. They came from psychiatric clinics and children's hospitals, from old age homes and welfare institutions, from military hospitals and internment camps. The number of victims is huge, the number of offenders who were sentenced, small.

A link between Aktion T4 and the Holocaust has been found by historians. Gerald Reitlinger, in his *Early History of the Final Solution*, notes the direct connection between the personnel and gas chamber technology of the T4 killing centers and the Final Solution, officially put into words at the Wannsee conference in January 1942.

The historian Raul Hilberg, in *The Destruction of the European Jews*, 1985 edition, also noted the connection between the Aktion T4 program and the subsequent annihilation of Jews: *Euthanasia was a conceptual as well as a technological and administrative prefiguration of the final solution in the death camps.*

In addition, Michael Burleigh, Wolfganger Wippermann, and Henry Friedlander, in *The Racial State: Germany 1933–45*, posit that the connection between the Aktion T4 program and the Final Solution goes well beyond personnel, technology, and procedure, and that they were two campaigns in the same crusade. They state that the killing of the handicapped and of the Jews were two essential elements of the Nazis' attempted creation of a racial utopia—the former to clear Germany of "degenerate and defective elements" and then the latter to "destroy the ultimate enemy."

After the war, Dr. Karl Brandt was tried along with twenty-two others at the Palace of Justice in Nuremberg, Germany, in a trial officially designated *The United States of America v. Karl Brandt et al.* but more often called the Doctors' Trial, one of the Nuremberg Trials. Brandt was found guilty and, with six other doctors, was sentenced to death by hanging.

To forget the dead would be akin to killing them
a second time.

—Elie Wiesel, *Night*

Acknowledgments

As always, thank you, Noel MacNeal. And Matthew MacNeal.

Thank you to Idria Barone Knecht, one of the sharpest minds I've ever encountered—and one of the loveliest people, as well—for her time and editing insights.

I am grateful to Victoria Skurnick (a.k.a. Agent V) at the Levine Greenberg Agency, the best agent imaginable at the best agency ever, who makes everything possible.

Thanks to the always-patient Kate Miciak, who believed Maggie's story could continue and even asked for a third and a fourth book.

Thank you to Maggie Hope's Random House team, especially Gina Wachtel, Jane von Mehren, Susan Corcoran, Lindsey Kennedy, Randall Klein, Maggie Oberrender, Vincent La Scala, and Susan M. S. Brown.

Special thanks to the intrepid Random House sales force, who also believed Maggie Hope's adventures could continue, about whom I can never say enough great things.

Thank you to Dr. Ronald Granieri, for his patience with German-history-related questions and help in translating German.

Special thanks to expat Londoner (and Blitz survivor) Phyllis Brooks Schafer for reading and helping with *It's That Man Again*'s schedule, as well as myriad other facts of life during the Blitz.

Thanks to Audra Branum Rickman, my Berlin travel companion.

Thank you to Dr. Daniel Levy, Director, Synthetic Chemistry, and Principal Consultant at DEL BioPharma in San Francisco for answering questions about the use of fluoride in World War II.

I owe a huge debt of gratitude to Dr. Meredith Norris, who patiently answered many, many medical questions.

Thanks to musician friends for verifying that people really *can* be transported in instrument cases: Karen Podd, Jessi Rosinski, Frank Scinia, Louis Toth, Lilly Tao, and Doug Wyatt.

Thanks to early readers Monica Byrne, Deborah Ellis, Shannon Halprin, Lauren Marchisotto, Jana Riess, Liza Wachman Percer, Kathryn Plank, Sarah Bermingham Quinn, and Jennifer Valvo McCann.

A special thank-you to Yeoman Warden Jim Duncan, at the Tower of London, who answered my many questions about where various Nazi prisoners, including Rudolf Hess, were kept. (It's not part of the usual tour of the Tower of London—apparently, guests find the chronologic proximity to World War II too disturbing, and the Tower tour deliberately leaves it out.)

If you enjoyed *His Majesty's Hope*, you won't want to miss the next ingenious suspense novel in the Maggie Hope series. Read on for an exciting early look at *The Prime Minister's Secret Agent* by Susan Elia MacNeal.

Published by Bantam Books Trade Paperbacks

Chapter One

Maggie Hope had thought that summer in Berlin was hell, but it was nothing compared to the inferno of darkness that raged in her own head, even as she was "safe as houses" now in Arisaig, Scotland.

A mixture of shame, anger, guilt, and sadness had become a miasma of depression. It followed her everywhere, not at all helped by the lack of sunlight in Scotland in November. She'd once heard Winston Churchill describe his own melancholy as his "black dog," but never understood it then. She'd pictured a large black dog with long silky fur and dark, sad eyes, silently padding after his master.

But now she knew the truth: the black dog of depression was dirty and scarred, feral and rabid. He lurked in the night, yellow eyes gleaming, waiting for a chink in the armor, a weakness, a vulnerability, a memory. And then, jaws wide and fangs sharp, he would leap.

Maggie had a few moments in the morning, when she first woke up, when she didn't remember. Those were blessed moments, innocent and sweet. Until her mind started working again, and the sharp ache returned to her heart. Remembered what had happened in Berlin. Remembered that her German contact was dead—a devout Catholic who'd killed himself rather than be taken by the Gestapo for questioning.

That she herself had killed a man. "It was self-defense," the Freudian analyst she'd been ordered to see by Peter Frain had told her. "It's war. You don't need to torture yourself." And yet, even though he'd shot her first, and she'd killed him in self-defense, the dead man's eyes haunted her.

As did those of the little Jewish girl being pushed into a cattle car in Berlin, destined for Poland. "I'm thirsty, Mama," she'd cried, "so thirsty." What had happened to her? Maggie often wondered. Had she died on the train, or later in the camp? Because now that Maggie—and most of the rest of the world—knew that the Nazis were capable of killing their own children, she didn't hold any hope at all for the children of Jews.

And, as if that weren't enough burden, her mother, Clara Hess, was a Nazi Abwehr agent imprisoned in the Tower of London—and asking to talk with her. No wonder every breath Maggie took caused her pain.

She turned over beneath the heavy wool blankets, reflexively reaching for her ribs, the hard outline of the German boy's bullet, which had just managed to miss her heart. Dumb luck was all that had saved her. The doctors in Switzerland, and then in London—even one of her best friends, Chuck, a nurse—had wanted her to have it removed, but she wouldn't. She called it her "Berlin souvenir."

I'm dead inside, she thought, not for the first time since she'd made it to Arisaig. *Worse than dead—if I were dead at least I wouldn't have to remember everything anymore.*

On her nightstand the green glass clock ticked, and she reached over to turn it off before the alarm rang. The tear-off calendar propped up against her lamp read November 1, 1941.

Finally, Maggie rose, washed, and changed her clothes, putting on the blue twill jumpsuit all the instructors wore over layers of thermal underwear and wool socks, plus standard-issue thick-soled boots. She twisted and then pinned up her long red hair with her tortoiseshell clip. If she'd been doing office work, she would have put on the pearl earrings that her aunt Edith had given to her when she'd graduated from Wellesley in '37—but not only were they completely inappropriate for her job as an instructor at an SOE camp, she'd lost them somewhere in London after returning from Berlin.

Pale and gaunt, with violet shadows under her eyes, Maggie shrugged into her thick wool coat, pulled on a scarf and Fair Isle stocking cap, and then left the gardener's cottage to which she'd been assigned, heading to the manor house. Although her body ached and felt as if it were made from spun glass, she walked quickly to warm up her muscles before breaking into a run up the path of the rockery, taking the steep, lichen-covered flagstone steps up to the manor house at a brisk jog. The view was lost on her—the snow-covered mountains, the ancient forests, the white sheep grazing in the neighbor's field, the blue-green ocean in the distance.

Arisaig House was the administrative heart of the War Office for Special Operations Executive—or SOE, as it was better known. SOE was neither MI-5 nor MI-6, but a black ops operation, training agents to be dropped into places such as France and Germany, and helping local resistance groups "set Europe ablaze," as Winston Churchill had urged. The SOE used great houses all over Britain to train their would-be spies, sparking the joke that SOE really stood for "Stately 'Omes of England." While most training camps were preliminary schools specifically dedicated to parachute jumping or radio transmission, Arisaig was the place where trainees received intense training in demolition, weapons, reconnaissance, and clandestine intelligence work.

Isolated on the far Western coast of Scotland, closed off by military roadblocks, the rocky mountains and stony beaches of

Arisaig were ideal for pushing trainees to their physical and mental limits. Arisaig House was the administrative hub. Other great houses in the area were used for training: Traigh House, Inverailort Castle, Camusdarach, and Garramor, just to name a few. Maggie's lips twisted in a smile as she recalled how a group of trainees from Norway, Italy, and Spain had stumbled over the Scottish names.

But it was the perfect place for Maggie, still recovering from her gunshot wound—and also from everything she'd seen and done in Berlin.

As an instructor, she trained her charges harder than Olympians—swimming in the freezing ocean, running over stones, navigating obstacle courses in the cold mud, and mastering rope work. Under other instructors, the trainees learned fieldcraft, demolition, Morse code, weapons training, and Sykes and Fairbairn methods of silent killing. Anything and everything they might need to know when sent to France, or Germany, or wherever a local resistance group might need aid.

Maggie hadn't always been a draconian instructor; in fact, the very idea would have made her former bookish and dreamy self laugh in disbelief. She'd planned to obtain her Ph.D. in mathematics from MIT, but had instead found herself in London when war broke out. Maggie had found a job in Winston Churchill's secretarial pool, and, after finding a secret code in an innocuous advertisement, and then foiling an IRA bomb plot, had been tapped for MI-5. She'd been sent to one of the preliminary training camps in Scotland as a trainee in the fall of 1940. Not surprisingly, while she was excellent at Morse code and navigating by stars, she flamed out spectacularly at anything that required the least bit of physical fitness.

Maggie remembered how angry she'd been when she'd washed out of the SOE program and Peter Frain of MI-5 had placed her at

Windsor Castle to look after the young Princesses. But, in retrospect, the Windsor assignment had done her a lot of good. She had grown stronger both mentally and physically, and was able to help foil a kidnapping plot.

After her adventures at Windsor with the Royals, she'd returned to SOE training in the spring of 1941. She made it through all the various schools and, as a newly minted agent, was sent on a secret mission to Berlin. Now, she had returned once more to Arisaig House—but this time as an instructor.

As she opened the thick oak door and paused, the bells in the clock tower chimed eight times. The vestibule of the large stone manor house led into the great hall, which SOE had turned into a lobby of sorts, with a desk for a telephone and a receptionist. Sheets protected the grand house's wooden paneling from the government workers, while a Miss Astley Nicholson, owner of Arisaig and Traigh Houses, had been relocated to a smaller cottage up the road for the duration of the war. However, the spacious, high-ceilinged entrance hall with its mullioned windows, staircase elaborately carved with birds and thistles, and views over fields dotted with white sheep leading down to the jagged coastline made it clear instantly this was no ordinary office.

"Yes," the girl on receptionist duty said into the black Bakelite telephone receiver, twisting the metal cord. She was short, sturdy, and a bit stout, with a wide grin and eyes that crinkled when she smiled, which was often. Her name was Gwen Glyn-Jones and she was from Cardiff, Wales, but her mother was French, and she had a perfect accent from summers spent just outside Paris. She was training to become a radio operator—if she survived the physical training at Arisaig. Gwen scribbled something down on a scrap of paper. "Yes, miss—I'll make sure Miss Hope receives the message as soon as possible." She hung up.

"Message for Lady Macbeth?" one of the other girls in the room asked. Yvonne had been born and raised in Brixton, London, but her grandfather was French, and she was bilingual.

"The one and only." The girls, both trainees, giggled. Maggie was strict. She was hard on her students. She never smiled. None of the women at Arisaig House liked her. None of the men liked her much either, for that matter.

Gwen grimaced. "I hate being in Lady Macbeth's section."

Yvonne leaned in. "Why does everyone call her Lady Macbeth?"

"Because she's a monster." Gwen lowered her plummy Welsh-inflected voice. "Rumor is, she has *blood* on her hands."

Yvonne's eyes popped open wide. "Really?"

"I heard she killed a man in France."

Two trainees walking down the staircase, a man and a woman, had overhead their conversation. "I heard she killed three men in Munich," the woman offered.

The man said, "I heard she was interrogated by the Gestapo and never talked—"

All right, that's enough. Maggie swept inside, giving them what she'd come to call her "best Aunt Edith look."

"Two, Five, and Eight—aren't you supposed to be out running?" Maggie had given her trainees numbers instead of names. She didn't want to become too attached to them.

There was a lengthy silence, punctuated only by the ticking of a great mahogany longcase clock. Then, "I'm on desk duty . . ."

"And I was waiting . . ."

Maggie held up one hand. "Stop making excuses."

"I'm—I'm sorry, Miss Hope," Gwen stuttered.

"And stop apologizing. In fact, stop speaking entirely." Maggie looked them all up and down. "You, stay here and do your job. You two—go run on the beach. Relay races on the stony part of the shore—they're good for your ankles and knees and will help with your parachute jumps. I'll be there shortly."

Her charges stared, frozen in place.

Maggie glared. "I said, *go!*"

They nearly fell over themselves in their haste to get away from her.

Mr. Harold Burns, a fit man in his fifties with smile lines etched around his eyes and rough skin dotted with liver spots, walked in from one of the other huge rooms of the house now used as administrative offices. The instructor favored her with a wintry smile. Maggie was a physical education instructor and Mr. Burns was her commanding officer. "Impressive, Miss Hope. I remember a time when you could barely run a mile without passing out. Or twisting your ankle. Or dropping your fellow trainees in the mud."

Maggie put a finger to her lips. "Shhhhh, Mr. Burns. That's our little secret."

"When you first trained with me, you were terrible. One of the worst. But you came back. And you worked hard. I've heard of some of the things you've accomplished, Miss Hope, and I must say I'm proud." Mr. Burns was a survivor of the Great War. Maggie could see in his eyes that, like her, he had seen things.

The clock struck. Maggie started, breath quickening, pupils dilating.

"It's all right," Mr. Burns said gently, nearly putting a hand on her arm, and then withdrawing it. "You're safe here, Miss Hope."

Safe. Who's safe, really? Certainly not children with any sort of illness in Germany. Certainly not the Jews. Certainly not young men who just happen to be on the wrong side of a gun. But Maggie liked Mr. Burns, she did, even though he'd been hard on her when she'd been in his section. In fact, much of what he taught her had helped keep her alive in Berlin.

"Thank you, Mr. Burns."

He shifted his weight from side to side. "You know, I served, too—over in France, in the trenches. I was a soldier then. Oh, you wouldn't know it now, but once I was young—almost handsome, too. We all were, back then. Saw a lot of my friends killed, better men than I ever was, and killed a fair number myself."

"Mr. Burns—"

"I don't remember their faces anymore, but I still think of them. What I try to remember is the Christmas truce—Christmas of fourteen, we had a ceasefire over in France. We even sang songs, if you can believe—us with *Silent Night*, and them with *Stille Nacht*. Same melody, though. We even had a game of football that afternoon, the 'Huns' versus the 'Island Apes.' Then, the next day, back to the trenches. . . ." He shook his head. "I'll leave you to read your message, Miss Hope." He turned back to the mail cubbies and extracted a packet of letters from his slot, and began to go through them. The girl at the desk pretended to be very interested in the contents of a folder.

"Thank you, Mr. Burns." Maggie looked at the note the girl had written: *Sarah Sanderson called to say that the Vic-Wells Ballet is performing La Sylphide at the Royal Lyceum Theatre in Edinburgh. Possibility she may be going on as the Sylph (she says, "the lead one, not one of the idiot fairies fluttering uselessly in the background"). She'll put house seats on hold for you this weekend. She hopes you can make it.*

Long-legged and high-cheekboned, Sarah was one of Maggie's closest friends. Once upon a time, Sarah and Maggie had been flatmates in London. At first Maggie had found Sarah intimidating—she was so worldly, after all, so beautiful and glamorous, with the slim figure of a fashion model, dark sparkling eyes, and long dark hair. But Sarah had a droll sense of humor and was given to witty retorts in a decidedly Liverpudlian accent. She was truly herself.

Maggie had only seen Sarah a few times since they'd parted ways in London the summer of the attempted bombing of St. Paul's Cathedral, and missed her terribly. If it were at all possible, she decided, she'd make it to Edinburgh for the performance. The trouble was the black dog. Would the black dog let her? Sometimes it was hard to know.

"Mr. Burns—" Maggie called over to him.

"Yes, Miss Hope?"

"I haven't taken any leave since I arrived here three months ago. A friend of mine is in Edinburgh this weekend, and I'd really like to see her."

"Go, Miss Hope"—Mr. Burns waved a leathery hand—"with my blessing. As I've been telling you, you need a change of scene. Go, and if there's a decent bottle of single malt to be had, bring it back for me."

Maggie picked up the telephone receiver. Black dog or no, she wasn't going to miss seeing her friend. She dialed and waited, then: "Yes, please tell Miss Sarah Sanderson that Maggie Hope returned her call. And let her know that I'll be at Saturday evening's performance."

There, now I have to go, Maggie thought. *Take that, black dog.*

The coastline of Arisaig, even in November—perhaps especially in November—was stunning. Snow-covered mountains poked into leaden clouds in the distance, while the stony shoreline melted into green water. The islands of Rhum, Eigg, and Muck peeked through the mist in the distance, as well as a few smaller, unnamed islands, home to gray seals.

Maggie jogged from the House to the shore, over well-trampled paths lined with lurid green moss on stones and tree trunks, the roar of rushing streams in the air. The trainees were on a different part of the shore, hidden from her view. Exhausted by her vigorous pace, Maggie leaned against a lichen-covered rock, taking a moment to gulp burning breaths. The cold, damp air tasted of salt and seaweed. Blood pounded in her ears as a hawk circled overhead.

Since she'd arrived in Arisaig, she'd often found herself on the jagged shore, sitting on one of the larger rocks, watching the water as the tide rushed in or out. It was a beautiful part of the world, if you could ignore the occasional loud bang from the training groups learning to use explosives on various parts of the grounds. The neighboring sheep had gotten used to the noise, placidly grazing despite the explosions, but it still startled the birds, who would chirp and twitter in alarm from the ancient oaks.

Looking out over the water, she remembered one of the American literature classes she'd taken at Wellesley where they'd read Kate Chopin's novel *The Awakening*. In the end, the heroine, Edna Pontellier, walked into the Gulf of Mexico.

She'd written a paper for that class on the ending—did Edna commit suicide? Or did she swim back to shore? Did she literally die to be reborn or was it a metaphorical death? Most people assumed Edna died, despite the fact Miss Chopin had left the ending vague. Maggie remembered how in her paper she'd argued for Edna's actual death: the clues the author left were in the allusions to Walt Whitman's poem "Out of the Cradle Endlessly Rocking." The ocean, a background chorus in Whitman's poem, was like the wise mother who reveals the word that awakened Whitman's own songs: "*And again death, death, death, death . . . Creeping thence steadily up to my ears and laving me softly all over.*"

Looking out into the grim gray water, Maggie thought about death, as she had so many times since she'd arrived. She thought how easy it would be to load up her pockets with stones—like

Shelley and Virginia Woolf, like Ophelia and Edna Pontellier—and walk into that cold water never to come back, putting an end to the pain. No more heartache, no more guilt, no more sleepless nights . . . no more black dog. If she died, he would die along with her. And, she had to admit, there was a certain satisfaction in that.

Out of the corner of her eye, she spotted a young man who had just arrived, leaning against one of the lichen-stained boulders. *What's Three doing here? And why isn't he running?* Her eyes narrowed as she watched the young man, who'd lit a cigarette, the blue smoke surrounding his head like the tentacles of a Portuguese man-o'-war. *Trainees,* Maggie thought with a flicker of annoyance. *They're everywhere. I can't even contemplate my own suicide in peace.* She rose.

As she walked closer, stepping silently over broken shells and seaweed left by the tide, she stared him down with her best Aunt Edith look, which she relied on as a trainer. "You're supposed to be running."

Seagulls screeched in the distance. "I'm a fast runner, so I have time for a smoke." His eyes twinkled. "And to look for mermaids. Although we're more likely to see seals. That's what the sailors of yore mistook for mermaids, most likely."

His accent was posh, she noted. He was handsome. She looked at his hands: they were white and soft. *A gentleman,* she thought dispassionately. *Let's see if he makes it through to the end.*

"Yes, seals, most likely." Maggie had no energy left to admonish him; keeping the black dog at bay absorbed it all. She watched the waves crest and break over the rocky shore. Another explosion sounded in the distance.

Three kicked at a thick rotting rope left behind by the family, when the beach had been used as a launch, the wind ruffling his straight dark hair. "They're blowing up bridges today."

"So I've heard." Then, "It's not good to run and smoke."

"Who says?"

"I do. When I came back here, I quit. It was affecting my time."

Three gave a crooked grin and smiled at her through thick black eyelashes. She noticed his eyes were preternaturally green. He threw away his cigarette. "You don't recognize me, do you?"

"Of course I do, Three. Decent at Morse code, not a bad shot, but always end of the pack in any race."

He laughed. "No, I mean, you don't recognize *me*."

Maggie raised an eyebrow. *Who is this arrogant twit?* "Should I?"

"Most people around here do, or at least think they do. Although I always thought—who better to be a spy than an actor."

"You're an actor, then." Maggie knew the type—good-looking, charming, utterly self-absorbed. "Sorry, but I don't think I've seen anything you've done."

"Really?" His face drooped in disappointment. "*Home Away from Home? Dead Men Are Dangerous? The Girl Must Live?*" He rubbed the back of his neck. "Well, how about theatre, then—I played Jack Favell, the first Mrs. de Winter's lover, in *Rebecca*. West End, summer of forty."

"Ah," Maggie said. Her twin flatmates had been the stage manager and costume assistant for *Rebecca*, and of course she and the other flatmates had gone to see it. Maggie remembered him now: handsome with a mustache and slick Brylcreemed hair. Decent chemistry with Mrs. Danvers. "Yes, I saw that." She realized that, puppy-like, he was waiting for more, so she added, "You were quite good."

The young man pushed away from the rock and gave a small bow. "At your service, Lady Macbeth."

Maggie's face twisted into a smile. "Yes, that's what this group calls me. The last one called me Nessie."

He looked blank.

Maggie sighed impatiently. "Nessie? You know—the Loch Ness Monster?"

Three did his best to hide a smile behind a hand. "Ahem, I'm afraid so. But it's better to be feared than to be loved, isn't it?"

"If you're Machiavelli. Or a prince." Her smile turned grim. "Or a spy, for that matter."

"My actual name is Charles Campbell, by the way. The press calls me Good Time Charlie."

"Hello, Charles." She tilted her head. "Where are you from?"

"Glasgow, actually." Maggie was surprised; he didn't have the distinctive accent. "Aye, lassie—ye pro'ly think we all wear kilts, eat haggis with tatties and neeps, an' get drunk on whisky ev'ry day!" He switched from Glaswegian back to his upper-crust enunciation. "It's true, actually, but only on Sunday."

"How—?"

Charles smiled. "I watched films, imitated the voices. When I started to make some real money, I hired an accent coach, a regular Henry Higgins of a fellow. Trained all my bad habits out of me. Now I can speak with almost any accent—used them in plenty of films, some even in Hollywood."

"The ability to switch accents—that's useful, for a spy."

Charles looked deep into her eyes. Maggie looked back, coolly. "You're not in love with me, are you?" he asked, sounding just a touch disappointed.

Despite the razor in her heart, Maggie nearly choked with laughter. *Love?* Love was the *last* thing on her mind these days. "In love with you? I just met you!"

"Most of the girls here are in love with me." He said it factually, not bragging. "Or at least the *image* of me they have from my films. It can be quite annoying, really."

My goodness he's young. "Well," Maggie replied, "never fear. Not only have I never seen your films, but I have no interest in romance, whatsoever. Ever again."

"What's your type?"

"Type? Tall, dark, and damaged. Or tall, fair, and damaged. And really, Charles, you're not nearly tall or damaged enough to be considered."

Charles clapped her on the back and grinned. Maggie could see how he could easily be a matinee idol. Still, with the black dog so close and ready to leap at any moment, romance was out of the question. "Then we shall get along very well," he said.

Maggie shot him a warning look. "First, don't do that."

He removed his hand.

"Second, don't *ever* do that again."

He had the grace to redden.

"And third"—she pushed back her sleeve to take a look at her watch—"start running."

Charles straightened, crushed out his cigarette in a mound of slippery seaweed, and then gave a crisp salute. "Yes, ma'am!"

When he trotted off, Maggie took a few more moments to look out over the water. Then she spotted something by the shore, where the waves gently lapped. A gray seal? A large stone? Driftwood?

Curious, she walked closer. It was a sheep. Or rather the carcass of a sheep, dead some time, from the look of the body. *Poor thing must have gotten away from the flock and fallen into the water. . . .* Maggie examined the body more closely. She saw the clips in its ears, two notches not one, and a dyed red dot on its rump, indicating it didn't belong to the local farmer's flock, whose sheep had just one ear notch and a blue stripe on the shoulders.

Maggie also noted that the corpse was encrusted with open, oozing black sores.

After the day's training sessions were completed, Maggie washed, changed into clean clothes, and bicycled in the dark to the small village of Arisaig to see the town veterinarian, Angus McNeil. It was still early evening, but overhead, the stars burned blue.

The doctor was an older man, tall—well over six feet—with a tuft of white hair sprouting from each ear. He might have started out the day with what was left of his hair neatly combed, but now the red and white strands—pink, almost—were standing straight up, like prawn antennae. His features were large and blunt, like an ancient Lewis chess piece. While his long legs were thin, his midsection was full, and he moved like a great circus bear on its hind legs.

"What do you want, lass?" he said, scowling, as she entered the office. His words were spoken with a thick burr, his voice low and rumbling.

"I found a dead sheep on the beach near Arisaig House—" she began.

"If it's dead, you don't need a veterinarian."

Score one for the ginger-haired brute from Barra. "At first I thought it was one of the neighboring flock that had somehow gotten through a fence and accidentally fallen in and drowned, but it's from a different flock."

"So? Could have fallen in somewhere else, then washed ashore near Arisaig House."

"Then I noticed it was covered in black sores."

The vet's face creased. "What kind of black sores?"

"About an inch or two across, looked like blisters."

"And this sheep—did it have any other markings on it?"

I'm a bloody spy, you addlepated giant, she thought impatiently. *I've been trained not just to see, but to observe. All this idiot sees is a woman.* "I noticed two triangular-shaped notches in his right ear, and a dot of red paint on his rump."

"That sheep belongs to Archie MacDonald, then." The vet rubbed his head, further disturbing his hair. "But his flock doesn't graze anywhere near the coast. . . .'"

"I just thought someone should know."

"Yes, yes . . ." growled the vet, lost in thought. "You didn't touch the beast, did ye, Doreen?"

"No, I most assuredly did not. And my name's not Doreen."

"*Doreen*'s Gaelic for a sourpuss—and your puss is most definitely a sour one."

From the back room came a mewing sound. "What's that?" Maggie asked.

"Stray cat."

"Is he all right?"

"It's a cat, miss. I'm a vet—I deal with sheep and cows and horses. *Not* cats."

"Then what's he doing here?"

"Pub owner brought him in, didn't want him hanging around, begging for food. He's an older cat, not a great mouser. I'd guess he was an indoor cat for most of his life—maybe when his owner died, no one wanted him, so they dumped him in the country. He probably doesn't have much time left anyway."

"But why is he here? Are you taking him in?"

The doctor looked down at her from his immense height with a mixture of annoyance and pity. "I'm going to euthanize him, miss. Can't fend for himself, since he's a pampered indoor cat. It's kinder this way, really."

"What?" Maggie exclaimed. "No!" She pushed past the doctor and opened the door to his office. Two eyes glowed phosphorescent in the darkness. Maggie switched on the light. There, on the vet's pinewood desk, sat a reddish tabby cat. He was painfully thin, with rough fur and bald patches and a torn ear. He looked up at Maggie with emerald eyes, pupils narrowing to slits. *Goodness gracious, you look as bad as I feel,* she thought.

"*Meh,*" the red tabby proclaimed. The disdainful sound was expressed in a peculiar and irritating nasal tone.

"*Meh?*" Maggie looked up at the doctor, who'd followed her in. "I thought cats said *meow.*"

The vet shrugged. "He's a talker, that one is. Talk your ear off. I think whoever he belonged to lived alone and talked to him. Talked to him day and night, and fed him from her plate. That's why the old boy's no good as a mouser. Thinks he's human, he does."

Maggie went up to the cat and held out her hand for him to sniff. She knew cats from the Prime Minister's office, where they roamed freely, along with a few of the Churchills' dogs.

The cat acquiesced to sniff her hand, then walked close to her. Raising himself on his haunches, he put one paw on her left shoulder and one paw on her right, holding her in place as he looked into her eyes with laser-like intensity. Maggie looked back, slightly disconcerted by the scrutiny.

"*Meh,*" he said finally, then dropped back down to all fours and rubbed against her, beginning to purr. Something passed between them; she had passed the test. Although no words had been spoken, Maggie knew, as clear as she knew her name or the day of the week, that she and this cat belonged together. Or, at least, he had chosen her, for whatever reason, and she was powerless to say no.

"Bold as brass, that one," Dr. McNeil said. "Looks like he's decided on you. Whether you fancy him or no."

"I'll take him," Maggie said impulsively, scooping him up in her arms. "My little Schrödinger."

"Don't know his name, lass." The cat settled in, purring loudly and glaring at Dr. McNeil. "*Meh!*" the cat spat at him.

"I just meant—" Maggie wasn't up to explaining the paradox of Schrödinger's cat.

"Suit yourself, miss," the vet said, as Maggie turned to leave, cat in her arms. "But don't think he'll be catching any mice for you."

"Come on," she whispered to the cat, unbuttoning her coat and slipping him inside, where he clung to her, simultaneously purring loudly and glaring at the vet. "We're going home."

After she was well out of earshot, Dr. McNeil reached for the telephone. "Put me through to Archie MacDonald's farm. It's *urgent*."

PHOTO: © LESLEY SEMMELHACK

SUSAN ELIA MACNEAL is the Edgar Award– and Dilys Award–nominated author of the Maggie Hope mystery series, including *Mr. Churchill's Secretary*, *Princess Elizabeth's Spy*, and *His Majesty's Hope*. She lives in Brooklyn, New York, with her husband and child, and is at work on the fourth Maggie Hope mystery, *The Prime Minister's Secret Agent*, to be published by Bantam.